MORGAWR

THE VOYAGE OF THE
JERLE SHANNARA

MORGAWR

TERRY BROOKS

BALLANTINE BOOKS • NEW YORK

A Del Rey® Book
Published by The Random House Publishing Group
Copyright © 2002 by Terry Brooks
Excerpt from *The High Druid of Shannara: Jarka Ruus* copyright © 2003 by Terry Brooks

This book contains an excerpt from *The High Druid of Shannara: Jarka Ruus* by Terry Brooks. This excerpt has been set for this edition only and may not reflect the final content of the forthcoming edition.

Del Rey is a registered trademark and the Del Rey colophon is a trademark of Random House, Inc.

www.delreydigital.com

ISBN 0-345-43575-3

Manufactured in the United States of America

First Hardcover Edition: September 2002
First DomesticMass Market Edition: September 2003

OPM   10   9   8   7   6   5   4   3   2   1

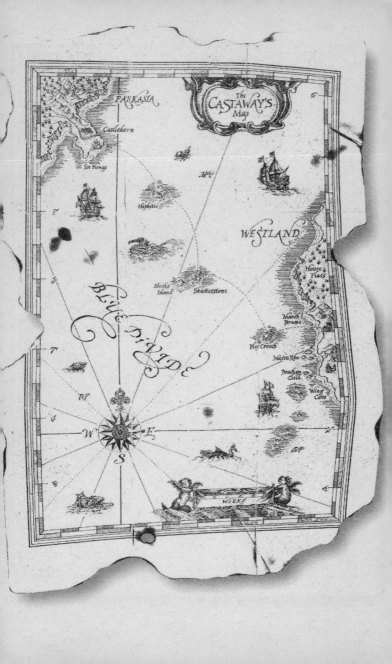

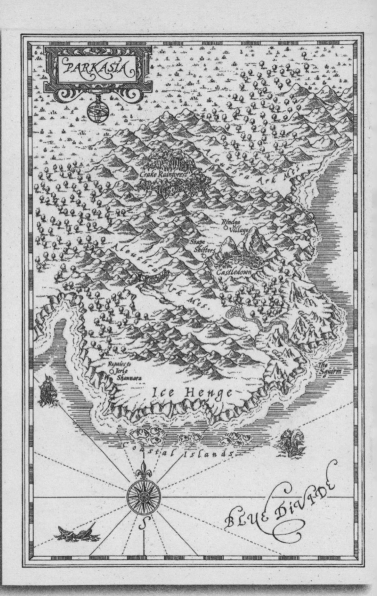

ONE

The figure appeared out of the shadows of the alcove so quickly that Sen Dunsidan was almost on top of it before he realized it was there. The hallway leading to his sleeping chamber was dark with nightfall's shadows, and the light from the wall lamps cast only scattered halos of fuzzy brightness. The lamps gave no help in this instance, and the Minister of Defense was given no chance either to flee or defend himself.

"A word, if you please, Minister."

The intruder was cloaked and hooded, and although Sen Dunsidan was reminded at once of the Ilse Witch he knew without question that it was not she. This was a man, not a woman—too much size and bulk to be anything else, and the words were rough and masculine. The witch's small, slender form and cool, smooth voice were missing. She had come to him only a week earlier, before departing on her voyage aboard *Black Moclips*, tracking the Druid Walker and his company to an unknown destination. Now this intruder, cloaked and hooded in the same manner, had appeared in the same way—at night and unannounced. He wondered at once what the connection was between the two.

Masking his surprise and the hint of fear that clutched at his chest, Sen Dunsidan nodded. "Where would you like to share this word?"

"Your sleeping chamber will do."

A big man himself, still in the prime of his life, the Minister of Defense nevertheless felt dwarfed by the other. It was more than simply size; it was presence, as well. The intruder exuded strength and confidence not usually encountered in ordinary men. Sen Dunsidan did not ask how he had managed to gain entry to the closely guarded, walled compound. He did not ask how he had moved unchallenged to the upper floor of his quarters. Such questions were pointless. He simply accepted that the intruder was capable of this and much more. He did as he was bidden. He walked past with a deferential bow, opened his bedroom door, and beckoned the other inside.

The lights were lit here, as well, though no more brightly than in the hallway without, and the intruder moved at once into the shadows.

"Sit down, Minister, and I will tell you what I want."

Sen Dunsidan sat in a high-backed chair and crossed his legs comfortably. His fear and surprise had faded. If the other meant him harm, he would not have bothered to announce himself. He wanted something that a Minister of Defense of the Federation's Coalition Council could offer, so there was no particular cause for concern. Not yet, anyway. That could change if he could not supply the answers the other sought. But Sen Dunsidan was a master at telling others what they expected to hear.

"Some cold ale?" he asked.

"Pour some for yourself, Minister."

Sen Dunsidan hesitated, surprised by insistence in the other's voice. Then he rose and walked to the table at his bedside that held the ice bucket, ale pitcher nestled within it, and several glasses. He stood looking down at the ale as he poured, his long silver hair hanging loose about his shoulders save where it was braided above the ears, as was the current fashion. He did not like what he was feeling now, uncertainty come so swiftly on the heels of newfound confidence. He had better be careful of this man; step lightly.

He walked back to his chair and reseated himself, sipping at the ale. His strong face turned toward the other, a barely visible presence amid the shadows.

"I have something to ask of you," the intruder said softly.

Sen Dunsidan nodded and made an expansive gesture with one hand.

The intruder shifted slightly. "Be warned, Minister. Do not think to placate me with promises you do not intend to keep. I am not here to waste my time on fools who think to dismiss me with empty words. If I sense you dissemble, I will simply kill you and have done with it. Do you understand?"

Sen Dunsidan took a deep breath to steady himself. "I understand."

The other said nothing further for a moment, then moved out from the deep shadows to the edges of the light. "I am called the Morgawr. I am mentor to the Ilse Witch."

"Ah." The Minister of Defense nodded. He had not been wrong about the similarities of appearance.

The cloaked form moved a little closer. "You and I are about to form a partnership, Minister. A new partnership, one to replace that which you shared with my pupil. She no longer has need of you. She will not come to see you again. But I will. Often."

"Does she know this?" Dunsidan asked softly.

"She knows nowhere near as much as she thinks." The other's voice was hard and low. "She has decided to betray me, and for her infidelity she will be punished. I will administer her punishment when I see her next. This does not concern you, save that you should know why you will not see her again. All these years, I have been the force behind her efforts. I have been the one who gave her the power to form alliances like the one she shared with you. But she breaches my trust and thus forfeits my protection. She is of no further use."

Sen Dunsidan took a long pull on his ale and set the glass aside. "You will forgive me, sir, if I voice a note of skepticism. I don't know you, but I do know her. I know what she can do. I know what happens to those who betray her, and I do not intend to become one of them."

"Perhaps you would do better to be afraid of me. I am the one who stands here in front of you."

"Perhaps. But the Dark Lady has a way of showing up when least expected. Show me her head, and I will be more than happy to discuss a new agreement."

The cloaked figure laughed softly. "Well spoken, Minister. You offer a politician's answer to a tough demand. But I think you must reconsider. Look at me."

He reached up for his hood and pulled it away to reveal his face. It was the face of the Ilse Witch, youthful and smooth and filled with danger. Sen Dunsidan started in spite of himself. Then the girl's face changed, almost as if it were a mirage, and became Sen Dunsidan's—hard planes and edges, piercing blue eyes, silvery hair worn long, and a half smile that seemed ready to promise anything.

"You and I are very much alike, Minister."

The face changed again. Another took its place, the face of a younger man, but it was no one Sen Dunsidan had ever seen. It was nondescript, bland to the point of being forgettable, devoid of interesting or memorable features.

"Is this who I really am, Minister? Do I reveal myself now?" He paused. "Or am I really like this?"

The face shimmered and changed into something monstrous, a reptilian visage with a blunt snout and slits for eyes. Rough, gray scales coated a weathered face, and a wide, serrated mouth opened to reveal rows of sharply pointed teeth. Gimlet eyes, hate-filled and poisonous, glimmered with green fire.

The intruder pulled the hood back into place, and his face

disappeared into the resulting shadows. Sen Dunsidan sat motionless in his chair. He was all too aware of what he was being told. This man had the use of a very powerful magic. At the very least, he could shape-shift, and it was likely he could do much more than that. He was a man who enjoyed the excesses of power as much as the Minister of Defense did, and he would use that power in whatever way he felt he must to get what he wanted.

"I said we were alike, Minister," the intruder whispered. "We both appear as one thing when in truth we are another. I know you. I know you as I know myself. You would do anything to further your power in the hierarchy of the Federation. You indulge yourself in pleasures that are forbidden to other men. You covet what you cannot have and scheme to secure it. You smile and feign friendship when in truth you are the very serpent your enemies fear."

Sen Dunsidan kept his politician's smile in place. What was it this creature wanted of him?

"I tell you all this not to anger you, Minister, but to make certain you do not mistake my intent. I am here to help you further your ambitions in exchange for help you can in turn supply to me. I desire to pursue the witch on her voyage. I desire to be there when she does battle with the Druid, as I am certain she must. I desire to catch her with the magic she pursues, because I intend to take it from her and then to take her life. But to accomplish this, I will need a fleet of airships and the men to crew them."

Sen Dunsidan stared at him in disbelief. "What you ask is impossible."

"Nothing is impossible, Minister." The black robes shifted with a soft rustle as the intruder crossed the room. "Is what I ask any more impossible than what you seek?"

The Minister of Defense hesitated. "Which is what?"

"To be Prime Minister. To take control of the Coalition

Council once and for all. To rule the Federation, and by doing so, the Four Lands."

A number of thoughts passed swiftly through Sen Dunsidan's mind, but all of them came down to one. The intruder was right. Sen Dunsidan would do anything to make himself Prime Minister and control the Coalition Council. Even the Ilse Witch had known of this ambition, though she had never voiced it in such a way as this, a way that suggested it might be within reach.

"Both seem impossible to me," he answered the other carefully.

"You fail to see what I am telling you," the intruder said. "I am telling you why I will prove a better ally than the little witch. Who stands between you and your goal? The Prime Minister, who is hardy and well? He will serve long years before he steps down. His chosen successor, the Minister of the Treasury, Jaren Arken? He is a man younger than you and equally powerful, equally ruthless. He aspires to be Minister of Defense, doesn't he? He seeks your position on the council."

A cold rage swept through Sen Dunsidan on hearing those words. It was true, of course—all of it. Arken was his worst enemy, a man slippery and elusive as a snake, cold-blooded and reptilian through and through. He wanted the man dead, but had not yet figured out a way to accomplish it. He had asked the Ilse Witch for help, but whatever other exchange of favors she was willing to accept, she had always refused to kill for him.

"What is your offer, Morgawr?" he asked bluntly, tiring of this game.

"Only this. By tomorrow night, the men who stand in your way will be no more. No blame or suspicion will attach to you. The position you covet will be yours for the taking. No one will oppose you. No one will question your right to lead.

This is what I can do for you. In exchange, you must do what I ask—give me the ships and the men to sail them. A Minister of Defense can do this, especially when he stands to become Prime Minister."

The other's voice became a whisper. "Accept the partnership I am offering, so that not only may we help each other now, but we may help each other again when it becomes necessary."

Sen Dunsidan took a long moment to consider what was being asked. He badly wanted to be Prime Minister. He would do anything to secure the position. But he mistrusted this creature, this Morgawr, a thing not entirely human, a wielder of magic that could undo a man before he had time to realize what was happening. He was still unconvinced of the advisability of doing what he was being asked to do. He was afraid of the Ilse Witch; he could admit that to himself if to no one else. If he crossed her and she found out, he was a dead man; she would hunt him down and destroy him. On the other hand, if the Morgawr was to destroy her as he said he would, then Sen Dunsidan would do well to rethink his concerns.

A bird in the hand, it was commonly accepted, was worth two in the bush. If a path to the position of Prime Minister of the Coalition Council could be cleared, almost any risk was worth the taking.

"What sort of airships do you need?" he asked quietly. "How many?"

"Are we agreed on a partnership, Minister? Yes or no. Don't equivocate. Don't attach conditions. Yes or no."

Sen Dunsidan was still uncertain, but he could not pass up the chance to advance his own fortunes. Yet when he spoke the word that sealed his fate, he felt as if he were breathing fire. "Yes."

The Morgawr moved like liquid night, sliding along the edges of the shadows as he eased across the bedchamber. "So be it. I will be back after sunset tomorrow to let you know what your end of the bargain will be."

Then he was through the doorway and gone.

Sen Dunsidan slept poorly that night, plagued by dreams and wakefulness, burdened with the knowledge that he had sold himself at a price that had yet to be determined and might prove too costly to pay. Yet, while lying awake between bouts of fretful sleep, he pondered the enormity of what might take place, and he could not help but be excited. Surely no price was too great if it meant he would become Prime Minister. A handful of ships and a complement of men, neither of which he cared overmuch about—these were nothing to him. In truth, to gain control of the Federation, he would have obligated himself for much more. In truth, he would have paid any price.

Yet it still might all come to nothing. It might prove nothing more than a fantasy given to test his willingness to abandon the witch as an ally.

But when he woke and while he was dressing to go to the Council chambers, word reached him that the Prime Minister was dead. The man had gone to sleep and never woken; his heart stopped while he lay in his bed. It was odd, given his good health and relatively young age, but life was filled with surprises.

Sen Dunsidan felt a surge of pleasure and expectation at the news. He allowed himself to believe that the unthinkable might actually be within reach, that the Morgawr's word might be better than he had dared to hope. *Prime Minister Dunsidan,* he whispered to himself, deep inside, where his darkest secrets lay hidden.

He arrived at the Coalition Council chambers before he learned that Jaren Arken was dead, as well. The Minister of the Treasury, responding to the news of the Prime Minister's sudden passing, had rushed from his home in response, the prospect of filling the leadership void no doubt foremost in his thoughts, and had fallen on the steps leading down to the street. He had struck his head on the stone carvings at the bottom. By the time his servants had reached him, he was gone.

Sen Dunsidan took the news in stride, no longer surprised, only pleased and excited. He put on his mourner's face, and he offered his politician's responses to all those who approached—and there were many now, because he was the one the Council members were already turning to. He spent the day arranging funerals and tributes, speaking to one and all of his own sorrow and disappointment, all the while consolidating his power. Two such important and effective leaders dead at a single stroke; a strong man must be found to fill the void left by their passing. He offered himself and promised to do the best job he could on behalf of those who supported him.

By nightfall, the talk was no longer of the dead men; the talk was all of him.

He sat waiting in his chambers for a long time after sunset, speculating on what would happen when the Morgawr returned. That he would, to claim his end of the bargain, was a given. What exactly he would ask was less certain. He would not threaten, but the threat was there nevertheless: if he could so easily dispose of a Prime Minister and a Minister of the Treasury, how much harder could it be to dispose of a recalcitrant Minister of Defense? Sen Dunsidan was in this business now all the way up to his neck. There could be no talk of backing away. The best he could hope for was to mitigate the payment the Morgawr would seek to exact.

It was almost midnight before the other appeared, slipping soundlessly through the doorway of the bedchamber, all black robes and menace. By then, Sen Dunsidan had consumed several glasses of ale and was regretting it.

"Impatient, Minister?" the Morgawr asked softly, moving at once into the shadows. "Did you think I wasn't coming?"

"I knew you would come. What do you want?"

"So abrupt? Not even time for a thank you? I've made you Prime Minister. All that is required is a vote by the Coalition Council, a matter of procedure only. When will that occur?"

"A day or two. All right, you've kept your end of the bargain. What is mine to be?"

"Ships of the line, Minister. Ships that can withstand a long journey and a battle at its end. Ships that can transport men and equipment to secure what is needed. Ships that can carry back the treasures I expect to find."

Sen Dunsidan shook his head doubtfully. "Such ships are hard to come by. All we have are committed to the Prek-kendorran. If I were to pull out, say, a dozen—"

"Two dozen would be closer to what I had in mind," the other interrupted smoothly.

Two dozen? The Minister of Defense exhaled slowly. "Two dozen, then. But that many ships missing from the line would be noticed and questioned. How will I explain it?"

"You are about to become Prime Minister. You don't have to explain." There was a hint of impatience in the rough voice. "Take them from the Rovers, if your own are in short supply."

Dunsidan took a quick sip of the ale he shouldn't be drinking. "The Rovers are neutral in this struggle. Mercenaries, but neutral. If I confiscate their ships, they will refuse to build more."

"I said nothing of confiscation. Steal them, then lay the blame elsewhere."

"And the men to crew them? What sort of men do you require? Must I steal them, as well?"

"Take them from the prisons. Men who have sailed and fought aboard airships. Elves, Bordermen, Rovers, whatever. Give me enough of these to make my crews. But do not expect me to give them back again. When I have used them up, I intend to throw them away. They will not be fit for anything else."

The hair stood on the back of Sen Dunsidan's neck. Two hundred men, tossed away like old shoes. Damaged, ruined, unfit for wear. What did that mean? He had a sudden urge to flee the room, to run and keep running until he was so far away he couldn't remember where he had come from.

"I'll need time to arrange this, a week perhaps." He tried to keep his voice steady. "Two dozen ships missing from any- where will be talked about. Men from the prisons will be missed. I have to think about how this can be done. Must you have so many of each to undertake your pursuit?"

The Morgawr went still. "You seem incapable of doing anything I ask of you without questioning it. Why is that? Did I ask you how to go about removing those men who would keep you from being Prime Minister?"

Sen Dunsidan realized suddenly that he had gone too far. "No, no, of course not. It was just that I—"

"Give me the men tonight," the other interrupted.

"But I need time."

"You have them in your prisons, here in the city. Arrange for their release now."

"There are rules about releasing prisoners."

"Break them."

Sen Dunsidan felt as if he were standing in quicksand and sinking fast. But he couldn't seem to find a way to save himself.

"Give me my crews tonight, Minister," the other hissed softly. "You, personally. A show of trust to persuade me that my efforts at removing the men who stood in your path were justified. Let's be certain your commitment to our new part- nership is more than just words."

"But I—"

The other man moved swiftly out of the shadows and snatched hold of the front of the Minister's shirt. "I think you require a demonstration. An example of what happens to those who question me." The fingers tightened in the fabric, iron rods that lifted Sen Dunsidan to the tips of his boots. "You're shaking, Minister. Can it be that I have your full attention at last?"

Sen Dunsidan nodded wordlessly, so frightened he did not trust himself to speak.

"Good. Now come with me."

Sen Dunsidan exhaled sharply as the other released his grip and stepped away. "Where?"

The Morgawr moved past him, opened the bedchamber door, and looked back out of the shadows of his hood. "To the prisons, Minister, to get my men."

TWO

Together, the Morgawr and Sen Dunsidan passed down the halls of the Minister's house, through the gates of the compound, and outside into the night. None of the guards or servants they passed spoke to them. No one seemed even to see them. *Magic,* Sen Dunsidan thought helplessly. He stifled the urge to cry out for help, knowing there was none.

Insanity.

But he had made his choice.

As they walked the dark, empty streets of the city, the Minister of Defense gathered the shards of his shattered composure, one jagged piece at a time. If he was to survive this night, he must do better than he was doing now. The Morgawr already thought him weak and foolish; if he thought him useless, as well, he would discard him in an instant. Walking steadily, taking strong strides, deep breaths, Sen Dunsidan mustered his courage and his resolve. *Remember who you are,* he told himself. *Remember what is at stake.*

Beside him, the Morgawr walked on, never looking at him, never speaking to him, never evidencing even once that he had any interest in him at all.

The prisons were situated at the west edge of the Federation Army barracks, close by the swift flowing waters of the Rappahalladran. They formed a dark and formidable collection of pitted stone towers and walls. Narrow slits served as windows, and iron spikes ringed the parapets. Sen Dunsidan, as Minister of Defense, visited the prisons regularly, and he had heard the stories. No one ever escaped. Now and then those incarcerated would find their way into the river, thinking to swim to the far side and flee into the forests. No one ever made it. The currents were treacherous and strong. Sooner or later, the bodies washed ashore and were hung from the walls where others in the prisons could see them.

As they drew close, Sen Dunsidan mustered sufficient resolve to draw close again to the Morgawr.

"What do you intend to do when we get inside?" he asked, keeping his voice strong and steady. "I need to know what to say if you want to avoid having to hypnotize the entire garrison."

The Morgawr laughed softly. "Feeling a bit more like your old self, Minister? Very well. I want a room in which to speak with prospective members of my crew. I want them brought to me one by one, starting with a Captain or someone in authority. I want you to be there to watch what happens."

Dunsidan nodded, trying not to think what that meant.

"Next time, Minister, think twice before you make a promise you do not intend to keep," the other hissed, his voice rough and hard-edged. "I have no patience with liars and fools. You do not strike me as either, but then you are good at becoming what you must in your dealings with others, aren't you?"

Sen Dunsidan said nothing. There was nothing to say. He kept his thoughts focused on what he would do once they were inside the prisons. There, he would be more in control of things, more on familiar ground. There, he could do more to demonstrate his worth to this dangerous creature.

Recognizing Sen Dunsidan at once, the gate watch admitted them without question. Snapping to attention in their worn leathers, they released the locks on the gates. Inside, the smells were of dampness and rot and human excrement, foul and rank. Sen Dunsidan asked the Duty Officer for a specific

interrogation room, one with which he was familiar, one removed from everything else, buried deep in the bowels of the
prisons. A turnkey led them down a long corridor to the room
he had requested, a large chamber with walls that leaked
moisture and a floor that had buckled. A table to which had
been fastened iron chains and clamps sat at its center. To one
side, a wooden rack lined with implements of torture was
pushed against the wall. A single oil lamp lit the gloom.

"Wait here," Sen Dunsidan told the Morgawr. "Let me persuade the right men to come to you."

"Start with one," the Morgawr ordered, moving off into the
shadows.

Sen Dunsidan hesitated, then went out through the door
with the turnkey. The turnkey was a hulking, gnarled man
who had served seven terms on the front, a lifetime soldier in
the Federation Army. He was scarred inside and out, having
witnessed and survived atrocities that would have destroyed
the minds of other men. He never spoke, but he knew well
enough what was going on and seemed unconcerned with it.
Sen Dunsidan had used him on occasion to question recalcitrant prisoners. The man was good at inflicting pain and
ignoring pleas for mercy—perhaps even better at that than
keeping his mouth shut.

Oddly enough, the Minister had never learned his name.
Down here, they called him Turnkey, as if the title itself were
name enough for a man who did what he did.

They passed down a dozen small corridors and through a
handful of doors to where the main cells were located. The
larger ones held prisoners who had been taken from the Prekkendorran. Some would be ransomed or traded for Free-born
prisoners. Some would die here. Sen Dunsidan indicated to
the turnkey the one that housed those who had been prisoners
longest.

"Unlock it."

The turnkey unlocked the door without a word.

Sen Dunsidan took a torch from its rack on the wall. "Close the door behind me. Don't open it until I tell you I am ready to come out," he ordered.

Then he stepped boldly inside.

The room was large, damp, and rank with the smells of caged men. A dozen heads turned as one on his entry. An equal number lifted from the soiled pallets on the floor. Other men stirred, fitfully. Most were still asleep.

"Wake up!" he snapped.

He held up the torch to show them who he was, then stuck it in a stanchion next to the door. The men were beginning to stand now, whispers and grunts passing between them. He waited until they were all awake, a ragged bunch with dead eyes and ravaged faces. Some of them had been locked down here for almost three years. Most had given up hope of ever getting out. The small sounds of their shuffling echoed in the deep, pervasive silence, a constant reminder of how helpless they were.

"You know me," he said to them. "Many of you I have spoken with. You have been here a long time. Too long. I am going to give all of you a chance to get out. You won't be doing any more fighting in the war. You won't be going home—not for a while. But you will be outside these walls and back on an airship. Are you interested?"

The man he had depended upon to speak for the others took a step forward. "What are you after?"

His name was Darish Venn. He was a Borderman who had captained one of the first Free-born airships brought into the war on the Prekkendorran. He had distinguished himself in battle many times before his ship went down and he was captured. The other men respected and trusted him. As senior officer, he had formed them into groups and given them positions, small and insignificant to those who were free men, but of crucial importance to those locked away down here.

"Captain." Sen Dunsidan acknowledged him with a nod.

"I need men to go on a voyage across the Blue Divide. A long voyage, from which some may not return. I won't deny there is danger. I don't have the sailors to spare for this, or the money to hire Rover mercenaries. But the Federation can spare you. Federation soldiers will accompany those who agree to accept the conditions I am offering, so there will be some protection offered and order imposed. Mostly, you will be out of here and you won't have to come back. The voyage will take a year, maybe two. You will be your own crew, your own company, as long as you go where you are told."

"Why would you do this now, after so long?" Darish Venn asked.

"I can't tell you that."

"Why should we trust you?" another asked boldly.

"Why not? What difference does it make, if it gets you out of here? If I wanted to do you harm, it would be easy enough, wouldn't it? What I want are sailors willing to make a voyage. What you want is your freedom. A trade seems a good compromise for both of us."

"We could take you prisoner and trade you for our freedom and not have to agree to anything!" the man snapped ominously.

Sen Dunsidan nodded. "You could. But what would be the consequences of that? Besides, do you think I would come down here and expose myself to harm without any protection?"

There was a quick exchange of whispers. Sen Dunsidan held his ground and kept his strong face composed. He had exposed himself to greater risks than this one, and he was not afraid of these men. The results of failure to do what the Morgawr had asked frightened him a good deal more.

"You want all of us?" Darish Venn asked.

"All who choose to come. If you refuse, then you stay where you are. The choice is yours." He paused a moment, as if considering. His leonine profile lifted into the light, and a reflective look settled over his craggy features. "I will make a bargain with you, Captain. If you like, I will show you a map of the place we are going. If you approve of what you see, then you sign on then and there. If not, you can return and tell the others."

The Borderman nodded. Perhaps he was too worn down and too slowed by his imprisonment to think it through clearly. Perhaps he was just anxious for a way out. "All right, I'll come."

Sen Dunsidan rapped on the door, and the turnkey opened it for him. He beckoned Captain Venn to go first, then left the room. The turnkey locked the door, and Dunsidan could hear the scuffling of feet as those still locked within pressed up against the doorway to listen.

"Just down the hallway, Captain," he advised loudly for their benefit. "I'll arrange for a glass of ale, as well."

They walked down the passageways to the room where the Morgawr waited, their footsteps echoing in the silence. No one spoke. Sen Dunsidan glanced at the Borderman. He was a big man, tall and broad shouldered, though stooped and thin from his imprisonment, his face skeletal and his skin pale and crusted with dirt and sores. The Free-born had tried to trade for him many times, but the Federation knew the value of airship Captains and preferred to keep him locked away and off the battlefield.

When they reached the room where the Morgawr waited, Sen Dunsidan opened the door for Venn, motioned for the turnkey to wait outside, and closed the door behind him as he followed the Borderman in. Venn glanced around at the implements of torture and chains, then looked at Dunsidan.

"What is this?"

The Minister of Defense shrugged and smiled disarmingly. "It was the best I could do." He indicated one of the three-legged stools tucked under the table. "Sit down and let's talk."

There was no sign of the Morgawr. Had he left? Had he decided all this was a waste of time and he would be better off handling matters himself? For a moment, Sen Dunsidan pan-icked. But then he felt something move in the shadows—*felt*, rather than saw.

He moved to the other side of the table from Darish Venn, drawing the Captain's attention away from the swirling dark-ness behind him. "The voyage will take us quite a distance from the Four Lands, Captain," he said, his face taking on a serious cast. Behind Venn, the Morgawr began to materialize. "A good deal of preparation will be necessary. Someone with your experience will have no trouble provisioning the ships we intend to take. A dozen or more will be needed, I think."

The Morgawr, huge and black, slid out of the shadows with-out a sound and came up behind Venn. The Borderman neither heard nor sensed him, just stared straight at Sen Dunsidan.

"Naturally, you will be in charge of your men, of choosing which ones will undertake which tasks . . ."

A hand slid out of the Morgawr's black robes, gnarled and covered with scales. It clamped on the back of Darish Venn's neck, and the airship Captain gave a sharp gasp. Twisting and thrashing, he tried to break free, but the Morgawr held him firmly in place. Sen Dunsidan stepped back a pace, his words dying in his throat as he watched the struggle. Darish Venn's eyes were fixed on him, maddened but helpless. The Mor-gawr's other hand emerged, shimmering with a wicked green light. Slowly the pulsating hand moved toward the back of the Borderman's head. Sen Dunsidan caught his breath. Clawed fingers stretched, touching the hair, then the skin.

Darish Venn screamed.

The fingers slid inside his head, pushing through hair and skin and bone as if the whole of it were made of soft clay. Sen Dunsidan's throat tightened and his stomach lurched. The Morgawr's hand was all the way inside the skull now, twisting slowly, as if searching. The Captain had stopped screaming and thrashing. The light had gone out of his eyes, and his face had gone slack. His look was dull and lifeless.

The Morgawr withdrew his hand from the Borderman's head, and it was steaming and wet as it slid back into the black robes and out of sight. The Morgawr was breathing so loudly that Sen Dunsidan could hear him, a kind of rapturous panting, rife with sounds of satisfaction and pleasure.

"You cannot know, Minister," he whispered, "how good it feels to feed on another's life. Such ecstasy!"

He stepped back, releasing Venn. "There. It is done. He is ours now, to do with as we wish. He is a walking dead man with no will of his own. He will do whatever he is told to do. He keeps his skills and his experience, but he no longer cares to think for himself. A useful tool, Minister. Take a look at him."

Reluctantly, Sen Dunsidan did so. It was not an invitation; it was a command. He studied the blank, lifeless eyes, revulsion turning to horror as they began to lose color and definition and turn milky white and vacant. He moved around the table cautiously, looking for the wound in the back of the Borderman's head where the Morgawr's hand had forced entry. To his astonishment, there wasn't one. The skull was undamaged. It was as if nothing had happened.

"Test him, Minister." The Morgawr was laughing. "Tell him to do something."

Sen Dunsidan fought to keep his composure. "Stand up," he ordered Darish Venn in a voice he could barely recognize as his own.

The Borderman rose. He never looked at Sen Dunsidan or gave recognition that he knew what was happening. His eyes stayed dead and blank, and his face had lost all expression.

"He is the first, but only the first," the Morgawr hissed, anxious now and impatient. "A long night stretches ahead of us. Go now, and bring me another. I am already hungry for a fresh taste! Go! Bring me six, but bid them enter one by one. Go quickly!"

Sen Dunsidan went out the door without a word. An image

of a scaly hand steaming and wet with human matter was fixed in his mind and would not give up its hold on him.

He brought more men to the room that night, so many he lost count of them. He brought them in small groups and had them enter singly. He watched as their bodies were violated and their minds destroyed. He stood by without lifting a finger to aid them as they were changed from whole men into shells. It was strange, but after Darish Venn, he couldn't remember any of their faces. They were all one to him. They were all the same man.

When the room grew too crowded with them, he was ordered to lead them out and turn them over to the turnkey to place in a larger chamber. The turnkey took them away without comment, without even looking at them. But once, after maybe fifty or so, the ruined face and the hard eyes found Sen Dunsidan with a look that left him in tears. The look bore guilt and accusation, horror and despair, and above all unmitigated rage. This was wrong, the look said. This went beyond anything imaginable. This was madness.

And yet the turnkey did nothing either.

The two of them, accomplices to an unspeakable crime.

The two of them, silent participants in the perpetration of a monstrous wrong.

So many men did Sen Dunsidan help destroy, men who walked to their doom with nothing to offer in their defense, decoyed by a politician's false words and reassuring looks. He did not know how he managed it. He did not know how he survived what it made him feel. Each time the Morgawr's hand emerged wet and dripping with human life, another feasting complete, the Minister of Defense thought he would run screaming into the night. Yet the presence of Death was so overpowering that it transcended everything else in those terrible hours, paralyzing him. While the Morgawr feasted, Sen Dunsidan watched and was unable even to look away.

Until finally, the Morgawr was sated. "Enough for now," he

hissed, glutted and drunk on stolen life. "Tomorrow night, Minister, we will finish this."

He rose and walked away, taking his dead with him into the night, shadows on the wind.

The dawn broke and the day came, but Sen Dunsidan saw none of it. He shut himself away and did not come out. He lay in his room and tried to banish the image of the Morgawr's hand. He dozed and tried to forget the way his skin crawled at the slightest sound of a human voice. Queries were made after his health. He was needed in the Council chambers. A vote on the position of Prime Minister was imminent. Reassurances were sought. Sen Dunsidan no longer cared. He wished he had never put himself in this position. He wished he were dead.

By nightfall, the turnkey was. Even given the harshness of his life and the toughness of his mind, he could not bear what he had witnessed. When no one else was about, he went down into the bowels of the prison and hung himself in a vacant cell.

Or did he? Sen Dunsidan could not be certain. Perhaps it was murder made to look like suicide. Perhaps the Morgawr did not want the turnkey alive.

Perhaps Sen Dunsidan was next.

But what could he do to save himself?

The Morgawr came again at midnight, and again Sen Dunsidan went with him into the prisons. This time Dunsidan dismissed the new turnkey and handled all the extraneous work himself. He was numb to it by now, inured to the screams, the wet and steaming hand, the grunts of horror from the men, and the sighs of satisfaction from the Morgawr. He was no longer a part of it, gone somewhere else, somewhere so far away that what happened here, in this place and on this night, meant nothing. It would be over by dawn, and when it was, Sen Dunsidan would be another man in another life. He would transcend this one and leave it behind. He would begin anew. He would remake himself in a way that cleansed him of the wrongs he had done and the atrocities he had abetted. It was not so hard. It was what soldiers did when they came home from a war. It was how a man got past the unforgivable.

More than 250 men passed through that room and out of the life they had known. They disappeared as surely as if they had turned to smoke. The Morgawr changed them into dead things that still walked, into creatures that had lost all sense of identity and purpose. He turned them into something less than dogs, and they did not even know it. He made them into his airship crews, and he took them away forever. All of them, every last one. Sen Dunsidan never saw any of them again.

Within days, he had secured the airships the Morgawr had requested and delivered them to fulfill his end of the bargain. Within a week, the Morgawr was gone out of his life, departed in search of the Ilse Witch, in quest of revenge. Sen Dunsidan didn't care. He hoped they destroyed each other. He prayed he would never see either of them again.

But the images remained, haunting and terrible. He could not banish them. He could not reconcile their horror. They haunted him in his sleep and when he was awake. They were never far away, never out of sight. Sen Dunsidan did not sleep for weeks afterwards. He did not enjoy a moment's peace.

He became Prime Minister of the Federation's Coalition Council, but he lost his soul.

THREE

Now, months later and thousands of miles away off the coast of the continent of Parkasia, the fleet of airships assembled by Sen Dunsidan and placed under the command of the Morgawr and his Mwellrets and walking dead materialized out of the mist and closed on the *Jerle Shannara*. Standing amidships at the port railing, Redden Alt Mer watched the cluster of black hulls and sails fill the horizon east like links in an encircling chain.

"Cast off!" the Rover Captain snapped at Spanner Frew, spyglass lifting one more time to make certain of what he was seeing.

"She's not ready!" the burly shipwright snapped back.

"She's as ready as she's going to get. Give the order!"

His glass swept the approaching ships. No insignia, no flags. Unmarked warships in a land where until a few weeks ago there had never been even one. Enemies, but whose? He had to assume the worst, that these ships were hunting them. Had the Ilse Witch brought others besides *Black Moclips*, ships that had lain offshore until now, waiting for the witch to bring them into the mix?

Spanner Frew was yelling at the crew, setting them in action. With Furl Hawken dead and Rue Meridian gone inland, there was no one else to fill the role of First Mate. No one stopped to question him. They had seen the ships, as well. Hands reached obediently for lines and winches. The tethering line was released, giving the *Jerle Shannara* her freedom. Rovers began tightening down the radian draws and lanyards, bringing the sails all the way to the tops of the masts, where they could catch the wind and light. Knowing what he would find, Redden Alt Mer glanced around. His crew was eight strong, counting Spanner and himself. Not nearly enough to fully man a warship like the *Jerle Shannara*, let alone fight a battle against enemies. They would have to run, and run fast.

He ran himself, breaking for the pilot box and the controls, heavy boots thudding across the wooden decking. "Unhood the crystals!" he yelled at Britt Rill and Jethen Amenades as he swept past them. "Not the fore starboard! Leave it covered. Just the aft and amidships!"

No working diapson crystal in the fore port parse tube, so to balance the loss of power from the left he was forced to shut down its opposite number. It would cut their power by a third, but the *Jerle Shannara* was swift enough even at that.

Spanner Frew was beside him, lumbering toward the mainmast and the weapons rack. "Who are they?"

"I don't know, Black Beard, but I don't think they are friends."

He opened the four available parse tubes and drew down power to the crystals from the draws. The *Jerle Shannara* lurched sharply and began to rise as ambient light converted to energy. But too slow, the Rover Captain saw, to make a clean escape. The invading ships were nearly on top of them, an odd assortment, all sizes and shapes, none of them recognizable save for their general design. A mix, he saw, mostly Rover built, a few Elven. Where had they come from? He could see their crews moving about the ships' decking, slow and unhurried, showing none of the excitement and fever he was familiar with. Calm in the face of battle.

Po Kelles, aboard Niciannon, flew past the pilot box off the starboard side. The big Roc banked so close to Redden Alt Mer that he could see the bluish sheen of the bird's feathers.

"Captain!" the Wing Rider yelled, pointing.

He was not pointing at the ships, but at a flurry of dots that had appeared suddenly in their midst, small and more mobile. War Shrikes, acting in concert with the enemy ships, warding their flanks and leading their advance. Already they were ahead of the ships and coming fast at the *Jerle Shannara*.

"Fly out of here!" Big Red yelled back at Po Kelles. "Fly inland and find Little Red! Warn her what's happening!"

The Wing Rider and his Roc swung away, lifting swiftly into the misty sky. A Roc's best chance against Shrikes was to gain height and distance. In a short race, the Shrikes had the advantage. Here, they were still too far away. Already, Niciannon was opening the gap between them. With the navigational directions Po Kelles had been given already, he would have no trouble reaching Hunter Predd and Rue Meridian. The danger now was to the *Jerle Shannara*. A Shrike's talons could rip a sail to shreds. The birds would soon attempt just that.

Alt Mer's hands flew to the controls. Shrikes in league with enemy warships. How could that be? Who controlled the birds? But he knew the answer as soon as he asked himself the question. It would take magic to bring War Shrikes into line like this. Someone, or something, aboard those ships possessed such magic.

The Ilse Witch? he wondered. Come out from inland, where she had gone to find the others?

There was no time to ponder it.

"Black Beard!" he yelled down to Spanner Frew. "Place the men on both sides, down in the fighting pits. Use bows and arrows and keep those Shrikes at bay!"

His hands steady on the controls, he watched the warships and birds loom up in front of him, too close to avoid. He couldn't get above them or swing around fast enough to put sufficient distance between them. He had no choice. On his first pass, he would have to go right through them.

"Hold fast!" he yelled to Spanner Frew.

Then the closest of the warships were on top of them, moving swiftly out of the haze, all bulk and darkness in the early morning gloom. Redden Alt Mer had been here before, and he knew what to do. He didn't try to avoid a collision. Instead, he initiated one, turning the *Jerle Shannara* toward the smallest ship in the line. The radian draws hummed as they funneled the ambient light into the parse tubes and the diapson crystals turned it to energy, a peculiar, tinny sound. The ship responded with a surge as he levered forward on the controls, tilted the hull slightly to port, and sliced through the enemy ship's foremast and sails, taking them down in a single sweep that left the vessel foundering.

Shrikes wheeled about them, but in close quarters they could not come in more than two at a time, and the bowmen fired arrows at them with deadly accuracy, causing injuries and screams of rage.

"Helm port!" Big Red shouted in warning as a second vessel tried to close from the left.

As the crew braced, he swung the wheel all the way about, bringing the rams to bear on this new threat. The *Jerle Shannara* shuddered and lurched as the parse tubes emitted fresh discharges of converted light, then shot forward across the enemy's stern, raking her decking and snapping off pieces of railing like deadwood. Redden Alt Mer had only a few moments to glance over at the enemy crew. A Mwellret clutched the helm, crouched down in the pilot box to weather the impact of the collision. He gestured and yelled toward his men, but their response was oddly slow and mechanical, as if they were just coming out of a deep sleep, as if further information was needed before action could be taken. Redden Alt Mer watched their faces turn toward him, blank and empty, devoid of emotion or recognition. Eyes stared up at him, as hard and milky white as sea stones.

"Shades!" the Rover Captain whispered.

They were the eyes of the dead, yet the men themselves

were still moving around. For a moment, he was so stunned that he lost his concentration completely. Though he had seen other strange things, he had never seen dead men walk. He had not believed he ever would. Yet he was seeing them now.

"Spanner!" he shouted down at the shipwright.

Spanner Frew had seen them, as well. He looked at Redden Alt Mer and shook his wooly black head like an angry bear.

Then the *Jerle Shannara* was past the second ship and lifting above the others, and Alt Mer brought her all the way around and headed her inland, out of the fray. The enemy ships gave chase at once, coming at her from all directions, but they were strung out along the coastline and too far away to close effectively. How had they found her in the first place? he wondered. For a second, he considered the possibility of betrayal by one of his men, but quickly dismissed the idea. Magic, possibly. If whoever commanded this fleet could enslave Shrikes and make the dead come alive, he could find a band of Rovers easily enough. It was more than likely that he had used the Shrikes to track them.

Or *she* had, if it was the Ilse Witch returned.

He cursed his ignorance, the witch, and a dozen other imponderables as he flew the airship inland toward the mountains. He would have to turn south soon to stay within his bearings. He could not trust to the shorter overland route. Too much danger of losing the way and missing Little Red and the others. He could not afford to do that, to leave them abandoned to these things that gave pursuit.

A sharp *whang*! cut through the rush of wind as the amidships radian draw off the port railing broke loose and began to whip about the decking like a striking snake. The Rovers, still crouched in their fighting pits, flattened themselves protectively. Spanner Frew leapt behind the mainmast, taking cover as the loose draw snapped past, then wrapped itself around the aft port line and jerked it free.

At once the airship began to lose power and balance, both

already diminished by the loss of the forward draws, now thrown off altogether by the breaking away of the entire port bank. If the lines were not retethered at once, the ship would circle right back into the enemy ships, and they would all be in the hands of the walking dead.

Redden Alt Mer saw those eyes again, milky and vacant, devoid of humanity, bereft of any sense of the world about them.

Without stopping to consider, he cut power to the amidships starboard tube and thrust the port lever all the way forward. Either the *Jerle Shannara* would hold together long enough for him to give them a fighting chance to escape or it would fall out of the sky.

"Black Beard!" he yelled down to Spanner Frew. "Take the helm!"

The shipwright lumbered up the steps and into the pilot box, gnarled hands reaching for the controls. Redden Alt Mer took no time to explain, but simply bolted past him down the steps to the decking and forward to the mainmast. He felt exhilarated and edgy, as if nothing he might do was too wild to consider. Not altogether a bad assessment, he decided. Wind, wild and shrieking in his ears, whipped at his long red hair and brilliant scarves. He could feel the airship rocking under him, fighting to maintain trim, to keep from diving. He was impressed. Three draws lost; she should already be going down. Another ship wouldn't have lasted this long.

To his left, the entangled draws snapped and wrenched at each other, threatening to tear loose at any moment. He risked a quick glance over his shoulder. Their pursuers had drawn closer, taking advantage of their troubles. The Shrikes were almost on them.

"Keep them at bay!" he shouted down to the Rovers crouched in the fighting pits, but his words were lost in the wind.

He went up the foremast using the iron climbing pins

hammered into the wood, pressing himself against the thick timber to keep from being torn loose and thrown out into the void. His flying leathers helped to protect him, but even so, the wind was ferocious, blowing out of the mountains and toward the coast in a cold, hard rush. He did not look behind him or over at the draws. The dangers were obvious and he could do nothing about them. If the draws worked loose before he got to them, they could easily whip about and cut him in half. If the Shrikes got close enough, they could rip him off his perch and carry him away. Neither prospect was worth considering.

Something flashed darkly at the corner of his vision. He caught just a glimpse as it whizzed past. Another whipped by. Arrows. The enemy vessels were close enough that longbows could be brought into play. Perhaps the Mwellrets and walking dead were not proficient with weapons. Perhaps some small part of the luck that had saved him so many times before would save him now.

Perhaps was all he had.

Then he was atop the mast and working his way out along the yardarm to where the renegade draw was fastened topside. He clung to the yardarm with numb, bruised fingers, his strength seeping away in the frigid wind. Below, upturned faces shifted back and forth as men fired arrows at the approaching Shrikes then glanced up at him to check his progress. He saw the worry in those hard faces. *Good,* he thought. He would hate not to be missed.

A Shrike swept past him from above, screaming. Its talons snatched at his back, and the flying leathers jerked and tore. A wash of pain rushed through him as the bird's claws ripped into his skin. He wrenched himself sideways and nearly fell, his legs losing their grip so that he was hanging from the yardarm by his fingers. The sail billowed into him like a balloon, and he lay across it, gathering his strength. While he was buried in the sail, another Shrike swept past but couldn't get close enough. It banked away in frustration.

Don't stop, he told himself through a haze of weariness and pain. *Don't quit!*

He crawled back up on the yardarm, then dragged himself to its end, swung out from the spar, and slid down the length of the midships draw to where it had tangled in the aft, his boots clearing the lines as he descended. Battered and worn, but still clinging desperately to both stays, he hollered out to his crew for help. Two of them leapt from the port fighting pits and were beside him in moments, taking hold of the draws and hauling them back toward the parse tubes from which they had broken loose, ignoring the diving Shrikes and the hail of arrows from the pursuing ships.

Redden Alt Mer collapsed on the deck, his back burning with pain and wet with blood.

"That's more than enough heroics from you, Captain," Britt Rill growled, appearing out of nowhere to take hold of one arm and haul him to his feet. "Down below for you."

Alt Mer started to object, but his throat was so dry he couldn't get the words out. Worse, his strength had failed him completely. It was all he could do to stand with Rill's help. He glanced at the other and nodded. He had done what he could. The rest was up to the ship, and he would bet on her in any race.

Belowdecks, Britt Rill helped him off with his flying leathers and began to wash and clean his wounds. "How bad is it?" Redden Alt Mer asked, head bent forward, arms resting on his knees, hands clasped, and the whole of him knotted with pain. "Did it sever the muscles?"

"Nothing so bad, Captain," the other answered quietly. "Just a few deep cuts that will give you stories to tell your grandchildren, should you ever have any."

"Not likely."

"Be a blessing for the world, I expect."

Rill applied salve to the wounds, bound him up with strips of cloth, gave him a long pull from the aleskin strapped to his waist, and left him to decide for himself what he would do next. "The others will be needing me," Rill called back as he went out the cabin door.

And me, Alt Mer thought. But he didn't move right away. Instead, he sat there on his bed for several minutes more, listening to the sound of the wind outside the shuttered windows, feeling the movement of the ship beneath him. He could tell from its sway and glide that it was doing what it should, that power was back in sufficient amounts to keep it aloft and moving. But the battle wasn't over yet. Pursuers with magic enough to summon Shrikes and command the walking dead would not give up easily.

He went topside moments later, his shredded flying leathers pulled back in place. Stepping out into the wind, he cast about momentarily to gauge their position, then moved over to the pilot box to stand next to Spanner Frew. Content to let the shipwright guide them, he didn't ask for the helm. Instead, he spent a few long moments looking back at the clutch of dark shapes that were still in pursuit but beginning to fade into the haze. Even the Shrikes seemed to have given up the chase.

Spanner Frew glanced over at him, took note of his condition, and said nothing. The Rover Captain's look did not encourage conversation.

Alt Mer glanced at the surrounding sky. It was all grayness and mist, with a darker wash north that meant rain approached. Mountains loomed ahead and on both sides as they advanced inland toward the ice fields they must traverse in order to reach Rue and the others.

Then he saw the scattering of dots ahead and off to the starboard where the coastline bent inward in a series of deep coves.

"Black Beard!" he said in the other's ear, pulling on his shoulder and pointing.

Spanner Frew looked. Ahead, the dots began to take shape, to grow wings and sails. "More of them!" the big man growled, a hint of disbelief in his rough voice. "Shrikes, as well, if I'm seeing right. How did they get ahead of us?"

"The Shrikes know the coastline and cliffs better than we do!" Alt Mer had to fight to be heard above the wind. "They've found a way to cut us off. If we stick to our flight line, they'll have us. We have to get further inland, and we have to get there quickly."

His companion glanced around at the mist-shrouded mountains. "If we fly into these in this mist, we'll end up in splinters."

Alt Mer caught his eye and held it. "We don't have any choice. Give me the wheel. Go forward and signal back whenever you think I need it. Hand signals only. Voices might give us away. Do your best to keep us off the rocks."

Having repaired the broken draws and swept aside the bits of wreckage, the crew was standing by on the lines. Spanner Frew called out to them as he passed, sending them to their stations, warning of what was happening. No one replied. They were schooled in the Rover tradition of keeping faith in those who had the luck. No one had more of it than Redden Alt Mer. They would ride a burning ship into a firestorm if he told them to do so.

He took a deep breath, glanced once more at the shapes ahead and behind. Too many to evade or to fight. He swung the wheel hard to port toward the bank of mist. He let the airship maintain speed until they were into the soup, then cut back to dead slow, watching the vapor gather and fade, wispy sheets of white wrapping the darker edges of the mountains. If they struck a peak at this height, in this haze, with a third of their power already gone, they were finished.

But the Shrikes couldn't track them, and their pursuers were faced with the same problem they were.

It was oddly silent in the mist, in the cradle of the peaks, empty of all sound as the *Jerle Shannara* glided like a bird. All about them the mountains seemed afloat, dark masses appearing and fading like mirages. Alt Mer read the compass, then put it away. He would have to navigate by dead reckoning and gut instinct, then hope he could get back on course when the mist cleared. If it cleared. It might stay like this even further inland, beyond the mountain peaks. If it did, they were as lost as if they had never had a course to begin with.

He could just make out Spanner Frew standing at the bow. The big Rover was hunched forward, his concentration riveted on the shifting layers of white. Now and then he would signal by hand—go left, go right, go slow—and Redden Alt Mer would work the controls accordingly. The wind whistled past in sudden gusts, then died, baffled by a cliff face or air current. Mist swirled through the peaks, empty and aimless. Only the *Jerle Shannara* disturbed its ethereal fabric.

The rain returned, a gathering of dark clouds that turned quickly into a torrent. It engulfed the airship and its crew, soaking them through, shrouding them in dampness and gloom, claiming them as the sea might a sinking ship. Alt Mer, who had weathered worse, tried not to think of the way in which rain distorted shapes and spaces, creating the appearance of obstacles where there were none, giving hints of passage where walls of rock stood waiting. He relied on his instincts rather than his senses. He had been a sailor all his life; he knew something of the tricks that wind and water could play.

Behind him, the mist and darkness closed about. There was no sign of their pursuers—no sign of anything but the sky and the mountains and the shifting rain and mist between.

Spanner Frew came back to stand with him in the pilot box.

There was no reason to remain in the bow. The world about them had disappeared into space.

The shipwright glanced over and gave Redden Alt Mer a fierce smile. The Rover Captain smiled back. There was nothing for either to say.

The *Jerle Shannara* sailed on into the gloom.

FOUR

Heat and light gave way to cool darkness, the odd tingling sensation to numbness, and the present to the past as the Ilse Witch was swept away by the power of the Sword of Shannara. One moment, she was deep underground in the catacombs of Castledown, alone with her enemy, with the Druid Walker, surrounded by the wreckage of another age. In the next, she was gone so far inside herself that she had no sense of where she was. In the blink of an eye, she was transformed from a creature of flesh and blood to nothing more substantial than the thoughts that bore her away.

She had only a moment to wonder what was happening to her, and then it was done.

She went alone into the darkness, and yet she was aware of Walker being there with her, not in recognizable form, not even wholly formed, more a shadow, a shade that trailed after her like the flow of her long, dark hair. She could feel the pulse of him in the talisman she gripped like a lifeline. He was only a presence in the ether, but he was with her and he was watching.

When she emerged from the darkness, she was in another time and place, one she recognized instantly. She was in the home from which she had been taken as a child. She had thought she would never see it again and yet there it was, just as she remembered it from her childhood, wreathed in the shadows of an approaching dawn, cloaked in silence and danger. She could feel the coolness of the early morning air and

36

smell the pungent scent of the lilac bushes. She recognized
the moment at once. She had returned to the morning in
which her parents and brother had died and she had been
stolen away.

She watched the events of that morning unfold once more,
but this time from somewhere outside herself, as if they were
happening to someone else. Again, old Bark was killed when
he went out to investigate. Again, the cloaked forms slid past
her window in the faint predawn light, moving toward the
front doorway. Again, she fled, and again, it was in vain. She
hid her brother in the cellar and tried to escape the fate of her
parents. But the cloaked forms were waiting for her. She saw
herself taken by them as her house burned in a smoky red
haze. She watched them spirit her away, unconscious and
helpless, into the brightening east.

It was just as she remembered it. Yet it was different,
too. She saw herself surrounded by dark forms huddled in
conference as she lay trussed, blindfolded, and gagged. But
something was not right. They did not have the look of the
shape-shifters she knew to have taken her. Nor was there any
sign of the Druid Walker. Had she seen him go past the windows of her home this time as she remembered him doing before? She did not think so. Where was he?

As if in response to her question, a figure appeared out of
the trees, tall and dark and hooded like her captors. He had
the look of a Druid, a part of the fading night, a promise of
death's coming. He gestured to her captors, brought them
close to him momentarily, spoke words she could not hear,
then stepped away. In a flurry of activity, her captors squared
off like combatants and began to fight with one another. But
their struggle was not harsh and brutal; it was merely an exercise. Now and then, one would pause to glance at her, as if to
measure the effect of this pretense. The cloaked form let it go
on for a time, waiting, then suddenly reached down for her,

snatched her up, and spirited her away into the trees, leaving the odd scenario behind.

As he ran, she caught a glimpse of his forearms. They were scaly and mottled. They were reptilian.

Her mind spun with sudden recognition. *No!*

She was carried deep into the woods to a quiet place, and the dark-cloaked figure set her down. She watched him reveal himself, and he was not the Druid, as she now knew he would not be, could not be, but the Morgawr. *Betrayer!* The word shrieked at her. *Liar!* But he was much worse, of course. He was beyond anything words could describe, anything recognizably human. He was a monster.

She knew it was the truth she was seeing. She knew it instinctively, even doubting that it could be so. The images drawn on the magic of the Sword of Shannara could not lie. She could feel it in her bones, and it made perfect sense to her. How had she not known it before? How had she let herself become deceived so easily?

Yet she was only six years old then, she reminded herself. She was still nothing but a child.

Besieged by emotions that tore through her like hungry wolves, she would have screamed in rage and despair had she been able to do so. But she could not give voice to what she was feeling. She could only watch. The magic of the sword would allow nothing more.

She heard the Morgawr speak to her, his words soft and cajoling and treacherous. She watched herself slowly come to terms with his lies, to accept them, to believe that he was what he claimed and that she was the victim of a Druid's machinations. She watched him spirit her away aboard his Shrike, deep into his underground lair in the Wilderun. She watched herself close the door on her own prison, a willing fool, a pawn in a scheme she was beginning to understand for the first time. She watched herself begin another life—a small, misguided child driven by hatred and determination.

She watched herself, knowing she would never be the same, helpless to prevent it, to do anything more than despair at her fate.

Still the images continued, spinning themselves out, revealing to her the truth that had been concealed from her all these years. She watched a shape-shifter burrow through the smoking ruins of her home to retrieve her still-living baby brother. She watched him carry her brother away to a solitary fortress that she quickly recognized as Paranor. She saw him give her brother over to the Druid Walker, who in turn took him into the Highlands of Leah to entrust to a kind-faced man and his wife, who had children of their own and a debt to repay. She watched her brother grow in that family, his tiny baby's face changing with the passing of the years, his features slowly becoming recognizable.

She might have gasped or even cried out as she realized she was looking at the boy who had come to this distant land with Walker, who had confronted her and told her he was Bek. There was no mistaking him. He was the boy she had disbelieved, the boy she had hunted with the caull and almost killed. Bek, the brother she was so certain had died in the fire . . .

She could not finish these thoughts, any of them. She could barely force herself to confront them. Nor was there any time for a balanced consideration, for a coming to terms with what she was absorbing. Other images swiftly appeared, a wave of them, inundating her so thoroughly that her chest constricted and her breathing tightened under their crushing weight.

Now the images were ones of her training under the Morgawr, of her long, harsh schooling, of her mastery of self-discipline and her hardening of purpose as she set about learning how to destroy Walker. She saw herself grow from a girl into a young woman, but not with the same freedom of life and spirit that had invested Bek. Instead, she saw herself change from something human into something so like the

Morgawr that when all was said and done she was different from him on the outside only, where her skin set her apart from his scales. She had become dark and hate-filled and ruthless in the same way he was. She had embraced her magic's poisonous possibilities with his eagerness and savage determination.

She watched herself learn to use her magic as a weapon. All of her long, dark experience was replayed for her in numbing, sickening detail. She watched as she maimed and killed those who stood in her way. She watched herself destroy those who dared to confront or question her. She saw herself strip them of their hope and their courage and reduce them to slaves. She saw herself ruin people simply because it was convenient or suited her purpose. The Addershag died so that she could gain power over Ryer Ord Star. Her spy in the home of the Healer at Bracken Clell died so that he could never reveal his connection to her. Allardon Elessedil died so that the voyage the Druid Walker sought to make might not have Elven support.

There were others, so many she quickly lost count. Most she did not even remember. She watched them appear like ghosts out of the past and watched them die anew. At her hand or by her command, they died all the same. Or if they did not die, they often had the look of men and women who wished they had. She could feel their fear, helplessness, frustration, terror, and pain. She could feel their suffering.

She who was the Ilse Witch, who had never felt anything, who had made it a point to harden herself against any emotion, began to unravel like an old garment worn too often.

No more, she heard herself begging. *Please! Please!*

The images shifted yet again, and now she saw not the immediate acts she had perpetrated, but the consequences of those acts. Where a father died to serve her needs, a mother and children were left to starve in the streets. Where a daughter was subverted for her use, a brother was inadvertently put in harm's path and destroyed. Where one life was sacrificed, two more were made miserable.

It did not end there. A Free-born commander broken in spirit and mind at her whim cost his nation the benefit of his courage and left it bereft of leadership for years. The daughter of a politician caught in the middle of a struggle between two factions was imprisoned when her wisdom might have settled the dispute. Children disappeared into other lands, spirited away so that those who obeyed her might gain control over the grief-stricken parents. Tribes of Gnomes, deprived of sacred ground she had claimed for the Morgawr, blamed Dwarves, who then became their enemies. Like the rippling effect of a stone thrown on the still waters of a pond, the results of her selfish and predatory acts spread far beyond the initial impact.

All the while, she could feel the Morgawr watching from afar, a silent presence savoring the results of his duplicitous acts, his lies and deceits. He controlled her as if she was his puppet, tugged and pulled by the strings he wielded. He channeled her anger and her frustration, and he never let her forget against whom she must direct it. All that she did, she did in expectation of destroying the Druid Walker. But seeing her past now, stripped of pretense and laid bare in brightest daylight, she could not understand how she had been so misguided. Nothing of what she had done had achieved her supposed goals. None of it was justifiable. Everything had been a travesty.

The shell of self-deception in which she was encased broke under the deluge of images, and for the first time she saw herself for what she was. She was repulsive. She was the worst of what she could imagine, a creature whose humanity had been sacrificed in the false belief that it was meaningless. In sacrifice to the monster she had become, she had given up everything that had been part of the little girl she had once been.

Worst of all was the realization of what she had done to Bek. She had done more than betray him by assuming him dead in the ashes of her home. She had done worse than fail to discover if he might be whom he claimed when he confronted her. She had tried to put an end to him. She had hunted him down and nearly killed him. She had made him her prisoner, taken him back with her to *Black Moclips*, and given him over to Cree Bega.

She had abandoned him.

Again.

In the silence of the Sword of Shannara's quieting magic, the images faded momentarily, and she was left alone with her truth, with its starkness, with its razor's edge. Walker was still there, still close, his pale presence watching her come to terms with herself. She felt him like a pall, and she could not shake him off. She fought to break free of the tangle of deceits and treacheries and wrongdoings that draped her like a thousand spiderwebs. She struggled to breathe against the suffocating darkness of her life. She could do neither. She was as trapped as her victims.

The images began again, but she could no longer bear to watch them. Tumbling through the kaleidoscope of her terrible acts, she could not imagine how forgiveness could ever be granted to her. She could not imagine she had any right even to ask for it. She felt bereft of hope or grace. Finding her voice at last, she screamed in a mix of self-hatred and despair. The sound and the fury of it triggered her own magic, dark and swift and sure. It came to her aid in a rush, collided with the magic of the Sword of Shannara, and erupted within her in a fiery conflagration. She felt herself explode in a whirl of images and emotions. Then everything began to spiral off into a vast, depthless void, and she was swept away into clouds of endlessly drifting shadows.

*   *   *

Bek Ohmsford stiffened at the sound. "Did you hear that?" he asked Truls Rohk.

It was an unnecessary question. No one could have missed it. They were deep underground now, back within the catacombs of Castledown, searching for Walker. They had come down through the ruins, finding doors once hidden now open and waiting. No longer did the fire threads and creepers protect this domain. No sign of life remained. The world of Antrax was a graveyard of metal skeletons and dead machines.

Truls Rohk, cloaked and hooded even here, looked around slowly as the echo of the scream died away. "Someone is still alive down here."

"A woman," Bek ventured.

The shape-shifter grunted. "Don't be too sure."

Bek tested the air with his magic, humming softly, reading the lines of power. Grianne had passed this way not long ago. Her presence was unmistakable. They were following her in the belief that she would be following Walker. One would lead to the other. If they were quick enough, they could reach both in time. But until now, they had not been so sure that anyone was left alive. Certainly they had found no evidence of it.

Bek started ahead again, running his hand through his hair nervously. "She's gone this way."

Truls Rohk moved with him. "You said you had a plan. For when we find her."

"To capture her," Bek declared. "To take her alive."

"Such ambition, boy. Do you intend to tell me the details anytime soon?"

Bek kept going, taking time to think his explanation through. With Truls, you didn't want to overcomplicate things. The shape-shifter was already prepared to doubt the possibility of any plan working successfully. He was already thinking of ways to kill Grianne before she had a chance to kill him. All that was preventing it was Bek's passionate demand that Truls give his way a chance.

"She cannot harm us unless she uses her magic," he said quietly, not looking over at the other as they walked. He picked his way carefully through collapsed cables and chunks of concrete that had been shaken loose from the ceiling by an enormous blast and a quake that they had felt even aboveground. "She cannot use her magic unless she can use her voice. If we stop her from speaking or singing or making any sound whatsoever, we can take her prisoner."

Truls Rohk slid through the shadows and flickering lights like a massive cat. "We can accomplish what's needed by just killing her. Give this up, boy. She isn't going to become your sister again. She isn't going to accept what she is."

"If I can distract her, then you can get behind her," Bek continued, ignoring him. "Put your hands over her mouth and muffle her voice. You can do this if we can keep her from discovering you are there. I think it is possible. She will be intent on finding the Druid and dealing with me. She won't be looking for you."

"You dream big dreams." Truls Rohk did not sound convinced. "If this fails, we won't get a second chance. Either one of us."

Something heavy crashed to the floor of the passageway ahead, adding to the mounds of debris already collected. Steam hissed out of broken pipes, and strange smells gathered in niches and slid through cracks in the walls. Within the catacombs, every passageway looked exactly the same. It was a maze, and if they hadn't had Grianne's distinctive aura to track, they would have long since become lost.

Bek kept his voice even. "Walker would want us to do this," he ventured. He glanced over at the shape-shifter's dark form. "You know that to be true."

"What the Druid wants is anyone's guess. Nor is it necessarily the right thing. It hasn't gotten us much of anywhere so far."

"Which is why you chose to come with him on this quest," Bek offered quietly. "Which is why you have gone with him so many times before. Is that right?"

Truls Rohk said nothing, disappearing back inside himself so that all that remained was his cloaked shadow passing along in the near darkness, more presence than substance, so faint it seemed he might disappear in the blink of an eye.

Ahead, the tunnel widened. The damage here was more severe than anything they had encountered so far. Whole chunks of ceiling and wall had fallen away. Shattered glass and twisted metal lay in heaps. Though flameless lamps lit the passageway with pale luminescence, their light barely penetrated the heavy shadows.

A vast and cavernous chamber at the end of the corridor opened onto a pair of massive cylinders whose metal skin was split like overripe fruit. Steam hissed through the wounds like blood leaking from a body. The ends of severed wires flashed and snapped in small explosions. Struts and girders wrenched free of their fastenings with long, slow groans.

"There," Bek said softly, reaching out to touch the other's cloak. "She's there."

No movement or sound reached out to them, no indication that anyone living waited at the end of the passage amid the massive destruction. Truls Rohk froze momentarily, listening. Then he started ahead, this time leading the way, no longer trusting Bek, taking charge of what might become a deadly situation. The boy followed wordlessly, knowing he was no longer in control, that the best he could hope for was a chance to make things work out the way he thought they should.

A sudden hissing shattered the stillness, the sibilance punctuated by popping and cracking. The sounds reminded Bek of animals feeding on the bones of a carcass.

As they reached the opening, Truls Rohk moved swiftly into the shadows of one wall, motioning for Bek to stay back. Unwilling to lose contact, Bek retreated perhaps a pace, no more. Flattening himself against the smooth wall, he strained to hear something above the mechanical noises.

Then the shape-shifter faded into a patch of shadow and simply disappeared. Bek knew at once that he was trying to get to Grianne first. Bek charged after him, frightened that he had lost all chance of saving his sister. He breached the rubble at the entrance to the chamber in a rush and stopped.

The chamber was in ruins, a scrap heap of metal and glass, of shattered creepers and broken machines. Grianne knelt at its center beside a fallen Walker, her head lifting out of the shadow of her dark hair, her pale face caught in a slow flicker of light from a tangle of ruptured wires that sparked and fizzed. Her eyes were open as she stared toward the ceiling, but they did not see. Her hands were fastened securely about the handle of the Sword of Shannara, which rested blade downward against the smooth metal of the floor.

There was blood on those hands and on that handle and blade. There was blood all over her clothing and on Walker's, as well. There was blood on the floor, pooled in a crimson lake that trickled off into thin rivulets winding their way through the wreckage.

Bek stared at the scene in horror. He could not help what he was thinking. Walker was dead and Grianne had killed him.

To one side, a blade's sharp edge flashed momentarily in the shadows, and from the gathered gloom a deeper darkness eased silently forward.

Truls Rohk had reached the same conclusion.

FIVE

Hugging each other like frightened children, Ahren Elessedil and Ryer Ord Star made their way through the silent, dust-choked passageways of Castledown toward the city ruins above. The seer was still sobbing uncontrollably, her head bent into the Elven Prince's shoulder, her arms clinging as if she was afraid she might lose him. Leaving Walker had undone her completely, and though Ahren whispered reassurances to her as they went, trying to bring her back to herself, she seemed not to hear him. It was as if by leaving the Druid, she had left the better part of herself. The only indication she gave that she was still present was in the way she flinched when fresh chunks of wall or ceiling gave way or something exploded in the darkening recesses through which they fled.

"It will be all right, Ryer," Ahren kept repeating, even long after it was clear the words had no meaning for her.

Stirred by the events of the past few hours, his thoughts were jumbled and uncertain. The effects of the Elfstone magic had worn off, leaving him quieted and at peace again, no longer filled with fire and white rage. He had tucked the stones safely away inside his tunic pocket for when they would be needed again. A part of him anticipated such use, but another part hoped it might never happen. He felt vindicated and satisfied at having recovered them, having successfully summoned up their magic, and having used the blue fire against the hateful machines that had destroyed so many of his friends and companions from the *Jerle Shannara*. He felt renewed within, as if he had undergone a rite of passage and survived. He had come on this journey not much more than a boy, and now he was a man. It was his odyssey in gaining possession of the Elfstones that lent him this feeling of fresh identity, of new confidence. The experience had been horrific but empowering.

None of which made him feel any better about what had happened to Walker or what was likely to happen now to them. That Walker was dying when they left him was indisputable. Not even a Druid could survive the sort of wounds he had received. He might last a few minutes more, but there was no chance for him. So now the company, or what remained of it, must continue on without him. But continue to where? Continue for what reason? Walker himself had said that with the death of Antrax the knowledge of the books of magic was lost to them. He had made a choice in destroying the machine, and the choice had cost them any chance of recovering what they had come to find. It was an admission of failure. It was an acknowledgment that their journey had been for nothing.

Yet he could not help feeling that somehow this wasn't so, that there was something more to what had transpired than what was immediately obvious.

He wondered about the others of the company. He knew Bek had been alive when Ryer had fled the Ilse Witch and come back into the ruins to find Walker. The Elven Tracker Tamis had escaped, too. There would be others, somewhere. What must he do to find them? Find them he must, he knew, because without an airship and a crew, they were stranded indefinitely. With the Ilse Witch and her Mwellrets hunting them.

But he knew what he could do to gain help. He could use the Elfstones, the seeking stones of legend, to find a way to the others. The problem was that using the magic would alert the Ilse Witch to their presence. It would tell her exactly where they were, and she would come for them at once. They couldn't afford to have that happen. Ahren didn't think for a moment that he was a match for the Witch, even with the magic of the Elfstones to aid him. Stealth and secrecy were better weapons to employ just now. But he wasn't sure that stealth and secrecy would be enough.

He had been navigating the passageways for several hours, lost in his thoughts, when he became aware of the fact that Ryer had stopped crying. He glanced down at her in surprise, but she kept her face buried in his shoulder, pressed against his chest, concealed in the curtain of her long silvery hair. He thought that she might be working her way through her grief and should not be disturbed. He let her be. Instead, he concentrated anew on regaining the surface. The debris that had clogged the lower corridors was not so much in evidence here, as if the explosions had been centered more deeply. The air seemed fresher, and he thought they must be close to breaking free.

He found he was right. Within only minutes they passed through a pair of metal doors that stood unhinged and ajar, ducked under the collapsed framework, and stepped out into the open. They emerged from the tower into which Walker had disappeared days earlier, there in the center of the deadly maze that had ravaged the remainder of the company. It was night still, but dawn's approach was signaled by a faint lightening along the eastern horizon. Overhead, moonlight flooded out of a cloudless, starlit sky.

Ahren stopped just outside the tower entry and looked around cautiously. He could trace the outline of the walls of the maze and discern the clutter of broken creepers and weapons. Beyond, the ruins of the city spread away in a jumble of shattered buildings. No sounds came from that wasteland. It felt as if they were the only living creatures in the world.

But that was deceptive, he knew. The Mwellrets were still out there, searching for them. He must be very careful.

With Ryer still clinging to him, he knelt and put his mouth to her ear. "Listen to me," he whispered.

She went still, then nodded slowly. "We have to try to find the others—Bek and Tamis and Quentin. But we have to be very quiet. The Mwellrets and the Ilse Witch will be hunting us. At least, that's what we have to assume. We can't afford to let them catch us. We have to get out of these ruins and into the cover of the trees. Quickly. Can you help me?"

"We shouldn't have left him," she replied so softly he could barely make out the words. Her fingers tightened on his arms. "We should have stayed."

"No, Ryer," he said. "He told us to go. He told us there was nothing else we could do for him. He told us to find the others. Remember?"

She shook her head. "It doesn't matter. We should have stayed. He was dying."

"If we fail to do what he asked of us, if we allow ourselves to be captured or killed, we will have failed him. That makes his dying an even bigger waste." His voice was low, but fierce. "That isn't what he expects of us. That isn't why he sent us away."

"I betrayed him." She sobbed.

"We all betrayed each other at some point on this voyage." He forced her head out from his shoulder and lifted her chin so that she was looking at him. "He isn't dying because of anything we did or failed to do. He is dying because he chose to give up his life to destroy Antrax. He made that choice."

He took a deep breath to calm himself. "Listen to me. We serve him best now by honoring his last wishes. I don't know what he intended for us, what he thought would happen now that he is gone. I don't know what we've accomplished. But there's nothing more we can do for him beyond getting ourselves out of here and back to the Four Lands."

Her pale, drawn face tightened at the harshness of his words, then crumpled like old parchment. "I cannot survive without him, Ahren. I don't want to."

The Elven Prince reached out impulsively and stroked her fine hair. "He said he would see you again. He promised. Maybe you should give him the chance to keep that promise." He paused, then bent forward and kissed her forehead. "You say you can't survive without him. If it makes any difference, I don't think I can survive without you. I wouldn't have gotten this far if it hadn't been for you. Don't abandon me now."

He rested his cheek against her temple and held her, waiting for a response. It was a long time coming, but at last she lifted away and placed her small hands against his cheeks.

"All right," she said quietly. She gave him a small, sad smile. "I won't."

They rose and walked out of the shadow of the black tower and into the maze, then back through the ruins. They kept to the shadows and did not hurry, stopping frequently to listen for sounds that would warn them of danger. Ahren led, holding Ryer Ord Star's hand, the link between them oddly empowering. He had not lied when he told her he still needed her. Despite his recovery of the Elfstones and his successful battle against the creepers, he did not yet feel confident about himself. He had passed out of boyhood, but he was still inexperienced and callow. There were lessons still to be learned, and some of them would be hard. He did not want to face them alone. Having Ryer there to face them with him gave him a confidence he could not entirely explain but knew better than to ignore.

Yet he thought he understood at least a part of it. What he felt for the girl was close to love. It had grown slowly, and he was only just beginning to recognize it for what it was. He was not certain how it would resolve itself or even if it would survive another day. But in a world of turmoil and uncertainty, of monsters and terrible danger, it was reassuring to have her close, to be able to ask her advice, just to touch her hand. He drew strength from her that was both powerful and mysterious—not in the way of magic, but in the way of spirit. Maybe it was as simple as not being entirely alone, of having another person with whom to share whatever happened. But maybe, too, it was as mystical as life and death.

They walked a long time through the ruins without hearing or seeing anything or anyone. They moved in a southerly direction, back the way they had come, toward the bay in which the *Jerle Shannara* had once anchored. She was in the hands of the Ilse Witch now, of course—unless things had changed, which was possible. Things changed quickly in this land. Things changed without warning. Maybe this time they would change in a way that would favor Walker's company rather than the Witch's.

Suddenly Ryer Ord Star drew up short, her slim body rigid and trembling. Ahren turned back to her at once. She was staring into space, into some place he could not see, and her face reflected such dismay that he found himself quickly scanning his surroundings to find its cause.

"He's dead, Ahren," she said in a small, grief-stricken whisper.

She sank to the ground, crying. Her hand still clutched his, as if that were all that held her together. He knelt beside her, putting his arms about her, holding her close.

"Maybe he's at peace," he said, wondering if that was possible for Walker Boh.

"I saw him," she said. "In my vision, just now. I saw him being carried by a shade into a green light over an underground lake. He wasn't alone. On the shore were three people. One was Bek, the second a cloaked form I didn't recognize. The third was the Ilse Witch."

"The Ilse Witch was with Bek?"

Her hand tightened on his. "But she wasn't doing anything threatening. She wasn't even seeing him. She was just there, physically present, but at the same time she wasn't. She looked lost. Wait! No, that isn't right. She didn't look lost; she looked stunned. But that isn't all, Ahren. The vision changed, and she was holding Bek and he was holding her. They were somewhere else, somewhere in the future, I think. I don't know how to explain this, but they were the same person. They were joined."

Ahren tried to make sense of this. "One body and one face? The same in that way?"

She shook her head. "It didn't look like that, but it felt like that. Something happened to connect them. But it was as much a spiritual as a physical joining. There was such pain! I could feel it. I don't know whom it was coming from, who had generated it. Maybe both. But it was released through the connection they formed, and it was a trigger for something else, something that was going to happen after. But I didn't see that; I wasn't permitted."

Ahren thought. "Well, maybe it has something to do with them being brother and sister. Maybe that was the connection you sensed. Maybe the Ilse Witch discovered it was true, and that was what released all this pain you felt."

Her eyes were huge and liquid in the moonlight. "Maybe."

"Do you think Bek and the Ilse Witch are down in Castledown with Walker?"

She shook her head. "I don't know."

"Should we go back and look for them?"

She just stared at him, wide-eyed, frightened.

There was no way to know, of course. It was a vision, and visions were subject to misleading and false interpretations. They revealed truths, but not in terms that were immediately apparent. That was their nature. Ryer Ord Star saw the future better than most. But even she was not permitted to catch more than a glimpse of it, and that glimpse might mean something other than what it suggested.

Going back for any reason suddenly seemed unthinkable

to Ahren, and he abandoned the idea. Instead, they rose and walked on. Frustrated and troubled by the seer's words, Ahren found himself hoping that when she had another vision, she would have one they could do something about. Like finding a way out of their present dilemma, for instance. Visions of other people in other places were of precious little use just now. It was a selfish attitude, and he was immediately ashamed of it. But he couldn't help thinking it nonetheless.

They continued on. It would be morning soon. If they hadn't reached the shelter of the trees by then, they would be in trouble. They had the remnants of buildings to hide in, but if they were detected, they would be easily trapped. If they kept on after it grew light, they would be left exposed on the open roadways. Ahren didn't know if it made any difference what he did at this point since they were without a destination or a plan for rescue. All he knew to do was to try to find a way to keep out of the hands of the Ilse Witch and the Mwellrets. Or maybe only the latter, if Ryer's vision proved prophetic. Was it possible that Bek had made the witch a prisoner, had found some way to subdue her? He had magic, after all, magic strong enough to shatter creepers. Was it sufficient to overcome the witch, as well?

Ahren wished he knew more about what was happening. But he had wished that from the beginning.

They were close to the edge of the forest when he heard movement ahead. It was soft and furtive, the kind that comes from someone trying not to be discovered. Ahren dropped into a crouch, pulling Ryer down with him. They were deep in the shadows of a wall, so they would not be easily seen. On the other hand, it was slowly growing lighter and they couldn't stay where they were indefinitely.

He motioned for her to keep silent and follow his lead. Then he rose and began to make his way forward, but more slowly. Moments later, he heard the noise again, a scraping of boots on stone, very close now, and he dropped back into the shadows once more.

Almost instantly, a Mwellret slid out of the darkness and made its way across the open ground in front of them. There was no mistaking what it was or its intent. It carried a battle-ax in one hand and a short sword strapped about its waist. It was searching for someone. It might not be them, Ahren accepted, but that wouldn't help them if they were found.

He waited until the ret was out of sight, and started ahead again. Maybe they could get behind it. Maybe there was only the one.

But as they angled left, away from the first, they encountered a second, this one coming right for them. Ahren ducked back into the cover of a building's roofless shell, then led Ryer across the open floor to another exit. He picked his way carefully over piles of debris, but his boots made small scraping sounds that he could not seem to avoid. Outside again, he scuttled in a crouch to another building, Ryer at his heels, and made his way through. Enough dodging, he hoped, would lose any pursuers.

Outside, he stopped and looked around. Nothing was familiar. He could see the outline of the treetops some distance off, but he had no idea in which direction he had been going or where the Mwellrets were. He listened for sound of them, but heard nothing.

"There's someone behind us," Ryer whispered in his ear.

He tugged her forward again, making for the cover of the trees, hoping that they could reach it in time. It was steadily growing lighter, the sun just beginning to crest the horizon, leaving the ruins bathed in a dangerous combination of light and shadows that could easily deceive the eyes. Ahren thought he heard a sudden grunt from somewhere close, and he wondered if they had been discovered after all.

Maybe he should use the Elfstones, even if they gave him away. But the magic wasn't any good against rets or any other creatures not motivated by magic. Nor would it respond if he wasn't physically threatened.

He put his free hand on the handle of his long knife, his only other weapon, hesitating. He was deliberating over what to do when a movement off to his right stopped him. He faded back against a wall with Ryer, holding his breath as a cloaked form shouldered into view through the buildings. He could not make out who it was. Or even what, human or Mwellret. Ryer was pressed so close against him he could feel her breathing. He tightened his grip on her hand, feeling nothing himself of the reassurance he was trying to convey to her.

Then the cloaked form was gone. Ahren exhaled slowly and began to move ahead again. It wasn't far to the trees. Beyond the ruins, only a hundred yards or so away, he could make out limbs and clusters of leaves in the new light.

As he stepped around the corner of a partially collapsed wall, he glanced back momentarily at Ryer to be certain she was all right. The look in her eyes changed just as he did so, her wariness giving way to outright terror.

Quickly he looked back, but he was too slow. Sudden movement confronted him.

Then everything went black.

SIX

When he saw Truls Rohk move toward his sister, Bek Ohmsford didn't take time to consider the consequences of what he did next. All he knew was that if he failed to act, the shape-shifter would kill her. It didn't matter what the other had promised earlier, in a moment of rational thought, away from the carnage in which they found themselves now. Once Truls saw her kneeling at the side of the fallen Walker, the Sword of Shannara in hand and blood everywhere, that promise might as well have been written on water.

If Bek had allowed his emotions to get the better of him, perhaps he would have reacted the same way as Truls Rohk. But Bek could see from his sister's face that something was very wrong with her. She was staring skyward, but she wasn't seeing anything. She held the Sword of Shannara, but not as if it was a weapon she had just used. Nor did he think she would rely on the talisman to take the life of the Druid. She would rely on her own magic, the magic of the wishsong, and if she had done so here, there would not be this much blood.

Once he got past his initial shock, Bek knew there was more to what he was seeing than appearances indicated. But Truls Rohk was behind Grianne and couldn't see her face. Not that it would have mattered, since he was not inclined to feel the same way Bek did. For the shape-shifter, the Ilse Witch was a dangerous enemy and nothing less, and if there was any reason to suspect she might harm them, he wouldn't think twice about stopping her.

So Bek attacked him. He did so in a reaction born out of desperation, intending to hold the other back without really harming him. But Truls Rohk was so enormously strong that Bek couldn't afford to employ half measures when calling up the power of the wishsong. He hadn't mastered it yet anyway, not in the way that Grianne had, having only just discovered a few months earlier that he even had the use of it. The best he could do was to hope it had the intended effect.

He sent it spinning out in an entangling web of magic that snared Truls and sent him tumbling head over heels through the wreckage of the chamber. The shape-shifter went down, but he was back up again almost at once, throwing off his concealment, revealing himself instantly, big and dark and dangerous. With the long knife held before him, he rushed Grianne a second time. But Bek knew enough by now to appreciate how strong Truls was, and he had already assumed his first attempt at slowing the shape-shifter would fail. He sent a second wave of magic lancing out, a wall of sound that snared the other and sent him flying backwards. Bek cried out, but he did not think Truls even heard him, so caught up was he in his determination to get at Grianne.

But Bek reached her first, dropped to his knees, and wrapped his arms about her protectively. She did not move when he did so. She did not respond in any way.

"Don't hurt her," he started to say, turning to find Truls Rohk.

Then something hit him so hard that it knocked him completely free of Grianne and sent him sprawling into the remains of a shattered creeper. Stunned, he dragged himself to his knees. "Truls . . . ," he gasped as he peered over at Grianne helplessly.

The shape-shifter was bent over her, a menacing shadow, his blade at her exposed throat. "You haven't the experience for this, boy," he hissed at Bek. "Not yet. But that doesn't make you less of an irritation, I'll give you that. No, don't try to get up. Stay where you are."

He was silent a moment, tensed and ready as he leaned closer to Bek's sister. Then the knife lowered. "What's wrong with her? She's in some sort of trance."

Bek climbed back to his feet in spite of the warning and stumbled over, shaking off the disorienting effects of the blow. "Did you have to hit me so hard?"

"I did if I wanted to be certain you would remember what it meant to use your magic against me." The other shifted to face him. "What were you thinking?"

Bek shook his head. "Only that I didn't want you to hurt her. I thought you would kill her outright when you saw Walker. I didn't think you could see her face, so you wouldn't know she couldn't hurt us. I just reacted."

Truls Rohk grunted. "Next time, think twice before you do." The blade disappeared into the cloak. "Take the sword out of her hands and see what she does."

He was already bent over the Druid, probing through the blood-soaked robes, searching for signs of life. Bek knelt in front of the unseeing Grianne and carefully pried her fingers loose from the Sword of Shannara. They released easily, limply, and he caught the talisman in his hand as it fell free. There was no sign of recognition in her eyes. She did not even blink.

Bek laid down the sword and moved Grianne's arms to her sides. She allowed him to do this without responding in any way. She might have been made of soft clay.

"She doesn't know anything that's happening to her," he said quietly.

"The Druid lives," Truls Rohk responded. "Barely."

He straightened the ragged form and tore strips of cloth from his own clothing to stem the flow of blood from the visible wounds. Bek watched helplessly, appalled by the extent of the damage. The Druid's injuries seemed more internal than external. There were jagged wounds to his chest and stomach, but he was bleeding from his mouth and ears and nose and even his eyes, as well. He seemed to have suffered a major rupture of his organs.

Then abruptly, unexpectedly, the penetrating eyes opened and fixed on Bek. The boy was so startled that for a moment he quit breathing and just stared back at the other.

"Where is she?" Walker whispered in a voice that was thick with blood and pain.

Bek didn't have to ask whom he was talking about. "She's right beside us. But she doesn't seem to know who we are or what's going on."

"She is paralyzed by the sword's magic. She panicked and used her own to try to ward it off. Futile. It was too much. Even for her."

"Walker," Truls Rohk said softly, bending close to him. "Tell us what to do."

The pale face shifted slightly, and the dark eyes settled on the other. "Carry me out of here. Go where I tell you to go. Don't stop until you get there."

"But your wounds—"

"My wounds are beyond help." The Druid's voice turned suddenly hard and fierce. "There isn't much time left, shape-shifter. Not for me. Do as I say. Antrax is destroyed. Castle-down is dead. What there was of the treasure we came to find, of the books and their contents, is lost." The eyes shifted. "Bek, bring your sister with us. Lead her by the hand. She will follow."

Bek glanced at Grianne, then back at Walker. "If we move you . . ."

"Druid, it will kill you to take you out of here!" Truls Rohk snapped angrily. "I didn't come this far just to bury you!"

The Druid's strange eyes fixed on him. "Choices of life and death are not always ours to make, Truls. Do as I say."

Truls Rohk scooped the Druid into the cradle of his arms,

slowly and gently, trying not to damage him further. Walker made no sound as he was lifted, his dark head sinking into his chest, his good arm folding over his stomach. Bek strapped the Sword of Shannara across his back, then took Grianne's hand and pulled her to her feet. She came willingly, easily, and she made no response to being led away.

They passed out of the ruined chamber and back down the passageway through which they had come. At the first juncture, Walker took them in a different direction than the one that had brought them in. Bek saw the dark head move slightly and heard the tired voice whisper instructions. The ends of the Druid's tattered robes trailed from his limp form, leaving smears of blood on the floor.

As they progressed through the catacombs, Bek glanced at Grianne from time to time, but never once did she look back at him. Her gaze stayed fixed straight ahead, and she moved as if she was sleepwalking. It frightened the boy to see her like this, more so than when she was hunting him. She seemed as if she was nothing more than a shell, the living person she had been gone entirely.

Their progress was slowed now and again by heaps of stone and twisted metal that barred their passage. Once, Truls was forced to lay the Druid down long enough to force back a sheet of twisted metal tightly jammed across their passage. Bek watched the Druid's eyes close against his pain and weariness, saw him flinch when he was picked up again, his hand clawing at his stomach as if to hold himself together. How Walker could still be alive after losing so much blood was beyond the boy. He had seen injured men before, but none who had lived after being damaged so severely.

Truls Rohk was beside himself. "Druid, this is senseless!" he snapped at one point, stopping in rage and frustration. "Let me try to help you!"

"You help me best by going on, Truls," was the other's weak response. "Go, now. Ahead still."

They walked a long way before finally coming out into a vast underground cavern that did not look as if it was a part of Castledown, but of the earth itself. The cavern was natural, the rock walls unchanged by metal or machines, the ceiling studded with stalactites that dripped water and minerals in steady cadence through the echoing silence. What little light there was emanated from flameless lamps that bracketed the cavern entry and a soft phosphorescence given off by the cavern rock. It was impossible to see the far side of the chamber, though bright enough to discern that it was a long distance off.

At the center of the chamber was a huge body of water as black as ink and smooth as glass.

"Take me to its edge," Walker ordered Truls Rohk.

They made their way along the uneven cavern floor, which was littered with loose rock and slick with damp. Moss grew in dark patches, and tiny ferns wormed through cracks in the stone. That anything could grow down here, bereft of sunlight, surprised Bek.

He squeezed Grianne's hand reassuringly, an automatic response to the encroachment of fresh darkness and solitude. He glanced at her immediately to see if she had noticed, but her gaze was still directed straight ahead.

At the water's edge, they stopped. On Walker's instructions, Truls Rohk knelt to lay him down, cradling him so that his head and shoulders rested in the shape-shifter's arms. Bek found himself thinking how odd it seemed, that a creature who was himself not whole, but bits and pieces held together by smoky mist, should be the Druid's bearer. He remembered when he had first met Walker in the Highlands of Leah. The Druid had seemed so strong then, so indomitable, as if nothing could ever change him. Now he was broken and ragged, leaking blood and life in a faraway land.

Tears came to Bek's eyes as swiftly as the thought, his response to the harsh realization that death approached. He did not know what to do. He wanted to help Walker, to make him whole again, to restore him to who he had been when they had first met all those months ago. He wanted to say something about how much the Druid had done for him. But all he could do was hold his sister's hand and wait to see what would happen.

"This is as far as I go," Walker said softly, coughing blood and wincing with the pain the movement caused.

Truls Rohk wiped the blood away with his sleeve. "You can't die on me, Druid. I won't allow it. We've too much more to do, you and I."

"We've done all we're allowed to do, shape-shifter," Walker replied. His smile was surprisingly warm. "Now we must go our separate ways. You'll have to find your own adventures, make your own trouble."

The other grunted. "Not likely I could ever do the job as well as you. Game-playing has always been your specialty, not mine."

Bek knelt beside them, pulling Grianne down with him. She let him place her however he wished and did nothing to acknowledge she knew he was there. Truls Rohk edged away from her.

"I'm done with this life," Walker said. "I've done what I can with it, and I have to be satisfied with that. Make certain, when you return, that Kylen Elessedil honors his father's bargain. His brother will stand with you; Ahren's stronger than you think. He has the Elfstones now, but the Elfstones won't make the difference. He will. Remember that. Remember as well what we made this journey for. What we have found here, what we have recovered, belongs to us."

Truls Rohk spat. "You're not making any sense, Druid. What are you talking about? We have nothing to show for what we've done! We've claimed nothing! The Elfstones?

They weren't ours to begin with! What of the magic we sought? What of the books that contained it?"

Walker made a dismissive gesture. "The magic contained in the books, the magic I spoke of to both Allardon Elessedil and his son, was never the reason for this voyage."

"Then what was?" Truls Rohk was incensed. "Are we to play guessing games all night, Druid? What are we doing here? Tell us! Has this all been for nothing? Give us something to hope for! Now, while there's still time! Because I don't think you have much left! Look at you! You're—"

He couldn't make himself finish the sentence, biting off the rest of what he was going to say in bitter distaste.

"Dying?" Walker spoke the word for him. "It's all right to say it, Truls. Dying will set me free from promises and responsibilities that have kept me in chains for longer than I care to remember. Anyway, it's only a word."

"You say it, then. I don't want to talk to you anymore."

Walker reached up with his good hand and took hold of the other's cloak. To Bek's surprise, Truls Rohk did not pull away.

"Listen to me. Before I came to this land, before I decided to undertake this voyage, I went into the Valley of Shale, to the Hadeshorn, and I summoned the shade of Allanon. I spoke with him, asking what I could expect if I chose to follow the castaway's map. He told me that of all the goals I sought to accomplish, I would succeed in only one. For a long time, Truls, I thought that he meant I would recover the magic of the books from the Old World. I thought that was what I was supposed to do. I thought that was the purpose of this voyage. It wasn't."

His fingers tightened on the shape-shifter's cloak. "I made the mistake of thinking I could shape the future in the way I sought. I was wrong. Life doesn't permit it, not even if you are a Druid. We are given glimpses of possibilities, nothing more. The future is a map drawn in the sand, and the tide can wash it away in a moment. It is so here. All of our efforts in coming to this land, Truls, all of our sacrifices, have been for something we never once considered."

He paused, his breathing weak and labored, the effort of speaking further too much for him.

"Then what did we come here for?" Truls Rohk asked impatiently, still angered by what he was hearing. "What, Druid?"

"For her," Walker whispered, and pointed at Grianne.

The shape-shifter was so stunned that for a moment he could not seem to find anything to say in response. It was as if the fire had gone out of him completely.

"We came for Grianne?" Bek asked in surprise, not sure he had heard correctly.

"It will become clear to you when you are home again," Walker whispered, his words almost inaudible, even in the deep silence of the cavern. "She is your charge, Bek. She is your responsibility now, your sister recovered as you wished she might be. Return her to the Four Lands. Do what you must, but see her home again."

"This makes no sense at all!" Truls Rohk snapped in fury. "She is our enemy!"

"Give me your word, Bek," Walker said, his eyes never leaving the boy.

Bek nodded. "You have it."

Walker held his gaze a moment longer, then looked at the shape-shifter. "And you, as well, Truls. Your word."

For a moment, Bek thought Truls Rohk wasn't going to give it. The shape-shifter didn't say anything, staring at the Druid in silence. Tension radiated from his dark form, yet he refused to reveal what he was thinking.

Walker's fingers kept their death grip on the shape-shifter's cloak. "Your word," he whispered again. "Trust me enough to give it."

Truls Rohk exhaled in a hiss of frustration and dismay. "All right. I give you my word."

"Care for her as you would for each other," the Druid continued, his eyes back on Bek. "She will not always be like this. She will recover one day. But until then, she needs looking after. She needs you to ward her from danger."

"What can we do to help her wake?" Bek pressed.

The Druid took a long, ragged breath. "She must help herself, Bek. The Sword of Shannara has revealed to her the truth about her life, about the lies she has been told and the wrong paths she has taken. She has been forced to confront who she has become and what she has done. She is barely grown, and already she has committed more heinous wrongs and destructive acts than others will commit in a lifetime. She has much to forgive herself for, even given the fact that she was so badly misled by the Morgawr. The responsibility for finding forgiveness lies with her. When she finds a way to accept that, she will recover."

"What if she doesn't?" Truls Rohk asked. "It may be, Druid, that she is beyond forgiveness, not just from others, but even from herself. She is a monster, even in this world."

Bek gave the shape-shifter an angry glance, thinking that Truls would never change his opinion of Grianne, that to him she would always be the Ilse Witch and his enemy.

The Druid had a fit of coughing, then steadied. "She is human, Truls—like you," he replied softly. "Others labeled you a monster. They were wrong to do so. It is the same with her. She is not beyond redemption. But that is her path to walk, not yours. Yours is to see that she has the chance to walk it."

He coughed again, more deeply. His breathing was so thick and wet that with every breath it seemed he might choke on his own blood. The sound of it emanated from deep in his chest, where his lungs were filling. Yet he lifted himself into a sitting position, freed himself from Truls Rohk's arms, and motioned him away.

"Leave me. Take Grianne and walk back to the cavern entrance. When I am gone, follow the passageway that bears left all the way to the surface. Seek out the others who still live— the Rovers, Ahren Elessedil, Ryer Ord Star. Quentin Leah, perhaps. One or two more, if they were lucky. Sail home again. Don't linger here. Antrax is finished. The Old World has gone back into the past for good. The New World, the Four Lands, is what matters."

Truls Rohk stayed where he was. "I won't leave you alone. Don't ask it of me."

Walker's head sagged, his dark hair falling forward to shadow his lean face. "I won't be alone, Truls. Now go."

Truls Rohk hesitated, then rose slowly to his feet. Bek stood up, as well, taking Grianne's hand and pulling her up with him. For a moment no one moved, then the shape-shifter wheeled away without a word and started back through the loose rock for the cavern entrance. Bek followed wordlessly, leading Grianne, glancing back over his shoulder to look at Walker. The Druid was slumped by the edge of the underground lake, his dark robes wet with his blood, the slow, gentle heave of his shoulders the only indication that he still lived. Bek had an almost uncontrollable urge to turn around and go back for him, but he knew it would be pointless. The Druid had made his choice.

At the cavern entrance, Truls Rohk glanced back at Bek, then stopped abruptly and pointed toward the lake. "Druid games, boy," he hissed. "Look! See what happens now!"

Bek turned. The lake was roiling and churning at its center, and a wicked green light shone from its depths. A dark and spectral figure rose from its center and hung suspended in the air. A face lifted out of the cloak's hood, dusky-skinned and black-bearded, a face Bek, without ever having seen it before, knew at once.

"Allanon," he whispered.

*　　*　　*

Walker Boh dreamed of the past. He was no longer in pain, but his weariness was so overwhelming that he barely knew where he was. His sense of time had evaporated, and it seemed to him now that yesterday was as real and present as today. So it was that he found himself remembering how he had become a Druid, so long ago that all those who were there at the time were gone now. He had never wanted to be one of them, had never trusted the Druids as an order. He had lived alone for many years, avoiding his Ohmsford heritage and any contact with its other descendants. It had taken the loss of his arm to turn him to his destiny, to persuade him that the blood mark bestowed three hundred years earlier by Al-lanon on the forehead of his ancestor, Brin Ohmsford, had been intended for him.

That was a long time ago.

Everything was so long ago.

He watched the greenish light rise out of the depths of the underground lake, breaking the surface of its waters in shards of brightness. He watched it widen and spread, then grow in intensity as a path from the netherworld opened beneath. It was a languid, surreal experience and became a part of his dreams.

When the cloaked figure appeared in the light's emerald wake, he knew at once who it was. He knew instinctively, just as he knew he was dying. He watched with weary anticipation, ready to embrace what waited, to cast off the chains of his life. He had borne his burden of office for as long as he was able. He had done the best he could. He had regrets, but none that gave him more than passing pause. What he had accomplished would not be apparent right away to those who mattered, but it would become clear in time. Some would embrace it. Some would turn away. In either case, it was out of his hands.

The dark figure crossed the surface of the lake to where

Walker lay and reached for him. His hand lifted automatically in response. Allanon's dark countenance stared down, penetrating eyes fixing on him. There was approval in those eyes. There was a promise of peace.

Walker smiled.

As Bek and Truls Rohk watched, the shade reached Walker's side. Green light played about their dark forms, slicing through them like razors, slashing them with emerald blades. There was a hiss, but it was soft and distant, the whisper of a dying man's breath.

The shade bent for Walker, the effort strong and purposeful. Walker's hand came up, perhaps to ward it off, perhaps to welcome it; it was difficult to tell. It made no difference. The shade lifted him into his arms and cradled him like a child.

Then together they made a slow retreat back across the lake, gliding on air, their dark forms illuminated by shards of light that gathered about them like fireflies. When both were encased in the glow, it closed around completely and they slowly disappeared into its brilliant center until nothing remained but a faint rippling of the lake's dark waters. In seconds, even that was gone, and the cavern was still and empty once more.

Bek realized suddenly that he was crying. How much of what Walker had hoped to see accomplished in this life had he lived to witness? Not anything of what had brought him here. Not anything of what he had envisioned of the future. He had died the last of his order, an outcast and perhaps a failure. The thought saddened the boy more than he would have believed possible.

"It's finished," he said quietly.

Truls Rohk's response was surprising. "No, boy. It's just begun. Wait and see."

Bek looked at him, but the shape-shifter refused to say

anything more. They stood where they were for a few seconds, unable to break away. It was as if they were expecting something more to happen. It was as if something must. But nothing did, and at last they quit looking and began to walk back through the passageways of Castledown to the world above.

SEVEN

Rue Meridian flew *Black Moclips* through the last hours of night and into the first light of morning before beginning her search of Castledown's ruins. She would have started sooner, but she was afraid to attempt anything complicated until it was light enough to see what she was doing. Airships were complex mechanisms, and flying one alone, even using the controls situated in the pilot box, was no mean feat. Just keeping the vessel airborne required all her concentration. To make out anything in the darkness, she would have had to place herself at the railing, outside the box and away from the controls. She would not have lasted long that way.

She still had Hunter Predd to help her, but the Wing Rider was not a sailor and knew almost nothing of how airships functioned. He could perform small tasks, but nothing on the order of what would be required if anything went wrong. Besides, he was needed aboard Obsidian if they were to have any real chance of finding the missing members of the company. The Roc's eyes were better than their own, and it had been trained to search for what was lost and needed finding. For now, the giant bird was keeping pace with the airship, staying just off her sails as it wheeled back and forth across the skies, waiting for his master to rejoin him.

"No chance of persuading that Federation Commander or any of his crew to help us, I don't suppose," Hunter Predd ventured at one point, looking doubtful even as he voiced the possibility.

She shook her head. "He says he won't do anything that contradicts his orders, and that includes helping us." She brushed back stray strands of her long red hair. "You have to understand. Aden Kett is a soldier through and through, trained to follow orders, to accept the hierarchy of command. He isn't a bad man, just a misguided one."

They hadn't heard anything from the imprisoned Federation crew since she had locked them away in the storeroom below. Twice she had sent the Wing Rider to check on them, and both times he had reported back that other than muffled conversation, there was nothing to be heard. Apparently the crew had decided that for the time being it was better to wait this business out. She was more than content to let them do so.

Still, it would have been nice to have help. As soon as it was light enough, she planned to send Hunter off on Obsidian in search of Walker, Bek, and the others. In a freewheeling search, he would have a better chance than she would of spotting something. If he was successful, she could bring *Black Moclips* close enough to pick them up. The risk to the airship was minimal. In daylight, from the safety of the skies, she would be able to see for miles. It was not likely that anything would be able to get close enough to threaten, especially now that she had control of the Ilse Witch's vessel.

Of course, she could not discount the possibility that the witch had other weapons at her disposal, ones that could affect even an airship in flight. The witch was down there somewhere in the ruins, hunting Walker, and they might be unlucky enough to encounter her in their search. Rue Meridian had to hope that Obsidian would spy out any sign of the witch before they got close enough for her to do them any damage. She also had to hope that they would find Bek or Walker or any of the others who still lived before the witch did.

She yawned and flexed her gloved fingers where they gripped the flying levers. She had been awake for twenty-four hours, and she was beginning to feel the strain. Her wounds, even padded and sealed within her flying leathers, were throbbing painfully, and her eyes were heavy with the need for sleep. But there was no one to relieve her at the controls, so there was no point in dwelling on her deprivations. Maybe she would get lucky and find Bek at first light. Bek could fly *Black Moclips*. Big Red had taught him well enough. With Bek at the controls, she could get some sleep.

Her thoughts settled momentarily on the boy. No, he was not a boy, she corrected herself quickly. Bek wasn't a boy— not in any way that mattered. He was young in years, but old already in life experience. Certainly he was more mature than those Federation fools she had been forced to suffer on the Prekkendorran. He was smart and funny, and he exuded genuine confidence. She thought back to their conversations on the flight out from the Four Lands, remembering how they had joked and laughed, how they had shared stories and confidences. Hawk and her brother both had been surprised. They didn't understand the attraction. But her friendship with Bek was different from the ones she was accustomed to; it was grounded in their similar personalities. Bek was like a best friend. She felt she could trust him. She felt she could tell him anything.

She shook her head and smiled. Bek put her at ease, and that wasn't something many men did. He didn't invite her to be anyone other than who she really was. He didn't expect anything from her. He wasn't looking to compete, wasn't trying to impress. He was a bit in awe of her, but she was used to that. The important thing was that he didn't let it interfere with or intrude on their friendship.

She wondered where he was. She wondered what had happened to him. Somehow he had fallen into the hands of the

Mwellrets and the Ilse Witch, been brought aboard *Black Moclips* and imprisoned. Then someone had rescued him. Who? Had he really lost his voice, as Aden Kett had said, or was he just pretending at it? She felt frustrated by her ignorance. She had so many questions and no way to determine the answers without finding Bek first. She did not like to think of him being hunted down there. But Bek was resourceful, able to find his way through dangers that would overwhelm other men. He would be all right until she found him.

Hawk would laugh at her, if he were there. *He's just a boy,* he would say, not making the distinction she had. *He's not even one of us, not even a Rover.*

But that didn't matter, of course. Not to her, at least. What mattered was that Bek was her friend, and she could admit to herself, if to no one else, that she didn't have many of these.

She brushed the matter aside and returned her attention to the task at hand. The first faint streaks of light were appearing in the east, sliding through gaps in the mountains. Within an hour, she would begin her search. By nightfall, perhaps they could be gone from this place.

Hunter Predd, who had been absent for a time, reappeared at her elbow. "I took a quick look below. Nothing happening. Some of them are asleep. There's no sign of any attempt to break out. But I don't like the situation anyway."

"Nor do I." She shifted her position to relieve her cramped and aching muscles. "Maybe Big Red will reach us before the day is out."

"Maybe." The Wing Rider looked east. "It's growing light. I should start searching. Will you be all right alone?"

She nodded. "Let's find them, Wing Rider. All of them we left behind. Bek, for one, is still alive—along with whoever saved him from the Mwellrets. We know that much, at least. Maybe a few of the others are down there, as well. Whatever happens, we can't abandon them."

Hunter Predd nodded. "We won't."

He went back down out of the pilot box and across the deck to the aft railing. She watched him signal into the night, then lower himself over the side on a rope. Moments later, he flew by aboard Obsidian, giving her a wave of reassurance before disappearing into the gloom. She could just make him out through the fading darkness. Wheeling *Black Moclips* in the direction he was taking, she moved out of the forested hill country and over the ravaged landscape of the ruins, the airship rocking gently in the wind.

She glanced down perfunctorily. Everything below looked flat and gray. It would have to grow much lighter before she could hope to see anyone. Even then, she doubted she would have much luck. Any rescue of the missing members of the company from the *Jerle Shannara* would rely almost entirely on the efforts of the Wing Rider and his Roc.

Don't let us fail them, she thought. *Not again.*

She took a deep breath and put her back to the wind.

Hunter Predd swung down the rope from the airship railing, his keen eyes picking out Obsidian's sleek shape moving up obediently through the darkness. The Roc drifted into place below him, then rose so that his rider could settle aboard. Once Hunter Predd felt the harness between his legs, he reached down for the grips, released the rope, and with a nudge of his knees sent his carrier winging away.

Dawn was a faint gray smudge to the east, but its light was beginning to creep over the landscape. Flying out over the ruins, he could already make out the shattered buildings and debris-strewn roadways, empty and silent. Obsidian would be seeing much more. Even so, this search would not be easy. He had a feeling that Rue Meridian believed that all they needed to do was complete a sweep of the city and they would find anyone who was still alive down there. But Castledown was huge, miles and miles of rubble, and there was every chance that they would fail in their efforts to unmask its secrets. Those they sought must find a way to make themselves known if they were to be discovered other than by chance. To do that, they must be looking skyward in order to see the Roc. It had been almost two weeks since the *Jerle Shannara* had deposited the missing company on the shores of that bay to make the journey inland. By now, they might well have given up hope of being found. They might not be looking for help at all. They might not be alive.

It did no good to speculate, of course. He had come with the Rover girl to find whoever still survived, so it was pointless to start throwing up obstacles to their search before they had even begun it. After all, Obsidian had found smaller specks in larger expanses against greater odds. The chances were there; he simply had to make the best of them.

He flew in widening circles for the duration of the sunrise, searching all the while for movement on the ground, for something that looked a little out of place, for anything that would indicate a foreign presence. As he did so, he found himself thinking back on his decision to make this journey and wondering if he would have been better off staying home. It wasn't just that it had turned out so badly; it was that nothing much seemed to have been accomplished for the effort. If it turned out that Walker was dead, then following Kael Elessedil's map would have been for nothing. Worse, it would have cost lives that could have been spared. Wing Riders were strong believers in letting well enough alone, in living their own lives and not messing in the lives of others. It had taken considerable compromise for him to come on this voyage, and it was taking considerable compromise now for him to stick things out. Common sense said he should turn around and fly home, that the longer he stayed, the shorter the odds grew that he would ever leave. Certainly the Rovers must feel the same way. Rovers and Wing Riders were alike, nomads by choice, mercenaries by profession. Their loyalty and sense of obligation could be bought and paid for, but they never let that get in the way of their common sense.

But he wouldn't leave, of course. He wouldn't abandon those on the ground, no matter the odds, if there was any chance at all that they were still alive. It was just that he couldn't help second-guessing himself, even if it wouldn't make any difference in what he perceived as his commitment to his missing comrades. What if this? What if that? It was the sort of game you played at if you spent enough time alone and in dangerous circumstances. But it was only a game.

The sun crested the horizon, daylight broke across the land, and the ruins stretched away as silent and empty as before. He glanced back to where Rue Meridian flew *Black Moclips*, a solitary figure in the pilot box. She was dangerously tired, and he wasn't sure how much longer she could continue to fly the airship alone. It had been an inspired idea to steal the vessel from the Ilse Witch, but it was going to turn into a liability if she didn't get help fast. He wasn't sure at the moment where that help was going to come from. He would give it if he could, but he knew next to nothing about airships. The best he could do was to pluck her off the deck if things got out of hand.

He caught sight of something odd at the edge of the ruins north, and he swung down for a closer look. He discovered a scattering of bodies, but they were not the bodies of his companions from the *Jerle Shannara* or even the bodies of any people he had ever encountered. These people had burnished skin and red hair, and they were dressed like Gnomes. He had never seen their like, but they had a tribal look to their garb and he assumed they were an indigenous people. How they had come to this sorry end was a mystery, but it looked as if they had been ripped apart by something extraordinarily powerful. Creepers, perhaps.

He flew over the still forms for a few moments more, hoping he would spy something that would help him discover what had happened. He thought it might be worth setting down to see if there was any indication that members of the *Jerle Shannara* had been involved, but decided against it. The information wouldn't do him any good unless he tried to follow up on foot, and that was too dangerous. He glanced over his shoulder to where *Black Moclips* hovered several hundred feet away, drifting in the wind. He signaled to Rue Meridian to swing by for a look, then began a slow sweep back out over the ruins. The Rover girl could make her own decision about what to do. He would continue on. If nothing else turned up, he would come back later.

He had barely settled into a fresh glide over the blasted expanse of the city when he caught sight of something flying toward them from the northeast. Obsidian saw it, as well, and gave a sharp cry of recognition.

It was Po Kelles aboard Niciannon.

Rue Meridian had just maneuvered *Black Moclips* over the collection of dead men at the edge of the ruins and was wondering what to make of it when she glanced back at Hunter Predd and saw the second Wing Rider. She knew it had to be Po Kelles, and she felt fresh hope that his arrival signaled the approach of her brother aboard the *Jerle Shannara*. With two airships searching, she would have a much better chance of finding Bek and the others. Perhaps she could take on a couple of Rovers to help her fly *Black Moclips* so that she could catch a few hours of sleep.

She watched the two riders circle in tandem, talking and gesturing from the backs of their Rocs. Holding her course, she peered back toward the coast, for some sign of the other ship. But there was nothing to be seen as yet, so she returned her attention to the Wing Riders. The discussion had become animated, and the first vague feelings of uneasiness crept through her. Something about the way they communicated, even from a distance, didn't look right.

You're imagining things, she thought.

Then Hunter Predd broke away from Po Kelles and flew back to where she waited, swinging about to come alongside before dropping down and below the aft railing. Taking hold of the line he had left dangling from before, the Wing Rider swung down off the bird and pulled himself up, hand over hand, until he was back on board. A hand signal to Obsidian sent the Roc wheeling away to take up a position beside them, flying to keep pace.

Rue Meridian waited as the Elf hurried over to the pilot box and climbed inside. Even in the faint new light, she could tell that he was upset.

"Listen to me, Little Red." His weathered face was calm, but strained. "Your brother and the others are flying this way, but they are being chased. A fleet of enemy airships appeared off the coast yesterday at dawn. The *Jerle Shannara* barely got away from them. She's been flying this way ever since, trying to shake them off. But fast as she is, she can't seem to lose them. They tracked her all through the mountains, all the way inland, even after she'd changed course to go another way entirely, and now they're almost here."

Enemy airships? All the way out here, so far from the Four Lands? She took a moment to let the information sink in. "Who are they?"

He made a dismissive gesture with one hand. "I don't know. No one does. They fly no flag, and their crews act like dead men. They walk around, but they don't seem to see anything. Po Kelles got a close look late yesterday when the Rovers set down to rest, thinking they'd lost them. Not an hour passed, and there they were again. The ones he could see were men, but they didn't act like men. They acted like machines. They didn't look as if they were alive. They were all stiff and empty-eyed, not seeing anything. One thing is certain. They know where they're going, and they don't seem to need a map to find us."

She glanced around at the brightening day and the ruins below, her hopes for continuing the search fading. "How far away are they?"

"Not half an hour. We have to fly out of here. If they catch you in *Black Moclips* by yourself, you won't stand a chance."

She stared at him without speaking for a moment, anger and frustration blooming inside. She understood the need for flight, but she had never been good at being forced to do anything. Her instincts were to stand and fight, not to run. She hated abandoning yet again those she was searching for, leaving them to an uncertain fate at the hands of not only the Mwellrets and the Ilse Witch, but now this new threat, as well. How long would they last on their own? How long would it be before she could come back and give them any help?

"How many of them are there?" she asked.

The Wing Rider shook his head. "More than twenty. Too many, Little Red, for us to face."

He was right, of course. About everything. They should break off the search and flee before the intruders caught sight of them. But she could not help feeling that Bek and the others were down there, some of them at least, waiting for help. She could not shake off the suspicion that all that was needed was just a little more time. Even a few minutes might be enough.

"Tell Po Kelles to take up watch for us," she ordered. "We can look just a little longer before giving up."

He stared at her. She knew she had no right to give him orders, and he was debating whether or not to point that out. She knew, as well, that he understood what she was feeling.

"The weather is turning, too, Little Red," he said softly, pointing.

Sure enough. Dark clouds were rolling in from the east, borne by coastal winds, and they looked menacing even from a distance. She was surprised she hadn't noticed them. The air had grown colder, too. A front was moving through, and it was bringing a storm with it.

She looked back at him. "Let's try, Wing Rider. For as long as we can. We owe them that much."

Hunter Predd didn't need to ask whom she was talking about. He nodded. "All right, Rover girl. But you watch yourself."

He jumped down out of the pilot box and sprinted back across the decking to the aft railing and disappeared over the side. Obsidian was already in place, and in seconds they were winging off to warn Po Kelles. Rue Meridian swung the airship back around toward the ruins, heading in. Already she was searching the rubble.

Then it occurred to her, a sudden and quite startling revelation, that she was flying an enemy airship, and those on the ground wouldn't know who she was. Rather than come out of hiding to reveal themselves, they would simply burrow deeper. Why hadn't she realized this before? Had she done so, perhaps she could have devised a way to make her intentions known. But it was too late now. Maybe the presence of the Wing Rider would reassure anyone looking up that she wasn't the Ilse Witch. Maybe they would understand what she was trying to do.

Just a few minutes more, she kept telling herself. *Just give me a few minutes more.*

She got those minutes and then some, but she saw no sign of anyone below. The clouds rolled in and blocked the sun, and the air turned so cold that even though she pulled her cloak tight about her, she was left shivering. The landscape was spotted with shadows, and everything looked the same. She was still searching, still insistent on not giving up, when Hunter Predd swung right in front of her and began to gesture.

She turned and looked. Two dozen airships had materialized from out of the gloom, black specks on the horizon. One led all the others, the one being chased, and she knew from its shape that it was the *Jerle Shannara*. Po Kelles was flying

Niciannon toward it already, and Hunter Predd was calling to her to tack east and head for the mountains. With a final glance down, she did so. *Black Moclips* lurched in response to her hard wrench on the steering levers and the surge of full power from the radian draws she sent down to the parse tubes and their diapson crystals. The airship shuddered, straightened, and began to pick up speed. Rue Meridian could hear the shouts and cries of the imprisoned Federation crew, but she had no time for them just now. They had made their choice in this matter, and they were stuck with things as they were, like it or not.

"Shut up!" she shrieked, not so much at the men as at the wind that whipped past her ears, taunting and rough.

At full speed, her anger a catalyst that made her as ready to fight as to flee, she flew into the mountains.

EIGHT

In the slow, cool hours before sunrise, Quentin Leah buried Ard Patrinell and Tamis. He lacked a digging tool to provide a grave, so he lowered them into the wronk pit and filled it in with rocks. It took him a long time to find the rocks in the darkness and then to carry them, sometimes long distances, to be dropped into place. The pit was large and not easily covered over, but he kept at it, even after he was so weary his body ached.

When he was finished, he knelt by the rough mound and said good-bye to them, talking to them as if they were still there, wishing them peace, hoping they were together, telling them they would be missed. An Elven Tracker and a Captain of the Home Guard, star-crossed in every sense of the word—perhaps they would be united wherever they were now. He tried to think of Patrinell as the Captain was before his changing, a warrior of unmatched fighting skills, a man of courage and honor. Quentin did not know what lay beyond death, but he thought it might be something better than life and that maybe that something allowed you to make up for missed chances and lost dreams.

He did not cry, he was all done crying. But he was hollowed out and bereft, and he felt a bleakness that was so pervasive it threatened to undo him completely.

Dawn was breaking when he stood again, finished at last. He reached down for the Sword of Leah where he had cast it away at the end of his battle, and picked it up again. The bright, dark surface was unmarked save for streaks of blood and grime. He wiped it off carefully, considering it as he did so. It seemed to him that the sword had failed him completely. For all its magic properties, for all that it was touted to have accomplished in its long and storied history, it had proved to be of little use to him here in this strange land. It had not been enough to save Tamis or Ard Patrinell. It had not even been enough to enable him to protect Bek, whom he had sworn to protect no matter what. That Quentin was alive because he had possession of it was of little consolation. His own life seemed to have been purchased at the cost of others. He did not feel deserving of it. He felt dead inside, and he did not know how he could ever feel anything else.

He put the blade back into its sheath and strapped it across his back once more. The sun was cresting the horizon, and he had to decide what he would do next. Finding Bek was a priority, but to do so he had to leave the concealment of the forest and go back into the ruins of Castledown. That meant risking yet another confrontation with creepers and wronks, and he did not know if he could face that. What he did know was that he needed to be away from this place of death and disappointment.

So he began walking, watching the shadows about him fade back into the trees as sunlight seeped through the canopy and dappled the forest floor. He dropped down from the hills surrounding Castledown to the level stretches he had abandoned in his flight from the Patrinell wronk two days earlier. Walking made him feel somewhat better. The bleakness in his heart lingered, but something of his loss of direction and purpose disappeared as he considered his prospects. There was nothing to be gained by standing about. What he must do, no matter what it took, was find Bek. It was Quentin's insistence on making the journey that had persuaded his cousin to come with him. If he accomplished nothing else, at least he must see Bek safely home again.

He believed that Bek was still alive, even though he knew that many others in the company had perished. He believed this because Tamis had been with his cousin before she found Quentin and because in his heart, where instincts sometimes gave insights that eyes could not, he felt nothing had changed. But that didn't mean that Bek wasn't in trouble and in need of help, and Quentin was determined not to let him down.

Some part of him understood that his intensity was triggered by a need to grasp hold of something to save himself. He was aware that if he faltered, his despair would prove overwhelming, his bleakness of heart so complete that he would be unable to make himself move. If he gave way, he was lost. Moving in any direction, seizing on any purpose, kept him from tumbling into the abyss. He didn't know how realistic he was being in trying to find Bek, all alone and unaided by any useful magic, but the odds didn't matter if he could manage to stay sane.

He was not far from the ruins when he caught sight of an airship flying out ahead of him, distant and small against the horizon. He was so surprised that for a moment he stopped where he was and stared at it in disbelief. It was too far away for him to identify, but he decided at once that it must be the *Jerle Shannara* searching for the members of the company. He felt fresh hope at this and began walking toward it at once.

But in seconds the airship had drifted into the haze of a massive bank of clouds coming out of the east and was lost from view.

He was standing in an open clearing, trying to find it again, when he heard someone call. "Highlander! Wait!"

He turned in surprise, trying to identify the voice, to determine from where the speaker was calling. He was still searching the hills unsuccessfully when Panax walked out of the trees behind him.

"Where have you been, Quentin Leah?" the Dwarf demanded, out of breath and flushed with exertion. "We've been hunting for you all yesterday and last night! It was pure luck that I caught sight of you just now!"

He came up to Quentin and shook his hand warmly. "Well met, Highlander. You look a wreck, if you don't mind my saying. Are you all right?"

"I'm fine," Quentin answered, even though he wasn't. "Who's been looking for me, Panax?"

"Kian and I. Obat and a handful of his Rindge. The wronk tore them up pretty thoroughly. The village, the people, everything. Scattered the tribe all over the place, those it didn't kill. Obat pulled the survivors together up in the hills. At one point, they were planning to rebuild their village and go on as before, but no longer. They're not going back. Things have changed."

He stopped suddenly, taking a close look at Quentin's face, finding something in it he hadn't seen before. "Where's Tamis?" he asked.

Quentin shook his head. "Dead. Ard Patrinell, as well. They killed each other. I couldn't save either one." His hands were shaking. He couldn't seem to stop them. He stared down, confused. "We set a trap, Tamis and I. We hid in the forest by a pit and let the wronk find us, thinking we could drop it in. We used a decoy, a trick, to lure it over. It worked, but then it climbed out, and Tamis . . ."

He trailed off, unable to continue, tears coming to his eyes once more, as if he were a child reliving a nightmare.

Panax took Quentin's hands in his own, steadying them, holding on until the shaking stopped. "You don't look as if you escaped by much yourself," he said quietly. "I expect there wasn't anything you could have done to save either that you didn't try. Don't expect too much of yourself, Highlander. Even magic doesn't always provide the answers we seek. The Druid may have found that out himself, wherever he is. Sometimes, we have to accept that we have limitations. Some things we can't prevent. Death is one."

He let go of Quentin's hands and gripped him by his shoulders. "I'm sorry about Tamis and Ard Patrinell, truly sorry. I expect they fought hard to stay alive, Highlander. But so did you. I think you owe it to them and to yourself to make that count for something."

Quentin looked into the Dwarf's brown eyes, coming back to himself as he did so, able to form a measure of fresh resolve. He remembered Tamis' face at the end, the fierce way she had faced her own death. Panax was right. To fall apart now, to give in to his sadness, would be a betrayal of everything she had fought to accomplish. He took a deep breath. "All right."

Panax nodded and stepped back. "Good. We need you to be strong, Quentin Leah. The Rindge have been out exploring since early this morning, before dawn. They went into the ruins. Castledown is littered with creepers, none of them functioning. The fire threads are down. Antrax, it seems, is dead."

Quentin stared at him, not comprehending.

"Well and good, you might say, but look over there." The Dwarf pointed east to a steadily advancing cloudbank, a huge wall of darkness that stretched across the entire horizon. "What's coming is a change in the world, according to the Rindge. They have a legend about it. If Antrax is destroyed, the world will revert to what it once was. Remember how the Rindge insisted that Antrax controlled the weather? Well before that time, this land was all ice and snow, bitter cold and barely habitable. It only turned to something warm and green after Antrax changed it eons ago. Now it's changing back. Feel the nip in the air?"

Quentin hadn't noticed it before, but Panax was right. The air was growing steadily colder, even as the sun rose. There was a brittle snap to it that whispered of winter.

"Obat and his people are going over the mountains and into

Parkasia's interior," the Dwarf continued. "Better weather over there. Safer country. If we don't find another way out of here pretty quick, I think we'd better go with them."

Suddenly Quentin remembered the airship. "I just saw the *Jerle Shannara*, Panax," he said quickly, directing the other's attention toward the front. "It was visible for a moment, right over there. I saw it while I was standing where you found me, and then I lost it in those clouds."

They stared into the darkness together for a several moments without seeing anything. Then Panax cleared his throat. "Not that I doubt you on this, but are you sure it wasn't *Black Moclips*?"

The possibility hadn't occurred to Quentin. He was so eager for it to be the *Jerle Shannara*, he supposed, that he had never stopped to consider that it might be the enemy airship. He had forgotten about their nemesis.

He shook his head slowly. "No, I guess I'm not sure at all."

The Dwarf nodded. "No harm done. But we have to be careful. The witch and her Mwellrets are still out there."

"What about Bek and the others?"

Panax looked uncomfortable. "Still no sign. I don't know if we can find them, Highlander. Obat's people still won't go into the ruins. They say it's a place of death even with Antrax gone and the creepers and fire threads down. They say it's cursed. Nothing has changed. I tried to get them to come with me this morning, but after they saw what had happened, they went right back up into the hills to wait." He shook his head. "I guess I don't blame them, but it doesn't help us much."

Quentin faced him. "I'm not leaving Bek, Panax. I'm all done with running away, with watching people die and not doing anything about it."

The Dwarf nodded. "We'll keep looking, Highlander. For as long as we can, we'll keep searching. But don't get your hopes up."

"He's alive," Quentin insisted.

The Dwarf did not reply, his weathered, bluff face masking his thoughts. His gaze shifted skyward to the north, and Quentin turned to look, as well. A line of black specks had appeared on the horizon, coming down parallel to the storm front, strung out across the morning sky.

"Airships," Panax announced softly, a new edge to his rough voice.

They watched the specks grow larger and begin to take shape. Quentin could not understand where so many airships had come from, seemingly out of nowhere, all at once. Whose were they? He glanced at Panax, but the Dwarf seemed as confused as he did.

"Look," Panax said, pointing.

The airship Quentin had seen earlier had reappeared out of the darkness, moving swiftly across the sky east toward the mountains. There was no mistaking it this time; it was *Black Moclips*. A cry for help died on the Highlander's lips, and he froze in place as it passed overhead and receded into the distance. They could see now that it was attempting to cut off another ship, one farther ahead. The distinctive rake of the three masts marked it instantly as the *Jerle Shannara*. The witch and her Mwellrets were in pursuit of the Rovers, and these new airships were chasing both.

"What's going on?" Quentin asked, as much of himself as of Panax.

A moment later, the pursuing fleet split into two groups, one going after *Black Moclips* and the *Jerle Shannara*, the other breaking off toward the ruins of Castledown. This second group was the smaller of the two, but was commanded by the largest of the airships. In a line, the vessels swung over the ruins, where they prepared to set down.

"I don't think we should stand out in the open like this," Panax offered after a moment.

Quickly, they moved into the cover of the trees, then retreated back up into the hills until they found a vantage point from which they could look down on what was taking place. It didn't take them long to decide that they had made the right decision. Rope ladders had been lowered from the airships, which hovered a dozen feet off the ground, and knots of Mwellrets were climbing down and spreading out. On board the airships, the crews kept their stations. But there was something odd about their stance. They stood frozen in place like statues, not moving about, not even talking with one another. Quentin stared at them for a long time, waiting for any sort of reaction at all. There was none.

"I don't think they're friends," Panax declared softly. He paused. "Look at that."

Something new had been added to the mix—a handful of creatures that lacked any recognizable identity. They were being placed in slings and lowered by winches from the largest airship, one after the other. They looked a little like humans grown all out of proportion, with massive shoulders and arms, thick legs, and hairy torsos. They hunched forward as they walked, using all four limbs like the apes of the Old World. But their heads had a wolfish look to them, with narrow, sharp snouts, pointed ears, and gimlet eyes. Even at a distance, their features were unmistakable.

"What are those?" Quentin breathed.

The search parties fanned out through the ruins, dozens of Mwellrets in each, armed and armored, a decidedly hostile invader. Secured on lengths of chain and ordered to track, the odd hunched creatures were being used like dogs. Noses to the ground, they began making their way through the rubble in different directions, the Mwellrets trailing. Within the ruins, there was no response from Antrax. No creepers appeared and no fire threads lanced forth. It appeared the Rindge were right about what had happened. But it only made Quentin wonder all the more about Bek.

Burly, dark-skinned Kian appeared suddenly out the trees,

moving over to join them. He nodded a greeting to Quentin as he came up, but didn't speak.

"We've got a problem, Highlander," Panax said without looking at him.

Quentin nodded. "They're searching for us. Eventually, they'll find us."

"All too quickly, I expect." The Dwarf straightened. "We can't stay. We have to get away."

Quentin Leah stared down at the searchers as they trickled into the city, tiny figures still, like toys. Quentin understood what Panax was saying, but he didn't want to speak the words aloud. Panax was saying that they had to give up the search for Bek. They had to put as much distance as possible between themselves and whoever was down there hunting them.

He felt something shrivel up and die inside at the prospect of abandoning Bek yet again, but he knew that if he stayed, he would be found. That would accomplish nothing useful and might result in his death. He tried to think it through. Maybe Bek stood a better chance than Quentin thought. Bek had the use of magic; Tamis had told them so. She had seen him use it, a power that could shred creepers. His cousin wasn't entirely helpless. In truth, he might be better off than they were. Maybe he had even found Walker, so that the two of them were together. They might have already fled the ruins and gone into the mountains themselves.

He stopped himself angrily. He was rationalizing. He was trying to make himself feel better about abandoning Bek, about breaking his promise once more. But he didn't really believe what he was telling himself. His heart wouldn't let him.

"What do we do?" he asked finally, resigned to doing the one thing he had sworn he wouldn't.

Panax rubbed his bearded chin. "We go into the Aleuthra Ark—those mountains behind us—with Obat and his people. We go deeper into Parkasia. The airships were flying that way. Maybe we can catch up to one of them. Maybe we can signal it." He shrugged wearily. "Maybe we can manage to stay alive."

To his credit, he didn't say anything about coming back for Bek and the others, or resuming the search somewhere further down the line. He understood that such a thing might not happen, that they might never return to the ruins. He was not about to make a promise he knew he could not keep.

None of this helped Quentin with his feelings of betrayal, but it was better to be honest about the possibilities than to cling to false hopes.

I'm sorry, Bek, he said to himself.

"They're coming this way," Kian said suddenly.

One of the search parties had emerged at the edge of the ruins below and found the bodies of the Rindge that the Patrinell wronk had killed two days earlier. Already, the hunched creatures were sniffing the ground for tracks. A wolfish head lifted and looked toward where they crouched in the trees, as if aware of them, as if able to spy them out.

Without another word, the Dwarf, the Elf, and the Highlander melted into the trees and were gone.

It took them the better part of an hour to reach the clearing where Obat and his Rindge were assembled. They were high up on the slopes of the hills fronting the Aleuthra Ark, which ran down the interior of Parkasia from northwest to southeast like a jagged spine. The Rindge were a ragged and dispirited-looking group, although not disorganized or unprepared. Sentries had been posted and met the three outlanders long before they reached the main body of Rindge. Weapons had been recovered, so that all the men were armed. But the larger portion of survivors was made up of women and children, some of the latter only babies. There were at least a hundred Rindge and probably closer to two hundred. They had their belongings piled about them, tied up in bundles or stuffed into cloth sacks. Most sat quietly in the shadows, talking among themselves, waiting. In the dappled forest light, they looked like hollow-eyed and uncertain ghosts.

Obat came up to Panax and began talking to him immediately. Panax listened, then replied, using the ancient Dwarf tongue he had employed successfully when they had first met. Obat listened and shook his head no. Panax tried again, pointing back in the direction from which they had come. It was clear to Quentin that he was telling Obat about the intruders from the airships. But Obat didn't like what he was hearing.

Exasperation written all over his face, Panax turned to the Highlander. "I told him we have to move quickly, that the belongings must be left behind. As it is, it will take everything we have to move this bunch to safety without having to deal with all this stuff. But Obat says this is all his people have left. They won't leave it."

He turned to Kian. "Go back up the trail with a couple of the Rindge and keep watch."

The Elven Hunter turned without a word, beckoned a couple of the Rindge to come with him, and disappeared into the trees at a quick trot.

Panax turned back to Obat and tried again. This time he made unmistakable gestures indicating what would happen if the Rindge were too slow in the attempt to escape. His broad face was flushed and angry, and his voice was raised. Obat stared at him, impassive.

We're wasting time, Quentin thought suddenly. *Time we don't have.*

"Panax," he said. The Dwarf turned. "Tell them to pick up their things and start walking. We can't take time to argue about this any longer. Let them find out for themselves whether or not it's worth it to haul their possessions. Set a pace the women and children can follow and go. Leave me a dozen Rindge. I'll see what I can do to slow our pursuers down."

The Dwarf gave him a hard look and then nodded. "All right, Highlander. But I'm staying, as well. Don't argue the matter. As you say, we don't have time for it."

He spoke quickly to Obat, who turned to his people and began shouting orders. The Rindge assembled at once, belongings in place. Led by a handful of armed men, they set out along a narrow forest path into the hills, moving silently and purposefully. Quentin was surprised at how swiftly they got going. There was no hesitation, no confusion. Everyone seemed to know what to do. Perhaps they had done it before. Perhaps they were better prepared for the move than Panax thought.

In seconds, the clearing was empty of everyone but Quentin, Panax, and a dozen or so Rindge warriors. Obat had chosen to stay, as well. Quentin wasn't sure this was a good idea, since Obat was clearly the leader of the tribe and losing him might prove disastrous. But it wasn't his decision to make, so he left it alone.

He turned to look off in the direction of the ruins, wondering how much time they had before the Mwellrets and those hunched creatures discovered them. Perhaps it wouldn't happen as quickly as he feared. There would be other tracks to distract them, other trails to follow. They might choose one that would lead them in another direction entirely. But he didn't believe that for a minute.

He thought about his failures on his journey from the Highlands of Leah, of his missed opportunities and questionable choices. He had set out with such high hopes. He had thought himself capable of dictating the direction of his life. He had been wrong. In the end, it had been all he could do to stay afloat in the sea of confusion that surrounded him. He could not even determine whom he would use the magic of his vaunted sword to protect. He could use it to help only those whom fate placed within his reach, and maybe not even those.

The Rindge were among them. He could leave them and go on, because in the end they didn't really have anything to do with him, his reasons for coming to Parkasia, or his promise to Bek. If anything, they were a hindrance. If he was to have any chance at all of catching up to one of the airships and finding a way out of this land, speed might make the difference. But in the wake of his failure to save Tamis or Ard Patrinell or to find Bek, he felt a compelling need to succeed in helping *someone*. The Rindge were giving him that opportunity. He could not make himself walk away from it. He could not let anyone else be hurt because of him.

He would do what he could for those he was in a position to help. If helping the Rindge was what fate had given him the chance to do, that would have to be enough.

Panax walked up beside him. "What happens now, Quentin Leah? How do we stop those things back there from catching up to Obat's people?"

The Highlander only wished he knew.

NINE

When Ahren Elessedil regained consciousness, he found himself lying on his side in Castledown's rubble looking at the boots of his captors. His hands were tied behind his back, and his head ached from the blow he had received. Even without having witnessed the particulars, he knew at once what had happened and was awash in despair and frustration. He had stumbled into a Mwellret trap, one set for him as he tried to move through the ruins with Ryer Ord Star. How could he have been so stupid? After what he had gone through to retrieve the Elfstones and escape Castledown, how could he have allowed himself to be caught so completely unawares?

There wasn't any answer for such questions, of course. Asking them only invited self-recrimination, and there was nothing to be gained from that.

He blinked against the dryness in his eyes and tried to sit up, but a heavy boot pushed him back again and settled on his chest.

"Little Elvess sstayss where they are," a voice hissed.

He glanced up at the big Mwellret standing over him and nodded. The boot and the Mwellret moved away a few steps, but the watchful eyes stayed fixed on him. He could see rets standing all about him, maybe a dozen or so, heavy reptilian bodies cloaked against the dawn light, heads bent between heavy shoulders, voices low and sibilant as they conversed among themselves. None of them seemed to be in a hurry to go anywhere or to get anything done. They seemed to be waiting for something. He tried to imagine what it might be. The Ilse Witch, perhaps. She must have gone further into the ruins. Perhaps she had gone underground in search of Walker.

He thought suddenly of Ryer Ord Star, and from his prone position he scanned as much of the area as he could in an effort to find her. He spotted her finally, seated in an open space, alone and ignored. He stared at her for a long time, waiting to be noticed, but she never looked his way. She kept her gaze lowered, her face shadowed by her long silver hair. She might have had her eyes closed; he couldn't tell. She was unfettered, and no Mwellrets stood over her as they did over him. They seemed unconcerned that she might try to escape.

Something about her situation bothered him. She didn't seem to be a prisoner at all.

He glanced around further, searching for any other members of the company who might have encountered the same misfortune. But no one else was in evidence, only the two of them. He shifted surreptitiously in an effort to see what else he might have missed from where he lay, but he saw only Mwellrets in the area.

Then he glanced skyward and saw the airships.

His throat tightened. There were six of them—no, wait, there were eight—hanging in the air, not far off the ground at the edge of the ruins, silhouetted against the morning sky. They were close enough that he could see crew members standing about, Mwellrets climbing down rope ladders, and hoists lowering animals that twisted and writhed and grunted loudly. He caught only glimpses of them against the bright sunrise as they slipped over the sides of the airships and disappeared down into the ruins, and he couldn't make out what they were.

Mwellrets and airships. He couldn't understand it. Where had they come from, all at once like this? Had the Ilse Witch brought them, keeping them back from *Black Moclips*, hiding them until they were needed? He tried to reason it through and failed.

He glanced again at Ryer Ord Star. The seer still hadn't looked up, hadn't changed position, hadn't done anything to evidence that she was even conscious. He wondered suddenly if perhaps she was in a trance, trying to connect to Walker. But the Druid had to be dead by now. He had been dying back there in the extraction chamber, his blood everywhere. Walker had sacrificed himself to destroy Antrax. Even Ryer must realize that she could no longer reach him.

So what was she doing?

Why wasn't she tied up like he was?

He waited for the answers to come, for her to respond to his mental summons, for something to happen that would reveal her condition—without success.

All of a sudden, he remembered the Elfstones. He was astonished that he had forgotten about them, that he had somehow failed to remember the one weapon he still had at his disposal. Maybe. He had tucked them into his tunic on fleeing the ruins, in a pocket near his waist. Were they still there? He didn't think he could reach them with his hands tied, but he could at least determine if he had them. The Mwellrets would have searched him for weapons, not for the Stones. They wouldn't even know what they were.

He glanced about quickly, but no one was looking at him. He rolled onto his other side, moving slowly, trying not to attract attention. He squirmed down against the hard earth, searching for the feel of the Elfstones against his body. He could not find them. His hopes sank. He shifted positions, trying to see if they were somewhere else, but he could not feel them anywhere.

He was still searching when he heard a mix of heavy footfalls, rough voices, and deep growls. The Mwellret who had pushed him down came over at once and hauled him to his feet with a jerk, standing him upright and propping him against a section of wall.

"Sseess now what becomess of you, little Elvess," he muttered before turning away.

Ahren glanced over at Ryer Ord Star. She was on her feet, as well, still alone and still not looking at him. She stood with her arms wrapped about her slender body, looking frail and tiny. Something was going on with her that he didn't understand, and she wasn't doing anything to let him know what it was.

A clutch of Mwellrets strode into the clearing. Two of the burliest held the ends of chains that were fastened to a collar strapped about the neck of one of the most terrifying creatures Ahren had ever seen. The creature tugged and twisted against the collar like a huge dog, grunts and growls emanating from deep within its throat as it did so. Its body was hunched over and heavily muscled. Four human limbs that ended in clawed fingers and massive shoulders were covered in thick black hair. Its torso was so long and sinuous that it allowed the creature to almost double back on itself as it twisted about angrily, trying to bite at the chains. Its head was wolfish, its jaws huge, and its teeth long and dark. It had the look of something bred not just to hunt, but to destroy.

When it saw Ahren, it lunged for him, and the Elf pressed back against the building wall in fear.

A tall, black-cloaked figure stepped forward, blocking the creature's path. The beast cringed and backed away.

The cloaked figure turned and looked at him. Ahren could just make out the other's face. It might have been human once, but now it was covered with gray scales like the rets, flat and expressionless, its green eyes compressed into narrow slits that regarded him with such coldness that he forgot all about the wolf creature.

"Cree Bega," the cloaked figure called, still watching Ahren.

The Mwellret who had been standing guard over him came at once. Big as he was, he looked small next to the newcomer. Even so, he did not do anything to acknowledge the other's authority, neither bowing nor nodding. He simply stood there, his gaze level and fixed.

"Cree Bega," the other repeated, and this time there was a hint of menace in his voice. "Why is this Elf still alive?"

"He iss an Elesssedil. He hass the power to ssummon the magic of the Elfsstoness."

"You have seen this for yourself?"

Cree Bega shook his head. "But the sseer tellss me thiss iss sso."

Ahren felt as if the ground had dropped away beneath him. He glanced quickly at Ryer, but she was still staring blankly.

"She is the witch's tool," the cloaked figure declared softly, looking over at the seer.

"Her eyess and earss aboard little Elvess sship." Cree Bega glanced at Ahren. "Not anymore. Belongss to uss now. Sservess uss."

Ahren refused to believe what he was hearing. Ryer Ord Star would never go back to serving their enemies, not after what she had gone through, not after breaking free of the Ilse Witch. She had said she was finished with that. She had sworn it.

Stunned, he watched as his captors turned away from him and walked to where the seer stood. Bent close, the cloaked one began speaking to her. The words were too faint for Ahren to hear, but Ryer Ord Star nodded and then replied. The conversation lasted just minutes, but it was clear that some sort of agreement had been reached.

He moved his elbows down close to his sides, pressing them against his ribs, shifting first one way and then the other, straining at the cords that bound his wrists as he tried to determine if the Elf stones were indeed gone. It seemed they were; he could find no trace of their presence.

Close by, the chained beast growled and snapped at him again, trying to break free, all size and teeth and claws as it fought against its restraints. Ahren quit moving and stood as still as he could manage, staring into the creature's eyes. He was surprised to find that they were almost human.

The cloaked figure walked back across the clearing and stood looking down at him. "I am the Morgawr," he said, his voice soft and strangely warm, as if he sought to reassure Ahren of his friendship. "Do you know of me?"

Ahren nodded.

"What is your name?"

"Ahren Elessedil," he answered, deciding there was no reason to hide it.

"Youngest son of Allardon Elessedil? Why isn't your brother here?"

"My brother wanted me to come instead. He wanted an Elessedil presence, but not his own."

The flat face nodded. "I am told you can invoke the power of the Elfstones, the ones Kael Elessedil carried on his voyage thirty years ago. Is that so?"

Ahren nodded, disappointment welling up inside him. Ryer Ord Star had betrayed him. He wished he had never trusted her. He wished he had left her behind in the catacombs of Castledown.

"Where are the Stones now?" the Morgawr asked.

Ahren was so surprised by the question that for a moment he just stared. He had assumed that the Mwellrets had taken them from him when he was captured. Had they failed to do so? Was he mistaken about having them still?

He had to say something right away, so he said, "I don't know where they are."

It was the truth, which was all to the good because he could see the Morgawr reading his eyes. The Morgawr knew about the Elfstones, but didn't know where they were. How could that be? Ahren had carried them out of Castledown. They

were hidden inside his tunic when he was knocked unconscious. Could Cree Bega have taken them for himself? Could
one of the other rets? Would any of them dare to do that?

The Morgawr touched his face with one scaly finger. "I am
keeping you alive because the seer assures me you will use
the Elfstones once I find them. She does not lie, does she?"

Ahren took a deep breath, fighting down his fear and
anger. "No."

"I am mentor to the Ilse Witch. I trained her and schooled
her and gave her my protection. But she betrays me. She
seeks the magic of Castledown for herself. So I have come to
eliminate her. You and the seer will help me find her. She is
talented, but she cannot escape the seeking light of the Elfstones. Nor can she avoid her connection to the seer. She es-
tablished it for the purpose of tracking the Druid and his
airship; now we will use it, in turn, to track her. One or the
other of you will reveal the witch to me. If you provide your
help, I will set you free when I am done with her."

Ahren didn't believe this for a minute, but he held his
tongue.

The gimlet eyes fixed on him. "You should welcome this
offer."

Ahren nodded. As confused as he was about the disappear-
ance of the Elfstones, he knew what to say. "I will do what I
can."

The Morgawr's finger slid away. "Good. The Ilse Witch has
gone underground to find the Druid. The seer says you left
him there, dying. What wards this safehold is dying, too, so
we have nothing to fear. You will take us down there."

A chill swept through Ahren. He did not want to go back
into Castledown for any reason, least of all to help the Morgawr. But he knew that if he refused, he would be made to go
anyway, and he would be watched afterwards all the more
closely. If they didn't just kill him and have done with it. It
was better to do what was asked of him for now, to go along

with the Morgawr's wishes. Antrax was dying when Ryer and he had ascended the passageways and would be as dead as Walker by now. What could it hurt to go into the catacombs a final time?

Even so, he was not comfortable with the idea. He glanced at Ryer Ord Star across the way, but she was looking down again, her face lost in the shadow of her long hair. She would have agreed already, of course. By making herself an ally to the Morgawr and the Mwellrets, she would have promised to help them track the Ilse Witch. She had good reason to hate the witch, but not reason enough to bring harm to Ahren and the others of the company of the *Jerle Shannara*. Didn't she realize that the Morgawr and Cree Bega were no more trustworthy than the witch? He could not believe she had compromised herself so completely.

"Cut him loose," the Morgawr ordered Cree Bega, his silky voice a whisper of comfort and reassurance.

The Mwellret severed the cords that bound Ahren's wrists, and the Elven Prince rubbed the circulation back into them. Straightening his clothes, he sought one final time to locate the Elfstones. Perhaps they were shoved way down inside his tunic. His hands and fingers ran swiftly down his sides. Nothing. The Elfstones were gone.

The Morgawr moved away, beckoned for Ahren to follow, motioned Cree Bega toward Ryer, and called out instructions to the other Mwellrets. Ahren went without hesitating, still rubbing his wrists, already thinking of ways he might escape. He would find a way, he promised himself. He would not be part of this business for one moment longer than he had to. He would flee the Morgawr and his rets at the first opportunity and continue his search for his missing friends.

He glanced wistfully at Ryer Ord Star, who was moving just ahead and still not looking at him. He tried to move over to her, but almost instantly the Morgawr blocked his way.

"Don't think that because I have released you I am not

watching you," he said softly, leaning close. "If you try to escape, if you attempt to flee, if you fail to do as I ask, I will set the caull on you."

He motioned to the wolfish animal that had moved into the forefront of their party, tugging so hard on its chains that it dragged its handlers like dead weights behind it.

"No secrets, no tricks, no foolish acts, Elven Prince," the Morgawr cautioned in his smooth, quiet voice. "Do you understand?"

Ahren nodded, his eyes riveted on the caull.

The Morgawr touched Ahren's cheek with that odd caressing motion. "You don't understand fully. Not yet. But you will. I will see to it that you do."

He moved away again, and Ahren rubbed at his cheek to erase the unpleasant feeling of the scaly touch. He had no idea what he was going to do to escape. Whatever it was, it had better work because he would get only one chance. But he could not imagine where that chance would come from if he did not regain possession of the Elfstones. His memory of what it had been like to wield the magic was still strong. Finding them and invoking their power had transformed him. He had redeemed himself in his own eyes, at least, from his cowardice in the ruins, and in doing so had discovered something of the man he had hoped to become. He had evidenced courage and strength of will, and he did not want to lose those. But without the Elfstones, he was afraid he might.

His eyes drifted skyward, to where the airships still hovered against the horizon. West, the sky was black and thick with rolling clouds. The temperature was dropping, as well. A storm was coming, and it looked to be severe.

They were moving deeper into the ruins, back the way they had come. The caull and its handlers led, but Ryer Ord Star and the Morgawr were close behind, whispering back and forth as if kindred with a common goal. Cree Bega shoved at Ahren, urging him to catch up to them, to lend whatever input he might have to give. The Elven Prince put aside his thinking and increased his pace until he was right behind the seer, following in her footsteps, close enough to reach out and touch her.

Look at me, he thought. *Say something!*

She did neither. He might not have been there at all, for all the difference his presence made to her. He could not escape the feeling that she was ignoring him deliberately. Was her sense of guilt at betraying him so strong? It seemed as if she was rejecting everything she had tried to become since finding him and was reverting to the creature she had been when in the service of the witch. It felt as if her sense of loyalty had died with Walker. He could not understand that.

Then she was pointing out something in the ruins to the Morgawr, and as the warlock turned to look, she lost her footing and stumbled, careening backwards into Ahren. He caught her without thinking, holding her upright. Without looking at him, she straightened and pushed him away.

It was over in seconds, and they were moving ahead once more, Ryer Ord Star back beside the Morgawr, Cree Bega and his Mwellrets all about. But in those seconds, when she was pressed up against him, she whispered, so clearly he could not mistake what she said, two words.

Trust me.

TEN

Less than a quarter of a mile away Bek Ohmsford crouched in a pool of deep shadows formed by the juncture of two broken walls and waited for Truls Rohk to return. He heard the approach of the Mwellrets and whoever was with them, the sound of their voices and the scrape of their boots carrying clearly in the early morning silence. He had already seen the airships hanging in the distance over the ruins, dark hulls and masts empty of insignia or flags. He had watched them disgorge their Mwellret passengers and creatures like the caull his sister had used to track the shape-shifter and himself. He knew they were in trouble.

Truls Rohk had gone to investigate. He had not returned.

Bek's hand tightened about Grianne's, and he glanced over at her to reassure himself that she was all right. Well, to reassure himself that nothing had changed, at least. She was hunched down next to him in the darkness, staring at nothing. He had pulled back her hood to let the light find her face. Her pale skin looked ghostly in the shadows, and her strange blue eyes were empty and fixed. She was compliant to his directions, but unresponsive to anything around her. She did not speak, did not look at him, and did not react to what was happening. He did not know much about the catatonic state, about what it would take to release her from it, but he supposed she was in a great deal of emotional or psychological pain and that was the reason for her condition. She would regain consciousness when she was ready, Walker had said. But after several hours of traveling with and watching her, he was not sure he believed it.

"Grianne," he said softly.

He reached over with his free hand and touched her cheek, running his finger over her smooth skin. There was no reaction. He wished there was something he could do for her. He could only imagine what it must have been like for her to confront the truth about herself. The magic of the Sword of Shannara had drawn back the veil of lies and deception, letting in the light she had kept out for so many years. To be made to see yourself as you really were when you had committed so many atrocities, so many ugly and terrible acts, would be unbearable. No wonder she had retreated so far into herself. But how were they to help her if she remained there?

Not that Truls Rohk believed they should. The shapeshifter saw her as no different from before, save for the fact that she was helpless and at present not a danger to them. But he also saw her as a sleeping beast. When she awoke, she could easily erupt into a frenzy of murderous rage. There was nothing to say that the magic of the talisman would prevent it, nothing to say that she was any different now from what she had been before. There was no guarantee she would not revert to form. In fact, there was every reason to believe she would.

Bek had chosen not to argue the point. On their trek out, winding their way back up the passageways of Castledown to the surface of the ruins, he had kept silent on the matter. Walker had given them their charge—to care for Grianne at any cost, to see her safely home again, to accept that she was important in some still unknowable way. It didn't matter what Truls Rohk thought of her; it didn't matter what he really believed. The Druid had made them promise to ward her, and the shape-shifter had sworn that promise alongside Bek. Like it or not, Truls Rohk was bound by his word.

In any case, Bek thought it better to let the matter alone. If the Druid, even while dying, had been unable to convince the shape-shifter of Grianne's worth, there was little chance that Bek could now. Not right away, at least. Perhaps time would provide him with a way to do so. Perhaps. Meanwhile, he would have to find a way to stay alive.

He took a steadying breath and tried to fight down the panic he felt at his dwindling prospects of being able to do so. They had fought their way clear of one trap and now found themselves facing another. Antrax and the creepers and fire threads might be gone, but now a mix of enemy airships and Mwellrets confronted them. That they were allied in some way with his sister was an unavoidable conclusion. It was too big a coincidence to believe they had come all this way for any other reason. Cree Bega would have linked up with the newcomers and advised them of his presence. They would be looking for Bek and for whoever had helped him escape from *Black Moclips*. If he stayed where he was for much longer, they would find him. Truls had better hurry.

As if reading his mind, the shape-shifter materialized across the way, sliding into the light like a phantasm, blacker than the shadows out of which he came. Concealing cloak swirling gently with the movement of his body, he crouched next to the boy.

"We have fresh trouble," he announced. "The airships are commanded by the Morgawr. He's brought Mwellrets, caulls, and some men who look as if they have been turned into wooden toys. Besides the airships we see, at least a dozen more have gone off in pursuit of the *Jerle Shannara* and *Black Moclips*."

"*Black Moclips?*" Bek shook his head in confusion.

"Don't ask me, boy. I don't know what happened aboard ship after we escaped, but it seems the rets managed to lose control of her. Someone else got aboard and took her over, sent her skyward, and sailed her right out from under their noses. Good news for us, perhaps. But not soon enough to make a difference just now."

The sounds of their pursuit broke into Bek's thoughts, but he forced himself to stay calm. "So now they're hunting us, following our tracks or our scent, using these fresh caulls?"

Truls Rohk laughed. "You couldn't be more wrong. They don't care about us! It's the witch they're looking for! She's done something to convince the Morgawr she wants the magic for herself—or at least convinced him she's too dangerous to trust anymore. He's come to take possession of the magic and do away with her. He doesn't realize there isn't any magic to take possession of and the witch has already done away with herself! It's a good joke on him. He's wasting his time and he doesn't even realize it."

The cowled head turned in the direction of Grianne. "Look at her. She's as dead as if she'd quit breathing. The Druid thinks she has a purpose in all this, but I think his dying blinded him. He wanted something useful to come of all this, something that would give meaning to the lives wasted and the chances lost. But wishing doesn't make it so. When he destroyed Antrax, he destroyed what he had come to find. The Old World books are lost. There isn't anything else. Nothing!"

"Maybe we just don't see it," Bek ventured quietly. He heard snarls and growls from the approaching caull. "Look, we have to get out of here."

"Yes, boy, we do." The hard eyes peered out from the shadows, reflective stone amid a sea of shifting mist and bits of matter. "But we don't need to take her." He gestured at Grianne. "Leave her for the Morgawr. Let them do with her what they choose. They won't bother with us if we do. She's what they want."

"No," Bek said at once.

"If we take her, they will keep after us, all the way inland to wherever we run, to wherever we hide. If she could find us earlier, they can find us now. Sooner or later. She's a weight around our necks and not one we need carry."

"We promised Walker we would protect her!"

"We promised it so that the Druid could die at peace." Truls Rohk spit. "But it was a fool's promise and given without any cause beyond that. We don't need her. We don't want her. She serves no purpose now and never will. What she is has destroyed her. She isn't coming back, newly born, your sister returned; you're not going to be a happy family reunited. Thinking otherwise is foolish."

Bek shook his head. "I'm not leaving her. You do what you want."

For just an instant, Bek thought that Truls Rohk was going to do just that. The shape-shifter went as still as the shadows on a windless night, all dark presence and hidden danger. Bek could feel the tension in him, a sort of singing sound that was more vibration than noise, a cord become taut on a bow drawn back.

"You persist in being troublesome," Truls Rohk whispered. "Have you no capacity for rational behavior?"

Bek almost laughed at the words, spoken with such seriousness but rife with irony. He shook his head slowly. "She is my sister, Truls. She doesn't have anyone else to help her."

"She's going to disappoint you. This isn't going to turn out like you think."

Bek nodded. "I don't suppose it will. It hasn't so far." He kept his eyes locked on the shape-shifter as the sounds of approach intensified. "Can we go now?"

Truls Rohk stared at him a moment longer, as if trying to decide. Then he came forward, all blackness even in the early morning light, picked up Grianne like a rag doll, and tucked her under his arm.

"Try to keep up with me, boy," he said. "Carrying one of you is load enough."

He sprang atop the nearest remnant of wall and began to

navigate its length like a tightrope walker in a street fair, crouched low and moving swiftly. The feel of his sister's hand in his a lingering warmth, Bek watched him for a moment, then hurried after.

Ahren Elessedil listened with growing concern as the snarls of the caull leading the Morgawr's party deeper into the ruins grew more anxious. Clearly, it had come across something, tracks or scent that it recognized and wanted to pursue. Its handlers had not released it, however. Nor was the Morgawr giving it much attention; his focus was on Ryer Ord Star as they walked next to each other, engaged once again in close conversation. What was it she was telling him? The boy was encouraged by her whispered words, but suspicious of her actions. She was asking him to trust her, but doing nothing to warrant it. He had thought she might at least try leading their captors in the wrong direction; instead she was taking them the way she had come, directly toward the entrance that led underground to where they had left Walker.

It appeared she had become the Morgawr's ally in his business, and the Elf was having trouble convincing himself that he should trust her at all.

They moved more quickly now, navigating the rubble to where the opening led downward into Castledown. Judging from the sounds emanating from the caull, its snout lowered to the ground as it tugged and pulled its handlers ahead, whomever they were tracking had come this way recently. He wondered briefly if it might be their own scent the caull had come across, but that would make the beast a good deal more stupid than the Elf was prepared to believe. Since it was the Ilse Witch the Morgawr was seeking, Ahren had to assume the caull had been given her scent. She could easily have come the same way they had and still managed to miss them in the catacombs.

They passed through the entry in a cautious knot. Creepers

lay in heaps just inside, unmoving. Flameless lamps still burned, casting a weak yellow glow from the passage walls, but the Mwellrets lit torches anyway. The smoky light lent the empty corridors an eerie, shadowy look as the group moved downward into the earth.

Several times Ahren thought to make a break for freedom, but fear and common sense kept him from acting on his impulse. He needed a better opportunity, and he needed to know more about what Ryer Ord Star was doing. He needed, as well, to know who had the Elfstones so that he could try to find a way to get them back. He hadn't made a conscious decision on the matter before this, but he knew now, thinking about it, that he wasn't going back to the Four Lands without them. It was ambitious for him to think about getting home at all, but at this point, he couldn't help himself. Thinking about it was all he had to keep his mind off his current predicament, and if he didn't concentrate on something, he was afraid his dwindling courage would collapse completely.

They walked a long time, back the way Ryer and he had come, following the very same passageways down into the bowels of Castledown. Sporadic sounds rose in the distance, but nothing solid appeared to hinder them. Antrax and Castledown had gone back into time to join the rest of the Old World, dead and lost.

When they reached the cavernous chamber where Antrax had housed its power, they found it empty. Walker was gone, though pools of his blood had dried dark and sticky on the metal floor. Twisted chunks of metal and broken cables littered the landscape, and fluids had begun leaking from tanks and lines, cloudy and thick. Excited by the blood and the lingering smells, the caull lunged this way and that, but there were no people to be found. The Morgawr walked around, looking at everything carefully, distancing himself from the rest of the party as he did so. He poked at the creepers, stood close to the massive twin cylinders, and entered the extraction chamber, where he remained alone for a long time. Ahren watched everyone, but particularly Ryer Ord Star. She stood only yards from him, staring off into space. She never glanced in his direction. If she sensed him looking at her, she kept it to herself.

When the Morgawr was finished with his examination, he emerged from the extraction chamber, brushing aside Cree Bega with a hiss of impatience. The caull leading the way, its massive body jerking at its chains in frustration, they set off in a new direction. The Ilse Witch had been here, Ahren knew. No one had said so, but the behavior of the Morgawr as he plunged ahead down this new passageway made the conclusion unavoidable. Perhaps they had just missed her. He found himself wondering what had become of Walker. Even if the witch had found him, she wasn't strong enough to move him herself.

He had his answer not long afterwards. They navigated the maze of empty, ruined corridors until they came to a vast cavern housing an underground lake. Illuminated by the dim phosphorescence that streaked the cavern's rocky walls, a trail of blood led down to the edge of the water, pooled anew on the rocky shore, and disappeared. The surface of the lake was still and perfectly smooth. There was no sign of Walker.

The Morgawr stood staring out across the lake for a moment, black cloak drawn close about him. No one tried to approach him or dared to speak.

"Get back from me," he told them finally.

They did so, and Ahren watched as scaly arms emerged from the Morgawr's cloak and began to weave in quick motions, drawing pictures or symbols on the air. A greenish light emanated from the fingertips, leaving trails of emerald fire in their wake. The hush of the empty cavern filled with a whisper of phantom wind, and from the depths of the lake rose a deep, ugly hiss that seemed as much a warning as a response to the Morgawr's conjuring. Still, the warlock continued his efforts, robes whipping about his dark body, spray bursting from the waters in sudden explosions. Faint images began to appear, shades cast upon the darkness by his magic's light, there one moment and gone the next. Ahren could not tell who they were meant to be; he could not even be sure of what his senses were telling him. Once, he thought he heard voices, rough whispers that rose and fell like the lake's dark spray. Once, he was sure he heard screams.

Then the wind increased, and the torches blew out. The Mwellrets dropped back a few paces, closer to the entrance to the cavern. Ahren went with them. Only Ryer Ord Star stood her ground, head lifted, a fierce look on her childlike face as she stared out across the lake into the darkness beyond. She was seeing something, as well, Ahren thought—maybe the strange images, maybe something else entirely.

Finally, the Morgawr's hands stopped moving, the wind and noise died away, and the lake went still. The Morgawr stepped back from the water's edge and walked to where his rets crouched watchfully at the cavern entrance, motioning for the seer to come with him as he passed her. Dutifully, she turned and followed.

"The Druid is dead," he declared as he came up to them.

Hearing someone speak the words gave their truth fresh impact. Ahren caught his breath in spite of himself, and it suddenly felt to him as if whatever hopes he had harbored that a way out of this terrible place, this savage land, might be found, had just been stolen away.

The Morgawr was looking at him, assessing his reaction. "Our little Ilse Witch, however, is alive." He kept his dangerous eyes fixed on Ahren. "She's come and gone, and she's not alone. She's with that boy you let escape from *Black Moclips*, Cree Bega—and someone else, someone I can't put a name to." He paused. "Can you, Elven Prince?"

Ahren shook his head. He had no idea who Bek might be with if it wasn't Tamis or one of the other Elves.

The Morgawr came forward and reached out to touch his cheek. The cavern air turned colder with that touch, and its silence deepened. Ahren forced himself to stand his ground, to repress the repulsion and fear that the touch invoked in him. The touch lingered a moment and then withdrew like the sliding away of sweat.

"They brought the Druid here, down to the water's edge, and left him for the shades of his ancestors to carry off." The Morgawr's satisfaction was palpable. "And so they did, it seems. They bore his corpse away with them, down into the waters of that lake. Walker is gone. All the Druids are gone. After all these years. All of them."

His gaze shifted from Ahren. "Which leaves us with the witch," he whispered, almost to himself. "She may not be as formidable as she once was, however. There is something wrong with her. I sense it in the way she moves, in the way she lets the other two lead her. She isn't what she was. It felt to me, as I studied the traces of her passing, as if she was asleep."

"Sshe dissembless," Cree Bega offered softly. "Sshe sseekss to confusse uss."

The Morgawr nodded. "Perhaps. She is clever. But what reason does she have to do so? She does not know of my presence yet. She does not know I've come for her. She has no reason to pretend at anything. Nor any reason to flee. Yet she is gone. Where?"

No one said anything for a moment. Even the caull had gone silent, crouched on the cavern floor, big head lowered, savage eyes gone to narrow slits as it waited to be told what to do.

"Perhapss sshe iss aboard the airsship," Cree Bega suggested.

"Our enemies control *Black Moclips*," the Morgawr replied. "They would seek to avoid her, Cree Bega. Besides, there was no time for her to reach them before they fled from us.

No, she is afoot with the boy and whoever goes with him—
his rescuer, from the ship. She is afoot and not far ahead
of us."

Suddenly he turned again to Ahren, and this time the sense
of menace in his voice was so overpowering that it froze the
boy where he was.

"Where are the Elfstones, Elven Prince?" the warlock
whispered.

The question caught Ahren completely by surprise. He
stared at the other wordlessly.

"You had them earlier, didn't you?" The words pressed
down against the boy like stones. "You used them back there
in that chamber where the Druid was mortally wounded. You
were there, trying to save him. Did you think I wouldn't
know? I sensed the Elfstone magic at once, found traces of its
residue in the smells and tastes of the air. What happened to
them, little boy?"

"I don't know," Ahren answered, unable to come up with
anything better.

The Morgawr smiled at Cree Bega. "You searched him?"

"Yess, of coursse," the Mwellret answered with a shrug.
"Little Elvess did not have them."

"Perhaps he hid them from you?"

"There wass no time for him to hide them. Hssst. Losst
them, perhapss."

The Morgawr took a moment to consider. "No. Someone
else has them." His gaze shifted quickly to Ryer Ord Star.
"Our quiet little seer, perhaps?"

Cree Bega grunted. "Ssearched her, alsso. No sstoness."

"Then our little witch has them. Or that boy she is with."
He paused. "Or the Druid carried them down with him into
the netherworld, and no one will ever see them again."

He did not seem bothered by that. He did not seem concerned at all. Ahren watched his flat, empty face look off a fi-

nal time toward the underground lake. Then the sharp eyes flicked back to his.

"Boy, I have no further need of you."

The chamber went so still that there might have been no one left alive, that even those who stood waiting to see what would happen next had been turned to stone. Ahren could feel the beating of his heart in his chest and the pulsing of his blood in his veins; he could hear the rasp of his breathing in his throat.

"Perhaps you do," Ryer Ord Star said suddenly. They all turned to look at her, but her eyes were fixed on the Morgawr. "The Druid brought the prince on the journey because his brother the King insisted, but also because the Druid knew something of the prince's worth beyond that. I have seen it in a vision. One day, Ahren Elessedil will be King of the Elves."

She paused. "Perhaps, with training, he could learn to become *your* King."

Ahren had never heard any such speculation, and he certainly didn't like hearing it now, particularly given the twist that the seer was putting to it. He was so shocked he just stared at her, not trying to hide anything of what he was feeling, a mix of emotions so powerful he could barely contain them. *Trust me,* she had urged him. But what reason did he have for doing so now?

The Morgawr seemed to consider this, and then he nodded. "Perhaps." He gestured vaguely toward the girl. "You seek to demonstrate your worth by sharing what you know, little seer. I approve."

His eyes flicked back to Ahren. "You will come with me. You will do what you can to help me in my search. Together, we will track our little witch. Wherever she goes, we will find her. This will be over soon enough, and then I will decide what to do with you."

He looked at Cree Bega. "Bring him."

Then he motioned the caull to its feet, gave orders to its

handlers, and sent them away into the tunnels once more. He took Ryer Ord Star by the arm and followed, ignoring Ahren. Seeing him rooted in place, Cree Bega clipped the boy across the back of his head and sent him stumbling after the warlock.

"Little Elvess musst do ass they are told!" he hissed balefully.

Ahren Elessedil, saying nothing, trudged ahead in a sullen rage.

ELEVEN

Aboard the *Jerle Shannara*, Redden Alt Mer paused at the aft railing of the airship and looked back at *Black Moclips*. She was laboring heavily as she tried to outrun the approaching storm, her armored hull tossing and slewing like a heavy branch caught in rapids. The storm was a black wall coming inland off the eastern coast, a towering mass of lightning-laced clouds riding the back of winds gusting at more than fifty knots. Little Red was doing the best she could to sail the airship alone, but it would have been a difficult task under ordinary circumstances. It was an impossible one here. Even if she reached the relative safety of the mountains ahead, there was no guarantee she would be able to find shelter until the storm passed. Landing an airship in the middle of a mountain range, with cliffs and downdrafts to contend with, was tricky business in any case. In the teeth of a storm like this one, it would be extremely dangerous.

Behind *Black Moclips*, at least a dozen of the enemy airships continued to give chase. He had thought he might lose them with the approach of the storm, but he had been wrong. Since yesterday morning, he had tried everything to shake them, but nothing had worked. Each time he thought he had given them the slip, they had reappeared out of nowhere. They shouldn't have been able to do that. No one should have been able to find him so easily, especially not these ships, with their walking-dead crews and ship-shy Mwellrets.

They were tracking him somehow, tracking him in a way he hadn't yet been able to identify. He had better do so soon. The repairs to the *Jerle Shannara* had not been completed before they had been forced to flee the coast, and the strain of having to rely on four of their six parse tubes and diapson crystals, the radian draws reconfigured to allow for the transference of energy, was beginning to tell. The draws were threatening to snap from the additional strain, and the airship's maneuverability was less than he needed. Even though the *Jerle Shannara* was the faster airship, if something went wrong, their pursuers would be on them before they could make the necessary adjustment.

It didn't help that no one had slept for more than a couple of hours since yesterday, and everyone was dog-tired. Tired men made mistakes, and if they made one here, it would probably cost them their lives.

He tested the aft starboard draw, adjusted the tension, and looked back again at *Black Moclips*. She was struggling to keep up, losing ground at an increasing pace. The Wing Riders flew on either side of her, offering their presence as reassurance, but the Elves were of no help in the sailing of the ship. Po Kelles had flown back to tell him what Little Red had done, and at first Alt Mer had been elated. They had the witch's airship as well as their own, two chances to find a way out of this miserable country. But the convergence of their pursuers and the approach of the storm quickly made him realize that his sister might have seized too big a prize. Without a crew to assist her, she was seriously handicapped in her efforts to sail the captured ship. He would have put a couple of his own crew aboard to help her, but there was no way to do so without docking the airships; Rovers were skittish where Rocs were concerned.

A gust of wind howled through the rigging above him, producing a sharp and eerie whine, a wounded animal's cry. The temperature was dropping, as well. If this kept up, there would be snow in the mountains and conditions for flying would become impossible.

He left the railing and hurried across the aft decking and down to the main deck and the pilot box where Spanner Frew stood like a rock at the helm, guiding the airship ahead with his steady hand.

"Lines still holding?" he bellowed as Big Red jumped up beside him in the box.

"For now—I don't know for how much longer. We need to get down before that storm catches us!" They had to shout to be heard over the wind. He glanced over his shoulder at *Black Moclips*. "We have to do something to help Little Red. She's game, but as good as she is, she can't go it alone."

Spanner Frew's black-bearded face swung about momentarily, then straightened forward again. "If we could get a line to her, we could tow her."

"Not in this weather—not with all those airships chasing us. We'd be slowed down, even using her parse tubes to help."

The big man nodded. "Better get her off there, then! When that storm catches up, chances are pretty good she won't be able to stay aloft. If she starts to go down then, we won't be able to help her."

Redden Alt Mer had already come to that conclusion. He wasn't even sure he could manage to keep the *Jerle Shannara* flying. He toyed briefly with the prospect of changing over to *Black Moclips* and sailing her instead, since she was in better condition. But the *Jerle Shannara* was the faster, more maneuverable vessel, and he didn't want to give her up when it was speed and maneuverability that were likely to make the difference in a confrontation with their pursuers. The matter was moot in any case because there wasn't any real chance that he could get everyone off his ship and onto Little Red's with the weather this bad.

He pursed his lips. Rue was going to be furious if he told

her to give up her prize. She might not do it, even knowing how much trouble she was in.

He looked back again at *Black Moclips* and beyond to the enemy airships, black dots against the roiling darkness of the storm.

"How do they keep finding us?" he snapped at Spanner Frew, suddenly angry at how impossible things had gotten.

The shipwright shook his head and didn't answer. A new level of frustration crept through Big Red. It was bad enough that they had lost Walker and all those who had gone inland to the ruins. It was bad enough that they had nothing to show for having come all this way and might well return home empty-handed—if they were able to get home at all. But it was intolerable that these phantom airships continued to harass them like hunting dogs would a fleeing, wounded animal, finding their tracks or their scent where there should be no trace of their passing at all.

There was nothing he could do about it just now. But he could do something about Little Red. She was not yet recovered from her wounds and couldn't have had much more sleep than they had. She must be near exhaustion from flying *Black Moclips* alone, trying to manage everything from the pilot box, the wind howling past her like a demon set loose to tear her from the skies. She was a good pilot, almost as good as he was—and a better navigator. But it wouldn't be enough to save her from this.

"I'm taking her off, Black Beard!" he yelled over to the shipwright. "Drop our speed one quarter and hold steady toward that split in the peaks ahead."

"You want to take her off in a grapple?" Spanner Frew yelled back.

Redden Alt Mer shook his head. "It would take too long. She has to come to us. I'll send one of the Wing Riders in."

He jumped down to the main deck, shouting orders at the crew, telling them to find their places at the working parse tubes, to monitor the draws while he ran aft. At the railing, he dug through a wooden box and found the emerald pennant that meant he needed one of them to fly to him.

Of course, the signal wouldn't work if no one was looking. And in a bad storm like this one, they might not be.

He fastened the pennant's clips to a line and ran the piece of cloth up into the wind, where it snapped and cracked like ice breaking free in the Squirm. Facing back, he watched *Black Moclips* lurch and buck. Several of her draws had broken loose, and one of her sails was in tatters. She was flying on her pilot's skill and sheer luck.

Even as he watched, she faded farther back in the haze of clouds and mist. The Wing Riders were barely visible, still flying to either side. Their pursuers had disappeared entirely.

Redden Alt Mer pounded his fist on the railing cap. Neither Hunter Predd nor Po Kelles had seen the pennant.

"Look at me!" he screamed in frustration.

Lost in the howl of the wind, the words blew away from him.

A thousand yards back, so fatigued that she was near collapse, Rue Meridian fought to keep the *Jerle Shannara* in sight. Her world had narrowed down to this single purpose. Forgotten were her plans for coming inland to the ruins, for finding and rescuing Bek and the others of the company, for trying to salvage something from the disaster this voyage had become, for doing anything but keeping her vessel flying. Though her thoughts were clouded and her mind numb from concentrating on working the controls, she knew she was in trouble. The *Jerle Shannara* was drawing farther away and the airships pursuing her were drawing closer. Soon, any chance for escape would be lost.

Black Moclips shuddered anew as the winds preceding the storm buffeted her. The airship lurched sideways and down. The problem was simple enough to diagnose if not to solve. The ambient-light sails had been kept furled during the past few days, and no new power had been gathered for the diapson crystals. No new power was being collected now because she couldn't put up the sails in this storm—couldn't put them up at all, for that matter, storm or not, by herself. The limited power that remained was being exhausted. Personal attention at the various parse tubes was needed to distribute it more efficiently, but she couldn't leave the controls long enough to attempt that. The best she would do was to try to manipulate things from the pilot box, and while that was possible, it was never intended that an airship be flown by a single person.

She had a crew, but they were locked up belowdecks, and once she set them free she might as well lock herself up in their place.

The first flurries of snow blew past her face, and she was reminded again of how far the temperature had fallen. Winter seemed to be descending into a land that hadn't seen such weather in more than a thousand years.

She tried to coax more speed from the crystals, forcing herself to try a different combination of power allocations, feeling *Black Moclips* slew and skid on the wind from her efforts, fighting off her growing certainty that nothing she could do would make any difference.

She was so absorbed in her efforts that she failed to see Hunter Predd soar ahead into the misty gray toward the *Jerle Shannara*. Po Kelles kept pace with her off to the port side, but she didn't even glance at him. In her struggle to fly *Black Moclips*, she had all but forgotten the Wing Riders. Then Hunter Predd flew Obsidian right over her bow to catch her attention. She ducked in response to the unexpected movement, then turned as the Roc swung around and settled in off her starboard railing, almost close enough to touch, rocking back and forth with the force of the wind.

"Little Red!" Hunter Predd shouted into the wind, his words barely audible.

She glanced over and waved to let him know she heard.

"I'm taking you off the ship!" He waited a moment to let the impact of the words sink in. "Your brother says you have to come with me. That's an order!"

Angry that Big Red would even suggest such a thing, she shook her head no at once.

"You can't stay!" Hunter Predd shouted, bringing Obsidian in closer. "Look behind you! They're right on top of you!"

She didn't have to look; she knew they were there, the airships chasing her. She knew they were so close that if she turned, she could make out the blank faces of the dead men who flew them. She knew they would have her in less than an hour if something didn't happen to change her situation. She knew if they didn't catch her by then, it was only because she had gone down.

She knew, in short, that her situation was hopeless.

She just didn't want to admit it. She couldn't bear it, in fact.

"Little Red!" the Wing Rider called again. "Did you hear me?"

She looked over at him. He was hunched close to Obsidian's dark neck, arms and legs gripping the harness, safety lines tethering rider and bird. He looked like a burr stuck in the great Roc's feathers.

"I heard!" she shouted back.

"Then get off that ship! Now!"

He said it with an insistence that brooked no argument, an insistence buttressed by the knowledge that she must realize the precariousness of her situation as surely as her brother and he did. He stared at her from astride his bird, weathered features scrunched and angry, daring her to contradict him. She understood what he was thinking: if he didn't convince her here and now, it would be too late; already, the *Jerle Shannara* was nearly out of sight ahead and the storm upon her. She could still do what she chose, but not for very much longer.

She stared through the tangled, windblown strands of her

hair to the airship's controls. Dampness ran down the smooth metal and gleaming wood in twisting rivulets. She studied the way her hands fit on the levers and wheel. She owned *Black Moclips* now; it belonged to her. She had snatched it away from the thieves who had stolen her own ship. She had claimed it at no small risk to herself, and she was entitled to keep it. No one had a right to take it away from her.

But that didn't mean she was wedded to it. That didn't mean she couldn't give it up, if she chose. If it was her idea. After all, it was just something made out of wood and metal, not out of flesh and blood. It wasn't possessed of a heart and mind and soul. It was only a tool.

She looked back at Hunter Predd. The Wing Rider was waiting. She pointed aft and down, then at herself. He nodded and swung away from the ship.

She snatched up the steering bands and lashed the wheels and levers in place, then hurried down the steps and across the slippery surface of the decking to the main hatchway. She went down in a rush, before she had time to think better of it. She was curiously at peace. The anger she had felt moments earlier was gone. *Black Moclips* was a fine airship, but it was only that and nothing more.

She reached the storeroom door where Aden Kett and his Federation crew were locked away and banged on the door. "Aden, can you hear me?"

"I hear you, Little Red," the Commander replied.

"I'm letting you out and giving you back your ship. She's struggling in this storm and needs a full crew to keep her flying. I can't manage it alone. I own her, but I won't let her die needlessly. So that's that. You do what you can for her. All right?"

"All right." She could tell from the sound of his voice that he was pressed up against the door on the other side.

"You'll understand if I don't stay around to see how this turns out." She wiped at the moisture beading her forehead and dripping into her eyes. "You might have trouble doing the right thing by me afterwards. I'd hate to see you make a fool of yourself. So after I open this door, I'll be leaving. Do you think you and the others can refrain from giving in to your worst impulses and coming after me?"

She heard him laugh. "Come after you? We've had enough of you, Little Red. We'll all feel better knowing you're off the ship. Just let us out of here."

She paused then, leaning into the door, her face close to the cracks in the boards that formed it. "Listen to me, Aden. Don't stay around afterwards. Don't try to do the right thing. Forget about your orders and your sense of duty and your Federation training. Take *Black Moclips* and sail her home as quickly as you can manage it. Take your chances back there."

She heard his boots shift on the flooring. "Who's out there? We saw the other ships."

"I don't know. No one does, but it isn't anyone you want anything to do with. More than a dozen airships, Aden, but no flags, no insignia, nothing human aboard. Just rets and men who look like they're dead. I don't know who sent them. I don't care. You remember what I said. Fly out of here. Leave all this. It's good advice. Are you listening?"

"I'm listening," he answered quietly.

She didn't know what else to say. "Tell Donell that I'm sorry I hit him so hard."

"He knows."

She pushed away from the door and stood facing it again. "See you down the road, Aden."

"Down the road, Little Red."

She reached for the latch and threw it clear, then turned and bolted up the stairs without looking back. In seconds she was topside again, surprised to find sleet had turned the world white. She ducked her head against the bitter sting of the wind and slush and moved to the aft railing. The rope Hunter Predd had used earlier to climb down to Obsidian was still tied in place and coiled on the deck. She threw the loose end overboard and watched it tumble away into the haze. She could just barely make out the dark contours of the Roc's wings as it lifted into place below.

She looked back once at *Black Moclips*. "You're a good girl," she told her. "Stay safe."

Then she was gone into the gloom.

Minutes later, Redden Alt Mer stood at the port railing of the *Jerle Shannara* and watched his sister pause in her climb up the rope ladder. She had gotten off the Roc all right, taken firm hold of the ladder and started up. But now she hung there with her head lowered and her long red hair falling all around her face, swaying in the wind.

He thought he might have to go down the ladder and get her.

Thinking that, he was reminded suddenly of a time when they were children, and he had gone high up into the top branches of an old tree. Rue, only five years old, had tried to follow, working her way up the trunk, using the limbs of the tree as rungs. But she wasn't strong yet, and she tired quickly. Halfway up, she lost her momentum completely and stopped moving, hanging from the branches of that tree the way she was hanging from the rope ladder now. She was something of a nuisance back then, always tagging along after him, trying to do everything he was doing. He was four years older than she was and irritated by her most of the time. He could have left her where she was on the tree—had thought he might, actually. Instead, he had turned back and yelled down to her. "Come on, Rue! Keep going! Don't quit! You can do it!"

He could yell those same words down to her now, to the little sister who was still trying to do everything he did. But even as he considered it, she lifted her head, saw him looking at her, and began to climb again at once. He smiled to himself. She came on now without slowing, and he reached out to take her arm, helping her climb over the railing and onto the ship.

Impulsively, he gave her a hug and was surprised when she hugged him back.

He shook his head at her. "Sometimes you scare me." He looked into her wet face, reading the exhaustion in her eyes. "Actually, most of the time."

She grinned. "That's real praise, coming from you."

"Flying *Black Moclips* all by yourself in a bad piece of weather like you did would scare anyone. It should have scared you, but I suppose it didn't."

"Not much." She grinned some more, like the little kid she was inside. "I took her away from the witch, big brother. Crew and all. It was hard to give her up again. I didn't want to lose her, though."

"Better her than you. We don't need her anyway. It's enough if the witch doesn't have her." He gave his sister a small shove. "Go below and put on some dry clothes."

She shook her head stubbornly. "I don't need to change clothes just yet."

"Rue," he said, a hint of irritation creeping into his voice. "Don't argue with me about this. You argue with me about everything. Just do it. You're soaked through; you need dry clothes. Go change."

She hesitated a moment, and he was afraid she was going to press the matter. But then she turned around and went down through the main hatch to the lower cabins, water dripping from her across the decking.

He watched her disappear from sight, thinking as she did that no matter how old they grew or what happened to them down the road, they would never feel any differently about each other. He would still be her big brother; she would still be his little sister. Mostly, they would still be best friends.

He couldn't ask for anything better.

*   *   *

When she reemerged, the wind was blowing so hard it knocked her sideways. The rain and sleet had stopped, but the air was cold enough to freeze the tiny hairs in her nostrils. She wrapped her great cloak more tightly about her, warm again in dry clothes and boots, and pushed across the deck unsteadily to where her brother and Spanner Frew stood in the pilot box. Ahead, the mountains loomed huge and craggy against the skyline, a massing of jagged peaks and rugged cliffs piled one on top of the other until they faded away into the brume-shrouded distance.

She climbed into the pilot box, and her brother said at once, "Put on your safety harness."

She did so, noting that all of the Rover crew on the decks below were strapped in as well, hunched down against the weather, stationed at the parse tubes and connecting draws.

When she glanced over her shoulder, she found the world behind had disappeared in a thick, dark haze, taking with it any sign of the pursuing airships.

Big Red glanced over. "They disappeared sometime back. I don't know if they broke it off because of the weather or to go after *Black Moclips*. Doesn't matter. They're gone, and that's enough. We've got bigger problems to deal with."

Spanner Frew yelled something down to one of the Rovers amidships, and the crewman waved back, moving to tighten a radian draw. Big Red had stripped back all the sails, and the *Jerle Shannara* was riding bare-masted in the teeth of winds that sideswiped her as badly as they had *Black Moclips*. Rue saw that the radian draws had been reconfigured, strung away from two of the six parse tubes to feed power to the remaining four. Even those were singing with the vibration of the wind, straining to break free of their fastenings.

"I *left* a ship in better shape than this one," she declared, half to herself.

"She'd be in better shape if we hadn't had to leave quite so suddenly to find you!" Big Red grunted.

That wasn't true, of course. They would have had to leave in any case to flee the enemy airships, no matter whether or not they were searching for her. Repairs of the sort needed by the *Jerle Shannara* required that the airship be stationary, and that wasn't going to happen until they could set down somewhere.

"Any place we can land?" she asked hopefully.

Spanner Frew laughed. "You mean in an upright position? Or will a severe slant do?" His hands worked the steering levers with quick, anxious movements. "First things first. See those mountains ahead of us, Little Red? The ones that look like a big wall? The ones we're in danger of smashing into?"

She saw them. They lay dead ahead, rising across the skyline, barring their way. She glanced sideways and down and saw for the first time how high up they were. Several thousand feet at least—probably more like five thousand. Even so, they weren't nearly high enough to clear these peaks.

"Heading ten degrees starboard, Black Beard," she heard her brother order. "That's it. There, toward that cut."

She followed his gaze and saw a break in the peaks. It was narrow, and it twisted out of view at once. It might dead-end into the side of a mountain beyond, in which case they were finished. But Redden Alt Mer could read a passage better than anyone she had ever sailed with. Besides, he had the luck.

"Brace!" he yelled down at the crew.

They shot between the cliffs and into the narrow defile, skimming on the back of a vicious headwind that nearly drove them sideways in the attempt. Beyond, they saw the opening slant right. Spanner Frew threw the wheel over and fed what power he could to keep them steady. The passage narrowed further and cut back left. Rue felt the hair on the back of her neck lift as the massive cliff walls tightened about them like the jaws of a trap. They were so close that she could make out the depressions and ridges on the face of the stone. She could see rodent nests and tiny plants. There was no room to turn around. If the passage failed to run all the way through, they were finished.

"Steady," her brother cautioned to Spanner Frew. "Slow, now."

The winds had shifted away, and they were no longer being buffeted so violently. The *Jerle Shannara* canted left in response to Spanner Frew's handling of the controls, sliding slowly through the gap. They rounded a jagged corner, still close enough that Rue could reach out and touch the rock. Ahead, the defile began to widen, and the mountains opened out onto a deep, forested valley.

"We're through," she said, grinning in relief at her brother.

"But not yet safe." His face was tight and set. "Look ahead. There, where the valley climbs into that second set of peaks."

She did so, brushing away loose strands of her long red hair. There were breaks all through this range, but the movement of the clouds overhead suggested that the winds were much more turbulent than anything they had encountered before. Still, there was nowhere else to go except back, and that was unthinkable.

Spanner Frew glanced over at Big Red. "Where do we go? That gap on the right, lower down?"

Her brother nodded. "Where it might not be so windy. Good eye. But stay hard left to give us room to maneuver when the crosswind catches us."

They navigated the valley through a screen of mist, riding air currents that bucked and jittered like wild horses. The *Jerle Shannara* shuddered with the blows, but held her course under Spanner Frew's steady hand. Below, the forests were dark and deep and silent. Once, Rue caught sight of a thin ribbon of water where a small river wound along the valley floor, but she saw no sign of animals or people. Hawks soared out of the cliffs, fierce faces set against the light. Behind, the entire sky was dark with the storm they had left on the other side of the mountains. Everywhere else, the horizon was hazy and flat.

Rue listened to the wind sing through the taut lines of the vessel. It always seemed to her that the ship was calling to her when she heard that sound, that it was trying to tell her something. She felt that now, and her uneasiness grew.

When they reached the far side of the valley, they angled right, toward the draw that her brother had spied earlier, a deep cut in the peaks of the second range that offered clear passage to whatever lay beyond. More mountains, certainly, but perhaps something else, as well. She glanced skyward to where the clouds skittered over the peaks in frightened bursts of energy, blown by winds that channeled down out of the north. Since the weather was all behind them, she realized that these crosswinds must blow like this all the time. They would be dangerous, if that was so.

The *Jerle Shannara* lifted through the gap, catching the first rip of crosswind as she did, slewing sideways instantly. Spanner Frew brought her back on course again, keeping her low and down to the left. Ahead, more peaks and cliffs appeared, slabs of stone jutting from the earth like giant's hands lifted in warning. But the defile wormed through them, offering passage, so they continued on. Below, the floor of the canyon rose steadily as the mountains closed about, and they were forced to fly higher.

Rue Meridian took a deep breath and held it, feeling the tension radiate through her.

"Steady, Black Beard," she heard her brother say quietly. Then a burst of wind slammed into the airship and sent her spinning sideways for endless, heart-stopping seconds before Spanner Frew was able to bring her back around again.

Rue exhaled sharply. Big Red glanced over at her and broke into one of those familiar grins that told her how much he loved this.

"Hold on!" he shouted.

They bucked through the gap's twists and turns like a cork through rapids, knocked this way and that, fighting to stay steady at every turn. The winds thrust at them, then died away, then returned to hammer them again. Once they were blown so hard to starboard that they very nearly struck the cliff wall, only just managing to skip past an outcropping of rock that would have ripped the hull apart. Rue clung to the pilot box railing, her knuckles white with determination, thinking as she did so that this was much worse than what they had encountered coming through the Squirm, ice pillars notwithstanding. At any moment they could lose control completely and be smashed to bits against the rocks.

They climbed to a thousand feet as the floor of the pass rose ahead, forcing them to gain altitude beyond what Rue knew her brother had hoped would prove necessary; the winds at this elevation were too strong and unpredictable.

Then the mountains parted ahead, and far below they saw a vast forest cupped by the fingers of scattered peaks, deep and impenetrable and stretching away into the haze. There would be a landing site there, a place for them to set down and make repairs.

She had no sooner finished the thought than the aft port radian draw snapped at the masthead and fell away.

At once, the *Jerle Shannara* began to lose power and slip sideways. Spanner Frew fought to bring her nose up, but without both aft parse tubes in operation, he lacked the means to do so.

"I can't right her!" he grunted in frustration.

"Mainsail!" Big Red shouted instantly to the crew.

Kelson Riat and another of the Rovers leapt up at once from where they were crouched amidships and began to unfasten the lines and run up the sail. Without the use of the aft parse tubes, Big Red was going to rely on the sails for power. But the crosswinds were vicious; there was as much chance as not that they would fill the big sail and carry the airship right into the cliffs like a scrap of paper.

"Steady, steady, steady . . . ," Big Red chanted to Spanner Frew as the shipwright fought to hold the *Jerle Shannara* in place.

Fluttering and snapping, the mainsail went up. Then the wind caught it and drove the airship forward with a lurch. She bucked in the wind's strong grip, and another of the draws snapped and fell away.

"Shades!" Redden Alt Mer hissed. He snatched at the wheel as Spanner Frew lost his footing, struck his head on the pilot box railing, and blacked out.

They were still falling, but they were accelerating toward the gap, as well, the mountains widening on both sides. If they could stay high enough to miss the boulders clustered in the mouth of the pass, they might survive. It was going to be close. Rue willed the *Jerle Shannara* to lift, begged her silently to level off. But she was still falling, the rocky surface of the pass rising swiftly to meet her.

Her brother threw the levers that fed power to the diapson crystals all the way forward and brought the steering levers all the way back. The airship shuddered anew, lurched, and rose a final time. They surged through the gap, breaking into the clear air above the forest below. But even as they did so, the keel scraped across the boulders beneath them, making a terrible grinding, ripping noise. The *Jerle Shannara* shuddered and then dipped, the bow coming down sharply, pointing left and toward the forest a thousand feet below. The crosswind returned, sudden and vicious, snatching at the crippled vessel. The mainsail reefed as several of her lines snapped, and the *Jerle Shannara* plunged downward.

Rue Meridian, clinging to both her safety harness and the pilot box railing, thought they were dead. They spiraled down, out of control, the canopy of the trees rising to meet them with dizzying swiftness. Her brother, still struggling to

bring the bow up, cursed. Crew members slid along the decking. The safety line broke away on one, and she caught just
a glimpse of him as he flew out over the side of the ship and
disappeared.

Then the crosswind shifted, ripping along the cliff face and
carrying the *Jerle Shannara* sideways into the rock. Rue had
just a moment to watch the cliff wall fly toward them before
they struck in a shattering crunch of wood and metal. She lost
her grip on both her safety line and the railing and flew into
the pilot box control panel. Pain ratcheted through her left
arm, and she felt the stitches on her wounded side and leg
give. Her safety line snapped, and then she careened into her
brother, who was hanging desperately onto the useless steering
levers.

A moment later, everything went black.

TWELVE

As he finished tying off the bandages around Little Red's damaged torso, Redden Alt Mer was thinking things couldn't get any worse. Then Spanner Frew lumbered up the steps to the pilot box and knelt down beside him.

"We lost all the spare diapson crystals through the tear in the hull," he announced sullenly. "They've fallen somewhere down there."

His gesture made it clear that *somewhere down there* was the jungle below the wooded precipice on which the *Jerle Shannara* had finally come to rest, an impenetrable green covering of treetops and vines that spread away from the cliff face for miles.

Alt Mer rocked back on his heels and stared at the shipwright as if he were speaking in a foreign language. "All of them?"

"They were all in one crate. The crate fell out through a hole ripped in the hull." Spanner Frew reached up to touch the gash in his forehead, flinching as he did so. "As if I needed another headache."

"Can we fly with what we have?"

The shipwright shook his head. "We're down to three. We lost the port fore tube and everything with it on landing. What's left might let us fly in calm weather, but it won't get us off the ground. If we try it, we'll just go over the side and into the trees with the crystals."

He sighed. "The thing of it is, we came through this all right otherwise. We've got the timbers to repair the hole in the hull. We've got spare draws and fastenings. We've got plenty of sail. Even the spars and mast can be fixed with a little time and effort. But we can't go anywhere without those crystals." He rubbed his beard. "How's Little Red?"

Redden Alt Mer looked down at his sister. She was still unconscious. He had let her sleep while he worked on her injuries, but he thought he'd wake her soon in case she had suffered a concussion. He needed to know, as well, if there was damage inside that he couldn't see.

"She'll be all right," he said with a reassuring smile. He wasn't sure at all, but there was no point in worrying Black Beard unnecessarily. He had enough to concern him. "Who went over the side?"

"Jahnon Pakabbon."

Big Red grimaced. A good man. But they were all good men, which is why they had been chosen for the voyage. There wasn't a one he could bear to lose, let alone afford to. He had known Jahnon since they were children. The quiet, even-tempered Rover had a gift for innovation in addition to his sailing skills.

"All right." He forced himself to quit thinking about it, to concentrate on the problem at hand. "We have to go down there and bring him out. We'll look for the crystals when we do. Choose two men to go with me—and make sure you're not one of them. I need you to work on the repairs. We don't want to be stranded here any longer than necessary. Those airships with their Mwellrets and walking dead will come looking for us soon enough. I don't intend to be around when they do."

Spanner Frew grunted, stood up, and went back down the pilot box steps. The *Jerle Shannara* was canted to port at a twenty-degree angle perhaps a hundred yards from the precipice, the curved horn of her starboard pontoon lodged in a cluster of boulders. She wasn't in much danger of sliding over the edge, but she was fully exposed to anything flying overhead. Behind her, running back for perhaps another hundred yards, a forested shelf jutted from the cliff face of the mountain on which they had settled. They were lucky to be alive after such a crash, lucky not to have fallen all the way into the jungle below, from which extraction would have been impossible. That the *Jerle Shannara* had not broken into a million pieces was a testament to her construction and design. Say what you would about Spanner Frew, he knew how to build an airship.

Nevertheless, they were trapped, lacking sufficient diapson crystals to lift off, short one more crew member, and completely lost in a strange land. Big Red was normally optimistic about tough situations, but in this particular instance he didn't much care for their chances.

He glanced skyward, where clouds and mist hung like a curtain across the horizon, hiding what lay farther out in all directions. Nothing was visible but the emerald canopy of the jungle and the tips of a few nearby peaks, leaving him with the unpleasant feeling of being trapped on a rocky island, suspended between gray mist and green sea.

"Spanner!" he yelled suddenly. The burly shipwright trudged back over to stand below the box and looked up at him. "Cut some rolling logs, rig a block and tackle, and let's try to move the ship back into those trees. I don't like being out in the open like this."

The big man turned away without a word and disappeared over the side of the ship. Big Red could hear him yelling anew at the crewmen, laying into them with his shipyard vocabulary. He listened a moment and shook his head. He missed Hawk, who was always a step ahead in knowing what needed to be done. But Black Beard was capable enough, if a bit irksome. Give him some direction and he would get the job done.

Redden Alt Mer turned his attention to his sister. He bent down and gave her a gentle shake. She groaned and turned her head away, then drifted off. He shook her once more, a little more firmly this time. "Rue, wake up."

Her eyes blinked open, and she stared at him. For a moment, she didn't say anything. Then she sighed wearily. "I've been through this before—come back from the edge and found you waiting. Like a dream. Still alive, are we?"

He nodded. "Though one of us is a little worse for wear."

She glanced down at herself, taking in the bandages wrapped about her torso and leg where the clothing had been cut away, seeing the splint on her arm. "How bad am I?"

"You won't be flying off to rescue anyone for a while. You broke your arm and several ribs. You ripped open the knife wounds on your thigh and side. You banged yourself up pretty good, all without the help of a single Mwellret."

She started to giggle, then grimaced. "Don't make me laugh. It hurts too much." She lifted her head and glanced around, taking in as much as she could, then lay back. "We don't seem to be flying, so I guess I didn't dream that we crashed. Are we all in one piece?"

"More or less. There's damage, but it can be repaired. The problem now is that we can't fly. We lost all our spare diapson crystals through a break in the hull. I have to take a search party down into the valley and find them before we can get out of here." He shrugged. "Thank your lucky stars it wasn't worse."

"I'm busy thanking them that I'm still alive. That any of us are, for that matter." She licked her lips. "Got anything to drink that doesn't come from a stream?"

He brought her an aleskin, holding it up for her as she took deep swallows. "You hurt anywhere I can't see?" he asked when she was done. "A little honesty here wouldn't hurt, by the way."

She shook her head. "Nothing you haven't already taken care of." She wiped her lips and sighed deeply. "Good. But I'm really tired."

"Then you'd better sleep." He arranged the torn bit of sail he had folded under her head for a pillow and tucked in the ragged folds of her great cloak about her arms and legs. "I'll let you know when something happens."

Her eyes closed at once, which was what he had expected, given the strength of the sleeping potion he had dropped into her drink. He took the aleskin and tucked it away in a storage bin to one side of the control panel, out of sight but ready to use if he needed it again. But she wouldn't wake for twelve hours or better, if he'd measured the dosage right. He looked down at her, his little sister, tough as nails and so anxious to demonstrate it she would have insisted on getting up if he hadn't drugged her. She confused him sometimes, the way she was always trying to prove herself, as if she hadn't already done so a dozen times over. But better to be like that, he supposed, than to be content with the way things were. His sister set the standard, and she was always looking to improve on it. He could wish for more like her, but he wouldn't find them no matter how hard he looked. There was only one Little Red.

He yawned, thought he wouldn't mind a little sleep himself, then walked over to the ship's railing and looked down at Spanner Frew and the others as they placed the rolling logs under the pontoons. The block and tackle was already in place, strapped to a huge old oak fifty yards back with the rope ends clipped to iron pull rings that had been screwed into the aft horns just above the waterline.

"We could use another pair of hands!" the shipwright shouted up at Big Red as he took in the slack in the ropes with an audible grunt.

Redden Alt Mer climbed down the ship's ladder and joined the others as they picked up the lead rope, set themselves, and began to heave against the weight of the airship. Even after she had been pulled off the rocks and straightened so that her pontoons were resting on the logs, the *Jerle Shannara* was difficult to budge. Eventually, Big Red took three others forward and began to rock her. After some considerable effort and harsh words had been expended, she began to move. Once she got rolling, they worked swiftly. Pulling steadily on the ropes, they rotated the rolling logs under her floats as she lumbered backwards until they got her perhaps three dozen yards off the exposed flat and into a mix of trees and bushes.

After taking down the block and tackle and unhooking the ropes, Redden Alt Mer ordered Kelson Riat and the big Rover who called himself Rucker Bont to cut some of the surrounding brush and spread it around the decks of the airship as camouflage. It took them only a little while to change her appearance sufficiently that the Rover Captain was satisfied. With all the sails down and the decking partially screened, the *Jerle Shannara* might look like a part of the landscape, a hummock of rock and scrub or a pile of deadwood.

"Good work, Black Beard," he told Spanner Frew. "Now see what you can do with that hole in her side while I take a look down below for those crystals."

The big man nodded. "I've given you Bont and Tian Cross for company." He took hold of the Captain's arm and squeezed. "Little Red and I won't be there to look out for you. Watch yourself."

Redden Alt Mer gave him a boyish grin and patted the big, gnarled hand. "Always."

They went down the cliff face in a line, Big Red in front setting the pace and finding the most favorable route for them to follow. It wasn't a particularly steep or long descent, but a misstep could result in a nasty fall, so the three men were careful to take their time. They used ropes as safety lines where the descent was steepest; the other sections, where the slope broadened and there were footholds to be found in the jagged rock, they navigated on their own. It was mid-afternoon by now, and the hazy light was beginning to darken as the sun slid behind the canopy of clouds and mist. Big Red gave them another three hours at most before it would become too dark to continue the search. There wasn't as much time as he would have liked, but that was the way it went sometimes. You had to make the best of some situations. If they ran out of time today, they would just have to try again tomorrow.

The climb down took them almost an hour, and by the time they were inside the trees, everything was much darker. The canopy of limbs and vines was so thick that almost no light penetrated to the jungle floor. As a result, the undergrowth wasn't as thick as Big Red had anticipated, so they were able to advance relatively easily. They quickly discovered that they were in a rain forest, the temperature on the valley floor much higher than in the mountains. The air was steamy and damp and smelling of earth and plants. Life was abundant. Ferns grew everywhere, some of them very tall and broad, some tiny and fragile. Though most were green, others were milky white and still others a rust red. Their tiny shoots unfurled like babies' fingers, stretching for the light. Slugs oozed their way across the earth, leaving trails of moisture, sticky and glistening. Butterflies careened from place to place in bright splashes of color, and birds darted through the canopy overhead so fast the eye could barely follow. Now and again, they heard them singing, a mix of songs that seemed to come from everywhere at once.

The atmosphere was strange and vaguely unsettling, and they could feel the change immediately. The sound of the wind had disappeared. Over everything lay a hush broken only by birdsong and insect buzzes. In the silences between, there was a sense of expectancy, as if everything was waiting for the next sound or movement. They had the unmistakable feeling of being watched by things that they could not see, of eyes following them everywhere.

Some distance in, they stopped while Big Red took a reading

on his compass. It would be all too easy to become lost down here, and he wasn't about to let that happen. He had only a vague idea of where to look for Jahnon's body and the missing diapson crystals, so the best they could do was to navigate in that general direction and hope they got lucky.

He stared off into the hazy distance, thinking for a moment about the direction of his life. He could stand to take a compass reading on that, as well. At best he was drifting, tacking first one way and then another, a vessel with no particular destination in mind. He shouldn't spend a moment of time worrying about becoming lost down here given how lost he was in general. He might argue otherwise—did so often, in fact—but it didn't change the truth of things. His life, for as long as he could remember, had consisted of one escapade after the other. Rue had been right about their lives as mercenaries. Mostly, they had been centered on the size of the purse being offered. This was the first time they had accepted a job because they believed there was something more at stake than money.

Yet what difference did it make? They were still fighting for their lives, still careening about like ships adrift, still lost in the wider world.

Did Little Red now feel that coming on this voyage was worth it?

He supposed he was rethinking his own life because of hers. She had been injured twice in the past two weeks, and both times she had come close to being killed. It was bad enough that he risked his own life so freely; he shouldn't be so quick to risk hers. True, she was a grown woman and capable of deciding for herself whether or not she wanted to accept that risk. But he also knew she looked up to him, followed after him, and believed unswervingly in him. She always had. Like it or not, that invested him with a certain responsibility for her safety. Maybe it was time to give that responsibility some attention.

They said he had the luck. But everyone's luck ran out sooner or later. The odds in his case had to be getting shorter. If he didn't find a way to change that, he was going to pay for it. Or worse, Rue was.

They set off again, working their way through the jungle, and hadn't gone two hundred yards when Tian Cross spied the wooden crate that contained the crystals lying in a deep depression of its own making. Amazingly, the crate was still in one piece, if somewhat misshapen, the nails and stout wire securing it having held it together despite the fall from the precipice.

Big Red bent down to examine it. The crate was maybe two and a half feet on each side and weighed in the neighborhood of two hundred pounds. A strong man could carry it, but not far. He thought about taking out several of the crystals and tucking them into his clothing. But they were heavy and too awkward for that. Besides, he wanted to retrieve them all, not just some. It would take longer to haul out the entire crate, but there was no reason to think that on the long journey home they might not need replacement crystals again.

He stood up, pulled out the compass, and took another reading.

"Captain," Rucker Bont called over to him.

He glanced up. The big Rover was pointing ahead. There was a distinct gap in the wall of the jungle where trees and brush were missing and hazy light flooded down through the canopy. It was a clearing, the first they had come across.

He snapped shut the casing on the compass and tucked the instrument back into his pocket. Something about the break in the jungle roof didn't look right. He made his way through trees and vines for a closer look, leaving the crystals where they were. The other two Rovers followed. The brush was thicker here, and it took them several minutes to reach the edge of the clearing, where they slowed to a ragged halt and, still within the fringe of the trees, peered out in surprise.

A section of the forest had been leveled on both sides of a lazy stream that meandered through the dense undergrowth, its waters so still they were barely moving. Trees had been knocked down, bushes and grasses had been flattened, and the earth torn up so badly it had the look of a plowed field. A hole had been opened in the trees that tunneled back down the length of the stream and disappeared into the mist.

Rucker Bont whistled softly. "What do you suppose did that?"

Big Red shrugged. "A storm, maybe."

Bont grunted. "Maybe. Could have been wind, too." He paused. "Could also be that something bigger than us lives down here."

His eyes darting right and left watchfully, Big Red walked out of the trees and into the clearing, picking his way across the rutted, scarred earth. The other two waited a moment, then followed. At the clearing's center, he knelt to look for tracks, hoping he wouldn't find any. He didn't, but the ground was so badly churned he couldn't be sure of what he was looking at.

He glanced up. "I don't see anything."

Rucker Bont scuffed his boot in the dirt, glanced over at Tian Cross and then back at Alt Mer. "Want me to have a look around?"

Big Red peered down the debris-strewn length of the little stream, down the tunnel that burrowed into the trees. In places the damage was so severe that the stream's banks had collapsed entirely. Tree limbs and logs straddled the stream bed, wooden barriers that stuck out in all directions and smelled of shredded leaves and wood freshly ripped asunder. Everything he was seeing felt wrong for a windstorm or a flood. The damage was too contained, too geometrical, not random enough. Perhaps Bont wasn't as far off the mark as he had thought. This had the look of something done by a very big, very powerful animal.

Aware suddenly of a change in the forest, he stood up slowly. The birds and butterflies they had seen in such profusion only minutes ago had disappeared entirely and the jungle had gone very still. His hand strayed to the hilt of his sword.

He saw Jahnon Pakabbon then, his eyes drawn to the corpse as surely as if it had been pointed out to him. Across the clearing, less than fifty feet away, Pakabbon lay sprawled against a clump of rocks and deadwood. Only he didn't look the way he had when he was alive, and the fall alone wouldn't account for it. His body had been stripped of its flesh and his organs sucked out. His clothes hung on bleached bones. His eyes were missing. His mouth hung open in a soundless scream and seemed to be trying to bite at something.

At almost the same moment, Redden Alt Mer caught sight of the creature. It was crouched right over Jahnon, as green and brown as the jungle that hid it. He might not have seen it at all if the light hadn't shifted just a touch while he was staring at Pakabbon's corpse. Intent on retrieving the remains of his friend, he might have walked right up to it without knowing it was there. It was so well concealed that even as big as it was—and it had to be huge from the size of its head—it was virtually invisible. All that Redden Alt Mer could see of it now was a blunt reptilian snout with lidded eyes and mottled skin that hovered over Jahnon's dead body like a hammer about to fall.

He never had a chance to warn Rucker Bont and Tian Cross. He never had a chance to do anything. Redden Alt Mer had only just realized what he was looking at when the creature attacked. It catapulted out of the jungle, bursting from its concealment in a flurry of powerful, stubby legs, and seized Tian Cross in its jaws before the Rover knew what was happening. Tian screamed once, and then the jaws tightened, the needle-sharp teeth penetrated, and there was blood everywhere.

It had been a long time since Redden Alt Mer had panicked, but he panicked now. Maybe it was the suddenness of the creature's attack. Maybe it was the look of it, a lizard of some sort, all crusted and horned, or the sheer size of it, rearing up with Tian Cross's crushed body dangling from its jaws. He had never seen a creature so big move so fast. It had come out of the trees, out of its concealment, with the quickness of a striking snake. He could still see that movement in his mind, could feel the terror it induced rush through him like the touch of hot metal.

Drops of blood sprayed over him as the lizard shook his friend's dead body like a toy.

Redden Alt Mer bolted back through the jungle. He never stopped to think what he was doing. He never even considered trying to help Tian. Some part of him knew that Tian was dead anyway, that there was nothing he could do to help him, but that wasn't why he ran. He ran because he was terrified. He ran because he knew that if he didn't, he was going to die.

Running was all he could think to do.

At first, he thought the creature would not follow, too busy with its kill to bother. But within seconds he heard it coming, limbs and brush snapping, leaves and twigs tearing free, the earth shaking with the weight and force of its massive body. It exploded through the jungle like an engine of war set loose. Big Red picked up his pace, even though he had thought he was already running flat out. He darted and dodged through the heavier foliage until he was back where the trees opened up, and then he put on a new burst of speed. He cast aside his cumbersome weapons, useless in any case against such a behemoth. He lightened himself so that he could fly, and still he felt as if he were weighted in chains.

Alt Mer glanced back only once. Rucker Bont was running just as hard, only steps behind, features drained of blood and filled with terror, a mirror of his own. The lizard, thundering after them in a blur of mottled green and brown, jaws open, was right behind.

"Captain!" Bont cried out frantically.

Alt Mer heard him scream. The lizard was tearing at him, and the sounds of his friend's dying followed the Rover Captain as he fled.

Shades! Shades!

He never looked back. He couldn't bear to. He could only run and keep running, closing off everything inside but the fear. The fear drove him. The fear ruled him.

He gained the cliff wall and went up it in a scrambling rush, barely feeling the sharpness of the rock and roughness of the rope as he climbed. Forgotten were the crystals and Jahnon's body. Forgotten were his hopes for a quick exit from this valley. His companions lay dead in the valley below. His weapons lay discarded. He gave them no thought. He had no faculty for thinking. He had nothing left inside but a frantic, desperate need to escape—not so much what pursued him as what he was feeling. His fear. His terror. If he did not escape it, he knew, if he did not run fast enough, it would consume him.

He gained the heights after endless minutes of climbing through the fading afternoon light and the deepening haze of an approaching nightfall. He never stopped to see if he was being pursued, and it was only as Spanner Frew's big hands reached down to pull him over the lip of the precipice that he realized how quiet it was.

He looked back in wonder. Nothing was behind him, no sign of the lizard, no indication that anything had ever happened. There was no movement, no sound, nothing. The jungle had swallowed it all and gone as still and calm as the surface of the sea after a storm.

Spanner Frew saw his face, and the light in his own eyes darkened. "What happened? Where are the others?"

Redden Alt Mer stared at him, unable to answer. "Dead," he said finally.

He looked down at his hands and saw that they were shaking.

Later that night, when the others were asleep and he was alone again, he resolved to wake his sister and tell her what he had done. He would tell her not just that he had failed to retrieve the crystals or Jahnon Pakabbon and that the men who had gone into the valley with him were dead, but that he had panicked and run. It would be his first step toward recovery, toward finding a way back from the dark place into which he had fallen. He knew he could not live with himself if he did not find a way to face what had happened. It began with telling Rue, from whom he had no secrets, to whom he confided everything. He would not stint in his telling now, casting himself in the most unfavorable light he could imagine. What he had done was unthinkable. He must confess himself to her and seek absolution.

But when he rose and went to her and stood looking down, he imagined what that confession would feel like. He could see her face as she listened to his words, changing little by little, reflecting her loss of pride and trust in him, revealing her distaste for his actions. He could see the way her eyes would darken and veil, hiding feelings she had never before experienced, changing everything between them. Rue, the little sister who had always looked up to him.

He couldn't bear it. He stood there in the shadows without moving, studying her face, letting the moment pass, and then he left.

Back on deck, well away from where the watch stood at the airship's bow looking out toward the dark bowl of the valley, he leaned against the masthead and stared up at the hazy night sky. Glimpses of a half-moon and clusters of stars were visible through breaks in the clouds. He watched the way they came and went, thinking of his feckless courage and uncertain resolve.

After a time, he slid down to a sitting position, his back against the roughened timber, and lay his head back. As still as the mast itself, he lost himself in the fury of his bitter self-condemnation, and morning still hours away and redemption still further off, he closed his eyes and drifted off to sleep.

THIRTEEN

Imprisoned in the bowels of the Morgawr's flagship, Ahren Elessedil rode out the storm that had brought down the *Jerle Shannara*. He was not chained to the wall as Bek had been when held prisoner on *Black Moclips* a day earlier, but left free to wander about the locked room. The storm had caught up to them as they flew north into the interior of the peninsula, snatching at the airship like a giant's hand, tossing it about, and finally tiring of the game, casting it away. With the room's solitary window battened down and the door secured, he could see nothing beyond the walls of his prison, but Ahren could feel the storm's wrath. He could feel how it attacked and played with the airship, how it threatened to reduce her to a shattered heap of wooden splinters and iron fragments. If it did, his troubles would be over.

In his darker moments, he thought that perhaps this would be best.

An unwilling accomplice in the warlock's search for the Ilse Witch, he had been brought aboard by the Morgawr and his Mwellrets after leaving Castledown's ruins and taken directly to his present confinement. A guard had been posted outside, but had disappeared shortly after the storm had begun and not returned. Just before that, they had brought him some food and water, a small measure of both and only enough to keep him from losing strength entirely. No effort was made to communicate with him. From the way the Morgawr had left things, it was clear that he would be brought out only when it was felt he could be useful in some way.

Or when it was finally time to dispose of him. He held no illusions about that. Sooner or later, promises notwithstanding, that time would come.

Ryer Ord Star had disappeared with the warlock, and the Elven Prince still had no clear idea why she had turned against him. He had not stopped pondering the matter, not even during the storm, while he sat braced in a corner of the storeroom, pressed up against a wall between two heavy trusses to keep from being knocked around. She had been the willing tool of the Ilse Witch, and it did not require a great leap of faith to accept that she would take that same path with the Morgawr if she thought it meant the difference between living and dying. Walker was gone, and Walker had provided her with both strength and direction. Without him, she seemed frailer, smaller, more vulnerable—a wisp of life that a strong wind could blow away.

Even so, Ahren had thought she was his friend, that she had come to terms with what she had done and closed that door behind her. To have her betray him now, to reveal his identity and suggest a use for him to his enemy, was too much to bear. Like it or not, he was left with the unpleasant possibility that she had been lying to him all along.

Yet she had clearly mouthed the words *trust me* to him after they had been made prisoners. Why would she do that if she was not trying to let him know she was still his friend?

What sort of deception was she working?

He thought some more about the Elfstones, as well. He simply could not understand what had happened to them. They had most certainly been in his possession in Castledown. He remembered quite clearly tucking them away in his tunic. He did not think he had lost them since, did not see how that was possible, so someone must have taken them after he had been rendered unconscious. But who? Ryer Ord Star was the logical suspect, but Cree Bega had searched her. Besides, how could she have taken them after the Mwellrets took them prisoner? That left Cree Bega or another of the Mwellrets as suspects, but it would take an act of either supreme courage or foolishness to try to conceal the stones from the Morgawr. Ahren did not think that the Mwellrets would chance it.

He was still wrestling with his confusion when the storm abated and the ship settled back into a smooth and easy glide through the clearing skies. He could tell the sun had reappeared from the sudden brightening that shone through the chinks in his window shutters, and he could smell the sharp, clean air that always followed a heavy storm. He was standing with his face pushed up against the rough battens, trying to see something besides the brightness, when the lock on his door released with a *snap*. He turned. A Mwellret entered, mute and expressionless, carrying a tray of food and water. The Mwellret glanced about to make certain that nothing was amiss, then placed the tray on the floor by the entry, backed out, closed the door, and locked it anew.

Ahren ate and drank, hungrier and thirstier than he had imagined, and listened to renewed activity on the decks above, the sudden movement of booted feet amid a flurry of shouts and gruff exclamations. The airship tacked several times, swinging about, maneuvering in a series of fits and starts. The ones who sailed her were inexperienced or stiff-handed. Other than to note that they were Southlanders—Federation conscripts and sailors like the ones who fought on the Prekkendorran—he had paid no attention to the sailors on being brought aboard earlier. Mostly he had spent his time studying the layout of the decks and corridors he was moved along, thinking that at some point he might have a chance to escape and would need to know his way.

He closed his eyes and took a deep, steadying breath. That hope seemed impossibly naive just now.

A sudden jolt threw him backwards and knocked the tray

aside, spilling its contents. A slow grinding of wooden timbers and a screech of metal suggested that they were rubbing
up against something big. He sprawled on the floor, as the
ship lurched to a stop. He heard more activity overhead. For a
moment he-thought they were engaged in combat, but then
the sounds died away. Yet the movement of the ship had
changed, the earlier smooth, easy glide gone, replaced by a
stiffer sway, as if the ship was resting against something
solid.

Then the door to his prison opened again, and Cree Bega
stepped through, followed by two more Mwellrets. The latter
crossed to where he sat, hauled him roughly to his feet, and
propelled him toward the open door.

"Comess with uss, little Elvess," Cree Bega ordered.

They took him back up on deck. The sunlight was so bright
that at first he was blinded by it. He stood in the grip of the
Mwellrets, squinting through the glare at a cluster of figures
gathered forward. Most were Mwellrets, but there were Federation sailors, as well. The sailors were slack-jawed, their
faces empty of expression. They stood as if in a daze, staring
at nothing. Ahren realized that they were still airborne, riding
several hundred feet above a canopy of brilliant green forest
with the peaks of a mountain range visible off their bow, a rippling stone spine that disappeared into a hazy distance.

Then he saw that they were lashed to a second airship, one
he recognized immediately. It was *Black Moclips*.

"Besst now to pay closse attention," Cree Bega whispered
in his ear.

Ahren saw Ryer Ord Star then. She was standing beside the
Morgawr, almost at the bow, her small figure lost in his shadow.
The Morgawr warded her protectively, and she seemed to welcome the attention, glancing up at him regularly, leaning into
him as if his presence somehow gave her strength. There was
anticipation on her face, though the pale features still bore that
ghostly pallor, that look of otherworldliness that suggested she

was someplace else altogether. Ahren stared at her, waiting for her to notice him. She never even glanced his way.

Aboard *Black Moclips*, Federation sailors crowded the rail, making secure the fastenings that bound the two ships together. Their uneasy glances were unmistakable. Now and then, those glances would stray to their counterparts aboard the Morgawr's ship, then move quickly away. They saw what Ahren saw in the faces of those who crewed the Mwellret ship—emptiness and disinterest.

A pair of men had descended from *Black Moclips'* pilothouse and come forward. The Commander, recognizable by the insignia on his tunic, was a tall, well-built man with short-cropped dark hair. The other, his Mate perhaps, was tall as well, but thin as a rail, and had the seamed, browned face of a man who had spent his life as a sailor. The crew of the *Black Moclips* looked to them at once for guidance, closing about them in a show of support as they came to the railing. The Morgawr came forward and stood talking to them for a moment, the words too soft for Ahren to make out. Then the broad-shouldered Commander climbed onto the railing and stepped across to the Morgawr's ship.

"Comess closser, little Elvess," Cree Bega ordered. "Sseess what happenss."

The Mwellrets holding Ahren hauled him forward to where he could hear clearly. He glanced again at Ryer Ord Star, who had dropped back and was standing apart from everyone in the bow, her eyes closed and her face lifted, as if gone into a trance. She was dreaming, he realized. She was having a vision, but no one had noticed.

"She took you prisoner, commandeered your ship, and escaped—all of this with no one to help her but a Wing Rider?" the Morgawr was saying. His rough voice was calm, but there was an unmistakable edge to his words.

"She is a formidable woman," the Federation officer replied, tight-lipped and angry.

"No more so than your mistress, Commander Aden Kett, and you were quick enough to abandon her. I would have thought twice about doing so in your shoes."

Kett stiffened. He was staring into the black hole of the other's cowl, clearly intimidated by the dark, invisible presence within, by the other's size and mystery. He was confronted by a creature he now knew to have some sort of relationship to the Ilse Witch, which made him very dangerous.

"I thought more than twice about it, I assure you," he said.

"Yet you let her escape, and you did not give chase?"

"The storm was upon us. I was concerned more for the safety of my ship and crew than for a Rover girl."

Rue Meridian, Ahren thought at once. Somehow, after the Ilse Witch had gone ashore, Rue had boarded and gotten control of *Black Moclips*. But where was she now? Where were the rest of the Rovers, for that matter? Everyone had disappeared, it seemed, gone into the ether like Walker.

"So you have your ship back, but the Rover girl is gone?" The Morgawr seemed to shrug the matter aside. "But where is our little Ilse Witch, Commander?"

Aden Kett seemed baffled. "I've told you already. She went ashore. She never returned."

"This boy who escaped, the one she seemed so interested in when she brought him back to the ship—what do you think happened to him?"

"I don't know anything about that boy. I don't know what happened to either of them. What I do know is that I've had enough of being questioned. My ship and crew are under the command of the Federation. We answer to no one else, especially now."

A brave declaration, Ahren thought. A foolish declaration, given what he suspected about the Morgawr. If the Ilse Witch was dangerous, this creature, her mentor, was doubly so. He had come a long way to find her. He had gained control over an entire Federation fleet to manage the task. Mwellrets who were clearly in his thrall surrounded him. Aden Kett was being reckless.

"Would you go home again, Commander?" the Morgawr asked him quietly. "Home to fight on the Prekkendorran?"

This time Aden Kett hesitated before speaking, perhaps already sensing that he had crossed a forbidden line. The Mwellrets, Ahren noticed, had gone very still. Ahren could see anticipation on their flat, reptilian faces.

"I would go home to do whatever the Federation asks of me," Kett answered. "I am a soldier."

"A soldier obeys his commanding officer in the field, and you are in the field, Commander," the Morgawr said softly. "If I ask you to help me find the Ilse Witch, it is your duty to do so."

There was a long silence, and then Aden Kett said, "You are not my commanding officer. You have no authority over me. Or over my ship and crew. I have no idea who you are or how you got here using Federation ships and men. But you have no written orders, and so I am not obligated to follow your dictates. I have come aboard to speak with you as a courtesy. That courtesy has been exercised, and I am absolved of further responsibility to you. Good luck to you, sir."

He turned away, intent on reboarding *Black Moclips*. Instantly, the Morgawr stepped forward, his huge clawed hand lunging out of his black robes to seize the luckless Federation officer by the back of his neck. Powerful fingers closed about Aden Kett's throat, cutting off his futile cry. The Morgawr's other hand appeared more slowly, emerging in a ball of green light as his victim thrashed helplessly. Then, as Ahren Elessedil watched in horror, the Morgawr extended the glowing hand to the back of his prisoner's head and eased it through skin and hair and bone, twisting and turning inside like a spoon. Kett threw back his head and screamed in spite of the grip on his throat, then shuddered once and went still.

The Morgawr withdrew his hand slowly, carefully. The

back of Aden Kett's skull sealed as he did so, closing as if there had been no intrusion at all. The Morgawr's hand was no longer glowing. It was wet and dripping with brain matter and fluids.

It was finished in seconds. Aboard *Black Moclips*, the stunned Federation crew rushed to the railing, but the Mwell-rets blocked their way with pikes and axes. Pushing back the horrified Southlanders, the rets swarmed aboard, closing about and rendering them all prisoners. The sole exception was the rail-thin Mate, who hesitated only long enough to see the terrible, blasted look on his Commander's empty face, devoid of life and emotion, stripped of humanity, before going straight to the closest opening on the rail and throwing himself over the side.

The Morgawr squeezed what was left of Aden Kett's brain in his hand, pieces dripping onto the deck, dampness sliding down his scaly arm.

"Bring the others now," he said softly. "One by one, so I can savor them."

Unable to help himself, tears filling his eyes, Ahren Elessedil retched and threw up.

"Thiss iss what could happen to little Elvess who dissobey," Cree Bega hissed into Ahren's ear. "Thinkss how it feelss!"

Then he had the boy dragged belowdecks once more and into his prison.

At the bow, in the shadow of the curved rams, alone and forgotten while the subjugation of Aden Kett took place, Ryer Ord Star stood with her eyes closed and her mind at rest.

Walker.

There was no response. Borne aloft by the wind, the smell of the forest filled her nostrils. She could picture the trees, branches spread wide, leaves touching like fingers, a shelter and a home.

Walker.

–I am here–

At the sound of his voice, her tension diminished and the peace that always came when he was near began to replace it. Even in death, he was with her, her protector and her guide. As he had promised when he sent her from him out of Castledown, he had come to her again. Not in life, but in her dreams and visions, a strong and certain presence that would lend her the strength she so desperately needed.

How much longer must I stay here?

In her mind, the Druid's voice assumed shape and form and became the Druid as he had been in life, looking at her with kindness and understanding.

–It is not yet time to leave–

I am frightened!

–Do not be afraid. I am with you and will keep you from harm–

She kept her eyes closed and her face lifted, feeling the warmth of the sun and the cool of the wind on her skin, but seeing only him. To anyone who looked upon her, to Ahren in particular, who was watching, she seemed a small, fragile creature given over to a fate that only she would recognize when it came for her. She was prepared for that fate, accepting of it, and her features radiated a reassurance that she was ready to embrace it.

Her words, when she spoke them in the silence of her mind, were rife with her need.

I am so lonely. Let me be free.

–Your task is not yet finished. Grianne has not yet awakened. You must give her time to do so. She must remain free. She must escape the Morgawr long enough to remember–

How will she do that? How will she find her way back from where she has gone to hide from the truth?

She knew of Grianne Ohmsford and the Sword of Shannara. She knew what had befallen the Ilse Witch in the catacombs of Castledown. Walker had told her at the time of his first coming, when she was made a prisoner of the Mwellrets with Ahren. He had told her what had transpired and what he needed of her. She was so grateful to see him again, even in another form, in another place, that she would have agreed to anything he asked of her.

The soft, familiar voice whispered to her.

—She will come back when she finds a way to forgive herself. She will come back when she is reborn—

The seer did not know what this meant. How could anyone forgive themselves for the things the Ilse Witch had done? How could anyone who had lived her life ever be made whole again?

Walker spoke again.

—You must deceive the Morgawr. You must delay his search. You must lead him astray. No other possesses the skills or magic to find her. He, alone, threatens. If he captures her, everything will be lost—

She felt herself turn cold at the words. What did they mean? Everything? The entire world and all those who lived in it? Could that be possible? Could the Morgawr possess power enough to accomplish such a thing? Why was Grianne Ohmsford's survival so important to whether or not that happened? What could she do to change things, even should she find a way out of her madness and despair?

—Will you try—

I will try. But I must help Ahren.

For a moment it was as if he was touching her in the flesh. She watched his hand reach out to grip her shoulder. She felt his fingers close about, warm and solid and alive. She gave a small gasp of surprise and wonder.

Oh, Walker!

—Let the Elven Prince be. Do as you have been told. Do not speak to him. Do not look at him. Do not go near him. Carry through with your deception or everything I have worked for will be ruined–

She nodded and sighed, still lost in the feel of his hands, of his flesh. She knew what was expected of her. She knew she must act alone and in the best way she could. She wondered anew at his choice of words. *Carry through with your deception or everything I have worked for will be ruined.* What did that mean? What had he worked for that could be at risk? Why did it matter so to him that she be successful in deceiving the Morgawr? What was so important that she make it possible for Grianne Ohmsford to escape?

Then she saw it. It came to her in a flash of recognition, a truth so obvious that she did not understand how she could have missed it before. *Of course,* she thought. *How could it be anything else?* The enormity of her revelation left her so off balance that for a moment she lost her concentration completely and opened her eyes without thinking. The fierce glare of the midday sun was sharp and blinding, and she squeezed her eyes closed again instantly.

Too much light. Too much truth.

His voice cut through her confusion and her agitation like a gentle breeze.

–Do as I ask of you. One last time–

I will. I promise. I will find a way.

Then he was gone, and she was alone in the darkness of her mind, his words still lingering in small echoes, his presence still warm against her heart.

When she came back to herself again, out of her trance and unlocked from her vision—opening her eyes again, careful to shade them against the light—she could hear the screams of the Federation sailors from *Black Moclips* as the Morgawr fed on their souls.

FOURTEEN

Bek Ohmsford, Truls Rohk, and the catatonic Grianne escaped the ruins of Castledown just ahead of the searching Mwellrets and their caulls and fled into the surrounding forest. Their pursuers were so close that they could hear them moving through the trees, fanning out like beaters intent on flushing their prey. Their closeness infused Bek with a sense of helplessness that even the reassuring presence of the shape-shifter could not dispel entirely. He had a vision of what it must be like to be an animal tracked by humans and their dogs for sport, though there was nothing of sport in this. Only the movement generated by their flight kept his panic at bay.

They would not have escaped at all if Truls hadn't taken on the responsibility of carrying Grianne. Lacking any will of her own, she could not have moved at any sort of pace that would have allowed them to stay ahead of their enemies, and it was only the shape-shifter's unexpected decision to carry her that gave them any chance. Even so, with Truls bearing the burden of his sister and Bek running free on his own, they were harassed on all sides for the first two hours of their flight.

What gave them a fighting chance in the end was the coming of the same storm that had brought down the *Jerle Shannara*. It swept in off the coast in a black wall, and when it struck, pursued and pursuers alike were deep in the forest flanking the Aleuthra Ark and there was no hiding from it. It blanketed them in a torrent of rain and wave after wave of rolling thunder. Bolts of lightning struck the trees all around them in blinding explosions of sparks and fire. Bek shouted to Truls that they must take cover, but the shape-shifter ignored him and continued on, not even bothering to glance back. Bek followed mostly because he had no other choice. Darting and dodging through the blasted landscape with the fury of the storm sweeping over them like a tidal wave, they ran on.

When they finally stopped, the storm having passed, they were soaked through and chilled to the bone. The temperature had dropped considerably, and the green of the forest had taken on a wintry cast. The skies were still clouded and dark, but beginning to clear where night had faded completely and the silvery dawn of the new day had become visible. The sun was still hidden behind the wall of the storm, but soon it would climb high enough in the sky to brighten the land.

Bek was taking deep, ragged breaths as he faced Truls. "We can't keep up this pace. I can't, anyway."

"Going soft, boy?" The other's laugh was a derisive bark. "Try carrying your sister and see how you do."

"Do you think we've lost them?" he asked, having figured out by now why they had kept going.

"For the moment. But they'll find the trail again soon enough." The shape-shifter put Grianne down on a log, where she sat with limp disinterest, eyes unfocused, face slack. "We've bought ourselves a little time, at least."

Bek stared at Grianne a moment, searching for some sign of recognition and not finding it. He felt the weight of her inability to function normally, to respond to anything, pressing down on him. They could not afford to have her remain like this if they were to have any chance of escape.

"What are we going to do?" he asked.

"Run and keep running." Bek could feel Truls Rohk staring at him from out of the black oval of his cowl. "What would you have us do?"

Bek shook his head and said nothing. He felt disconnected from the world. He felt abandoned, an orphan left to fend for himself with no chance of being able to do so. With Walker gone and the company of the *Jerle Shannara* dead or scattered, there was no purpose to his life beyond trying to save his sister. If he let himself think about it, which he refused to do, he might come to the conclusion that he would never see home again.

"Time to go," Truls Rohk said, rising.

Bek stood up, as well. "I'm ready," he declared, feeling anything but.

The shape-shifter grunted noncommittally, lifted Grianne back into the cradle of his powerful arms, and set out anew.

They walked for the remainder of the day, traveling mostly over ground where it was wet enough that their tracks filled in and disappeared behind them and their scent quickly washed away. It was the hardest day Bek could remember having ever endured. They stopped only long enough to catch their breath, drink some water, and eat a little of what small supplies Truls carried. They did not slow their pace, which was brutal. But it was the circumstances of their flight that wore Bek down the most—the constant sense of being hunted, of fleeing with no particular destination in mind, of knowing that almost everything familiar and reassuring was gone. Bek got through on the strength of his memories of home and family and life before this voyage, memories of Quentin and his parents, of the world of the Highlands of Leah, of days so far away in space and time they seemed a dream.

By nightfall, they were no longer able to hear their pursuers. The forest was hushed in the wake of the storm's passing and the setting of the sun, and there was a renewed peace to the land. Bek and Truls sat in silence and ate their dinner of dried salt beef and stale bread and cheese. Grianne would eat nothing, though Bek tried repeatedly to make her do so. There was no help for it. If she did not choose to eat, he couldn't force her. He did manage to make her swallow a little water, a reflex action on her part as much as a response to his efforts. He was worried that she would lose strength and die if she didn't ingest something, but he didn't know what to do about it.

"Let her alone" was the shape-shifter's response when asked for his opinion. "She'll eat when she's ready to."

Bek let the matter drop. He ate his food, staring off into the darkness, wrapped in his thoughts.

When they were finished, the shape-shifter rose and stretched. "Tuck your sister in for the night and go to sleep. I'll backtrack a bit and see if the rets and their dogs are any closer." He paused. "I mean what I say, boy. Go to sleep. Forget about keeping watch or thinking about your sister or any of that. You need to rest if you want to keep up with me."

"I can keep up," Bek snapped.

Truls Rohk laughed softly and disappeared into the trees. He melted away so quickly that he might have been a ghost. Bek stared after him for a moment, still angry, then moved over to his sister. He stared into her cold, pale face—the face of the Ilse Witch. She looked so young, her features radiating a child's innocence. She gave no hint of the monster she concealed beneath.

A sense of hopelessness stole over him. He felt such despair at the thought of what she had done with her life, of the terrible acts she had committed, of the lives she had ruined. She had known what she was doing, however misguided in her understanding of matters. She had embraced her behavior and found a way to justify it. To expect her to shed her past as a snake would its skin seemed ludicrous. Truls was probably right. She would never be the child she had been. She would never even come back to being human.

Impulsively, he touched her cheek, letting his fingers stray down the smooth skin. He couldn't even remember her as a child. His image of her was formed solely from his imagination. She remembered him, but his own memory was built on a foundation of wishful thinking and imperfect hope. She looked enough like he did that no small part of his image of her was based on his image of himself. It was a flawed concoction. Thinking of her as he thought of himself was fool's play.

He reached out and gently drew her against him. She came compliantly, limply, letting him hold her. He imagined what she must feel, trapped inside her mind, unable to break free. Or did she feel anything? Was she conscious at all of what was happening? He pressed his cheek against hers, feeling the warmth of her, sharing in it. He couldn't understand why she invoked such strong feelings in him. He barely knew her. She was a stranger and, until lately, an enemy. Yet what he felt was real and true, and he was compelled to acknowledge it. He would not abandon her, not even if it cost him his own life. He could not. He knew that as surely as he knew that nothing about his life would ever be the same again.

Some part of his sense of responsibility for her, he admitted, was the result of his need to feel useful. His life was spinning out of control. With her, if with no one else, himself included, he was in a position of power. He was her caretaker and protector. She had enemies all about. She was more alone than he was. Accepting responsibility for her gave him a focus that would otherwise be reduced to little more than self-preservation.

He laid her down on a dry patch of ground beneath the sheltering canopy of a tree that the rains hadn't penetrated, and covered her carefully with her cloak. He stared down at her for a long time, at the clear features and closed eyes, at the pulse in her throat, at her chest rising and falling with each breath. His sister.

Then he stood and stared out into the darkness, tired but

not sleepy, his mind working through the morass of his troubles, trying to decide what he might do to help himself and Grianne. Surely Truls would do what he could, but Bek knew it was a mistake to rely too heavily on his enigmatic protector. He had done that before, and it hadn't been enough to keep him safe. In the end, as the shape-shifters in the mountains had warned him he must, he had relied on himself. He had waited for Grianne, confronted her, and changed the course of both their lives.

What he could not tell as yet was whether or not the change had been for the better. He supposed it had. At least Grianne was no longer the Ilse Witch, his enemy and antagonist. At least they were together and clear of the ruins and *Black Moclips* and the Mwellrets. At least they were free.

He sat down, closed his eyes to rest them, and in moments was asleep. His sleep was deep and untroubled, made smooth by his exhaustion and his willingness to let go of his waking life for just a little while. In the cool, silent blanket of the dark, he was able to make himself believe that he was safe.

He did not know how long he slept before he woke again, but he was certain of the cause of his waking. It was a voice summoning him from his dreams.

—Bek—

The voice was clear and certain, reaching out to him. His eyes opened.

—Bek—

It was Walker. Bek rose and stood staring about the empty clearing, the sky overhead clear and bright, filled with thousands of stars, their light a silvery wash over the forest dark. He looked around. His sister slept. Truls Rohk had not returned. He stood alone in a place where ghosts could speak and the truth be revealed.

—Bek—

The voice called to him not from the clearing, but from somewhere close by, and he followed the sound of it, moving into the trees. He did not fear for his sister, although he could not explain why. Perhaps it was the certainty that Walker would not summon him if it would put her in peril. Just the sound of the Druid's voice brought a sense of peace to Bek that defied explanation. A dead man's voice giving peace— how odd.

He walked only a short distance and found himself in a clearing with a deep, black pond at its center, weeds clustered along the edges and pads of night-blooming water lilies floating their lavender flags through the dark. The smells of the water and the forest mixed in a heady brew suffused with both damp and dry earth, slow decay and burgeoning life. Fireflies blinked on and off all across the pond like tiny beacons.

The Druid was at the far side of the pond, neither in the water nor on the shore, but suspended in the night air, a transparent shade defined by lines and shadows. His face was hidden in his cowl, but Bek knew him anyway. No one else had exactly that stance and build; Walker in death, even as in life, was distinctive.

The Druid spoke to him as if out of a deep, empty well.

—Bek. I am given only a short time to walk free upon this earth before the Hadeshorn claims me. Time slips away. Listen carefully. I will not come to you again—

The voice was smooth and compelling as it rose from its cavernous lair. It had the feel and resonance of an echo, but with a darker tone. Bek nodded that he understood, then added, "I'm listening."

—Your sister is my hope, Bek. She is my trust. I have given that trust to you, the living, since I am gone. She must be kept safe and well. She must be allowed to become whole—

Bek wanted to say that he was not the one to bear the weight of this responsibility, that he lacked the necessary experience and strength. He wanted to say that it was Truls who would make the difference; Bek was acting only as the shape-shifter's conscience in this matter so that Grianne would not be abandoned. But he said nothing, choosing instead to listen.

But Walker seemed to divine his reluctance.

—Physical strength is not what your sister needs, Bek. She needs strength of mind and heart. She needs your determination and commitment to see her safely back from where she hides—

"Hides?" he blurted out.

—Deep inside a wall of denial, of darkness of mind, of silence of thought. She seeks a way to accept what she has done. Acceptance comes with forgiveness. Forgiveness begins when she can confront the darkest of her deeds, the one she views as most unforgivable, the one that haunts her endlessly. When she can face that darkest of acts and forgive herself, she will come back to you—

Bek shook his head, thinking through what little he knew of the specifics of her life. How could one deed be darker than any other? What one deed would that be?

"This one deed . . . ," he began.

—Is known only to her, because it is the one she has fixed upon. She alone knows what it is—

Bek considered. "But how long will it take for such a thing to happen? How will it even come about?"

—Time—

Time we don't have, Bek thought. Time that slips away like night toward day, a certainty of loss that cannot be reversed.

"There must be something we can do to help!" he exclaimed.

—Nothing—

Despair settled through him, pulling down hopes and stealing away possibilities. All he could do, all anyone could do, was to keep Grianne out of the hands of the Morgawr and his Mwellrets. Keep running. Wait patiently. Hope she found a way clear of her prison. It wasn't much. It was nothing.

"Truls wants to leave her," he said quietly, searching for something more upon which to rely. "What if he does?"

–His destiny is not yours. Even if he goes, you must stay–

Bek exhaled sharply.

–Remember your promise–

"I would never forget it. She is my sister." He paused, rubbing at his eyes. "I don't understand something. Why is she so important to you, Walker? She was your enemy. Why are you trying so hard to save her now? Why do you say she is your hope and trust?"

Shards of moonlight knifed through the transparent form, causing it to shift and change. Below, the waters of the pond rippled gently.

–When she wakes, she will know–

"But what if she doesn't wake?" Bek demanded. "What if she doesn't come back from where she has hidden inside?"

–She will know–

He began receding into the dark.

"Walker, wait!" Bek was suddenly desperate. "I can't do this! I don't have the skills or experience or anything! How can I reach her? She won't even listen to me when she's awake! She won't tell me anything!"

–She will know–

"How can she know anything if I can't explain it to her?" Bek charged ahead a few steps, stopping at the edge of the pond. The Druid was fading away. "Someone has to tell her, Walker!"

But the shade disappeared, and Bek was left alone with his confusion. He stood without moving for a long time, staring at the space Walker had occupied, repeating his words over and over, trying to understand them.

She will know.

Grianne Ohmsford, his sister, the Ilse Witch, mortal enemy of the Druids and of Walker, in particular.

She will know.

There was no sense to it.

Yet in his heart, where such things reveal themselves like rainbows after thunderstorms, he knew it to be true.

FIFTEEN

Bek returned to the camp to find Grianne still sleeping and Truls Rohk not yet returned. The position of the stars told him it was after midnight, so he went back to sleep and did not wake again until he felt the shape-shifter's hand resting on his shoulder.

"Time to go," the other said quietly, eyes on the woods behind them.

"How close are they?" Bek asked at once. It was first light, the sunrise just a silvery glow east.

"Still a distance off, but getting closer. They haven't found our trail yet, but they will soon."

"The caulls?"

"The caulls. Mutations of humans captured and altered by magic." He shifted his gaze back to Bek. "Your sister's work, I would have said, if she wasn't here with us. So it must be the Morgawr. Wonder where he found his victims."

Bek sat up quickly. "Not Quentin or the others? Not the Rovers?"

Truls Rohk took his arm and pulled him to his feet. "Don't think about it. Think about staying one step ahead of them. That's worry enough for now."

He walked over to the supplies pack he carried and pulled out some of the bread. Breaking off a piece, he handed it to Bek. "If you were like me, you wouldn't need this." He

173

laughed softly. "Of course, if you were like me, you wouldn't be in this mess."

Bek took the bread and ate it. "Thanks for staying with us," he said, nodding toward the still-sleeping Grianne.

The shape-shifter grunted noncommittally. "Packs of caulls and Mwellrets are everywhere in these woods, dozens of them. They're not chasing only us, either. I heard the sounds of someone else fighting them off when I went back to scout—a larger group, somewhere off to our right, heading into the mountains. I didn't have time to see who it was. It probably doesn't bear thinking on, except that maybe it will draw some of the rets away."

He gestured impatiently, a faceless darkness within his hood. "Enough. Let's be off."

He scooped up Grianne, and they started out once more. They went swiftly and silently through the trees, then Truls moved them into a shallow stream, which they followed for several miles. It was as if they were repeating the events of less than a week ago. They were taking a different path, but traversing the same woods. Again, they were fleeing a hunter possessed of magic and a creature created to track them. Again, they were fleeing the ruins of Castledown, heading in-land. Again, they were running away from something and toward nothing.

Ironic and darkly comic, but pathetic, as well, Bek thought.

As the morning slipped away, in spite of his companion's warning not to do so, he found himself speculating on the fate of his missing friends. He could not bear to think of them made over into caulls, not after what they had already endured. An image of Quentin become a snarling animal flashed through his mind. Wouldn't he know if that had happened? Wouldn't he feel it? But he wasn't Ryer Ord Star, so he couldn't be sure. At this point, he couldn't even be certain his cousin was still alive. The wishsong was a powerful magic, but it didn't make him prescient. There was nothing he could know of what happened to anyone but Walker.

He reflected anew on last night's visit from Walker's shade. He had said nothing of it to Truls. He was not sure why, only that there didn't seem to be any reason for it. If Walker had wanted Truls to hear what he had to say, wouldn't he have appeared to both of them? It was difficult enough dealing with Truls without having to argue over Walker's enigmatic pronouncements. The Druid had been quick enough to let Bek know that his destiny was not tied to that of the shape-shifter. Though they traveled together and for the moment, at least, shared a common cause, that did not mean things wouldn't change. They had changed so often on this journey that Bek knew he could ill afford to take anything for granted. There was nothing in Walker's message that was meant for Truls, nothing that would help or inform him, nothing that would change what they were doing now.

Bek didn't like dissembling, and although he could argue that he wasn't doing that here, it was close enough to feel like it.

His thoughts shifted to his present situation. He wondered if there was any chance at all that one of the Wing Riders would catch sight of them from the skies. He knew how unlikely that was, given the size and depth of this forest. They were like ants down here, all but invisible from above. Only a ground creature like a caull could track them, and that was exactly what they didn't need.

He pushed away the idea of rescue. He was dreaming, he knew. He was grasping at anything that offered even a semblance of hope. He could not afford such desperation. Determination and perseverance were all that he was allowed.

They walked all that day and into the next, climbing steadily into the foothills that fronted the mountains. The Mwellrets and their caulls still tracked them, but seemed to draw no closer. Now and again, the Morgawr's airships cruised the skies overhead. They came across no animals or people, no indication that anything lived in these woods but birds and insects. It was an illusion, of course, but it gave Bek a feeling of such loneliness that at times he wondered if there was any hope for them at all. The air had turned steadily colder, and snow clouds ringed the peaks of the mountains. Summer had faded with the destruction of Antrax, and the climate was in flux.

On the second night, after trying and again failing to persuade Grianne to eat something, Bek confronted Truls Rohk.

"I don't get the feeling that running away is going to accomplish anything," he said. "Other than to keep us alive for another day."

The other's head was bowed, the black opening to the cowl lowered. "Isn't that enough, boy?"

"Don't call me 'boy' anymore, Truls. I don't like the way it sounds."

The cowl lifted now. "What did you say?"

Bek stood his ground. "I'm not a boy; I'm grown. You make me sound young and foolish. I'm not."

The shape-shifter went perfectly still, and Bek half expected one of those powerful hands to shoot out, snatch him by his tunic front, and shake him until his bones rattled.

"Sooner or later, we have to stop running," Bek said, forcing himself to continue. "We tried running last time, and it didn't work. I think we need a better plan. We need somewhere to go."

There was no response. The empty opening of the cowl faced him like a hole in the earth that would swallow him if he stepped too close.

"I think we ought to go back into the mountains and find the shape-shifters who live there."

The other exhaled sharply. "Why?"

"Because they might be able to tell us where we should go. They might help us in some way. They seemed interested in me when they appeared there last time, as if they saw something about me that I didn't. They were the ones who insisted I had to stand up to Grianne. I think they might help us now."

"Didn't they tell you not to come back?"

"They saved your life. Maybe it would be different if we went back together."

"Maybe it wouldn't."

Bek stiffened. "Do you have a better idea? Are we going to go up into those mountains and try to cross them without knowing what's on the other side? Or are we just going to stay down here in these woods until we run out of trees to hide in? What are we going to do, Truls?"

"Lower your voice when you speak to me or you won't have a chance to ask those kinds of questions again!" The shape-shifter rose and stalked away. "I'll think about it," he mumbled over his shoulder. "Later."

Maybe he did, and maybe he didn't. He was gone all night, out scouting, Bek presumed. But, gone deep inside himself, unreachable, Truls Rohk refused to talk to Bek on returning the next morning. They set out again at daybreak, the skies clear, the air sharp and cool, the sunlight pale and thin. Bek had told Truls not to call him a boy anymore, but in truth he still felt like a boy. He had endured tremendous hardships and confronted terrible revelations about himself, and while the experiences had changed him in many ways, they hadn't made him feel any more capable of dealing with life. He was still hesitant and unsure about himself. He might have the power of the wishsong and the heritage of the Sword of Shannara to fall back on, but none of it gave him a sense of being any more mature. He was still a boy running from the things that frightened him, and if it wasn't for the fact that he knew his sister needed him, he might have fallen apart already.

Truls Rohk's refusal to speak to him, even to acknowledge him, left him feeling more insecure than before. He half believed—had always half believed—that the shape-shifter's commitment to look after him was written on the wind. Nothing the other did or said suggested he felt particularly bound to honor that commitment, especially with Walker dead and gone. With one chase leading into another, with the effort of running wearing on the shape-shifter's nerves and nothing good coming from it, Bek felt the distance between himself and Truls growing wider.

Once, the shape-shifter had told him how much alike they were. It had been a long time since he had spoken in such terms, and Bek was no longer certain that Truls had really meant what he said. He had used Bek to poke needles into Walker, to play at the games they had engaged in for so many years. Nothing suggested to Bek there was anything more to his relationship with the shape-shifter than that.

It was mean-spirited thinking, but Bek was sullen and depressed enough by now that such thinking came easily. He resented it, regretted it the minute he was finished, but could not seem to help himself. He wanted more from Truls than what he was getting. He wanted the kind of reassurance that came from companionship, the kind he always used to get from Quentin. But Truls Rohk couldn't give him that. There wasn't enough of him that was human to allow for it.

They walked through the morning without speaking or stopping. It was nearing midday, when the shape-shifter brought them to an unexpected halt. He stood frozen in place, Grianne cradled in his arms as he lifted his head to smell the air.

"Something's coming," he said.

He pointed ahead, through the trees. They stood in a clearing ringed by old-growth cedars and firs, now high enough up in the foothills that the outlines of the peaks ahead were clearly visible. They were not far from the shape-shifter habitat that Bek had suggested they go to, and the boy thought at first that perhaps the mountain creatures were coming to meet them.

But Truls did not seem to think so. "It's tracking us," he said quietly, as if trying to make sense of the idea.

Indeed, it made no sense. Whatever it was, it was ahead of them, not behind. It was upwind, as well. It couldn't be following their footprints or their scent.

"How can that be?" Bek asked.

But the shape-shifter was already moving, taking them through the trees, perpendicular to the route they had been following and away from whatever was ahead. They worked through the deep woods, then across a narrow stream, backing down for almost a quarter of a mile before coming ashore again. All the while, Truls Rohk stayed silent, concentrating on what his senses could tell him. When Bek tried to speak, the shape-shifter motioned him silent.

Finally, they stopped on a wooded rise, where the shape-shifter set down Grianne, faced back in the direction they had been heading, then slowly pivoted to his right on a line parallel to the one they had been taking.

His rough voice was dark and hard. "It's moving with us, staying just ahead. It's waiting. It's waiting for us to come to it."

Bek had not missed the repeated use of the pronoun *it* in reference to whatever tracked them. "What is it, Truls?" he asked.

The shape-shifter stared into the distance for a moment without replying, then said, "Let's find out."

He picked up Grianne and started toward their stalker. Bek wanted to tell him that this was a bad idea and they should keep moving away. But trying to tell the shape-shifter what to do in this situation would just enrage him. Besides, if whatever tracked them could do so without following their scent or prints, it was not likely to be thrown off by a simple change of direction.

They moved ahead for a time, listening to the sounds of the forest. Slowly, those sounds died away. Within minutes, the woods had gone silent. Truls Rohk slowed, sliding noise-lessly through the trees, stopping now and then to listen be-fore continuing on. Bek stayed close to him, trying to move as quietly as the shape-shifter did, trying to be as invisible.

In a shallow vale through which a tiny stream meandered, the shape-shifter brought them to a halt. "There," he said, and pointed into the trees.

At first, Bek saw just a wall of trunks interspersed with clumps of brush and tall grasses. It was dark where they stood, the light shut away by a thick canopy of limbs. The floor of the vale sloped down to the stream, where a patch-work of shadows and hazy light carpeted the forest floor. The air was cold and still, unwarmed by the sun, unstirred by the wind.

Then he saw a shadow that didn't quite fit with everything else, squat and bulky, crouched back by the treeline where the dark trunks masked its features. He stared at it for a long time, and then it moved slightly, shifting position, and he saw the yellow glitter of its eyes.

A moment later, it detached itself from its concealment and padded into view. It was a massive creature, hump shoul-dered and broad chested, covered with coarse gray hair that stuck out in wild clumps. It had a wolf's head, but the head had mutated into something dreadful. The snout was long and the ears pointed like a wolf's, but the jaws were massive and broad, and when they split wide in a kind of panting grin, they revealed double rows of finger-long serrated teeth. Down on all fours, it moved with a shambling gait, its long forelegs dis-proportionate to its rear, which were short and powerful and sprouted from hindquarters dropped so low it appeared to be crouching.

It eased its way down into the vale until it was almost to the stream. There, it stopped, lifted its head, and emitted the most terrible mewling sound Bek had ever heard, a combination of wail and snarl that froze the woods into utter silence.

"What is it?" Bek whispered.

Truls Rohk's laugh was low and wicked. "Your sister's destiny, come back to claim her. That's the thing she made to track us when we fled from her before, the thing the shape-shifters saved me from. I thought it dead and gone, but they must have set it free outside their boundaries. It's a caull, but look at it! It's mutated beyond what even she had intended. It's become something even more monstrous. Bigger and stronger."

"What does it want with us?" Bek looked at him. "It tracks us, you said. What does it want?"

"It wants her," the shape-shifter answered softly. "It's come for her. See how it looks at her?"

It was true. The hard yellow eyes were fixed not on the men, but on the sleeping girl, locked on her as she slept in the shape-shifter's arms—focused on her with such intensity that its purpose was unmistakable.

"There's true madness," Truls whispered, a hint of wonder in his voice. "Captured, mutated, driven out, lost. It seeks only one thing. Revenge. For what has been done to it. For what has been stolen. A life. An identity. Who knows what it thinks and feels now? It must have tracked her through the connection of their magic, a joining of kindred. She created it, and it remains connected to her. It must be able to read her pulse or heartbeat. Or the sound of her breathing. Who knows? It sensed her and came."

The caull cried out again, the same high-pitched wail. The skin on the back of Bek's neck prickled and his stomach clenched. He had been afraid before on this journey, but never the way he was now. He couldn't tell if it was the look of the caull, all crooked and bristling, or the sound of its cry, or just the fact of its existence, but he was terrified.

"What are we going to do?" he asked, barely able to get the words out.

Truls Rohk snorted derisively. "We let it have her. She made it; let her deal with the consequences."

"We can't do that, Truls! She's helpless!"

The other turned on him. "This might be a good time for some rational thinking on your part, *boy*." He emphasized the word. "There are so many things waiting to kill your sister that we can't even begin to count them! Sooner or later, one of them will finish the job. All we do by interfering now is to prolong the process. You think you can save her, but you can't. Time to let go of her. Enough is enough!"

Bek shook his head. "I don't care what you say."

"She is the Ilse Witch! Your sister is dead! Why are you so stubborn about it? Bah, I've had enough of this! You do what you wish, but I'm leaving!"

Bek took a deep, calming breath. "All right. Leave. You don't owe me anything. It isn't fair to ask you to do more than you have. You've done enough already." He looked over at the caull as it hunched down at the edge of the stream. "I can take care of this."

Truls Rohk snorted. "You can?"

"The wishsong was powerful enough to stop Antrax's creepers. It can stop that thing." He stepped close to the shape-shifter. "Give her to me."

Without waiting for the other to respond, he reached in and took Grianne right out of his arms. Cradling her, he stepped away again. "She's my sister, Truls. No matter what you say."

Truls Rohk straightened and looked directly at Bek. "The wishsong is a powerful magic, Bek Ohmsford. But it isn't enough here. You still haven't mastered it. Your sister proved that to you already. That thing over there will be at your throat before you figure out what's needed."

Bek looked at the caull and went cold to the bone thinking of how it would feel to have those teeth and claws tearing into him. It would be over quickly, he guessed. The pain would be momentary. Then it would be Grianne's turn.

"You could do something for me," he said to the shape-shifter. "If you could draw its attention away, just for a moment, I might be able to catch it off guard."

Truls Rohk stared at him. Bek couldn't see the shape-shifter's eyes within the dark confines of his cowl, but he could feel the weight of their gaze, hard and certain. For a long moment, Truls didn't speak. He just kept looking at Bek.

"Don't do this," he said finally.

Bek shook his head. "I have to. You know that."

"You won't survive it."

"Then you can do what you wish with my sister, Truls." He gave the shape-shifter a defiant look. "I won't be there to stop you."

Another long silence stole away the seconds. Bek brushed at a stray lock of hair and felt a bead of sweat slide down his forehead. He was hot in spite of the chill in the air. He felt as if he might never be cool again.

The shape-shifter stood where he was a moment longer, still staring at Bek. "All right," he said finally, his voice harsh and angry. "I've said what I needed to say. Staying with her is up to you." He turned away. "I'll try to draw its attention. Maybe that will help, but I doubt it. Good luck to you, boy."

Bek watched as Truls Rohk angled down the gentle slope, moving with the grace and precision of a moor cat. Deformed and ill made, an aberration of nature, he was nevertheless beautiful to watch. Bek could not believe he was really leaving. They had been together since the beginning of the journey west out of the Wolfsktaag. Truls had saved him so many times Bek had lost count, had given him the insights he needed to come to terms with his heritage and his destiny. They had not always agreed on everything, and there had been a degree of mistrust and uncertainty between them, but the alliance had worked. It was shattering now to see that alliance end. Even watching the other go, Bek couldn't believe it was happening. It felt as if the shape-shifter was taking a part of Bek with him. His confidence. His heart.

Truls, he wanted to call out. *Don't go.*

The caull swung around to watch the shape-shifter; its powerful body flattened and tensed. Bek lowered Grianne to the ground, placing her carefully behind him before turning back to defend them. When the caull struck, it would do so swiftly. He would have only one chance to stop it.

He never got even that. Before he could prepare himself, the caull attacked, springing sideways with blinding speed and tearing across the stream and up the slope in a blur of churning legs and gaping jaws. Bek would have been dead an instant later but for Truls Rohk, who moved even faster. So quick that he seemed simply to leave one place and reappear at another, he intercepted the caull from the side, slammed into it, and knocked it sprawling.

Then he was on top of the beast, tearing at it like an animal himself, snarling with such ferocity that for an instant Bek wasn't sure that it was Truls at all. The shape-shifter ripped at the caull using weapons that Bek couldn't see—weapons he concealed beneath his cloak or perhaps just fashioned out of the mass of raw and jagged bone that comprised his ruined body. Whatever they were, they proved effective. Bits and pieces of the caull's body flew into the air, and blood jetted in dark spurts of inky green. The fighters careened across the vale, locked in combat, joined in purpose, lost in their desperate struggle to kill each other.

Bek recovered himself enough to remember to use the wishsong, but he could not think how to use it effectively. Shape-shifter and caull were so tightly fused that there was no opportunity to bring the magic to bear without striking both. Bek darted right and left at the edge of the battle, enveloped by its sound and fury, desperately seeking a way to intervene, unable to do so.

"Truls!" he screamed helplessly.

Bright fountains of red spurted out of the tangle, the shape-shifter's human blood released from a wound somewhere beneath the concealing cloak, a wound that Bek could not see. He heard Truls snarl in rage and pain, then tear at the caull with renewed fury, bearing it down against the earth. The caull screeched with a sound like metal tearing, writhing and snapping in a flurry of claws and teeth, but it could not break free.

Then Truls Rohk locked his arms about the caull's head and hauled back on its long, thick neck, twisting violently. Bek heard cartilage snap and ligaments tear. The caull shrieked with such fury that the sound matched the howl of the worst storm Bek had ever witnessed, of hurricane winds tearing past windows and walls, of funnel clouds ripping at the earth. The caull heaved upward in one last futile effort to dislodge the shape-shifter, then its head separated from its body and exploded into an unrecognizable ruin.

In the ensuing silence, cacophonous and empty both at once, Truls Rohk threw down the remains of the body. Still twitching, it fell to the forest floor, dark blood spreading everywhere. The shape-shifter stood over it a moment, bent to the stream to drink and wash, then strode back up the hill to where Bek waited.

Without pausing for even a second, he reached down and picked up Grianne, lifting her into the cradle of his arms.

"I changed my mind," he said, his voice harsh and broken, his breathing ragged.

Then he set off walking once more, leaving an astonished Bek to follow.

SIXTEEN

As the day went on and the trio climbed out of the foothills and onto the lower slopes of the mountains, two things became increasingly clear to Bek Ohmsford.

First, they had moved into shape-shifter territory. He knew this not because there were boundary markers or signposts or anything that would designate it as such. Having come a different way, he couldn't even be certain he recognized what he was looking at from his previous visit. He knew where he was because he could feel the shape-shifters watching him. He could feel their eyes. It was broad daylight and the sparsely wooded slopes offered few hiding places, so it didn't appear as if anyone was there. Yet they were, he knew, and not far away. He might have questioned this feeling once, but having experienced it not much more than a week earlier—having felt it so strongly he could barely breathe because the shape-shifters had been right on top of him—he wasn't questioning it now.

Second, Truls Rohk was failing. He had come away from his battle with the caull winded and clearly hurt, but seemingly not in any real danger. He had walked strongly for several hours, carrying Grianne and setting a quick pace for Bek to follow. But over the last two hours, with the fading of the afternoon and the approach of nightfall, he had begun to slow, then to stagger, his smooth gait turned into an uneven lurch.

"I have to rest," Bek said finally, in an effort to find out what was going on.

The shape-shifter continued ahead for another fifty yards, then all but collapsed beside a fallen tree trunk, barely managing to set Grianne down before dropping heavily beside her. He wouldn't have thought to sit close to her before this; now, it seemed he could not find the strength to move away.

Bek walked up next to him and reached down for the water skin. Truls handed it to him without looking up. A ragged gasping came from inside the cowl, and Bek saw the rise and fall of the shape-shifter's shoulders as he struggled to breathe. Seating himself, he drank from the skin and watched as Truls give a deep, involuntary shudder.

They sat together without speaking for a long time, looking out over the valley below, listening to the silence.

"We can camp here," Bek said finally.

"We have to keep moving," Truls said, his voice raspy and weak. It didn't even sound like Truls. "We need to get higher up on the slopes while there's still light."

The cowl lifted, shadowed emptiness facing the boy like a hole dropping away into the earth. "Do you know where we are?"

Bek nodded. "In the land of the shape-shifters."

A cough racked the other's body, and he doubled over momentarily before straightening again. "We have to get deep enough in that they'll have no choice, that they'll have to come to us."

"You've decided to ask for their help?"

He didn't answer. Another spasm shook his body.

"Truls, what's wrong?" Bek asked, leaning close.

"Get away from me!" the shape-shifter snapped angrily.

Bek moved back. "What's wrong?"

For a moment, there was no response. "I don't know. I don't feel right. The caull did something to me, but I don't know what. I didn't think those cuts and bites were much, but everything feels like it's breaking down." He gave a short, sharp laugh. "Wouldn't it be a joke on me if I died because of your sister? Protecting her when I don't even like her? The Druid would love that, if he were here!"

He laughed again, the sound weak and broken. Then he struggled back to his feet, picked up Grianne, and set off once more.

They walked on for another hour, the afternoon passing slowly into twilight, the air cooling swiftly to a chill that nipped at Bek's face. Shadows lengthened on the mountainside, dark fingers stretching, and the moon appeared in the sky, rising out of the hazy distance, half-formed and on the wane. Bek looked back the way they had come to see if anyone was following, an impossible attempt in this light, and quickly gave it up. He glanced at their surroundings, searching for the watchers, but the effort yielded nothing. He listened to the silence and was not reassured.

They reached a shelf of ground that angled back into a deep stand of conifers, and Truls collapsed again. This time he went down without warning, dropping Grianne in a heap, rolling away from her onto his back where he lay gasping for air. Bek rushed over at once, kneeling beside him, but the shape-shifter pushed him away.

"Leave me alone!" he snapped. "See to your sister!"

Grianne lay sprawled to one side, eyes open and unseeing, body limp. She appeared unhurt as Bek helped her back to a sitting position, straightening her clothing and brushing leaves and twigs from her hair before returning to Truls.

"I'm done," the shape-shifter rasped. "Finished. Build a fire back in the trees to warm yourself. Wait for them to come."

A fire might attract the attention of those who hunted them, but Bek knew that whatever happened now was in the hands of the shape-shifters. No harm would come to them if the spirit creatures didn't wish it—not in their habitat and not from caulls or Mwellrets or anything else. Truls Rohk knew this, as well. He was counting on it.

Bek set about gathering wood to build a fire. It wasn't until he'd set the wood in place that he realized he didn't have any tinder. When he went back to see if Truls had any, the shape-shifter was unconscious. Bek took Grianne to where he had stacked the wood, then returned for Truls, but found him too heavy to move. All those broken and missing body parts, and he still weighed so much. Bek left him and sat with Grianne by the useless wood. He thought about using the wishsong to trigger a fire, but he didn't know how to do that. He sat staring into the night, feeling helpless and alone.

Where were the shape-shifters?

Night descended, and darkness closed about. The stars appeared overhead and the silence deepened. Soon it was so cold that Bek was shivering. He pulled Grianne close to him, trying to keep them both warm, wondering if they might freeze to death before morning. They were high up on the mountainside; it was too cold already and it was going to get much colder.

Once, he rose and walked out to where Truls Rohk lay and tried to rouse him. The shape-shifter was awake and breathing, but he did not appear lucid. A terrible heat radiated from his body, as if he was burning with fever. Bek sat with him for a while, trying to think of something he could do. But Truls Rohk's physiology was so different that Bek didn't even know where to begin. In the end, he just spoke quietly to the other, trying to reassure him, to give him some small comfort.

Then Bek returned to Grianne and the waiting.

He must have dozed off finally, because the next thing he knew he awoke to find the fire burning brightly in front of him and the night air grown warm and comforting. He glanced at

Grianne, who sat next to him, awake and staring, unresponsive when he spoke her name. He looked around and saw nothing, stood and looked some more, and still saw nothing.

He started to walk out toward the edge of the flat to where Truls lay and stopped. A dozen dark shapes blocked his way, massive forms rising before him like great rocks. As he started to back away, more closed about from both sides, huge and menacing, features hidden by the darkness and a sudden mist.

Bek stopped where he was and stood his ground. He knew what they were; he had been waiting for them. What he didn't know was why they had waited so long to appear.

Why did you come back?

The voice was thin and hollow, almost a wail, and it came from all around and not from any single source.

"My friend is sick."

Your friend is dying.

The words were unexpected, spoken without a trace of emotion or interest. For a moment, Bek could not make himself reply. *No,* he said to himself. *No, that's wrong. That can't be.*

"He's hurt," he said. "Can you help him?"

The shadows faded and reappeared in the deep mist like creatures conjured out of imagination. There was that ethereal quality to the shape-shifters, that otherworldliness that defied explanation. They seemed so impermanent that nothing about them was quite real. But Bek remembered how quickly they could change to something hard and deadly.

The caull has poisoned him. Teeth and claws excreted poison and it seeped into his human half, infecting it. The poison leeches away his strength. When his human half dies, his shape-shifter half will die, as well.

"Is there an antidote?" Bek demanded, still trapped in a web of disbelief and shock. "Do you know of one?"

There is no cure.

Bek looked around in despair. "There must be something I can do," he said finally. "I'm not going to just let him die!"

As soon as he spoke the words, he knew they were what the shape-shifters had been waiting to hear. He could see them move in response, hear their expectant whispers as they did so. He could feel a change in the air. He thought at once to take back the words, but did not know how to do so and could not have made himself, anyway.

You were told that halflings have no place in the world. You said that you would make a place for this one. Would you do so now?

Bek took a deep breath. "What are you asking?"

Would you make a place for your friend? Would you give him a chance to live?

The voice was coldly insistent, uninterested in argument or reason, in anything but a direct answer to its question. The shape-shifters had gone still again, clustered about like stones. Bek could no longer see or feel the fire. He could no longer remember in which direction it lay. He was shrouded in darkness and enclosed by the spirit creatures, and all he could see of the world was the glitter of the stars overhead.

"I want to save him," he said finally.

He sensed a murmur of approval and, once again, of expectation. It was the answer they were hoping for, yet one that promised results he did not fully comprehend.

He must shed his human skin. He must cast it aside forever. He must become like us, all of one thing and none of the other. If he does this, the poison cannot hurt him. He will live.

Cast off his human skin? Bek was not sure what he was being told, but it didn't matter. He couldn't dismiss out of hand any offer that might save Truls. "What do you want me to do?" he asked.

Give us permission to make him one of us.

Bek shook his head quickly. "I can't do that. I have to ask him if that's what he wants. I don't have the right—"

He cannot hear you. He is lost in his sickness. He will die before he can give you an answer. There is no time. You must decide for him.

"Why do you need my permission?" Bek was suddenly frantic. "What difference does it make what I say?"

The whispers and movement stopped, and the night went completely still. Bek froze in place and held his breath like a man about to jump from a very high place.

A human must make this choice. It is his human side we would destroy. There is no one else but you. You said you were his friend. You said you would give up your life for him and he would give up his life for you. Should we make a place in the world for him? You must decide.

Bek exhaled sharply. "You have to tell me what will become of him. If I tell you to do this, whatever it is, if I give you my permission, what will become of Truls?"

There was a long pause.

He will become one with us, a part of us.

Bek stared. "What does that mean?"

We are one. We are a community. No one of us lives apart from the others. He would be joined.

Bek felt every bit a boy in that instant, a boy who had ventured out into the world and gotten himself into such trouble that he would never see home again. He closed his eyes and shook his head. He couldn't do this. He was being asked to save Truls, but he was also being asked to change him irrevocably. By saving Truls, he would transform him into something else completely—a communal creature, no longer separate and apart, but a part of a whole. What would that be like? Would Truls want this, even to save his life? How could Bek possibly know?

He stood there, adrift in a sea of profound uncertainty, knowing he was being offered the only choice available and hating that it was his to make. Truls Rohk had never been at peace in the world. He had been an outcast all his life with few friends and no family or home. He was an aberration created through forbidden breeding, a freak of nature that had never belonged. What place there was for him, he had made for himself. Maybe he would be better off changed into one of the spirit creatures, a part of a family and community at last. Maybe he would be happier.

But maybe not.

Bek wanted Truls to live—wanted it desperately—but not if the price was too high. How could he measure that?

Tell us your decision.

Bek closed his eyes. A chance at life was worth any price, too precious to give up for any reason. He could not know how this would turn out; he could not determine what Truls Rohk would do if he were able. He could do for Truls only what Bek would want done for himself in the same situation. He could fall back only on what he believed to be right.

"Save him," he said quietly.

There was a sudden rush of movement from the shapeshifters, an odd hissing that turned into a sigh. The wall of bodies that had gathered about him opened, and the darkness cleared to reveal the fire still blazing in front of his sister.

Go back to her. Sit with her and wait. When morning comes, take her and go into the mountains. You will find what you are looking for there. Do not fear for your safety. Do not worry about those who follow. They shall not pass.

Dark forms changed into the bristling monsters he had seen once before, terrible apparitions that could smash a life with barely a thought, things that existed in nightmares. They hovered close for an instant, their smell washing over him, their raw presence reinforcing the promise they had made.

Go.

He did as he was told, not yet at peace with himself, unable to gain the reassurance he sought. He could not bear to consider too closely what he had done. He did not want to ponder the result because he was afraid he might recognize something he had not considered and did not want to face. He went back to the warmth and comfort of the fire, seating himself next to Grianne, taking her hands in his and holding them while he stared into the flames. He did not look back at the shape-shifters, did not try to see where they went or what they did. He would not have been able to do so anyway, because his eyes could not penetrate the darkness beyond the firelight.

He stared instead at Grianne and tried to make himself believe that she had been worth everything that had happened— that saving her was not a Druid's whim or a brother's false hope, but a necessary act that would result in something more important and far-reaching than the losses it had caused.

After a time, he fell asleep. His dreams were vivid and charged with emotion, and they ranged across the length and breadth of his life. In them, Quentin reappeared to him, working on an ash bow, red hair hanging loose and easy, strong face cocky and smiling, laughter bright with reassurance. Coran and Liria looked in on him as he slept, and he could hear them speak of him with ambition and pride. The company of the *Jerle Shannara* filed past him one by one as he stood at the edge of a forest, and then Rue Meridian stepped away long enough to come over to him and touch his face with cool fingers that swept away thoughts of everything but her.

Finally, Walker stood looking down at him from a castle rampart, from a place that looked vaguely familiar. Truls Rohk stood next to him, then faded into a disembodied voice that whispered to him to be strong, to be steadfast, to remember always how alike they were. He was different than Bek remembered him, and after a moment Bek knew that it was because Truls was no longer a halfling, but a true shapeshifter. He was one with his new family, with his community, with the world that had given him a second chance at life.

There was a sense of completion about him, of having found a peace that he had never known before.

Bek watched and listened to a box of empty space, to a wall of darkness, hanging on the other's words as if to a lifeline, and the peace that Truls had found settled over him, as well.

When he came awake again, it was morning. A misty gray light rose out of the mountain peaks, east where the dawn was breaking. The fire had gone out, the smoking embers turned to dying ashes and charred stumps. He reached out his hand. The ashes were still warm. Beside him, Grianne slept, stretched out upon the ground, her eyes closed and her breathing slow and even.

He stared down at her a moment, then rose and went to find Truls Rohk.

He stopped at the edge of the flat where he had left his friend the night before. All that remained was a hooded cloak and a scattering of half-formed bones. Bek knelt and reached down to touch them, lifting the folds of the cloak away, half expecting to find something more. Truls Rohk had seemed so indestructible that it was impossible that this was all that was left of him. Yet there was nothing more. Not even bloodstains were visible on the hard, frost-covered ground.

Bek rose and stood looking at the bones and cloak a moment longer. Perhaps most of what Truls Rohk had been, what mattered and had value, had gone on to become a part of what he was now.

He wondered if the shape-shifters, Truls among them, were watching him. He wondered if he would ever know if he had done the right thing.

He walked back to the campfire, woke Grianne, took her hands in his, and brought her to her feet. She came willingly, her calm, blank expression empty of emotion, her limp acquiescence sad and childlike. He was all she had left, all that stood between her and random fate. He had become for her the protector he had promised he would be.

He was not sure he was up to it, only that he must try, that he must do what he could to save them both.

Holding hands like children, they began to climb.

SEVENTEEN

On the next mountain over from the one that Bek and Grianne were struggling to ascend, Quentin Leah looked up expectantly from his breakfast of bread and cheese as Kian appeared out of the trees below the trailhead and began to climb toward him. Further up, gathered in the copse of fir where they had spent the night, the remnant of Obat's Rindge waited for instructions on where to go next—all but Obat himself and Panax, who had gone on ahead to scout their way through the passes of the Aleuthra Ark. They had been fleeing the Mwellrets and their tracking beasts for two days, and Quentin had hoped they would not have to flee for a third.

"They found our trail," Kian growled. His dark, square face furrowed as he sank down next to the Highlander and mopped his brow. "They're coming."

He would not look at Quentin. No one would these days. No one wanted to see what was in his eyes. Not since they found him in the ruins of Castledown. Not since they heard what became of Ard Patrinell.

Quentin understood. He did not feel right about himself anymore either. Everything seemed out of joint.

He handed the Elven Hunter what was left of his bread and cheese and stared down in frustration. They were sitting on a rugged slope that had the look of a hunched-over Koden, all bristle-backed with conifers and jagged rocks. Forty-eight hours of running had brought them here—frantic hours spent trying to throw off their pursuers. Nothing had worked, and now, finally, they had been run to earth.

From the beginning, when Quentin, Panax, Kian, Obat, and a dozen Rindge had remained behind to slow down the hunt for the tribe, things had gone wrong. As a group, they possessed a lifetime of knowledge of hunting and tracking in wilderness terrain, and each knew a dozen tricks that would slow or stop anyone trying to follow them. They had employed them all. They had started with simple devices intended to create dozens of false trails that would take a hunting dog hours to unravel. But the beasts the rets were using to track them were far superior to dogs, and they separated the real trail from the false with uncanny quickness, coming after Quentin's group almost before they could make their escape. The Rindge next used extracts from plants to create strong scents that would throw off the creatures. That didn't work either. Kian and Panax led them into streams and even one river, using the water to hide their passage, but the tracking beasts found them again anyway.

In desperation, Obat lured them into a narrow ravine and set fire to the whole of the woods leading up, a strong wind blowing the fire right back down into the faces of the rets. The fire was intended not only to drive their pursuers back, but to obliterate their tracks and scent, as well. That bought them several hours, but in the end the rets and their beasts found them anyway.

Finally, in desperation, Quentin and his companions set an ambush, thinking to kill or disable the tracking beasts. The ambush caught the rets by surprise, and a handful were killed by bows and arrows and blowguns before the remainder had a chance to take cover. The tracking beasts were struck, too, but the projectiles seemed to have almost no effect on them. They shrugged off the barbs as if they were nothing more than bee stings and came after their attackers with astonishing fury. Loosed from their chains, they turned into a pack of savage killers. Quentin had been involved in many hunts over the years, but he had never seen anything like this. The tracking beasts, at least eight of them, had charged through the scrub and over the rocks like maddened wolves, voiceless monsters that vaguely resembled humans evolved into something bigger and more terrible than the gray wolves that hunted the Black Oaks east of Leah.

Having no other choice, Quentin and his companions stood their ground and fought back. But before anyone could prevent it, three of the Rindge were dead, the beasts covered in their blood. They might have all been killed but for the Sword of Leah, which lit up like a torch, the magic surging down its length in a streak of blue fire. That was when Quentin realized that these beasts had been created out of magic, and that it would take magic to stop them. He killed two of them in a flurry of shrieks and severed limbs before the rest fell back, not defeated or cowed, but wary now of the power of the sword and uncertain whether or not they were meant to continue.

Their hesitation allowed Quentin and his companions to escape, but use of the sword marked them, as well; it alerted their hunters that at least one among the pursued possessed magic, and that hardened their determination to continue the pursuit. Airships appeared in the skies overhead, and fresh units of Mwellrets and trackers were lowered to the ground to join those already gathered. Quentin couldn't tell how many there were, but it was more than enough to overpower him should he choose to stand and fight again. He couldn't be certain whom the rets thought they were tracking, but it was clear that they were serious about finding out.

The chase wore on through that first day and all through the second, with the Rindge working their way deeper into the Aleuthra Ark, higher into the rugged peaks, following a trail they knew would eventually take them over the mountains and into the broader grasslands beyond. Quentin was beginning to wonder what good that would do. If their pursuers were this determined, they would be caught sooner or later whether they fled over the mountains or not. If they were to escape, a more permanent solution had to be found, and it had to be found quickly because the women and children that comprised the bulk of the fugitives were tiring.

Quentin was tiring, as well, not so much physically as emotionally. He had lost something in his battle with the Ard Patrinell wronk—something of the fire that had driven him earlier, something of heart and purpose—so that now he felt more a shell than a whole person. With so many of the company dead and all the rest scattered and lost, his focus had become blurred. He was helping the Rindge because they needed it and because he didn't know what else to do. It gave him direction, but not passion. He had lost too much to find that again without a dramatic shift in his fortunes.

He didn't think Panax and Kian were much better off, although they seemed more hardened than he was, more accustomed to the idea of going on alone. Quentin was too young yet, unprepared to have experienced the kind of losses he had just endured, and the losses were affecting him more dramatically. At times, he collapsed inside completely. He saw Tamis again, covered in blood and dying. He saw Ard Patrinell's head, encased in metal and glass, an instant before he smashed it apart. He saw Bek, the way he remembered him in the Highlands, such a long time ago.

He was haunted and worn and disillusioned, and he could feel himself slipping notch by notch. He cried because he couldn't help himself, trying to mask his tears, to hide his weakness. Chills racked him in bright sunshine. Dark dreams haunted his sleep—dreams of what hunted him, of what awaited him, of fate and prophecy. He awoke shaking and afraid and went back to sleep cold and empty.

But he was also the best chance the others had of staying alive, and he was painfully aware of the fact. Without the magic of the Sword of Leah, they had no answer for the magic of the things that pursued them. Quentin might be slipping off the edge, but he could not afford to let go.

"How much time do we have?" he asked Kian after a moment.

The Elf shrugged. "The Rindge will try to slow them down, but won't succeed. So, maybe an hour, a little more."

Quentin closed his eyes. They needed help. They needed a miracle. He didn't think he could give it to them. He didn't know who could.

Kian finished the bread and cheese, took a drink from his water skin, and stood. He was coated with dust and debris, and his clothes were torn and streaked with blood. He was a mirror image of Quentin. They were refugees in need of a bath and some real sleep, and they were unlikely to get either anytime soon.

"We'd better get them up and moving," Kian said.

They went back up the trail to where the Rindge waited. Using gestures and the few Rindge words they had picked up, they got the tribe back on its feet and trudging ahead once more. The Rindge were a dispirited group, not so much because of their weariness as because nothing the men had tried had worked and time was running out. Still, they kept on without complaint, the very young and old, the women and children, all helping one another where help was needed, a people dispossessed from their home of centuries, driven out by forces over which they had no control. They were demonstrating a resolve that Quentin found surprising and heartening, and he took what strength he could from them.

Still, it was not much.

They had hiked for perhaps an hour when the Rindge rearguard appeared on the run. Their gestures were unmistakable. The Mwellrets and tracking beasts were catching up to them.

At the same moment, Panax and Obat appeared from the other direction. The Dwarf was excited as he hurried to reach Kian and the Highlander.

"I think we've found something that will help," he said, eyes bright and eager as they shifted from one face to the other. He rubbed vigorously at his thick beard. "The pass divides up ahead. One fork leads to a thousand-foot drop—no way around it. The other leads to a narrow ledge with room for maybe two people to pass, but no more. This second trail winds around the mountain, then farther up through a high pass that crosses to the other side. Here's what's important. You can get above the second trail by climbing up the mountainside farther on and doubling back. There's a spot, perfect for what we need, to trigger an avalanche that will sweep away the pass and anything on it. If we can get the Rindge through before they're caught by the rets, we might be able to start a rockslide that will knock those rets and their beasts right off the trail—or at least trap them on the other side of where we are."

"How far ahead is this place?" Kian asked at once.

"An hour, maybe two."

The Elven Hunter shook his head. "We don't have that kind of time."

"We do if I stay behind," Quentin said at once.

He spoke before he could think better of it. It was a rash and dangerous offer, but he knew even without thinking it through that it was right.

They stared at him. "Highlander, what are you saying?" Panax asked angrily. "You can't—"

"Panax, listen to me. Let's be honest about this. It's the magic that's attracting them. No, don't say it, don't tell me I don't know what I'm talking about—we both know it's true. We all know it. They want the magic, just like Antrax and its creepers did. If I stay back, I can draw them off long enough for you to get past the place on the mountain where you want to start the slide. It will buy you the time you need."

"It will get you killed, too!" the other snapped.

Quentin smiled. Now that there were so many of the tracking beasts, he had virtually no chance of withstanding a sustained assault. If he couldn't outrun them—and he knew he couldn't—they would be all over him, sword or no. He was proposing to give up his life for theirs, a bargain that didn't bear thinking on too closely if he was to keep it.

"I'll stay with you," Kian offered, not bothering to question the Highlander's logic, knowing better than to try.

"No, Kian. One of us is enough. Besides, I can do this better alone. I can move more quickly if I'm by myself. You and Panax get the Rindge through. That's more important. I'll catch up."

"You won't live that long," Panax said with barely contained fury. "This is senseless!"

Quentin laughed. "You should see your face, Panax! Go on, now. Get them moving. The faster you do, the less time I'll need to spend back here."

Kian turned away, dark features set. "Come on, Dwarf," he said, pulling at Panax's sleeve.

Panax allowed himself to be drawn away, but he kept looking back at Quentin. "You don't have to do this," he called back. "Come with us. We can manage."

"Watch for me," Quentin called after him.

Then the Rindge were moving ahead again, angling through the trees and up the trail. They wound through boulders and around a bend, and in minutes they were out of sight.

Everything went still. The Highlander stood alone in the center of the empty trail and waited until he could no longer hear them. Then he started back down the way he had come.

It didn't take Quentin very long to find what he was looking for. He remembered the defile from earlier, a narrow split through a massive chunk of rock that wound upward at a sharp incline and barely allowed passage for one. Quentin knew that if he tried to make a stand in the open, the tracking beasts would overwhelm him in seconds. But if he blocked their way through the split, they could come at him only one at a time. Sooner or later, they would succeed in breaking through by sheer weight of numbers or they would find another way around. But he didn't need to hold them indefinitely; he only needed to buy his companions a little extra time.

The split in the boulder ran for perhaps twenty-five feet, and there was a widening about halfway through. He chose this point to make his first stand. When he was forced to give way there, he could fall back to the upper opening and try again.

He glanced over his shoulder. Further back, another two or three hundred yards, was a deep cluster of boulders where he had stashed his bow and arrows. He would make his last stand there.

"Wish you could see this, Bek," he said aloud. "It should be interesting."

The minutes slipped away, but before too many had passed, he heard the approach of the tracking beasts. They did nothing to hide their coming, made no pretense of concealing their intent. Sharp snarls and grunts punctuated the sound of their heavy breathing, and their raw animal smell drifted on the wind. Further away, but coming closer, were the Mwellrets.

Quentin unsheathed the Sword of Leah and braced himself.

When the first of the beasts thrust its blunt head around the nearest bend in the split and saw him, it attacked without hesitating. Quentin crouched low and caught it midspring on the tip of his weapon, spitting it through its chest and pinning it to the earth where it thrashed and screamed and finally died as the magic ripped through it. A second and third appeared almost immediately, fighting to get past each other. He jabbed at their faces and eyes as they jammed themselves up in the narrow opening, and forced them to back away. From behind them, he heard the shouts of the rets and the snarls of other tracking beasts as they tried in vain to break through.

He fought in the defile for as long as he could, killing two of the creatures and wounding another before he made his retreat. He might have stayed there longer, but he feared that the rets would find a way around. If they trapped him in the defile, he was finished. He had bought as much time as he could at his first line of defense. It was time to fall back.

With the tracking beasts snapping at him, he backed through the split, then made his second stand at the upper end. Straddling the opening, he bottled up the frantic creatures, refusing to let them through, killing one and wedging it back inside so that the others could not pass it without climbing over. They tore at their dead companion until it was shredded and bloodied, and still they couldn't break free. Quentin fought with a wild and reckless determination, the magic driving through him like molten iron, sweeping away his weariness and pain, his reason and doubt, everything but the feel of the moment and its dizzying sense of power. Nothing could stop him. He was invincible. The magic of the sword buzzed and crackled through his body, and he gave himself over to it.

Even when the Mwellrets got around behind him, he stood his ground, so caught up in the euphoria generated by the magic that he would have done anything to keep it flowing. He drove back this fresh assault, then returned to battling the tracking beasts trying to emerge from the split, intent on doing battle with anything that challenged him.

It took a deep slash to his thigh to sober him up enough that he finally realized the danger. He turned and ran without slowing or looking back, gaining enough ground to enable him to clamber into the rocks and find his bow and arrows just before his pursuers caught up with him. He was a good marksman, but his pursuers were so close that marksmanship counted for almost nothing. He buried four arrows in the closest burly head before it was finally knocked back, blinded in both eyes and maddened with pain. He wounded two more, slowing them enough that the others could not get past. He shot every arrow he had, killing two of the rets, as well, then threw down the bow and began running once more.

There was nowhere reasonable left to stand and fight, so he sprinted for the ledge where he hoped Panax, Kian, and the Rindge would be waiting with help. It was a long run, perhaps two miles, and he soon lost track of time and place, of everything but movement. Still infused with the magic of the sword, its power singing in his blood, he found strength he did not know he possessed. He ran so fast that he outdistanced his bulky pursuers, leaving them to scramble over boulders and rock-strewn trails he scaled with ease.

Maybe, just maybe, he would find a way out of this.

"Leah, Leah!" he cried out, euphoric and wild-eyed, with reckless disregard for who might hear him. "Leah!" he howled.

They caught up to him finally at the near end of the ledge, forcing him to turn and fight. He stood his ground just long enough to throw them back again, then rushed out onto the ledge. The sweep of the Aleuthra Ark with its massive backdrop of peaks and valleys stretched like a painting across the horizon, somehow not quite real.

The tracking beasts came at him once more, but they did not have enough room. Two tumbled away, clawing and screaming as they fell. He glanced back down the slope he had just climbed; it was crawling with tracking beasts and Mwellrets. How many more could there be? Pressed against the cliff face, he retreated as swiftly as he could, slashing at the closest of his pursuers when they came within reach. He had been clawed and bitten in a dozen places, and the singing of the magic had taken on a high, frantic whine. His stamina and strength were nearly exhausted; when they were depleted, the magic of the Sword of Leah would fail, as well.

"Panax!" he called frantically, fighting to keep his newfound fear at bay, feeling the euphoria desert him as the brilliance of his blade began to dim.

He was perhaps a hundred feet out from where he had

started, the cliff wall to his left an almost vertical rise, the drop to his right deep and precipitous, when he heard Panax call back to him. He did not look away from his pursuers. They were crowded out onto the ledge behind him, still coming, rage and hunger reflected in their eyes, waiting for him to drop his guard.

Then he heard a rumble of rocks from above, and he turned and ran. He was too slow. The closest of the beasts was on top of him in a heartbeat, claws slashing. He whirled and knocked it backwards, slamming his closed fist into the rock wall with such force that he lost his grip on the sword. Knocked from his hand, it tumbled over the edge of the path and disappeared into the abyss.

He hesitated then, not quite believing what had just happened, and his hesitation cost him any chance of escape. Rocks and dirt showered down from above, pouring over everything in a thunderous slide that swept across the face of the cliff. Quentin tried to run through it, but he was too late. The avalanche was all around him, tearing away the mountainside, breaking off chunks of the ledge. The tracking beasts and their handlers disappeared in a roar of stone, then a massive section of the trail ahead tore free and was gone.

Quentin flattened himself against the cliff wall and covered his head. The entire mountain seemed to be coming down on top of him. For a moment, he held on, pressed against the stone. Then the avalanche plucked him from his perch like a leaf, and he was gone.

EIGHTEEN

The Highlander regained consciousness in a sea of mind-numbing blackness and bone-crushing weight. He could smell dust and grit and the raw odor of torn leaves and earth. At first he could not remember what had happened or where he was, and panic's sharp talons pricked at him. But he held fast, forcing himself to be patient, to wait for his mind to clear.

When it did, he remembered the avalanche. He remembered being swept over the narrow ledge and into the void, tumbling downward through a rain of rocks and debris, catching onto something momentarily before being torn free, tangling up in scrub thickets, all the while engulfed in a roar that dwarfed the fury of the worst storm he had ever endured. Then darkness had closed about in a wave and everything else disappeared.

His vision sharpened, and he realized that the avalanche had buried him in a cluster of tree limbs and roots. Through small openings in his makeshift tomb, he saw heavy gray clouds rolling across a darkening sky. He had no idea how much time had passed. He lay without moving, staring at the distant clouds and collecting his thoughts. He should, by all rights, be dead. But the roots and limbs, while trapping him in a jagged wooden cage, had saved him, as well, deflecting boulders that would otherwise have crushed him.

Even so, he was not out of trouble. His ears were ringing, and his mouth and nostrils were dry with dust. Every bone and muscle in his body ached from the pummeling he had received, and he could not tell as yet if he had broken anything in his fall.

When he tried to move, he found himself pinned to the ground.

He listened to the silence, a blanket that cloaked both his stone-encrusted prison and the world immediately outside. There wasn't the smallest rustle of life, not the tiniest whisper, nothing but the ragged sound of his breathing. He wondered if anyone would come looking for him—if anyone even could. There might be no one left to look. Half the mountain had fallen away, and there was no telling whom it had carried with it. Hopefully, Panax and the Rindge had escaped and the Mwellrets and their tracking beasts had not. But he could not be sure.

He tried not to think too hard on it, focusing instead on the problem at hand. He forced himself to relax, to take deep breaths, to gather his resources. Carefully, gingerly, he tested his fingers and toes to make certain they were all working—and still there—then tested his arms and legs, as well. Amazingly, nothing seemed broken, even though everything hurt.

Encouraged by his sense of wholeness, Quentin set about looking for a way to get free. There was only a little room to move in his cramped prison, but he took advantage of it. He was able to extricate his left leg and both arms through the exercise of a little time, patience, and perseverance, but the right leg was securely wedged beneath a massive boulder. It wasn't crushed, but it was firmly pinned. Try as he might, he could not work it free.

He lay back again, drenched in sweat. He was aware suddenly of how hot he was, buried in the earth like a corpse, covered over by layers of rock and debris. He was coated with dust and grime. He felt as if he knew exactly what it would be like to be dead, and he didn't care for it.

He wormed himself into a slightly different position, but

the smallness of the space and the immobility of his trapped leg prevented him from doing much. *Deep breaths,* he told himself. *Stay calm.* He felt raindrops on his face through the chinks in his prison and saw that the sky had darkened. The rainfall was slow and steady, a soft patter in the stillness. He licked at stray drops that fell on his lips, grateful for the damp.

He spent a long time after that working with an unwieldy piece of tree limb that he was able to drag within reach and position as a fulcrum. If he could shift the boulder just an inch, he might be able to wriggle free. But from his supine position, he could not get the leverage he needed, and the branch was too long to place properly in any event. Nevertheless, he kept working at it until it grew so dark he could no longer see what he was doing.

He fell asleep then, and when he woke, it was still dark, but the rain had stopped and the silence had returned. He went back to work with the branch, and it was morning before he gave the task up as impossible. Despair crept through him and he found himself wondering how desperate his situation really was. No one was coming to look for him; he would have heard them by now if they were. If he was going to survive, he was going to have to do so on his own. What would that cost him? Would he cut off his leg if there was no other way? Would he give up part of himself if it meant saving his life?

Sleep claimed him a second time, and he woke to daylight and sunshine flooding down out of a clear blue sky. He did not give himself time to dwell on the darker possibilities of his situation, but went back to trying to get free. This time, he used a sharp-ended stick to dig away at the rock and earth packed in beneath his leg. If he could tunnel under his leg, he reasoned, he might create enough space to worm loose. It was slow going, the digging often reduced to one pebble, one small chunk of hardened earth at a time. He had to start as far back as his knee and work his way down, inch by painful inch. He had to be careful not to disturb anything that supported the boulder. If it shifted, it would crush his leg and trap him for good.

He worked all day, ignoring his growing hunger and thirst, the aches in his body, and the heat of his cage. He had come too far and endured too much to die like this. He was not going to quit. He would not give up. He repeated the words over and over again. He made them into a song. He chanted them like a mantra.

It was almost dark again when he finally worked his leg free, leaving behind most of his pants leg and much of his skin. Immediately, he began digging his way out, burrowing upward through the debris toward the fading light, toward fresh air and freedom. He could not afford to stop and rest. He felt the panic taking over.

Night had fallen, a velvet soft blackness under a starlit sky, when he pulled himself from the rocks and earth and stood again in the open air. He wanted to weep with joy, but would not let himself, afraid that if he broke down, he might not recover. His emotions were raw and jangled from his ordeal, and his mind was not entirely lucid. He glanced around at the jumble of boulders and jutting trees, then upward to the darkened cliffs. In this light he could not determine from where he had fallen. He could tell only where he was, standing at one end of a valley that lay in the shadow of two massive mountains in the middle of the Aleuthra Ark.

It was cold, and he forced himself to move farther down the slope into the trees beyond the avalanche line so that he might find shelter. He found it in a grove of conifers, and he lay down and fell asleep at once.

He dreamed that night of the missing Sword of Leah, and he woke determined to find it.

In the daylight, he could see more clearly where he had been and what had happened. The slide that had carried him over the side had torn away much of the mountain below, stripping it of trees and scrub, leveling outcroppings and ledges, and loosening huge sections of cliffside, all of which had tumbled into a massive pile of rubble. Looking up, he could just make out where he had been standing when he had fallen. No trace remained of those with whom he had fled or from whom he had been fleeing.

He hunted for food and water, finding the latter in a small stream not far from where he had slept, but nothing of the former. Even his woods lore failed to turn up anything edible so high up in the mountains. He gave it up and went back to the slide to search for the Sword of Leah. He had no idea where to look, so for the entire morning he wandered about in something of a daze. The slide was spread out for almost half a mile, and in some places it was hundreds of feet deep. He kept thinking that it was impossible that he was still alive, impossible that he had ridden it out without being crushed. He kept telling himself that his survival meant something, that he was not going to die in this strange land, that he was meant to go home again to the Highlands.

By midday, the sun was burning out of the sky and the valley was steaming. He was beginning to hallucinate, seeing movement where there wasn't any, hearing the whisper of voices, feeling the presence of ghosts. He went back down into the trees to drink from the stream, then lay down to rest. He woke several hours later, feverish and aching, and went back to searching.

This time, the ghosts took on recognizable form. As he trudged through the rocks, he found them waiting for him at every turn. Tamis appeared first, rising out of the landscape, healed and new again, short-cropped hair pushed back from her no-nonsense face, eyes questioning his purpose as she stared at him. He spoke her name, but she did not respond. She regarded him for only a moment, as if measuring anew the depth of his commitment and the strength with which he intended to pursue it. Then she faded into the shimmer of the midday heat, into the tangle of the past.

Ard Patrinell appeared next, sliding out of the haze as a metal-shrouded wronk, transformed from human into something only partly so. He stared at Quentin, his trapped, doomed eyes begging for release even as he raised weapons to skewer the Highlander. Even knowing the image wasn't real, Quentin flinched from it. Words passed the lips of the Captain of the Home Guard, but they were inaudible behind his glassy face shield, empty of sound and meaning, as insubstantial as his spectre.

The image shimmered and lost focus, and Quentin dropped into a guarded crouch, closing his eyes to clear his vision, his head, and his mind. When he looked again, Ard Patrinell was gone.

Both dead, he reminded himself, Tamis and her lover, ghosts lost in the passage of time, never to return in any other form, memories only. He felt himself drawn to them, less a part of his surroundings than before, more ethereal. He was losing himself in the heat, fading away into his imaginings, in need of rest and food and something hard and fast to hold on to. A chance. A promise.

Neither appeared, and his stumbling hunt across the avalanche-strewn landscape yielded nothing of the missing talisman. The afternoon lengthened, and his exhaustion increased. He was not going to find the sword, he knew. He was wasting his time. He should leave this place and go on. But go on to what and to where? Did he have another purpose, now that he was alone and so lost? Was there something further he was meant to do?

His mind drifted into the past, to the Highlands, where he had spent his youth so carelessly, to the times he had spent hunting and fishing and exploring with Bek. He could see his cousin's face in the air before him, disembodied, but Bek all the same. Where was he now? What had become of him since the ambush in the ruins of Castledown? He had been alive when Tamis had seen him last, but had disappeared since. Bek was as much a ghost as the Tracker and Patrinell.

But alive, Quentin Leah swore softly. Even missing, even disappeared, Bek was alive!

Quentin found himself kneeling in the rocks, crying, his face buried in his hands, his shoulders heaving. When had he stopped to cry? How long had he been hunched down like this in the rubble?

He wiped at his eyes, angry and ashamed. Enough of this. No more.

When he put his right hand down to push himself back to his feet, his fingers closed about the handle of his sword.

For a second he was so stunned that he thought he was imagining it. But it was as real as the stone on which he knelt. He forced himself to look down, to see the blade lying next to him, coated with dirt and grime, its pommel nicked and scored, but its incomparable blade as smooth and unmarked as the day it was formed. His fingers tightened their grip, and he brought the weapon around so that he could see it more clearly, so that he could be certain. There was no mistake. It was his sword, his talisman, and his hope reborn.

It was impossible, of course, that he should have found it. It was a one-in-a-million chance that he would find it at all. He was not a strong believer in providence, in fate's hand reaching out, but there was no other explanation for this miracle.

"Shades," he whispered, the word a rustle of sound in the deep silence of the afternoon heat.

He took the offered gift as a sign and came back to his feet, infused with new purpose. A wayward spirit not yet ready to cross over to the land of the dead, he began to walk.

Daylight faded quickly to twilight, the sun sliding behind the western rim of the Aleuthra Ark, turning the horizon a brilliant purple and crimson, cloaking the valley in long, deep shadows. The heat faded, and the air turned crisp and raw. The unexpected shift in temperature marked the coming of another storm. Quentin hunched his shoulders and lowered his head as he pushed on through the valley and began to climb where the mountains met and formed a high pass. Clouds that had been invisible before slid into view in thick knots and gathered across the sky. The wind picked up, slow and unremarkable at first before changing to gusts that were both icy and sharp edged.

Ahead, where the pass narrowed and twisted out of view, the darkness deepened.

Quentin pressed on. There was no place to stop and no point in doing so. He was too exposed on the slopes to chance resting; what shelter he might find lay on the other side of the pass. He needed food and water, but he was unlikely to find either before morning. Darkness layered the earth; roiling storm clouds canopied the sky. Sleet spit at him, icy particles stinging his face as he ducked his head protectively. The wind howled down out of the mountains, rolling off empty slopes, gathering force as it whipped across the valley from the passes and defiles. Trying not to think about how far he still had to go to reach safety, Quentin bent and wavered before the wind's tremendous force.

By the time he gained the head of the high pass, the sleet had changed to snow, and a carpet twelve inches deep covered the ground he trod. He had strapped the Sword of Leah across his back using a length of cord he found in one pocket, a makeshift that allowed his hands to stay free. He was walking mostly uphill over uneven ground, the wind tearing at him from all sides and shifting rapidly. Light played tricks in the curtain of falling snow, and it was all Quentin could do to maintain his balance. He was still dizzy and feverish, hallucinating from dehydration and lack of food, but he could do nothing about that.

The ghosts of his past came and went, whispering words that made no sense, gesturing in ways he could not understand. They seemed to want something from him, but he could not tell what it was. Perhaps they simply wanted his company. Perhaps they waited for him to cross over from the world of the living. The idea seemed altogether too possible. If things did not change, they would not have long to wait.

He had lost his cloak, and so he had nothing to protect himself from the cold. He was shivering badly and afraid he would lose all his body heat before he reached shelter. He had been made strong and tough from his years in the Highlands, but his endurance was not limitless. He hugged himself as he slogged ahead through snow and sleet and cold, trying to hold together in body and spirit both, knowing he had to keep going.

At the head of the pass, he found something else waiting.

At first, he wasn't sure if what he was seeing was even real. It was big and menacing, rising out of the rocks beyond, vague and indistinct in the whirl of the storm. It was man-shaped, but something else, as well, the limbs and body not quite right for a human, not quite in proportion. It appeared to him all at once as he crested the pass and walked into a wind howling with such fury that it threatened to tear the clothes from his body. He watched it slide through veils of white snow, then fade away entirely. He moved toward it, drawn to it instinctively, afraid and intrigued both. He had the sword, he told himself. He was not unprepared.

The shape appeared anew, further in, waited a moment for his approach, then disappeared once more.

This game of hide-and-seek continued through the pass and down the other side, where the walls of the mountain were thickly grown with conifers and the force of the storm was lessened by their windbreak. He had left the mountain off which he had fallen and was now beginning to ascend the one adjoining it. The trail was narrow and difficult to follow, but the appearance of the ghost ahead kept him focused. He was convinced by now that he was being led, but there seemed no reason for concern. The ghost had not threatened him; it did not seem to mean him harm.

He climbed for a long time, winding his way westward around the mountainside, his path twisting and turning through sprawling stands of huge old trees, deep glades of pine needles dusted with snow, and rocky hillocks slick with dampened moss. The storm's fury had diminished. The snow still fell, but the wind no longer blew the flakes into his face like needles, and the cold seemed less pervasive. Ahead, the shape took on clearer definition, becoming almost recognizable. Quentin had seen that shape before somewhere, moving in the same way, a wraith of the woods in another time and place. But his mind was singing with fatigue, and he could not place it.

Not much farther, he told himself. *Not much longer.*

Placing one foot in front of the other, eyes shifting between the ground below and the swirling white ahead, between his own movements and the ghost's, he pushed on.

"Help me," he called out at one point, but there was no response.

Not much farther, he told himself again and again. *Just keep going.*

But his strength was failing.

He went down several times, his legs simply giving way beneath him. Each time, he struggled back to his feet without pausing to rest, knowing that if he stopped, he was finished. Daylight would bring light and warmth and a better chance to survive a sleep. But he could not chance it here.

In a clearing leading into a deep stand of cedar, he slowed and stopped. He could feel himself leaving his body, rising into the night like a shade. He was finished. Done.

Then the dark shape ahead seemed to transform into something else, not one but two shapes, smaller and less threatening.

They came out of the night together, walking hand in hand, angling toward him from his left—how had they gotten all the way over there? He stared at the new figures in disbelief, again uncertain that what he was seeing was real, that it wasn't some new form of phantasm.

The figures hesitated as well, as they caught sight of him. He moved toward them, peering through the curtain of snow, through space and time and hallucinations, through fatigue and a growing sense of recognition, until he was close enough to be certain whom he was seeing.

His voice was parched and ragged as he called out to the one who stood closest and who stared back at him wide-eyed in disbelief.

"Bek!"

NINETEEN

Bek Ohmsford's journey over the past two days had not been as eventful as Quentin's, but it had been just as strange.

After leaving the shape-shifters, and with Grianne in tow, he had continued into the Aleuthra Ark, the ghost of Truls Rohk an unwelcome guest borne with him. An image of the hooded cloak and scattered bones spread carelessly across the frozen ground lingered in the forefront of his thinking all that first day, a haunting that refused to be banished. He found himself remembering his protector in life, seemingly indestructible, offering his incomparable strength and unshakable reassurance. Though much of the time Truls Rohk had been an invisible presence, he had always kept close watch over Bek, fulfilling his promise to the Druid.

It seemed impossible that he was really gone. Bek could tell himself that it was so, that there was no mistake, but somehow he kept thinking that Truls would reappear, just as he always had before. He kept looking for Truls to do so. He couldn't help himself. At every turn, in every patch of shadows, Bek thought to find him waiting.

So that first day passed, a dream in which Bek walked with his catatonic sister and the ghost of his lost friend.

By nightfall, he was exhausted, having traveled far and rested little. He had given little thought to Grianne, taking for granted her compliance with the hard pace he had set, forgetting entirely that she could not speak and therefore would not complain. Aware suddenly of his failure, he sat her down and examined her feet. They were not blistered, so he turned his attention to feeding her. He had to do it by hand, and even so she was still barely taking anything. Mostly, she drank water, but he was able to get a little mashed cheese and bread down her throat, as well. She did not look different to him, but he could not tell what was going on inside her head. He trailed the tips of his fingers across her cheeks and forehead and kissed her. Her strange eyes stared through him to places he could not see.

He fed himself then, eating hungrily and drinking some of the ale he had salvaged from Truls's supplies. Night descended in a deep soft blackness, and the sky was awash in stars. He wrapped Grianne in her cloak and sat next to her in the silence, one arm draped about her protectively, his thoughts straying to the past they had lost and the future they might never share. He did not know what to do for her. He kept thinking there must be something that he had not tried, that her catatonia was a condition he could change if he could just figure out what was needed. He knew there was an answer to the puzzle if he could only put his finger on what it was. But the answer he sought would not come.

After a time, he sang to her, his voice barely more than a whisper, as if anything more might disturb the night. He sang songs he remembered from his childhood, songs he had sung with Coran and Liria in the Highlands as a child. It all seemed very long ago and far away. He had not been a child for years. He had not been a boy since he had come on this journey with Quentin.

On impulse, he tried using the wishsong. Perhaps the magic could affect Grianne. It was their strongest connection, the shared heritage of their bloodline. If he could not reach her in any other way, perhaps he could reach her in this. He had not used it this way, but he knew from the history of the Ohmsford family that others before him had. The trick was in finding a chink in the armor of her catatonia, in worming his way past her natural defenses to where she was hiding. If he could reach deep inside, he might be able to let her know he was there.

He began to sing to her again, nothing more than humming at first, a soft and gentle melody to soothe and comfort. He blended himself with the night, another of its sounds, a natural presence. Slowly, he worked his singing around to something more personal, using words—her name, his own, their lost family revisited. He kept to memories that he thought would make her smile or at least yearn for what she had lost. He did not use her known name—Ilse Witch. He used Grianne, and called himself Bek, and he linked them together in an unmistakable way. Brother and sister, family always.

For a very long time, slowly and patiently, he worked to draw her to him, to find a way inside her mind, knowing it would not be easy, that she would resist. He made himself repeat the same phrases over and over, the ones he thought might trigger a response, giving her a fresh look each time, another reason to reach out for him. He played with color and light, with smell and taste, infusing his music with the feel of the world, with life and its rewards. *Come back to me,* he sang to her, over and over. *Come out from the shadows, and I will help you.*

But nothing succeeded. She stared at the fire, at him, at the night, and did not blink. She looked through the world to an empty place that shielded her from real life, and she would not come away.

Frustrated, weary, he gave it up. He would try again tomorrow, he promised himself. He was convinced that he could do this.

He lay back, and in seconds he was asleep.

They climbed higher into the mountains on the following day, finding their path a snake of coiled switchbacks and rugged scrambles. Grianne followed after him compliantly, but had to be hauled over the rougher spots. It was hard going, and the sky west was darkening with the approach of a storm.

At one point, he heard the roar of a massive slide somewhere deeper in the mountains, and the eastern horizon was left cloudy with dust and debris in the aftermath.

By nightfall, it had begun to rain. They took shelter beneath the boughs of a massive spruce, lying on a bed of fallen needles that remained warm and dry. As the rain settled in, the temperature fell, spiraling downward with the change in the weather. Bek wrapped Grianne in her cloak and sang to her once more, and once more she stared through him to other places.

He lay awake much longer this night, listening to the soft patter of the rain and wondering what he was going to do. He had no idea where he had gotten to or where he was going. He was proceeding on faith, on the promise of the shape-shifters that he was moving toward something and not away from everything. He was adrift in the world with his stunned, helpless sister and with his friends and allies scattered or dead. He had one weapon, one talisman, one crutch on which he could lean, but no clear idea of how he might use it. He was so alone that he felt he would never find comfort or peace again.

When he slept, it was from exhaustion.

Morning dawned sullen and gray, a reflection of his mood as he rose sluggish and dispirited, and they started out once more. The storm caught up with them at midday, sliding past the high peaks north and curling down along the slopes on which he climbed. He had descended almost a thousand feet earlier, as the trail dipped and curved through a defile that opened deep into the mountain. Now, with the wind picking up and the cold penetrating his bones, he was high on the slopes anew and without suitable shelter. He picked up the pace, pulling Grianne after him with fresh urgency. He did not want to get caught out in the open if it began to snow.

It did, soon after, but the flakes were large and lazy and the way ahead remained clear. Bek pressed on, descending at a split in the trail, intent on gaining the forested stretches lower down. He did so just as the storm blew out of the high regions in a blinding sheet of sleet and rain. Everything beyond a dozen yards disappeared. The trees turned to phantoms that came and went to either side in the manner of soldiers at march. He held Grianne's hand as tightly as he could, not wanting to chance a separation that might prove permanent.

The storm worsened, something he had not thought possible. Sleet and rain turned to deep curtains of snow. The snow began to build underfoot, and soon it was approaching twelve inches deep even in the windswept clearings. Visibility lessened further until he was groping from tree to tree. He would have taken shelter if he could have found any, but in the blinding whirl of the blowing snow, everything looked the same.

Then he stumbled and fell and lost his grip on Grianne. In an instant, she was gone. She disappeared in the whiteout, stolen away as surely as his faith in his purpose in coming on this journey. He groped for her, turning first this way and then that, everything white and empty about him, everything the same. He could not find her. Panic overwhelmed him as he grasped at snow flurries and air and empty chances, and he screamed. He screamed not just for his lost sister or his helplessness, but for all the pent-up rage and frustration he had been carrying with him for weeks. He screamed because he had reached the breaking point, and he did not care what happened to him next.

In that moment, a shape appeared before him, huge and dark, rising up like a behemoth roused from sleep to put an end to his intrusion. He stumbled backwards from it, surprised and terrified. As he did so, his hands brushed against his sister. He pushed his face close to hers to make certain he was not mistaken, calling to her. Her pale, empty features stared back at him. She was kneeling in the snow, docile and unbothered.

Tears of relief blinded him as he brought her back to her feet, holding on to her with both hands, then deciding that wasn't enough, wrapping her with his arms. He wiped the tears away with his sleeve and looked for the phantom that had caused him to find her. It was there, just ahead of him, but smaller and moving away. Bek peered after it, sensing something familiar about it, something recognizable. It faded and then reappeared, prowling just at the limits of his vision, expectant and purposeful.

Then suddenly it turned and beckoned him.

Almost without realizing what he was doing, he obeyed. Both hands clasped tight on Grianne's slender wrist, he started ahead once more into the haze.

"Which is how I found you," he finished, passing the ale-skin back to Quentin, the pungent liquid warming his throat and stomach as he swallowed. "I don't know how long I was out there, but my guide stayed just ahead of me the whole way, obviously leading me toward something, keeping me on track. I didn't know where it was taking me, but after a while it didn't matter. I knew who it was."

"Truls Rohk," his cousin said.

"That's what I thought at the time, but now I'm not so sure. Truls is gone. He's become a part of the shape-shifter community, and no longer has a separate identity. Maybe I just want to believe it was him." Bek shook his head. "I don't guess it matters."

They were huddled in a shallow cave hollowed into the side of the mountain. Bek had started a fire, and it burned with little heat, but a steady, insistent flame that illuminated their faces. Grianne sat to one side, staring off into the night, unseeing. Every so often, Quentin looked at her, not quite sure yet what to make of having someone who had tried so hard to kill them sitting so close.

Bek watched Quentin take another deep swallow from the aleskin. The color was finally returning to Quentin's frozen body. He had been nearly gone when he had stumbled upon Bek and Grianne. Bek had wasted no time wrapping him in his cloak and finding shelter for them all. The fire and ale had brought Quentin around, and they had spent the last hour exchanging stories about what had happened since the ambush in the ruins of Castledown. They didn't rush it, taking their time, giving themselves a chance to adjust to the idea that the impossible had happened and they had found each other again.

"I never thought you were dead," Bek told his cousin, breaking the momentary silence. "I never believed it was so."

Quentin grinned, a hint of that familiar, cocky smile that marked him so distinctively. "Me either, about you. I knew when Tamis told me she had left you outside the ruins, that you would be all right. But this business about you having magic, that's another matter. I still can't quite believe it. You're sure you're an Ohmsford?"

"As sure as I can be after hearing everything Walker had to say." Bek leaned back on his elbows and sighed. "I suppose I really didn't believe it myself in the beginning. But after that first confrontation with Grianne, feeling the magic come alive inside me and break out like it did, I didn't have the same doubts anymore."

"So she's your sister."

Bek nodded. "She is, Quentin."

The Highlander shook his head slowly. "Well, there's something we'd have never guessed when we started out on this journey. But what are you supposed to do with her now that you know?"

"Take her home," Bek answered. "Keep her safe." He looked at Grianne a moment. "She's important, Quentin. Beyond the fact that she's my sister. I don't know how, but she is. Walker was insistent on it, when he was dying and afterwards when he returned as a shade. He knows something about her that he isn't telling me."

"Big surprise."

Bek smiled. "I guess that Walker keeping secrets isn't unusual, is it? Maybe there aren't any surprises left for you and me. No real ones, I mean."

Quentin exhaled a white plume that lofted into the chilly night. "I wouldn't be so sure. I'd thought that earlier, and then I found you again. You never know." He paused. "What do you think the chances are that anyone else is alive? Are they all dead, like Walker and Patrinell?"

Bek didn't say anything for a moment. All of the Elves were gone, save Kian and perhaps Ahren Elessedil. Ryer Ord Star might still be alive. The Wing Riders might be out there somewhere. And, of course, there were the Rovers.

"We saw the *Jerle Shannara* fly into these mountains," Bek ventured. "Maybe the Rovers are still searching for us."

Quentin gave him a hard look. "Maybe. But if you were Redden Alt Mer in this situation, what would you do—come looking for us or fly straight back to where you came from?"

Bek thought about it a moment. "I don't think Rue Meridian would leave us. I think she'd make her brother look."

His cousin snorted. "For how long? Chased by those Mwellret vessels? Outnumbered twenty to one?" He shook his head. "We'd better be realistic about it. They don't have any reason to think we're still alive. They were prisoners themselves; they won't want to chance being made prisoners again. They would be fools not to run for it. I wouldn't blame them. I would do the same thing."

"They'll look for us," Bek insisted.

Quentin laughed. "I know better than to try to change your mind, cousin Bek. Funny, though. I'm supposed to be the optimist."

"Things change."

"Hard to argue with that." The Highlander looked off into the falling snow and gestured vaguely. "I was supposed to look out for you, remember? I didn't do much of a job of it. I let us get separated, and then I ran the other way. I didn't even think of looking for you until it was too late. I want you to know how sorry I am that I didn't do a better job of keeping my word."

"What are you talking about?" Bek snapped, an edge to his voice. "What more were you supposed to do than what you did? You stayed alive, and that was difficult enough. Besides, I was supposed to look out for you, as well. Wasn't that the bargain?"

They stared at each other in challenge for a moment. Then the tension drained away, and in the way of friends who have shared a lifetime of experiences and come to know each other better than anyone else ever could, they began to grin.

Bek laughed. "Coward."

"Weakling," Quentin shot back.

Bek extended his hand. "We'll do better next time."

Quentin took it. "Much better."

The wind shifted momentarily, blowing snow flurries into their faces. They ducked their heads as it whipped about them, and the fire guttered beneath its rush. Then everything went still again, and they looked out into the darkness, feeling their efforts at getting through the day catching up to them, seeping away their wakefulness, nudging them toward sleep.

"I want to go home," Quentin said softly. He looked over at Bek with a pale, worn sadness in his eyes. "I bet you never thought you'd hear me say that, did you?"

Bek shrugged.

"I'm worn out. I've seen too much. I've watched Tamis and Patrinell die right in front of me. Some of the other Elves, as well. I've fought so hard to stay alive that I can't remember when anything else mattered. I'm sick of it. I don't even want to feel the magic of the sword anymore. I was so hungry for it. The feel of it, like a fire rushing through me, burning everything away, feeding me."

"I know," Bek said.

Quentin looked at him. "I guess you do. It's too much after a time. And not enough." He looked around. "I thought this would be our great adventure, our rite of passage into manhood, a story we would remember all our lives, that we would tell to our friends and family. Now I don't ever want to talk about it again. I want to forget it. I want to go back to the way things were. I want to go home and stay there."

"Me, too," Bek agreed.

Quentin nodded, looking off again, not saying anything. "I don't know how to make that happen," he continued after a moment. "I'm afraid now that maybe it can't."

"It can," Bek said. "I don't know how, but it can. I've been thinking about getting back home, about how to take Grianne there, like Walker said I should. It seems impossible, crazy. Walker's gone, so he can't help. Truls Rohk won't be going any farther. Half of everyone I came here with is dead and the other half is scattered. Until I found you, I was all alone. What chance do I have? But you know what? I just tell myself I'll find a way. I don't know what that way is, but I'll find it. I'll walk all the way home if I have to. Right over the Blue Divide. Or fly. Or swim. It doesn't matter. I'll find a way."

He looked at Quentin and smiled. "We got this far. We'll get the rest of the way, too."

They were brave words, but they sounded right, necessary, talismans against fear and doubt. Bek and Quentin were still fighting for small assurances, for bits of hope, for tiny threads of courage. The words gave them some of each. Neither wanted to challenge them just now. Look too closely at the battlements, and the cracks showed. That wasn't what they needed. They left the words where they were, undisturbed, an echo in their thoughts, a promise of what they believed might still be.

Taking comfort in the shelter of each other, because in the end it was the best sort of comfort they could hope to find, they went off to sleep.

The dawn was cloudy and gray; a promise of new snow reflected in the colorless canvas of the slowly brightening sky. The temperature had dropped to freezing, and the air was brittle with cold. They ate breakfast with few words exchanged, mustering their resolve. The confidence that had bolstered them the night before had dissipated like fog in sunlight. All about them, the mountains stretched away in an endless alternation of peaks and valleys. Save for the intensity of the light from the sunrise east, the horizons all looked the same.

"Might as well get going," Quentin muttered, standing up and slinging his sword over his shoulder.

Bek rose, as well, and did the same with the Sword of Shannara. He barely gave thought to the talisman anymore; it seemed to have served its purpose on this journey and had become something of a burden. He glanced self-consciously at Grianne, realizing he could say the same about her and most certainly had thought as much more than once.

Thinking to cover as much ground as possible before the next storm and not wanting to be caught out in the open again, they set a brisk pace. The frozen ground crunched like old bones beneath their boots, grasses and earth cratering with indentations of their prints. If their pursuers were still tracking them, they would have no trouble doing so. Bek considered the possibility and brushed it aside. The shapeshifters had promised him that his pursuers would not be allowed to follow. There was no reason to think that their protection extended this far, but he was weary and heartsick and needed to believe this one thing if he was to have any peace of mind. So he let himself.

They trudged on toward midday, following trails that wound through the valleys ahead. The horizons never changed. In the vast mountain coldness, the land seemed empty of life. Once, they saw a bird flying far away. Once, further down in the shadowed woods, they heard some creature cry. Otherwise, there was only silence, deep and pervasive and unbroken.

Time dragged, a dying candle, and Bek's spirits lagged. He found himself wondering if there was any sense to what they were doing, if there was a purpose for going on. He understood that it gave them a goal and that movement kept them alive. But the vastness of the range and the terrible solitude it visited on them gave rise to a growing certainty that they were simply prolonging the inevitable. They were never going to walk out of the mountains. They were never going to be able to find anyone else from the doomed company of the *Jerle Shannara*. They were trapped in a nightmare world that would deceive them, break them down, and in the end destroy them.

He was marking out the time that remained to him when a dark speck appeared in the sky to the north, faint and distant. It grew quickly larger, moving swiftly toward them, taking on a familiar look. Recognition flooded through Bek, and the sense of hopelessness that had possessed him only moments earlier fell away like old ashes in a new fire.

By the time Hunter Predd swung Obsidian down to a flat just ahead of them, one whipcord thin arm raised in greeting, Bek was ready to believe that in spite of what he had told Quentin earlier, there might still be a few surprises left.

TWENTY

For nearly a week after taking control of *Black Moclips*, cruising the skies like birds of prey, the Morgawr and his Mwellrets scoured the coastal and mountain regions of Parkasia in search of the *Jerle Shannara* and the remnants of her company. Their efforts were hampered by the weather, which proved exceedingly arbitrary, changing without warning from sun to rain, either of which was as likely to see high winds and downdrafts as calm air. During the worst of the storms, they were forced to land and anchor for almost twenty-four hours, sheltered in a cove off the coast where bluffs and woods offered protection from an onslaught of sleet and hail that otherwise would have leveled them.

During most of this time, Ahren Elessedil languished belowdecks in a storeroom that had been converted to a cell. It was the same room that had housed Bek Ohmsford when he was a prisoner of the Ilse Witch, although Ahren did not know this. The Elven Prince was kept alone and apart from everyone save the rets who brought him food or took him on deck for brief periods of exercise. The Morgawr had moved his personal contingent of Mwellrets onto *Black Moclips*, preferring its sleeker design and greater maneuverability to that of the larger, more cumbersome warship he had occupied previously. Reduced to mindless shells, sad remnants of better times, the doomed Aden Kett and his men were left to crew her. Cree Bega was given command. The Morgawr occupied the Commander's quarters, and while they sailed in search of the *Jerle Shannara*, the Elven Prince barely saw him.

He saw even less of Ryer Ord Star. Her absence fueled his already deep mistrust of her, and he found himself reexamining his feelings. He could not decide whether she had forsaken her promise to him and truly allied herself with the Morgawr or if she was playing a game he did not understand. He wanted to believe it was the latter, but try as he might he could not come to terms with her seeming betrayal of him when he was captured or her clear distancing from him since. She had told him in the catacombs of Castledown that she was no longer in thrall to the Ilse Witch, yet she seemed to have become very much the creature of the Morgawr. She had led the warlock on his search for the *Jerle Shannara*. She had directed him to *Black Moclips*. She had stood by while that Federation crew had been systematically reduced to members of the walking dead. She had watched it all as if in a trance, showing nothing of her feelings, as removed from the horror and degradation as if she were absent altogether.

Not once had she tried to make contact with Ahren after they had been brought aboard *Black Moclips*. Nothing had come of the words she'd whispered days earlier. *Trust me.* But why should he? What had she done, even once, to earn that trust? On reflection, the words now seemed to have been whispered to gain his confidence, to assure his compliance at a time when he still might have escaped. Now there was no chance. Aboard an airship, hundreds of feet off the ground, there was nowhere for him to go.

Not that he had any chance of getting beyond the door of his cell in the first place, he reminded himself bitterly, even if they were on the ground. Without the missing Elfstones or weapons of any sort to aid him, he had no hope of overpowering his captors.

Locked away as he was, he had not been witness to most of what had happened during the past few days. But he could tell from the slow and steady pace of the airship that they were still searching. Mostly, he could tell from the unchanging routine of his captors that they had found nothing.

He thought ceaselessly about escape. He imagined it over and over, thinking through the ways in which it could happen, the events that would precipitate it, the ways in which he would react, and the results that would follow. He pictured himself going through the motions—slipping through the door and down the passageway beyond, climbing the stairs to the decks above, crouching low against the mast, and waiting for a chance to gain the railing and go over the side. But in the end the mechanics always failed him and his chances never materialized.

One day, shortly after a storm had grounded them for almost twenty-four hours, he was on deck with Cree Bega when he caught sight of Ryer Ord Star standing at the bow. He was surprised to see her again, and for a moment he forgot himself and stared at her with undisguised longing and hope.

Cree Bega saw that look and recognized it. Touching Ahren lightly on his shoulder, he said, "Sspeakss to her, little Elvess. Tellss her of your feelingss."

The words were an open invitation for him to do something foolish. The Mwellret was suspicious of the seer, as much so as Ahren was. Cree Bega had never been persuaded that her alliance with the Morgawr was genuine. He showed it in his attitude toward her, ignoring her for the most part, making no effort to consult her, even while the Morgawr did so. He was waiting, Ahren judged, for her to reveal her treachery.

"Nothing to ssay, Prince of Elvess?" Cree Bega mocked, his face bent close, the rank smell of him strong in Ahren's nostrils. "Wassn't sshe your friend? Issn't sshe sstill?"

Ahren understood the nature of the questions. He hated himself for his uncertainty, but he stayed silent, bearing the weight of the Mwellret's taunts and his own doubts. Anything he did would reveal truths that would hurt either Ryer or himself. If she responded to him, it would suggest a hidden alliance. If she did not, he would be made even more painfully aware of how things between them had changed. He was too vulnerable for anything so raw just now. It would be smarter to wait.

He turned away. "You talk to her," he muttered.

Another opportunity arose a day later, when he was summoned to the Morgawr's quarters and, on entering, found the seer standing beside him. She had that distant look again, her face empty of expression, as if she was somewhere else entirely in spirit and only her body was present. The Morgawr asked him again about the members of the company of the *Jerle Shannara*—how many had set out, whom they were, where he had last seen them, what their relationship had been to the Druid. He asked again for a head count—how many were still alive. He had asked the questions before, and Ahren gave him the same answers. It was not hard to do so. Dissembling was not necessary. For the most part, he knew less than the Morgawr. Even about Bek, the Morgawr seemed to know as much as Ahren did. He had read the traces of magic left floating on the air in the catacombs of Castledown and knew that Bek had come and gone. He knew that Ahren's friend was still out there, running from the warlock, hiding his sister.

What little the Morgawr hadn't divined, Ryer Ord Star had told him. She had told him everything.

At times while the Morgawr interrogated Ahren, she seemed to come back from wherever she had gone. Her eyes would shift focus, and her hands twitched at her sides. She would become aware of her surroundings, but only momentarily and then she was gone again. The Morgawr did not seem bothered by this, although it caused Ahren no small amount of discomfort. Why wasn't the warlock irritated by her inattention to what he was saying? Why didn't he suspect that she was deliberately isolating herself?

It took Ahren a long time to realize what was really happening. She wasn't distancing herself at all. She was very much a part of the conversation, but in a way the Elven Prince hadn't recognized. She was hearing his words and using them to feed her talent. She was turning those words into images of his friends, trying to project visions of them. She was using him in an attempt to track them down.

He was so stunned by the revelation that for a moment he just stopped talking in midsentence and stared at her. The silence distracted her where his words had not. For a moment, she came back from where her visions had taken her, and she stared back at him.

"Don't do this," he told her softly, unable to conceal his disappointment.

She did not reply, but he could read the anguish in her eyes. The Morgawr immediately ordered him taken back to his cell, an angry and impatient dismissal. He saw his real use then—not as a hostage for negotiation or as a puppet King. Those were uses that could wait. The warlock's needs were more immediate. Ahren would serve him better as a catalyst for Ryer Ord Star's visions, as a trigger that would allow her to help find the Ilse Witch and the others who eluded him. Unsuspecting, naive, the boy would help without even realizing he was doing so.

Except he had realized.

Ahren was locked away once more, closed off in the storeroom and left to celebrate in fierce solitude his small victory. He had foiled the Morgawr's attempt to use him. He sat with his back against the wall of the airship and smiled into his prison.

Yet his elation faded quickly. His victory was a hollow one. Reality surfaced and crowded out wishful thinking. He was still a prisoner with no hope. His friends were still scattered or dead. He was still stranded in a dangerous, faraway land.

Worst of all, Ryer Ord Star had revealed herself to be his enemy.

In the Commander's quarters, the Morgawr paced with the restless intensity of a caged animal. Ryer Ord Star felt the tension radiating from him in dark waves of displeasure. It was unusual for him to display such emotion openly, but his patience with the situation was growing dangerously thin.

"He knows what we are trying to do. Clever boy."

She did not respond. Her thoughts were of Ahren's words and the way he had looked at her. She still heard the anguish in his voice and saw the disappointment in his eyes. Understandably confused and misguided, he had judged her wrongly, and she could do nothing to explain herself. If the situation had been bad before, it was spiraling out of control now.

The Morgawr stopped in front of the door, his back to her. "He has become useless to me."

She stiffened, her mind racing. "I don't need his cooperation."

"He will lie. He will dissemble. He will throw in enough waste that it will color anything good. I can't trust him anymore." He turned around slowly. "Nor am I sure about you, little seer."

She met his gaze and held it, letting him look into her eyes. If he believed she hid something, the game was over and he would kill her now.

"I've given you nothing but the truth," she said.

His dark, reptilian face showed nothing of what he was thinking, but his eyes were dangerous. "Then tell me what you have learned just now."

She knew he was testing her, offering her a chance to demonstrate that she was still useful. Ahren had been right about the game they were playing. She was feeding off his words and emotions in response to the Morgawr's questions in an effort to trigger a vision that would reveal something about the missing members of the company of the *Jerle Shannara*. He had been wrong about her intentions, but there was no way she could tell him that. The Morgawr must believe she could help him find the Ilse Witch. He must not begin to doubt that she was his willing ally in his search, or all of her plans to help Walker would fall apart.

She took a small step toward the warlock, a conscious act of defiance, a gesture that nearly took her breath away with the effort it cost her. "I saw the Ilse Witch and her brother surrounded by mountains. They were not alone. There were others with them, but their faces were hidden in shadow. They were walking. I did not see it, but I sensed an airship somewhere close. There were cliffs filled with Shrike nests. One of those cliffs looked like a spear with its tip broken off, sharp edged and thrust skyward. There was the smell of the ocean and the sound of waves breaking on the shore."

She stopped talking and waited, her eyes locked on his. She was telling him of a vision Ahren's words had triggered, but twisting the details just enough to keep him from finding what he sought.

She held her breath. If he could read the deception in her eyes and find in its shadings the truth of things, she was dead.

He studied her for a long time without moving or speaking, a stone face wrapped in cloak and shadow.

"They are on the coast?" he asked finally, his voice empty of expression.

She nodded. "The vision suggests so. But the vision is not always what I think it is."

His smile chilled her. "Things seldom are, little seer."

"What matters is that Ahren Elessedil's words generated these images," she insisted. "Without them, I would have nothing."

"In which case, I would have no further need of either of you, would I?" he asked. One hand lifted and gestured toward her almost languidly. "Or need of either of you if he can no longer be trusted to speak the truth, isn't that so?"

The echo of his words hung in the air, an indictment she knew she must refute. "I do not need him to speak the truth in order to interpret my visions," she said.

It was a lie, but it was all she had. She spoke it with conviction and held the warlock's dark gaze even when she could feel the harm he intended her penetrating through to her soul.

After a long moment, the Morgawr shrugged. "Then we must let him live a little longer. We must give him another chance."

He said it convincingly, but she could tell he was lying. He had made up his mind about Ahren as surely as Ahren had made up his mind about her. The Morgawr no longer believed in either of them, she suspected, but particularly in the Elven Prince. He might try using Ahren once more, but then he would surely get rid of him. He had neither time nor patience for recalcitrant prisoners. What he demanded of this land, of its secrets and magic, lay elsewhere. His disenchantment with Ahren would grow, and eventually it would devour them both.

Dismissed from his presence without the need for words, she left him and went back on deck. She climbed the stairs at the end of the companionway and walked forward to the bow. With her hands grasping the railing to steady herself, she stared at the horizon, at the vast sweep of mountains and forests, at banks of broken clouds and bands of sunlight. The day was sliding toward nightfall, the light beginning to fade west, the dark to rise east.

She closed her eyes when her picture of the world was clear in her mind, and she let her thoughts drift. She must do something to save the Elven Prince. She had not believed it would be necessary to act so soon, but it now seemed unavoidable. That she was committed to Walker's plan for the

Morgawr did not require committing Ahren, as well. His destiny lay elsewhere, beyond this country and its treacheries, home in the Four Lands, where his blood heritage would serve a different purpose. She had caught a glimmer of it in the visions she had shared with Walker. She knew it from what the Druid had said as he lay dying. She could feel it in her heart.

Just as she could feel with unmistakable certainty the fate that awaited her.

She breathed slowly and deeply to calm herself, to muster acceptance of what she knew she must do. Walker needed her to mislead the Morgawr, to slow him in his hunt, to buy time for Grianne Ohmsford. It was not something the Druid had asked lightly; it was something he had asked out of desperate need and a faith in her abilities. She felt small and frail in the face of such expectations, a child in a girl's body, her womanhood yet so far away that she could not imagine it. Her seer's mind did not allow for growing up in the ways of other women; it was her mind that was old. Yet she was capable and determined. She was the Druid's right hand, and he was always with her, lending his strength.

She held that knowledge to her like a talisman as she made her plans.

When nightfall descended, she acted on them.

She waited until all of the Mwellrets were sleeping, save the watch and the helmsman. *Black Moclips* sailed through the night skies at a slow, languorous pace, tracking the edge of the coastline north and east as Ryer Ord Star slipped from her makeshift bed in the lee of the aft decking and made her way forward. Aden Kett and his crew stood at their stations, dead eyes staring. She glanced at them as she passed, but her gaze did not linger. It was dangerous to look too closely at your own fate.

The airship rocked gently in the cradle of night winds blowing out of the west. The chill brought by the storms had not dissipated, and her breath clouded faintly. Below where they flew, where the tips of the mountain peaks brushed the clouds, snow blanketed the barren slopes. The warmth that had greeted them on their arrival into this land was gone, chased inland by some aberration linked to the demise of Antrax. That science had found a way to control the weather seemed incredible to her, but she knew that in the age before the Great Wars there had been many marvelous achievements that had since disappeared from the world. Yet magic had replaced science in the Four Lands. It made her wonder sometimes if the demise of science was for the better or worse. It made her wonder if the place of seers in the world had any real value.

She reached the open hatchway leading down into the storerooms and descended in shadowy silence, listening for the sounds of the guard who would be on watch below. Walker would not approve of what she was doing. He would have tried to stop her if he had been able. He would have counseled her to remain safe and concentrate on the task he had given her. But Walker saw things through the eyes of a man seeking to achieve in death what he had failed to achieve in life. He was a shade, and his reach beyond the veil was limited. He might know of the Ilse Witch and her role in the destiny of the Four Lands, of the reasons she must escape the Morgawr, and of the path she must take to come back from the place to which her troubled mind had sent her. But Ryer Ord Star only knew that time was slipping away.

The passageway belowdecks was shadowed, but she made her way easily through its gloom. She heard snores ahead, and she knew the Mwellret watch was sleeping. The potion she had slipped into his evening ale ration earlier had drugged him as thoroughly as anything this side of death. It had not been all that hard to accomplish. The danger lay in another of the rets discovering the guard to be asleep before she could reach Ahren.

At the door to his storeroom jail, she took possession of the keys from the sleeping ret and released the lock, all the while listening for the sounds of those who would put an end to her undertaking. She said nothing as she opened the door and slipped inside, a wraithlike presence. Ahren rose to face her, hesitating as he realized who it was, not certain what to make of her appearance. He kept silent, though—harking to the finger she put to her lips and her furtive movements as she came over to release him from his chains. Even in the dim cabin light, she could see the uncertainty and suspicion in his eyes, but there could be no mistaking her actions. Without attempting to intervene, he let her free him and followed her without argument when she was ready to leave, stepping over the sleeping guard where he was sprawled across the passageway, creeping behind her as she moved back toward the stairs leading up. *Black Moclips* rocked slowly, a cradle for sleeping men and a drowsy watch. The only sounds were those of the ship, the small, familiar stretchings and tightenings of seams and caulk.

They went up the stairs and emerged behind the helmsman, flattening themselves against the decking, scooting along the shadow of the aft rise and across to the rail. Wordlessly, she slipped over the side and crossed down the narrow gangway to the starboard pontoon, sliding swiftly to the furthest aft fighting port, a six-foot-deep compartment stacked with pieces of sail and sections of cross beam.

Cloaked in deep shadows, she moved to where the pontoon curved upward to form the aft starboard battering ram. She felt along the inside of the structure and released a wooden latch hidden in the surface of the hull. Instantly, a panel dropped down on concealed hinges. She reached inside and drew out a framework of flexible poles to which sections of lightweight canvas had been attached.

She passed the framework and canvas forward to Ahren,

where he crouched at the front of the fighting port, then moved up beside him.

"This is called a single wing," she whispered, her head bent close to his, her long silvery hair brushing the side of his face. "It is a sort of kite, built to fly one man off a failing airship. Redden Alt Mer had it hidden in the hull for emergencies." She reached up impulsively and touched his cheek.

"You never intended to help him, did you?" the Elven Prince whispered back, relief and happiness reflected in his voice.

"I had to save your life and mine, as well. That meant giving your identity away. He would have killed you otherwise." She took a deep breath. "He intends to kill you now. He thinks you're of no further use. I can't protect you anymore. You have to get off the ship tonight."

He shook his head at once, gripping her arm. "Not without you. I won't go without you."

He said it with such vehemence, with such desperate insistence, that it made her want to cry. He had doubted her and was trying to make up for it in the only way he knew. If it was called for, he would give up his life for hers.

"It isn't time for me to go yet," she said. "I made a promise to Walker to lead the Morgawr astray in his hunt. He thinks I intend to help, but I give him only just enough to keep him believing so. I'll come later."

She saw the uncertainty in his eyes and gestured sharply toward the single wing. "Quit arguing with me! Take this and go. Now! Unfold it, tie the harness in place, and lean out from the side with the wings extended. Use the bar and straps at the ends to steer. It isn't hard. Here, I'll help."

He shook his head, his eyes wondering. "How did you know about this?"

"Walker told me." She began undoing the straps that secured the framework, shaking it loose. "He learned about it from Big Red. The rets don't know of it. There, it's ready. Climb up on the edge of the pontoon and strap yourself in!"

He did as she instructed, still clearly dazed by what was happening, not yet able to think it through completely enough to see its flaws. She just had to get him off the ship and into the air, and then it would be too late. Things would be decided, insofar as she was able to make it so. That was as much as she could manage.

"You should come now," he argued, still trying to find a way to take her with him.

She shook her head. "No. Later. Fly inland from the coast when you get further north. Look for a rain forest in the heart of the mountains. That's where the others are, on a cliff overlooking it. My visions showed them to me."

He shrugged into the shoulder harness, and she cinched it tight across his back. She opened the wing frame so that it would catch the wind and showed him the steering bar and control straps. She glanced over her shoulder every few seconds toward the deck above, but the Mwellrets were not yet looking her way.

"Ryer," he began, turning toward her once more.

"Here," she said, reaching into her thin robes and extracting a pouch. She shoved it into his tunic, deep down inside so that it was snugged away. "The Elfstones," she whispered.

He stared at her in disbelief. "But how could you have—"

"Go!" she hissed, shoving him off the side of the pontoon and into space.

She watched the wind catch the canvas and draw the framework taut. She watched the single wing soar out into the darkness. She caught a quick glimpse of the Elven Prince's wondering face, saw the man he had become eclipse the boy she had begun her journey with, and then he was gone.

"Good-bye, Ahren Elessedil," she whispered into the night.

The words floated on the air feather-light and fading even as she turned away, alone now for good.

TWENTY-ONE

A hand shook his shoulder gently, and Bek Ohmsford stirred awake.

"If you sleep any longer, people will think you're dead," a familiar voice said.

He opened his eyes and blinked against the sunlight pouring out of the midday sky. Rue Meridian moved into the light, blocking it away, and stared down at him, a hint of irony in the faint twist of her pursed lips. Just seeing her warmed him in a way the sun never could and made him smile in turn.

"I *feel* like I'm dead," he said. He lay stretched out on the deck of the *Jerle Shannara*, cocooned in blankets. He took in the railings of the airship and the mast jutting skyward overhead as he gathered his thoughts. "How long have I been asleep?"

"Since this time yesterday. How do you feel?"

His memories of the past week flooded back as he considered the question. His flight out of Castledown with Grianne and Truls Rohk. Their struggle to escape the pursuit of the Morgawr and his creatures. The battle with the caull. Truls, dying. Their encounter with the shape-shifters and the lifesaving transformation of his friend. Climbing with Grianne into the mountains, trusting that they would somehow find their way. Finding Quentin after so long, a miracle made possible because of a promise made to a dead man.

And then, when it seemed the mountains would swallow

them whole, another miracle, as Hunter Predd, searching for the *Jerle Shannara*'s lost children, plucked them off the precipice and carried them away.

"I feel better than I did when I was brought here," Bek said. He took a deep, satisfying breath. "I feel better than I have in a long time." He took a good look at her, noting the raw marks on her face and the splint on her left arm. "What happened to you? Been wrestling with moor cats again?"

She cocked her head. "Maybe."

"You're hurt."

"Cuts and bruises. A broken arm and a few broken ribs. Nothing that won't heal." She punched him lightly. "I could have used your help."

"I could have used yours."

"Missed me, did you?"

She tossed the question out casually, as if his answer didn't mean anything. But he knew it did. For just an instant he was convinced it meant everything, that she wanted him to tell her she was important to him in a way that went beyond friendship. It was an improbable and foolish notion, but he couldn't shake it. Anyway, he liked the idea and didn't question it.

"Okay, I missed you," he said.

"Good." She bent down suddenly and kissed his lips. It was just a quick brush followed by a touching of his cheek with her fingers, and then she lifted away again. "I missed you, too. Know why?"

He stared at her. "No."

"I didn't think so. I only just figured it out for myself. Maybe with enough time, you will, too. You're pretty good at figuring things out, even for a boy." She gave him an ironic, mocking smile, but it wasn't meant to hurt and it didn't. "I hear you can do magic. I hear you're not who you thought you were. Life is full of surprises."

"Do you want me to explain?"

"If you want to."

"I do. But first I want you to tell me how you got all beat up. I want to hear what happened."

"This," she said sardonically, and she gestured at the airship. "This and a lot of other catastrophes."

He lifted himself on one elbow and looked around. The *Jerle Shannara's* decks stretched away in a jumble of makeshift patches and unfinished repairs. A new mast had been cut and shaped and set in place; he could tell from the new wood and fresh metal banding. Railings had been spliced in and damaged planks in the hull and decks replaced. Radian draws hung limply from cross beams and sails lay half mended. No one was in sight.

"They've deserted us," she advised, as if reading his thoughts.

He could hear voices nearby, faint and indistinguishable. "How long have you been here?"

"Almost a week."

He blinked in disbelief. "You can't fly?"

"Can't get off the ground at all."

"So we're trapped. How many of us are left?"

She shrugged. "A handful. Big Red, Black Beard, the Highlander, you, and me. Three of the crew. The two Wing Riders. Panax and an Elven Hunter. The Wing Riders found them yesterday, not too far from here, with a tribe of natives called Rindge. They're camped at the top of the bluff."

"Ahren?" he asked.

She shook her head. "Nor the seer. Nor anyone else who went ashore. They're all dead or lost." She looked away. "The Wing Riders are still searching, but so are those airships with their rets and walking dead. It's dangerous to fly anywhere in these mountains now. Not that we could, even if we wanted to."

He looked at the airship, then back at her. "Where's Grianne? Is she all right?"

The smile faded from Rue Meridian's face. "Grianne? Oh,

yes, your missing sister. She's down below, in Big Red's cabin, staring at nothing. She's good at that."

He held her gaze. "I know that—"

"You don't know anything," she interrupted, her voice oddly breezy. "Not one thing." She pushed back loose strands of her long red hair, and he could see the dangerous look in her green eyes. "I never thought I would find myself in a position where I would have to keep that creature alive, let alone look after her. I would have put a knife to her throat and been done with it, but you were raving so loudly about keeping her safe that I didn't have much of a choice."

"I appreciate what you've done."

Her lips tightened. "Just tell me you have a good reason for all this. Just tell me that."

"I have a reason," he said. "I don't know yet how good it is."

Bek told her everything then, all that had happened since he had left the *Jerle Shannara* weeks earlier and gone inland with Walker and the shore party. Some she already knew, because Quentin had told her. Some she had suspected. She had guessed at his imprisonment aboard *Black Moclips* and subsequent escape, but she had not realized the true reason for either. She was skeptical and angry with him, refusing at first to listen to his reasons for saving his sister, shouting at him that it didn't matter, that saving her was wrong, that she was responsible for all the deaths suffered by the company, especially Hawk's.

Rue told Bek her story then, relating the details of her imprisonment along with the other Rovers by the witch and her followers, and of her escape and battle aboard the *Jerle Shannara*, where Hawk had given his life to save hers. She told him of her struggle to regain control of the ship and the freeing of her brother. She told him of her search for Walker and the missing company, which led in turn to her regaining possession of *Black Moclips* and fleeing inland toward the safety of the mountains as the fleet of enemy airships pursued her. She told her story in straightforward fashion, making no effort to embellish her part in things, diminishing it, if anything.

He listened patiently, trying with small gestures to encourage and support, but she was having none of it. She hated Grianne to such an extent that she could find no forgiveness in her heart. That she had kept his sister alive at all spoke volumes about her affection for him. Losing Furl Hawken had been a terrible blow, and she held Grianne directly responsible. Rue Meridian refused to let Bek sit by passively, turning her anger and disappointment back on him, insisting that he respond to it. He did so as best he could, even though he was not comfortable doing so. So much had happened to both of them in such a short time that there was no coming to grips with all of it, no making sense of it in a way that would afford either of them any measure of peace. Both had suffered too many losses and were seeking comfort that required different responses from what each was willing to provide. Where the Ilse Witch was concerned, there could be no agreement.

Finally, Bek put up his hands. "I can't argue this anymore, not right now. It hurts too much to argue with you."

She snorted derisively. "It hurts you, maybe. Not me. I don't bruise so easily. Anyway, you owe me a little consideration. You owe me a chance to tell you what I think about your sister! You owe it to me to share some of what I feel!"

"I'm doing the best I can."

She reached down suddenly and hauled him all the way out of the blankets and shook him hard. "No, you're not! I don't want you to just sit there! I don't want you to just listen! I want you to do something! Don't you know that?"

Her red hair had shaken loose of its headband and strands of it were wrapped about her face like tiny threads of blood. "Don't you know anything?"

Her eyes had gone wild and reckless, and she seemed on the verge of doing something desperate. She stopped shaking him, instead gripping his shoulders so tightly he could feel her nails through his clothing. She was trying to speak, to say something more, but couldn't seem to make herself do so.

"I'm sorry about Hawk," he whispered. "I'm sorry it was Grianne. But she didn't know. She doesn't know anything. She's like a child, locked away in her mind, frightened of coming out again. Don't you see, Rue? She had to face up to what she is all at once. That's what the magic of the Sword of Shannara does to you. She had to accept that she was this terrible creature, this monster, and she didn't even know it. Her whole life has been filled with lies and deceits and treacheries. I don't know—she may never be made whole."

Rue Meridian stared at him as if he were someone she had never seen. There were tears in her eyes and a look of such anguish on her face that he was stunned.

"I'm tired, Bek," she whispered back. "I haven't even thought about it until now. I haven't had time for that. I haven't taken time." She wiped at her eyes with her sleeve. "Look at me."

He did so, having never looked away, in truth, but giving her what she needed, trying to find a way to help her recover. He said, "I just want you to try to . . ."

"Put your arms around me, Bek," she said.

He did so without hesitation, holding her against him, feeling her body press close. She began to cry, soundlessly, her shoulders shaking and her wet face pushing into the crook of his shoulder and neck. She cried for a long time, and he held her while she did, running his hand over her strong back in small circular motions, trying to give some measure of comfort and reassurance. It was so out of character for her to behave like this, so different from anything he had seen from her before, that it took him until she was finished to accept that it was really happening.

She brushed what remained of the tears from her face and

composed herself with a small shrug. "I didn't know I had that in me." She looked at him. "Don't tell anyone."

He nodded. "I wouldn't do that. You know I wouldn't."

"I know. But I had to say it." She stared at him a moment, again with that sense of not knowing exactly who he was, of perhaps meeting him for the first time. "My brother and the others are down at the edge of the bluff, talking. We can join them when you're ready."

He climbed to his feet, reaching for his boots. "Talking about what?"

"About what it's going to take to get us out of here."

"What *is* it going to take?"

"A miracle," she said.

Redden Alt Mer stood at the edge of the cliff face and stared down at the canopy of the Crake Rain Forest, very much the same way he had stared down at it for the previous five days. Nothing at all had changed during that time, save for the level of his frustration, which was rapidly becoming unmanageable. He had considered and reconsidered every option he could think of that would let him bypass the Graak and retrieve the diapson crystals they needed to get airborne again. But each option involved unacceptable risks and little chance of success, so he would toss it aside in despair, only to pick it up and reexamine it when he decided that every other alternative was even worse.

All the while, time was slipping away. They hadn't been discovered by the airships of the Morgawr yet, but sooner or later they would be. One had passed close enough yesterday for them to identify its dark silhouette from the ground, and even though they hadn't been spotted on that pass they likely would be on the next. If Hunter Predd and Po Kelles were right, there were only one or two this deep into the Aleuthra Ark; the bulk of the fleet was still searching for them out on the coast. When that effort failed to turn them up, the fleet would sail inland. If that happened and they were still grounded, they were finished.

Still, for the first time since the *Jerle Shannara* had crashed, he had reason to hope.

He glanced over at Quentin Leah. The Highlander was staring down into the Crake with a puzzled look on his lean, battle-damaged face. The look was a reflection of his inability to imagine what waited down there, having not as yet seen the Graak. No one had, except for himself. That was part of the problem, of course. He knew what they were up against, and although the others—Rovers and newcomers alike—might be willing to go down into the rain forest and face it, he was not. What had happened to Tian Cross and Rucker Bont was still fresh in his mind. He did not care to risk losing more lives. He did not want any more deaths on his conscience.

It was more than that, though. He could admit it to himself, if to no one else. He was afraid. It had been a long time—so long he could not remember the last occasion—since he had been frightened of anything. But he was frightened of the Graak. He felt it in his blood. He smelled it on his skin. It visited him in his dreams and brought him awake wide-eyed and shaking. He could not rid himself of it. Watching his men die, seeing them go down under the teeth and claws of that monster, feeling his own death so close to him that he could imagine his bones and blood spattered all over the valley floor, had unnerved him. Though he tried to tell himself his fear was only temporary and would give way to his experience and determination, he could not be sure.

He knew the only way to rid himself of this feeling was to go down into the Crake and face the Graak.

He was about to do that.

"I won't ask you to go with me," he said to Quentin Leah without looking at him.

"He won't ask, but he'll make it plain enough that he expects it," Spanner Frew snorted. "And then he'll find a way to make you end up thinking it was your idea!"

Alt Mer gave the shipwright a dark look, then smirked in spite of himself. Something about the other amused him even now—the perpetually dour look, the furrowed brow, the cantankerous attitude, something. Spanner Frew always saw the glass as half-empty, and he was ready and more than willing to share his worldview with anyone close enough to listen.

"Keep your opinions to yourself, Black Beard," he said, brushing a fly from his face. "Others don't find them so amusing. The Highlander is free to do as he chooses, as are all of us in this business."

Quentin Leah was looking better this morning, less ghostly and wooden than the day before when he was brought in with Bek and the witch. Alt Mer was still getting used to the idea of having her around, but he wasn't having as much trouble with it as his sister. Little Red hated the witch, and she was not likely to forgive her anytime soon for Hawk's death. Maybe having Bek back would help, though. She'd been upset at the thought of losing him, more so than by anything for a long time. He didn't understand the affection she felt for Bek, but was quick enough to recognize it for what it was.

He sighed. At any rate, there were more of them now than there had been three days ago, after Rucker and Tian had died. Down to only six, the Rovers had seen their numbers strengthened since. The Wing Riders had reappeared first, flying out of the clouds on a blustery day in which rain had soaked everything for nearly twelve hours. After that, Po Kelles had found Panax, the Elven Hunter Kian, and those odd-looking reddish people they called Rindge. It had taken the Rindge another two days of travel to reach them, but now they were camped several miles east in a forested flat high in the mountains, concealed from searchers while they waited to see what would happen down here.

Their leader, the man Panax called Obat, was the one who

told them that the valley was called the Crake. He knew about the thing that lived there, as well. Obat hadn't seen it, but when Panax brought him down to talk, and Alt Mer described it, he recognized it right away. He had gotten so excited that it looked as if he might bolt. Hand gestures and a flurry of words that even Panax had trouble translating testified to the extent of Obat's fear. It was clear that whatever anyone else did, neither Obat nor any other Rindge was going near whatever was down there—"A Graak," Obat told Panax over and over again. The rest of what he said had something to do with the nature of the beast, of its invincibility and domination of mountain valleys like the Crake, where it preyed on creatures who were foolish or unwary enough to venture too close.

Knowing what it was didn't help solve the problem, because Obat had no idea what they could do about the thing. Graaks were to be avoided, never confronted. His information did not aid Alt Mer in any measurable way. If anything, it further convinced him of his helplessness. What was needed was magic of the sort possessed by Walker.

Or by Quentin Leah perhaps, in the form of his sword, a weapon that had been effective against the creepers of Antrax.

But he could not say anything more to persuade the Highlander to help. If anything, he should advise against it. But then he would have to go into the Crake alone, and he did not think he could do that. Though he was a brave man, his courage had eroded so completely that he felt sick to his stomach even getting close enough to look down into the rain forest. He had concealed his fear from everyone, but it was there nevertheless—pervasive, inescapable, and debilitating. He couldn't confess it, especially to Little Red. It wasn't that she wouldn't understand or try to help. It was the look he knew he would see in her eyes. He was the brother on whom she had always relied and in whom she took such pride. He could not bear it if she found out that he had run away while his men were dying.

The Highlander looked over at him. "All right, I'll go."

Big Red exhaled slowly, keeping his face expressionless.

"I'll go," Quentin Leah continued, "but Bek stays. Whatever magic he's got is new to him, and he doesn't have the experience with it that I do. I won't risk his life."

Whatever magic the Highlander possessed was pretty new to him, too, from what the Druid had told Alt Mer. Still, he wasn't about to argue the matter. He would take whatever help he was offered if it meant getting his hands on the diapson crystals. He didn't know what they had accomplished by coming here in the first place, but he didn't think it was much. Mostly, they had succeeded in getting a lot of their friends killed, which was hardly a reason for going anywhere. You didn't have to come all the way here to get killed. His frustration with matters surfaced once more. He would do anything to get out of this place.

Before he could respond to the Highlander, Rue and Bek Ohmsford walked out of the trees from one side and Panax, having gone off earlier to try to find an easier way down the cliff face, appeared from the other.

"Morning, young Bek!" the Dwarf shouted cheerfully on spying him. A grin spread across his square, bluff face, and he gave a wave of one hand. "Back among the living, I see! You look much better today!"

Bek waved back. "You look about the same, but that's not something sleep will cure!"

They came together at the cliff edge with Spanner Frew, Quentin, and Alt Mer and clasped hands. The Highlander's face had gone dark as he realized what was about to happen and knew he couldn't prevent it. Alt Mer gave a mental shrug. Some things couldn't be helped. At least his sister seemed composed again. Almost radiant. He stared at her in surprise, but she wouldn't look at him.

"I've scouted the cliff edge all the way out and back," Panax informed them, oblivious to the Highlander's look of warning. "There's a trail farther on, not much of one, but enough to give us a way down that doesn't involve ropes. It opens onto a flat, so we'll be able to see what's waiting much better than Big Red could when he dropped into the trees."

He glanced at Bek. "I forgot. You just woke up. You don't know what's happened."

"About the Graak and the crystals?" Bek asked. "I know. I heard all about it on the walk down. When do we leave?"

"No!" Rue Meridian wheeled on him furiously. "You're not going! You're not healed yet!"

"She's right," Quentin Leah said, glaring at his cousin. "What's wrong with you? I just spent weeks worrying that you were dead! I'm not going through that again! You stay up here. Big Red and I can handle this."

"Wait a minute," Panax growled. "What about me?"

"You're not going either!" Quentin snapped. "Two of us is enough to risk."

The Dwarf cocked one eyebrow. "Have you suddenly gotten so much better at staying alive than the rest of us?"

Bek glared at Quentin. "What makes you think you have the right to decide if I go or not? I decide what's right for me, not you! Why would I agree to stay up here? What about our promise to look out for each other?"

"Well, I'm going if you're going!" Rue Meridian spat out the words defiantly. "I'm the one who's done the best job of looking out for everyone so far! You're not leaving me behind! No one's leaving me!" She shifted her angry gaze from one to the next. "Which one of you wants to try to stop me?"

They were face-to-face now, all of them, so angry they could barely make themselves stop shouting long enough to hear what anyone else was saying. Spanner Frew was quiet, his dark face lowered to hide the grin on his lips, his head shaking slowly from side to side. Alt Mer listened in dismay, wondering when to step in and if it would make any difference if he did.

Finally, he'd heard enough. "Stop shouting!" he roared.

They quit arguing and looked at him, faces red and sweating in the midday heat.

He shook his head slowly. "The Druid is dead, so I command this expedition. Both aboard ship and off. That means I decide who goes."

His eyes settled momentarily on Bek—Bek, who looked taller and stronger than he remembered, more mature. He wasn't a boy anymore, the Rover Captain realized in surprise. When had that happened? He glanced quickly at his sister, suddenly seeing things in a new light. She was staring at him as if she wanted to jump down his throat.

He looked away again quickly, out over the valley, out to where his fears were centered. He wondered again why he had come all this way. Money? Yes, that was a part of the agreement. But there had been a need to escape the Prekkendorran and the Federation, as well. There had been a need to see a new country, to journey to somewhere he hadn't been. There had been a need for renewal.

"There's not that many of us left," he said, more quietly now. "Just a handful, and we have to look out for each other. Arguing is a waste of time and energy. Only one thing is important, and that's getting back into the skies and flying out of here."

He didn't wait for their response. "Little Red, you stay here. If anything happens to me, you're the only one who can fly the *Jerle Shannara* home again. Bek might try, but he doesn't know how to navigate. Besides, you're all beat up. Broken ribs, broken arm—if you have to defend yourself down there, you'll be in trouble. I don't want to have to worry about saving you. So you stay."

She was furious. "You're worried about saving me? Who

was it who got you out of the Federation prison? Who was it who . . ."

"Rue."

". . . got *Black Moclips* back from the rets and would have kept her, too, with just a little help? What about Black Beard? Standing there with his head down and his mouth shut, hoping no one will remember he can sail an airship just as well as I can! Don't say a word about it, Spanner! Don't say anything that might help me!"

"Rue."

"No! It isn't fair! He can navigate just as well as I can! You can't tell me not to go just because I—"

"Rue!" His voice would have melted iron. "Four of us are risk enough. You stay."

"Then Bek stays with me! He's injured, too!"

Alt Mer stared at her. What was she talking about? Bek wasn't her concern. "Not like you. Besides, we might need his magic."

She glared at him for a moment, and he could see she was on the verge of breaking down. He had never seen her do that, never even seen her come close. For a moment, he reconsidered his decision, realizing that something about this was more important than what her words were telling him.

But before he could say anything, she wheeled away and stalked back toward the airship, rigid with anger and frustration. "Fine!" she shouted over her shoulder. "Do what you want! You're all fools!"

He watched her disappear into the trees, thinking that was that, there was nothing he could do about it. Anyway, his next confrontation was already at hand. If Rue Meridian was angry, Quentin Leah was livid. "I told you I wouldn't go if Bek went! Did you think I didn't mean it?" He could barely bring himself to speak. "Tell him he can't go, Big Red. Tell him, or I'm not going."

Bek started to speak, but Alt Mer held up his hand to silence him. "I can't do that, Highlander. I'm sorry things didn't work out the way you wanted, but I can't change that, so threats are meaningless. Bek has the right to decide for himself what he wants to do. So do you. If you don't want to go, you don't have to."

There was a long silence as the Rover and the Highlander stared each other down. There was a dangerous edge to Quentin Leah, as if nothing much mattered to him anymore. Alt Mer couldn't know what Quentin had gone through to get clear of Castledown and find them, but it must have been horrendous and it had left him scarred.

"I'm sorry, Highlander," he said, not knowing what he was sorry about, save for the look he saw in the other's eyes.

"Quentin," Bek interjected quietly, laying one hand on his shoulder. "Don't let's argue like this."

"You can't go, Bek."

"Of course I can. I have to. We promised to look out for each other from here on, remember? We made that promise only a day or so ago. That meant something to me. It should mean something to you. This is when we have to make it count. Please."

Quentin stayed silent for a moment, looking so desperate that Alt Mer wouldn't have been surprised at anything he did. Then Quentin shook his head and put his hand over Bek's. "All right. I don't like it, but all right. We'll both go."

They stood looking at each another for a moment, aware that Quentin's words had made final their commitment to undertake a task that on balance was far too dangerous even to consider. Yet it was only the latest in a long line, and their decision to take this one, as well, no longer had the edge to it that it might have had once. Gambling with their lives had become commonplace.

"We'll need a plan," Panax said.

Big Red glanced over his shoulder in search of his sister.

She was out of sight now, and he wished suddenly that they hadn't left things as they had between them.

"I have one," he said.

The Dwarf stared down into the leafy depths of the Crake. "When do we do this?"

Alt Mer considered. The sun had eased westward, but most of the afternoon light still remained, and the sky was clear. It would not get dark for hours.

"We do it now," he said.

TWENTY-TWO

Quentin Leah was not in the least mollified by Big Red's and Bek's attempts to justify Bek's foolhardy decision to brave the Graak. It did not matter what reasoning they used, the Highlander could not help feeling that this would end badly. He knew it wasn't his place to tell Bek not to come with them. He knew that none of them thought him any better qualified than they were to judge the nature of the danger they would face. If anyone had the right to do so, in fact, it was Redden Alt Mer, who had already done battle with the creature and lived to tell about it.

Nevertheless, Quentin saw himself as the one they should listen to. Panax and Alt Mer were both battle-tested and experienced in the Four Lands, but neither had survived the challenges in Parkasia that he had. He knew more of this world than they did. He had a better feel for it. More to the point, he had the use of magic that they did not, which in all probability was going to make the difference between whether they lived or died.

Bek had magic, too, but he had used it sparingly and only on creepers—on things metal and impersonal—and he had not done all that much of that. Mostly, he had gotten through because he'd had Truls Rohk to protect him and Walker to advise him. He had not fought against something like the Graak. It was not going to be the same experience for him, and Quentin wasn't at all sure his cousin was ready for it.

As they made their way along the bluff toward the pathway into the valley, he trailed the others, stewing in silence and thinking about what they were going to do and how best to protect them while they were doing it. If Big Red and two of his most seasoned Rovers had been dispatched so easily, there wasn't much hope that things would change without help from the Sword of Leah. He would use it, of course. He would employ it as he had against the Ard Patrinell wronk. Maybe it would even be enough. But he wasn't sure. He had no idea how strong the Graak was. He knew it was bigger than anything he had ever encountered in the Highlands, and that was cause enough for concern. He could not be certain how well his talisman would protect them until he saw for himself what he was up against. As with all magic, the effectiveness of the sword depended on the strength of the user— not only physical, but emotional, as well. Once, he had thought himself equal to anything. He had felt the power of the magic race through him like fire, and he hadn't thought there was anything he couldn't overcome.

He knew better now. He knew there were limits to everything, even the euphoric rush of the magic's summoning and the infusion of its power. Events and losses had drained him of his confidence. He had fought too long and too often to feel eager about this. He was bone-weary and sick at heart. He had watched those around him die too quickly, more often than not helpless to prevent it. He mourned them still—Tamis and Ard Patrinell, in particular. Their faces haunted him with a persistence that time and acceptance had failed to diminish.

Perhaps that was the problem here, he thought. He was afraid of losing someone else he cared about. Bek, certainly, but Redden Alt Mer and Panax, as well. He did not think he could bear that. Not after what he had been through these past few weeks. Bek and he had agreed only a day ago that they must look out for each other as they had promised, that they needed to do so if they were to get home again safely.

But the truth of the matter was that he was the one who should be shouldering the larger share of the burden. He was the older and more experienced. He was physically and emotionally tougher than Bek. It might be true that Bek's magic was the stronger; Tamis had made it sound as if it was. But it was the strength of the user that mattered. Although Bek had gotten the *Jerle Shannara* through the Squirm and had managed to get control of his sister, neither of those achievements was going to help him in a confrontation with the Graak.

Quentin did not deceive himself into thinking that his own strength would prove sufficient for what lay ahead. He thought only that of the two, he had the better chance of getting the job done.

But there was no way of convincing his three companions that this was so, especially Bek, so he would have to do what he could in spite of them. That meant putting himself at the forefront of whatever danger they encountered and giving the others a chance to escape when escape was the only reasonable option.

Given the nature of the plan that Big Red had devised, Quentin did not think it would be that difficult for him to arrange. They needed only to get close enough to the crate of diapson crystals to get three or four of them in hand. More would be better, but if recovery of just those few was all they could manage, that would be sufficient. Three would get the *Jerle Shannara* airborne once more. A lack of spares might prove a problem later on, but staying alive in the here and now was a much bigger and more immediate concern.

So the four would make for the clearing where the crate lay waiting, searching as they went for any sign of the Graak. With luck, it would have gone elsewhere by now, lured away by its need for food or by some other attraction. If it was gone, this would be easy. If it was lying in wait, then it was up to Quentin and Bek to slow it down long enough for Big Red and Panax to gather up the crystals and regain the trail leading up. Bek had only the magic of the wishsong to rely on, and he was honest enough to admit he was not certain of his command of it, or of its effectiveness. That meant Quentin, who was sure where the Sword of Leah was concerned, was the front line of defense for all of them.

With that in mind, and unable to press further his demand that his cousin remain behind, he had at least managed to persuade him to stay a few paces back on their advance into the rain forest to give Quentin room to intervene if they were attacked.

None of which changed the fact that he was feeling much the same way he had felt going into the ruins at Castledown. There had to be more to this business of the Graak than he was seeing. He was missing something. He didn't know what it was, but he knew it was there. His hunting skills and instincts were screaming at him that he was overlooking something obvious.

They reached the trailhead and started down. The valley swept away below them, a vast carpet of leaves and vines, all tangled in a profusion of greens and browns. From high up, the jungle had the appearance of a bottomless swamp where the unwary could sink and be lost with a single misstep. Even as they descended the switchback trail, Quentin experienced the sense of being swallowed.

Halfway down, Redden Alt Mer stopped and turned back to them. "We are a pretty good distance away from where we have to go," he advised quietly. "This trail leads us further away from the crystals than the other. When we get to the valley floor, we'll have to backtrack. We'll stick close to the base of the cliff before starting into the trees." He pointed. "Over there, that's about where the crystals were when I was down here before. So we'll turn in where that big tree leans against the cliff face."

No one said anything in response. There was nothing to say.

They started ahead once more, working their way carefully

down the narrow pathway, pressing back against the rock to keep their footing, grasping scrub and grasses for balance. It was difficult going for Quentin because he was wearing his sword strapped across his back and the tip kept snagging on roots and branches. Alt Mer carried a short sword, and Bek carried nothing at all. Only Panax bore a more cumbersome weight in the form of his huge mace, but his squat, stocky form allowed him to better manage the task. Quentin suddenly wished he had thought to bring a bow and arrows, something he could strike out with from a distance. But it was too late to do anything about it now.

On the valley floor, they angled back along the base of the cliff, moving swiftly and silently through the tall grasses and around trees that grew close against the rocks. The terrain was still open, not yet overgrown by the rain forest, and Quentin could see through the trees for several hundred yards. He watched closely for anything that seemed out of place. But nothing moved and everything pretty much looked like it belonged. The Crake was a wall of foliage that concealed everything in its mottled pattern. Sunlight sprayed its vines and branches in thin streamers, but failed to penetrate with any success. Shadows lay over everything, layered in dusky tones, moving and shifting with the passing of the clouds overhead. It was impossible to be certain what they were seeing. They would be on top of anything hiding out there before they realized what it was.

They had gone some distance when Big Red held up one hand and pointed into the trees. This was where they would leave the shelter of the cliff wall. Ahead, the trees grew in thick clumps and the vines twisted about them like ropes. Clearings opened at sporadic intervals, large enough to admit something of size. On looking closer, Quentin could see that some of the trees had been pushed aside.

Alt Mer led with Quentin following close behind, Bek third, and Panax trailing. They worked their way in a loose line through a morass of earthy smells and green color, the dampness in the air rising off the soggy earth with the heat, the silence deep and oppressive. No birds flew here. No animals slipped through the shadows. There were insects that buzzed and hummed, and nothing more. Shadows draped the way forward and the way back with the light touch of a snake's tongue. Quentin's uneasiness grew. Nothing about the Crake felt right. They were out of their element, intruders who didn't belong and fair game for whatever lived here.

Less than ten minutes later, they found the remains of one of the Rovers who had come down with Alt Mer six days before. His body lay sprawled among shattered trees and flattened grasses. Little remained but head, bones, and some skin; the flesh had been largely eaten away. Most of his clothing was missing. His face was twisted into a grimace of unspeakable horror and pain, a mask bereft of humanity. They went past the dead man quickly, eyes averted.

Then Big Red brought them to a halt, hand raising quickly in warning. Ahead, a crate lay broken open, slats sticking skyward like bones. Quentin could not make out the contents, but assumed they were the diapson crystals. He looked around guardedly, testing the air and the feel of the jungle, searching out any predator that might lie in wait. He had learned to do this in the Highlands as a child, a sensory reading of the larger world that transcended what most men and women could manage. He took his time, casting about in all directions, trying to open himself to what might lie hidden.

Nothing.

But his instincts warned him to be careful, and he knew better than to discount them. *Tamis was better at this than I am*, he thought. *If she were here, she would see what I am missing.*

Redden Alt Mer motioned for them to stay where they were, and he stepped from the trees into the clearing and started for the crystals. He moved steadily, but cautiously, and Quentin watched his eyes shift from place to place. The Highlander scanned the jungle wall.

Still nothing.

When he reached the remains of the crate, the Rover Captain signaled over his shoulder for the others to join him. Spreading out, they moved across the clearing in a crouch. Quentin and Panax had their weapons drawn, ready for use. When they reached Alt Mer, Panax knelt to help the Rover extract the crystals while Quentin and Bek stood watch. The jungle was a silent green wall, but Quentin felt hidden eyes watching. He glanced at Bek. His cousin seemed oddly calm, almost at peace. Sweat glistened on his forehead, but it was from the heat. He held himself erect, head lifted, eyes casting about the concealment of the trees in a steady sweep.

Alt Mer had extracted two of the crystals and was working on a third when a low hiss sounded from somewhere back in the trees. All four men froze, staring in the direction of the sound. The hiss came again, closer, deeper, and with it came the sound of something moving purposefully.

"Quick," Alt Mer said, handing two of the crystals to Panax. The crystals were less than two feet long, but they were heavy. Panax grunted with the weight of his load as he started away. Big Red extracted the fourth crystal from the crate, making more noise than he intended, but unwilling to work more slowly. The hiss sounded again, closer still. Something was approaching.

With two crystals cradled in his arms, Big Red backed across the clearing, eyes on the jungle wall. Quentin Leah and Bek flanked him, the Highlander motioning for his cousin to fall back, his cousin ignoring him. The tops of the trees were shaking now, as if a wind had risen to stir them. Quentin had no illusions. The Graak was coming.

They had gained the shelter of a stand of cedar ringed by scrub brush, perhaps a dozen feet beyond the edge of the clearing, when the monster emerged. It pushed through the trees and vines with a sudden surge, a massive dragon weighing thousands of pounds and measuring more than fifty feet in length. Its body was the color of the jungle and glistened dully where the sunlight reflected off its slick hide. Horns and spikes jutted in clusters from its head and spine, and a thick wattle of skin hung from its throat. Claws the size of forearms dug into the dank earth, and rows of teeth flashed when its tongue snaked from its maw.

Squatting on four stubby, powerful legs, the Graak swung its spiky head left and right in search of what had caught its attention. Alt Mer froze in place, and Quentin and Bek followed his lead. Perhaps the creature wouldn't see them.

The Graak cast about aimlessly, then began to sniff the ground, long tail thrashing against the foliage. Quentin held his breath. This thing was huge. He had felt how the ground trembled when it lumbered out of the trees. He had seen how it shouldered past those massive hardwoods as if they were deadwood. If they had to do battle with it, they were in a world of trouble.

The Graak lumbered up to the crystals and sniffed at them, then put one massive foot atop the crate and crushed it. Hissing again, it turned away from them, searching the trees in the opposite direction.

Alt Mer caught Quentin's attention. *Now*, he mouthed silently.

Slowly, carefully, they began to inch their way backwards. Bek, seeing what they were attempting, did the same. Turned away, sniffing the wind, the Graak remained unaware of them. *Don't trip*, Quentin thought to himself. *Don't stumble*. The jungle was so silent he could hear the sound of his own breathing.

The Graak turned back again, its blunt snout swinging slowly about. As one, they froze. They were far enough back in the trees that they could barely see the creature's head above the tall grasses. Perhaps it couldn't see them either.

The reptilian eyes lidded, and the long tongue flicked out. It studied the jungle a moment more, then turned and shambled back the way it had come. Within seconds, it was gone.

When it was clear to all that it was not coming back right away, they started swiftly through the trees. Quentin was astonished. He had thought they had no chance of escaping undetected. His every instinct had warned against it. Yet somehow the creature had failed to spy them out, and now they were within minutes of reaching the cliff wall and beginning the climb back out.

They caught up with Panax, who was not all that far ahead yet. The Dwarf nodded wordlessly.

"That was close!" Bek whispered with a grin.

"Don't talk about it," Quentin said.

"You thought it had us," the other persisted.

Quentin shot him an angry glance. He didn't like talking about luck. It had a way of turning around on you when you did.

"Back home," Bek said, breathing heavily from his exertion, "if it was a boar, say, we would have looked for the mate, too."

Quentin almost stumbled as he turned quickly to look at him. *The mate*? "No," he whispered, realizing what he had missed, fear ripping through him. He pushed ahead of Bek, running now to catch up to Redden Alt Mer and Panax. "Big Red!" he hissed sharply. "Wait!"

At the sound of his name, the Rover came about, causing the Dwarf to slow and turn, as well, which probably saved both their lives. In the next instant, a second Graak charged out of the trees ahead and bore down on them.

There was no time to stop and think about what to do. There was only time to respond, and Quentin Leah was already in motion when the attack came. Never breaking stride, he flew past Big Red and Panax, the Sword of Leah lifted and gripped in both hands. The magic was already surging down the blade to the handle and into his hands and arms. He went right at the Graak, flinging himself past the snapping jaws as they reached for him, rolling beneath its belly and coming back to his feet to thrust the sword deep into its side. The magic flared in an explosion of light and surged into the Graak. The monster hissed in pain and rage and twisted about to get its teeth into its attacker. But Quentin, who had learned something about fighting larger creatures in his battles with the creepers and the Patrinell wronk, sidestepped the attack, scrambled out of the Graak's line of sight, and struck at it again, this time severing a tendon in the creature's hind leg. Again the Graak swung about, tearing at the earth with its claws, dragging its damaged rear leg like a club, its tail lashing out wildly.

"Run!" Bek yelled to Panax and Big Red.

They did so at once, bearing the crystals away from the battle and back toward the cliff wall. But Bek turned to fight.

There was no chance for Quentin to do anything about that. He was too busy trying to stay alive, and the shift of the Graak's body as it sought to pin him to the earth blocked his view of his cousin. But he heard the call Bek emitted, something shrill and rough edged, predatory and dark, born of nightmares known only to him or to those who worked his kind of magic. The Graak jerked its head in response, clearly bothered by the sound, and twisted about in search of the caller, giving Quentin a chance to strike at it again. The Highlander rolled under it a second time and thrust the blade of his talisman deep into the chest, somewhere close to where he thought its heart must be, the magic surging out of him like a river.

The Graak coughed gouts of dark blood and gasped in shock. A vital organ had been breached. Covered in mud and sweat and smelling of the damp, fetid earth, Quentin rolled free again. Blood laced his hands and face, and he saw that one arm was torn open and his right side lacerated. Somehow he had been injured without realizing it. Trying to stay out of the Graak's line of sight he ran toward its tail, looking for a fresh opening. The Graak was thrashing wildly, writhing in fury as it felt the killing effects of the magic begin to work through it. Another solid blow, Quentin judged, should finish it.

But then the creature did the unexpected. It bolted for Bek, all at once and without even looking his way first. Bek stood his ground, using the power of the wishsong to strike back, but the Graak didn't even seem to hear it. It rumbled on without slowing, without pause, tearing up the earth with its clawed feet, dragging its damaged hind leg, hissing with rage and madness into the steamy jungle air.

"Bek!" Quentin screamed in dismay.

He flew after the Graak with complete disregard for his own safety, and caught up to the creature when it was only yards away from his cousin. He swung the Sword of Leah with every last ounce of strength he possessed, the magic exploding forth as he severed the tendons of the hind leg that still functioned. The Graak went down instantly, both rear legs immobilized, its useless hindquarters dragging it to an abrupt stop. But as it fought to keep going, to get at Bek, it rolled right into the Highlander, who, unlike Bek, did not have time to get out of the way. Though Quentin threw himself aside as the twisting, thrashing body collapsed, he could not get all the way clear, and the Graak's heavy tail hammered him into the earth.

It felt as if a mountain had fallen on top of him. Bones snapped and cracked, and he was pressed so far down into the earth that he couldn't breathe. He would have screamed if there had been a way to do so, but his face was buried in six inches of mud. The weight of the Graak rolled off him, then back on again, then off again. He managed to get his head out of the mire, to take a quick breath of air, then to flatten himself as the monster rolled over him yet again, this time missing him as it twisted back on itself in an effort to rise.

"Quentin, don't move!" he heard Bek cry out.

As if he could, he thought dully. The pain was beginning to surge through him in waves. He was a dead man, he knew. No one could survive the sort of damage he had just sustained. He was a dead man, but his body hadn't gotten the message yet.

Hands reached under him and rolled him over. The pain was excruciating. "Shades!" he gasped as bones grated and blood poured from his mouth.

"Hang on!" Bek pleaded. "Please, Quentin!"

His cousin pulled him to his feet, then led him away. Somewhere close by, the Graak was in its death throes. Somewhere not quite so close, its mate was coming. He couldn't see any of this, but he could be sure it was happening. He stumbled on through a curtain of bright red anguish and hazy consciousness. Any moment now, he would collapse. He fought against that with frantic determination. If he went down, Bek would not be able to get him away. If he went down, he was finished.

Oh well, he thought with a sort of fuzzy disinterest, he was finished anyway.

"Sorry, Bek," he said, or maybe he only tried to say it; he couldn't be sure. "Sorry."

Then a wave of darkness engulfed him, and everything disappeared.

TWENTY-THREE

It was dark when Bek finally emerged from belowdecks on the *Jerle Shannara*, walked to the bow, and looked up at the night sky. The moon was a tiny crescent directly over the mountain they were backed against, newly formed and barely a presence in the immensity of the sky's vast sweep. Stars sprinkled the indigo firmament like grains of brilliant white sand scattered on black velvet. He had been told once that men had traveled to those stars in the Old World, that they had built and ridden in ships that could navigate the sky as he had the waters of the Blue Divide. It seemed impossible. But then most wonderful things did until someone accomplished them.

He hadn't been on deck for more than a few moments when Rue Meridian appeared beside him, coming up so silently that he didn't hear her approach and realized she was there only when she placed a hand over his own.

"Have you slept?" she asked.

He shook his head. Sleep was out of the question.

"How is he?"

He thought about it a moment, staring skyward. "Holding on by his fingernails and slipping."

They had managed to get Quentin Leah out of the Crake alive, but only barely. With Bek's help, he had stumbled to within a hundred yards of the trail before collapsing. By then he had lost so much blood that when they had carried him out they could barely get a grip on his clothing. Rue Meridian knew something of treating wounds from her time on the Prekkendorran, so after tying off the severed arteries with tourniquets, she had stitched and bandaged him as best she could. The patching of the surface wounds was not difficult, nor the setting of the broken bones. But there were internal injuries with which she did not have the skill to deal, so that much of the care Quentin needed could not be provided. Healing would have to come from within, and everyone knew that any chance of that happening here was small.

Their best bet was to either get him to a healing center in the Four Lands or to find a local Healer. The former was out of the question. There simply wasn't time. As for the latter, the Rindge offered the only possibility of help. Panax had gone to see what they could do, but had returned empty-handed. When a Rindge was in Quentin's condition, his people could do no more for him than the company of the *Jerle Shannara* could for Quentin.

"Is he alone?" Rue asked Bek.

He shook his head. "Panax is watching him."

"Why don't you try to sleep for a few hours? There isn't anything more you can do."

"I can be with him. I can be there for him. I'll go back down in just a moment."

"Panax will look after him."

"Panax isn't the one he counts on."

She didn't reply to that. She just stood there beside him, keeping him company, staring up at the stars. The Crake was a sea of impenetrable black within the cup of the mountains, silent and stripped of definition. Bek took a moment to look down at it, chilled by doing so, the memories of the afternoon still raw and terrible, endlessly repeating in his mind. He couldn't get past them, not even now when he was safely away from their cause.

"You're exhausted," she said finally.

He nodded in agreement.

"You have to sleep, Bek."

"I left his sword down there." He pointed toward the valley.

"What?"

"His sword. I was so busy trying to get him out that I forgot about it entirely. I just left it behind."

She nodded. "It won't go anywhere. We can get it back to-morrow, when it's light."

"I'll get it back," he insisted. "I'm the one who left it. It's my responsibility."

He pictured it lying in the earth by the dead Graak, its smooth surface covered with blood and dirt. Had it been bro-ken by the weight of the monster rolling over it, broken as Quentin was? He hadn't noticed, hadn't even glanced at it. A talisman of such power, and he hadn't even thought about it. He'd just thought about Quentin, and he'd done that too late for it to matter.

"Why don't you stop being so hard on yourself?" she asked quietly. "Why don't you ease up a bit?"

"Because he's dying," he said fiercely, angrily. "Quentin's dying, and it's my fault."

She looked at him. "Your fault?"

"If I hadn't insisted on going down there with him, if I hadn't been so stubborn about this whole business, then maybe—"

"Bek, stop it!" she snapped at him. He looked over at her, surprised by the rebuke. Her hand tightened on his. "It doesn't help anything for you to talk like that. It happened, and no one's to blame for it. Everyone did the best they could in a dangerous situation. That's all anyone can ask. That's all any-one can expect. Let it alone."

The words stung, but no more so than the look he saw in her eyes. She held his gaze, refusing to let him turn away. "Losing people we love, friends and even family, is a conse-quence of going on journeys like this one. Don't you under-stand that? Didn't you understand it when you agreed to come? Is this suddenly a surprise? Did you think that nothing could happen to Quentin? Or to you?"

He shook his head in confusion, cowed. "I don't know. I guess maybe not."

She exhaled sharply and her tone of voice softened. "It wasn't your fault. Not any more so than it was my brother's or Panax's or Walker's or whoever's. It was just something that happened, a price exacted in consequence of a risk taken."

The consequence of a risk. As simple as that. You took a risk, and the person you were closest to paid the price. He began to cry, all the pent-up frustration and guilt and sadness releasing at once. He couldn't help himself. He didn't want to break down in front of her—didn't want her to see that—but it happened before he could find a way to stop it.

She pulled him against her, enfolding him like an injured child. Her arms came about him and she rocked him gently, cooing soft words, stroking his back with her hand. The hard wooden rods of the splint on her left forearm were digging into his back.

"Oh, Bek. It's all right. You can cry with me. No one will see. Let me hold you until." She pressed him into the softness of her body. "Poor Bek. So much responsibility all at once. So much hurt. It isn't fair, is it?"

He heard some of what she said, but comfort came not from the words themselves but from the sound of her voice and the feel of her arms wrapped about him. Everything released, and she was there to absorb it, to take it into herself and away from him.

"Just hold on to me, Bek. Just let me take care of you. Everything will be all right."

She had said he owed it to her to share the losses she had suffered. Losses as great as his own. Furl Hawken. Her Rover companions. He was reminded of it suddenly and wanted to give back something of the comfort she was giving to him.

He recovered his composure, and his arms went around her. "Rue, I'm sorry . . ."

"No," she said, putting her fingers over his mouth, stopping him from saying anything more. "I don't want to hear it. I don't want you to talk."

She replaced her fingers with her mouth and kissed him. She didn't kiss him softly or gently, but with urgency and passion. He couldn't mistake what was happening or what it meant, and he didn't want to. It took him only a moment, and then he was returning her kiss. When he did, he forgot everything but the heat she aroused in him. Kissing her was wild and impossible. It made him worry that something was wrong, but he couldn't decide what it was because everything felt right. She ran her hands all over him, pushing him up against the ship's railing until he was pinned there, fastening her mouth on his with such hunger that he could scarcely breathe.

When she broke away finally, he wasn't sure who was the most surprised. From the look on her face she was, but he knew what he was feeling inside. They stared at each other in a kind of awed silence, and then she laughed—a low, sudden growl that brought such radiance to her face that he was surprised all over again.

"That was unexpected," she said.

He couldn't speak.

"I want to do it some more. I want to do it a lot."

He grinned in spite of himself, in spite of everything. "Me, too."

"Soon, Bek."

"All right."

"I think I love you," she said. She laughed again. "There, I said it. What do you think of that?"

She reached out with her good arm and touched his lips with her fingers, then turned and walked away.

*   *   *

When he went inside the ship to the Captain's quarters to see about Quentin, he was still in shock from his encounter with Rue. Panax must have seen something in his face when Bek entered the room, because he immediately asked, "Are you all right?"

Bek nodded. He was not all right, but he had no intention of talking about it just yet. It was too new to share, still so strange in his own mind that he needed time to get used to it. He needed time just to accept that it was true. Rue Meridian was in love with him. That's what she had said. *I think I love you.* He tried the words out in his mind, and they sounded so ridiculous that he almost laughed aloud.

On the other hand, the way she had kissed him was real enough, and he wasn't going to forget how that felt any-time soon.

Did he love her in turn? He hadn't stopped to ask himself that. He hadn't even considered it before now because the idea of her reciprocating had seemed impossible. It was enough that they were friends. But he did love her. He had always loved her in some sense, from the first moment he had seen her. Now, kissed and held and told of her feelings, he loved her so desperately he could hardly stand it.

He forced himself to shift his thinking away from her.

"How is he doing?" he asked, nodding toward Quentin.

Panax shrugged. "The same. He just sleeps. I don't like the way he looks, though."

Neither did Bek. Quentin's skin was an unhealthy pasty color. His pulse was faint and his breathing labored and shallow. He was dying by inches, and there was nothing any of them could do about it but wait for the inevitable. Already emotionally overwrought, Bek found himself beginning to cry anew and he turned away self-consciously.

Panax rose and came over to him. He put one rough hand on Bek's shoulder and gently squeezed. "First Truls Rohk and now the Highlander. This hasn't been easy," he said.

"No."

His hand dropped away, and he walked over to where Gri-anne knelt on a pallet in the corner, eyes open as she stared straight ahead. The Dwarf shook his head in puzzlement. "What do you suppose she's thinking?"

Bek wiped away the last of his tears. "Nothing we want to know about, I'd guess."

"Probably not. What a mess. This whole journey, from start to finish. A mess." He didn't seem to know where else to go with his thoughts, so he went silent for a moment. "I wish I'd never come. I wouldn't have, if I'd known what it was going to be like."

"I don't suppose any of us would." Bek walked over to his sister and knelt in front of her. He touched her cheek with his fingers as he always did to let her know he was there. "Can you hear me, Grianne?" he asked softly.

"I don't know what I'm doing here anymore," Panax continued. "I don't know that there's a reason for any of us being here. We haven't done anything but get ourselves killed and injured. Even the Druid. I didn't think anything would ever happen to him. But then I didn't think anything could happen to Truls, either. Now they're both gone." He shook his head.

"When I get home," Bek said, still looking at Grianne's pale, empty face, "I'll stay there. I won't leave again. Not like this."

He thought again about Rue Meridian. What would happen to her when they got back in the Four Lands? She was a Rover, born to the Rover life, a traveler and an adventurer. She was nothing like him. She wouldn't want to come back to the Highlands and stay home for the rest of her life. She wouldn't want anything to do with him then.

"I've been thinking about home," Panax said quietly. He knelt down beside Bek, his bearded face troubled. "I never cared all that much for my own. Depo Bent was just the village where I ended up. I have no family, just a few friends, none of them close. I've traveled all my life, but I don't know if there's anything left in the Four Lands that I want to see. Without Truls and Walker to keep me busy, I don't know that there's anything back there for me." He paused. "I think maybe I'll stay here."

Bek looked at him. "Stay here in Parkasia?"

The Dwarf shrugged. "I like the Rindge. They're a good people and they're not so different from me. Their language is similar to mine. I kind of like this country, too, except for things like the Graak and Antrax. But the rest of it looks interesting. I want to explore it. There's a lot of it none of us have seen, all of the interior beyond the mountains, where Obat and his people are going."

"You would be trapped here, if you changed your mind. You wouldn't have a way to get back." Bek tried the words out on the Dwarf, then grimaced at the way they sounded.

Panax chuckled softly. "I don't see it that way, Bek. When you make a choice, you accept the consequences going in. Like coming on this journey. Only maybe this time things will turn out a little better for me. I'm not that young. I don't have all that much life left in me. I don't think I would mind finishing it out in Parkasia, rather than in the Four Lands."

How different the Dwarf was from himself, Bek thought in astonishment. Not to want to go home again, but to stay in a strange land on the chance that it might prove interesting. He couldn't do that. But he understood the Dwarf's reasoning. If you had spent most of your life as an explorer and a guide, living outside cities and towns, living on your own, staying here wouldn't seem so strange. How much different were the mountains of the Aleuthra Ark, after all, from those of the Wolfsktaag?

"Do you think you can manage without me?" Panax asked, his face strangely serious.

Bek knew what Panax wanted to hear. "I think you'd just

get in the way," he answered. "Anyway, I think you've earned the right to do what you want. If you want to stay, you should."

They were nothing without their freedom, nothing without their right to choose. They had given themselves to a common cause in coming with Walker in search of the Old World books of magic, but that was finished. What they needed to do now was to help each other find a way home again, whether home was to be found in the Four Lands or elsewhere.

"Why don't you get some sleep," he said to the Dwarf. "I'll sit with Quentin now. I want to, really. I need to be with him."

Panax rose and put his hand on Bek's shoulder a second time, an act that was meant to convey both his support and his gratitude. Then he walked through the shadows and from the room. Bek stared after him a moment, wondering how Panax would find his new life, if it would bring him the peace and contentment that the old apparently had not. He wondered what it would feel like to be so disassociated from everyone and everything that the thought of leaving it all behind wasn't disturbing. He couldn't know that, and in truth he hoped he would never find out.

He turned back to Quentin, looking at him as he lay white-faced and dying. Shades, shades, he felt so helpless. He took a deep, steadying breath and exhaled slowly. He couldn't stand this anymore. He couldn't stand watching him slip away. He had to do something, even if it was the wrong thing, so that he could know that at least he had tried. All of the usual possibilities for healing were out of the question. He had to try something else.

He remembered from the stories of the Druids that the wishsong had the ability to heal. It hadn't been used that way often because it required great skill. He didn't have that skill or the experience that might lend it to him, but he couldn't worry about that here. Brin Ohmsford had used the magic once upon a time to heal Rone Leah. If an Ohmsford had used the magic to save the life of a Leah once, there was no reason an Ohmsford couldn't do so again.

It was a risky undertaking. Foolish, maybe. But Quentin was not going to live if something wasn't done to help him, and there wasn't anything else left to try.

Bek walked over to the bed and sat next to his cousin. He watched him for a moment, then took his hand in his own and held it. He wished he had something more to work with than experimentation. He wished he had directions of some kind, a place to begin, an idea of how the magic worked, anything. But there was nothing of the sort at hand, and no help for it.

"I'll do my best, Quentin," he said softly. "I'll do everything I can. Please come back to me."

Then he called up the magic in a slow unfurling of words and music and began to sing.

TWENTY-FOUR

Because he had never done this before and had no real idea of how to do it now, Bek Ohmsford did not rush himself. He proceeded carefully, taking one small step at a time, watching Quentin closely to make certain that the magic of the wishsong was not having an adverse affect. He called up the magic in a slow humming that rose in his chest where it warmed and throbbed softly. He kept hold of Quentin's hands, wanting to maintain physical contact in order to give himself a chance to further judge if things were going as intended.

When the level of magic was sufficient, he sent a small probe into Quentin's ravaged body to measure the damage. Red shards of pain ricocheted back through him, and he withdrew the probe quickly. Fair enough. Investigating a damaged body without adequate self-protection was not a good idea. Shielding himself, he tried again and ran into a wall of resistance. Still humming, he tried coming in through Quentin's mind, taking a reading on what his cousin was thinking. He ran into another blank wall. Quentin's mind seemed to have shut down, or at least it was not giving off anything Bek could decipher.

For a moment, he was stumped. Both attempts at getting to where he could do some good had failed, and he wasn't sure what he should try next. What he wanted to do was to get close enough to one specific injury to see what the magic could do to heal it. But if he couldn't break down the barriers that Quentin had thrown up to protect himself, he wasn't going to be able to do anything.

He tried a more general approach then, a wrapping of Quentin in the magic's veil, a covering over of his mind and body both. It had the desired effect; Quentin immediately calmed and his breathing became steadier and smoother. Bek worked his way over his cousin's still form in search of entry, thinking that as his body relaxed, Quentin might lower his protective barriers. Slowly, slowly he touched and stroked with the magic, his singing smoothing away wrinkles of pain and discomfort, working toward the deeper, more serious injuries.

It didn't work. He could not get past the surface of Quentin's body, even when he brushed up against the open wounds beneath the bandages, which should have offered him easy access.

He was so frustrated that he broke off his attempts completely. Sitting silently, motionlessly beside Quentin, he continued to hold his cousin's hand, not willing to break that contact, as well. He tried to think of what else he could do. Something about the way in which he was approaching the problem was throwing up barriers. He knew he could force his way into Quentin's body, could break down the protective walls that barred his way. But he thought, as well, that the consequence of such a harsh intrusion might be fatal to a system already close to collapse. What was needed was tact and care, a gentle offering to heal that would be embraced and not resisted.

What would it take to make that happen?

He tried again, this time returning to what was familiar to him about the magic. He sang to Quentin as he had sung to Grianne—of their lives together as boys, of the Highlands of Leah, of family and friends, and of adventures shared. He sang stories to his cousin, thinking to use them as a means of lessening resistance to his ministrations. Now and then, he would attempt a foray into his cousin's body and mind, taking a story in a direction that might lend itself to a welcoming, the two of them friends still and always.

Nothing.

He changed the nature of his song to one of revelation and warning. *This is the situation, Quentin,* he sang. *You are very sick and in need of healing. But you are fighting me. I need you to help me instead. I need you to open to me and let me use the wishsong to mend you. Please, Quentin, listen to me. Listen.*

If his cousin heard, he didn't do anything to indicate it and did nothing to give Bek any further access. He simply lay on his bed beneath a light covering and fought to stay alive on his own terms. He remained unconscious and unresponsive and, like Grianne, locked away where Bek could not reach him.

Bek kept at it. He fought to use the magic for the better part of the next hour, maintaining contact through the touching of their hands while trying to heal with his song. He came at the problem from every direction he could imagine, even when he suspected that what he was trying was futile. He attacked with such determination that he completely lost track of everything but what he was doing.

All to no avail.

Finally, exhausted and frustrated, he gave up. He rocked back, put his face in his hands, and began to sob. All this crying felt foolish and weak, but he was so weary from his efforts that it was an impulsive, unavoidable response. It happened in spite of his efforts to stop it, boiling over in a rush that left him convulsed and shaking. He had failed. There was nothing left for him to try, nowhere else for him to go.

"Poor little baby boy," a voice soothed in his ear, and slender arms came around his neck and pulled him close.

At first he thought it was Rue Meridian, come down to the cabin when he wasn't looking. But he realized almost before he had completed the thought that it wasn't her voice. Gray robes fell across his face as he twisted his head for a quick look.

It was Grianne.

He was so shocked that for a moment he just sat there and let her hold him. "Little boy, little boy, don't be sad." She was speaking not in her adult voice, but with the voice of a child. "It's all right, baby Bek. Your big sister is here. I won't leave you again, I promise. I won't go away again. I'm so sorry, so sorry."

Her hands stroked his face, gentle and soothing. She kissed his forehead as she cooed to him, touching him as if he were a baby.

He glanced up again, looking into her eyes. She was looking back at him, seeing him for the first time since he had found her in Castledown. Gone were the vacant stare and the empty expression. She had come back from wherever she had been hiding. She was awake.

"Grianne!" he gasped in relief.

"No, no, baby, don't cry," she replied at once, touching his lips with her fingers. "There, there, your Grianne can make it all better. Tell me what's wrong, little one."

Bek caught his breath. She was seeing him, but not as he really was, only as she remembered him.

Her gaze shifted suddenly. "Oh, what's this? Is your puppy sick, Bek? Did he eat something bad? Did he hurt himself? Poor little puppy."

She was looking right at Quentin. Bek was so taken aback by this that he just stared at her. He vaguely remembered a puppy from when he was very little, a black mixed breed that trotted around the house and slept in the sun. He remembered nothing else about it, not even its name.

"No wonder you're crying." She smoothed Bek's hair back gently. "Your puppy is sick, and you can't make him better.

It's all right, Bek. Grianne can help. We'll use my special medicine to take away the pain."

She released him and moved to the head of the bed to stand looking down at Quentin. "So much pain," she whispered. "I don't know if I can make you well again. Sometimes even the special medicine can't help. Sometimes nothing can."

A chill settled through Bek as he realized that he might be mistaken about her. Maybe she wasn't his sister at all, but the Ilse Witch. If she was thinking like the witch and not Grianne, if she had not come all the way back to being his sister, she might cure Quentin the way she had cured so many of her problems. She might kill him.

"No, Grianne!" he cried out, reaching for her.

"Uh-uh-uh, baby," she cautioned, taking hold of his wrists. She was much stronger than he would have thought, and he could not shake free. "Let Grianne do what she has to do to help."

Already she was using the magic. Bek felt it wash over him, felt it bind him in velvet chains and hold him fast. In seconds, he was paralyzed. She eased him back in place, humming softly as she moved once more to the head of the bed and Quentin Leah.

"Poor puppy," she repeated, reaching down to stroke the Highlander's face. "You are so sick, in such pain. What happened to you? You are all broken up inside. Did something hurt you?"

Bek was beside himself. He could neither move nor speak. He watched helplessly, unable to intervene and terrified of what was going to happen if he didn't.

She was speaking to him again, her voice suddenly older, more mature. "Oh, Bek, I've let you down so badly. I left you, and I didn't come back. I should have, and I didn't. It was so wrong of me, Bek."

She was crying. His sister was crying. It was astonishing, and Bek would have felt a sense of joy if he hadn't been so frightened that it wasn't his sister speaking. He fought to say something, to stop her, but no words would come out.

"Little puppy," she whispered sadly, and her hands reached down to cup Quentin's face. "Let me make you all better."

Then she leaned down and kissed him gently on the lips, drawing his breath into her body.

Rue Meridian was sleeping in a makeshift canvas hammock she had strung between the foremast and the bow railing, lost in a dream about cormorants and puffins, when she felt Bek's hand on her shoulder and awoke. She saw the look on his face and immediately asked, "What's wrong?"

It was a difficult look to decipher. His face was troubled and amazed, both at once; it reflected uncertainty mixed with wonder. He appeared oddly adrift, as if he was there almost by accident. Her first thought was that his coming was a delayed reaction to what she had told him hours earlier. She sat up quickly, swung her legs over the side of the hammock, and stood. "Bek, what's happened?"

"Grianne woke up. I don't know why. The magic, maybe. I was using it to try to help Quentin, to heal him the way Brin Ohmsford did Rone Leah once. Or maybe it was when I cried. I was so frustrated and tired, I just broke down."

He exhaled sharply. "She spoke to me. She called me by name. But she wasn't herself, not grown up, but a child, speaking in a child's voice, calling me 'poor baby boy, little Bek,' and telling me not to cry."

"Wait a minute, slow down," she said, taking hold of him by his shoulders. "Come over here."

She led him to the bow and sat him down in the shadow of the starboard ram where the curve of the horn formed a shelter at its joining with the deck. She sat facing him, pulled her knees up to her breast, and wrapped her arms around her legs. "Okay, tell me the rest. She came awake and she spoke to you. What happened next?"

"You won't believe this," he whispered, clearly not believing it himself. "She healed him. She used her magic, and she healed him. I thought she was going to kill him. She called him a puppy—I guess that's what she thought he was. I tried to stop her, but she did something to me with the magic so that I couldn't move or speak. Then she started on him, and I was sure she meant to help him by killing him, to take away his pain and suffering by taking his life. That's what the Ilse Witch would have done, and I was afraid she was still the witch."

Rue leaned forward, hugging herself. "How could she heal him, Bek? He was all broken up inside. Half his blood was gone."

"The magic can do that. It can generate healing. I watched it happen to Quentin. He's not completely well yet. He isn't even awake. But I saw his color change right in front of me. I heard his breathing steady and, afterwards, when I could move again, felt that his pulse was stronger, too. Some of his wounds, the ones you bandaged, have closed completely."

"Shades," she whispered, trying to picture it.

He leaned back into the curve of the horn and looked at the night sky. "When she was done, she came back over to me and stroked my cheek and held me. I could move again, but I didn't want to interrupt what she was doing because I thought it might be helping her. I spoke her name, but she didn't answer. She just rocked me and began to cry."

His eyes shifted to find hers. "She kept saying how sorry she was, over and over. She said it would never happen again. Leaving me, she said. She wouldn't leave me like before, not ever. All this in her little girl's voice, her child's voice."

His eyes closed. "I just wanted to help her, to let her know I understood. I tried to hold her. When I did, she went right back into herself. She quit talking or moving. She quit seeing me. She was just like before. I couldn't do anything to bring her back. I tried, but she wouldn't respond." He shook his head. "So I left her and came to find you. I had to tell some-one. I'm sorry I woke you."

She reached out for him, pulled him close, and kissed him on the lips. "I'm glad you did." She stood and drew him up with her. "Come lie down with me, Bek."

She took him back to the canvas hammock and bundled him into it beside her. She pressed herself against him and wrapped him in her arms. She was still getting used to the idea that he meant so much to her. Her admission of this to him had surprised her, but she'd had no regrets about it after-wards. Bek Ohmsford made her feel complete; it was as if by finding him, she had found a missing part of herself. He made her feel good, and it had been a while since anyone had made her feel like that.

They lay without moving for a while, without talking, just holding each other and listening to the silence. But she wanted more, wanted to give him more, and she began kissing him. She kissed him for a long time, working her way over his mouth and eyes and nose, down his neck and chest. He tried to kiss her, as well, but she wouldn't let him, wanting every-thing to come from her. When he seemed at peace, she lay back again, placing his head in the crook of her shoulder. He fell asleep for a time, and she held him while he dreamed.

I love you, Bek Ohmsford. She mouthed the words silently. She thought it incredibly odd she should fall in love with some-one under such strange circumstances. It seemed inconvenient and vaguely ridiculous. Hawk would have been shocked. He never thought she would fall in love with anyone. Too inde-pendent, too tough-minded. She never needed anyone, never wanted anyone. She was complete by herself. She understood his thinking. It was what she had believed, as well, until now.

She put her hands inside of Bek's clothing and touched his skin. She placed her fingers over his heart. Counting the beats in her head, she closed her eyes and dozed.

When she woke again, he was still sleeping. Overhead, the sky was lightening with the approach of dawn.

"It's almost daylight," she whispered in his ear, waking him.

He nodded into her shoulder. He was silent for a moment, shaking off the last of his sleep. She could feel his breath on her neck and the strength in his arms.

"When we get back to the Four Lands," he began, and stopped. "When this is all over, and we have to decide where we—"

"Bek, no," she said gently, but firmly. "Don't talk about what's going to happen later. Don't worry about it. We're too far away for it to matter yet. Leave it alone."

He went silent again, pressed against her. She brushed back her hair where it had fallen into her face. His eyes followed the movement with interest, and he reached out to help. "I have to go down into the Crake," he said. "I have to get Quentin's sword back. I want it to be there for him when he wakes up."

She nodded. "All right."

"Will you look after Grianne for me while I'm gone?"

She smiled and kissed him on the lips. "I can't, Bek." She touched the tip of his nose. "I'm going with you."

When she said it, Bek panicked. He kept the panic in check on the surface, but inside, where his emotions could pretty much do whatever they wanted to, he was a mess. All he could think about was how afraid he was for her, how frightened that something bad would happen. It had already happened to Quentin, and his cousin had at least had the protection of the Sword of Leah. Rue wore a splint on one arm and had no magic at all. If he agreed to let her come, he would be taking on the responsibility for both of them. He was not sure he wanted to do that right after failing Quentin so miserably.

"I don't think that is a good idea," he told her, not sure

what else to say that wouldn't make her furious and even more determined.

She seemed to consider the merits of his objection, then smiled. "Do you know what I like most about you, Bek? Not how you look or think, not your laugh or the way you see the world, although I like those things, too. What I really like about you is that you don't ever act as if I'm not just as good as everyone else. You take it for granted that I am, and you treat me with respect. I don't have to fight you for that. I can expect it as a matter of course. I am your equal; I might even be a little better in some ways." She paused. "I wouldn't want to lose that."

There was not much he could say to her after that. So he simply nodded and smiled back, and she kissed him hard to show that she appreciated his understanding. He liked having her kiss him, but it didn't make him feel any better about taking her along.

But the issue was decided, so they slipped over the side of the ship and walked to the edge of the bluff, followed the precipice to the trailhead, and started down. It was light enough now that they could make out the shapes of the trees and the soft movement of leaves and branches in the slow morning wind. Bek cast about with his magic as they descended, taking no chances on being caught off guard, even if what he was doing somehow alerted the dead Graak's mate. If the mate was anywhere close, he had already decided they would turn right around. Even Little Red couldn't argue with that.

But fortune smiled on them, and they slipped into the Crake as invisible as wraiths. Bek used the magic of the wishsong to cloak them in the look and feel of the rain forest, choosing images and smells that would not attract a carnivore. Draped in trailers of mist and cooled by the morning wind, they slid through the trees with the ease and freedom of shadows, untroubled by the dangers that on this occasion were elsewhere. They found Quentin's sword muddied but still in one piece beside the body of the dead Graak, retrieved it, and made their way back again. The sun was cresting the jagged line of mountains east when they began their climb back up the trail.

That was so easy, Bek thought in surprise as they regained the bluff. Why couldn't it have been like that for Quentin? But then, of course, there would have been no reason for Grianne to come awake, and he would not have seen for himself that her responses to pain and suffering were no longer those of the Ilse Witch, but of his sister. He would not have discovered that maybe she could return to him after all when she was ready.

Rue Meridian turned to him, a mix of mischievousness and satisfaction mirrored in her green eyes. "Admit it. That wasn't so bad."

He shook his head and sighed. "No, it wasn't."

"Remember that the next time you think about doing something dangerous without me." She reached out and took hold of the back of his neck with both hands and pulled him close to her. "If you love me, if I love you, there shouldn't be any question of that ever happening. Otherwise, what we feel for each other isn't real. It doesn't mean anything."

He shook his head. "Yes, it does. It means everything."

She grinned, brushing loose strands of her long hair from her face. "I know. So don't forget it."

She picked up the pace and moved ahead of him. He stared after her, barely able to contain himself. In her words and smile, in everything she said and did, he saw a future that would transcend all his expectations of what he had ever imagined possible. It was only a dream, but wasn't reality conceived in dreams?

His euphoria peaked and faded in a wash of doubt. It was foolish, he thought, to let himself think like this, to allow his emotions to cloud his reason. Look at where he was. Look at what had befallen him. Where, in all of this, did dreams like his belong? He watched Rue Meridian's stride lengthen and as he did so, felt those dreams slip away, too frail to hold, too insubstantial to grasp. He was drawing pictures in the sand, and the tide was coming in.

When they reached the trailhead and walked back toward the *Jerle Shannara*, they found Redden Alt Mer and his Rovers gathered at the edge of the bluff, looking east. The Wing Riders were flying in from the coast, and they had somcone with them.

TWENTY-FIVE

When the Morgawr found that Ahren Elessedil was gone, he had Ryer Ord Star brought before him. She denied knowing anything about it, but she knew he could read the lie in her eyes and smell it on her breath. Already suspicious of their failure to find any trace of the *Jerle Shannara* and her crew or of the Ilse Witch and her brother, he wasted no time in deciding that the seer had helped the Elven Prince escape. Whatever usefulness she might have had, she had outlived it.

He gave her to Cree Bega and his Mwellrets, who stripped her naked and beat her savagely. They broke all her fingers and slashed the soles of her feet. They defiled her until she fainted. When she woke again, they hung her by her wrists from one of the yardarms, lashed her with a rawhide whip, and left her to bake in the midday sun. They gave her no water or clothing and did not treat her wounds. She hung ignored in a haze of pain and thirst that left her ravaged and delirious.

Only once did the Morgawr speak to her again. "Use your gift, little seer," he advised, standing just below her, touching the wounds on her body with interest. "Find those I have asked you to find, and I will let you die quickly. Otherwise, I will make sure your agony endures until I find them myself. There are other things I can have done to you, things that will hurt much more than those you have already experienced."

She was barely conscious when he spoke the words, but her reason was not yet gone. She knew that if she gave him what he wanted, if she told him where to find her friends, he would not kill her quickly as he had said, but would do to her what he had done to Aden Kett. He would want that experience, to feed on her mind, a seer's mind, to see what that would feel like. The only reason he had not done so yet was because he was still hoping she would lead him to those he hunted. Damaging her so significantly would prevent her from giving him any further help. His hunger for her could wait a few days. He was patient that way.

The day drifted toward nightfall. The ropes that held her suspended had cut her wrists almost to the bone. Blood streaked her arms and shoulders. She could no longer feel her hands. Her unprotected body was burned and raw from exposure to wind and sun and throbbed with unrelenting pain.

Her suffering triggered visions, some recognizable, some not. She saw her companions, both living and dead, but could not seem to differentiate between them. They floated in and out of her consciousness, there long enough for her to identify and then gone. Sometimes they spoke, but she rarely understood the words. She felt her mind going as her life drained out of her body, sliding steadily into an abyss of dark, merciful forgetfulness.

Walker, she called out in her mind, begging him to come to her.

Night descended, and the Mwellrets went to sleep, all save the watch and helmsman. No one came to her. No one spoke to her. She hung from the yardarm as she had all day, broken and dying. She no longer felt the pain. It was there, but it was so much a part of her that she no longer recognized it as being out of the ordinary. She licked her cracked lips to keep her mouth from sealing over and breathed the cool night air with relief. Tomorrow would bring a return of the burning sun and harsh wind, but she thought that perhaps by then she would be gone.

She hoped that Ahren was far away. The Morgawr and his

airships had been searching for him all day without success, so there was reason to think that the Elven Prince had escaped. He would be wondering when she would join him, if she would come soon. But she had never intended to leave *Black Moclips*. Her visions had told her of her fate, of her death aboard this vessel, and she was not foolish enough to believe she could avoid it. Just as Walker had seen his fate in her visions long ago, so she had seen hers. A seer's visions came unbidden and showed what they chose. Like those she advised, Ryer Ord Star could only accept what was revealed and never change it.

But what she had told the Elven Prince about himself and his own future was the truth, as well, a more promising fate than her own. His future awaited him in the Four Lands, long after she was gone, long after this voyage was a distant memory.

He would wonder what had become of her, of course. Or perhaps he would know when enough time had passed and she hadn't appeared. He would never know how she had hidden the Elfstones from the Morgawr and the Mwellrets. That secret would remain hers. And Walker's. She had been quick to take them from Ahren when he was felled in the attack, feigning concern for his injury, bending down to shield her movements. She had known she would be searched, and she had slipped the Stones into a crevice in the wall while the Mwellrets were still concentrating on Ahren. A simple ruse, but an effective one. Search her once, and the matter was settled. After that, she had needed only to get aboard *Black Moclips* before finding a new place of concealment. She had left the Stones hidden until it was time for Ahren to leave.

She would be lying to herself if she didn't admit that she had thought of giving him the Stones earlier so that he could use them on his captors. But Ahren was new to the magic, and the Morgawr was old, too powerful to be overcome by any save an experienced hand. Only Walker would have stood a chance, and while she wanted to live as much as the next person, she was not prepared to risk Ahren's life and fate on a gamble that would almost surely fail. She had sworn an oath to protect him, to do what she could to redeem herself for the harm she had caused while in the service of the Ilse Witch. No halfway measures were allowed in fulfilling that oath. She had much to atone for, and her death was small payment for her sins.

She lifted her head out of the tangle of her hair and tasted the night air on her lips. She wanted to die, but could not seem to. She wanted release from her pain, from her helplessness, but could not find it alone. She needed Walker to help her. She needed him to come.

She drifted in and out of half sleep, always aware that no true sleep would come, that only death would give her rest. She cried for herself and her failures, and she wished she could have grown to be a woman of some worth. In another time and place, in another life, perhaps that would happen.

It was during the deep sleep hours of early morning, the sky clear indigo and the stars a wash of brightness across the firmament, that he appeared at last, lifting out of the ether in a soft radiant light that bathed her in hope.

Walker, she whispered.

–I am here–

Ahren Elessedil flew north through the night after escaping *Black Moclips*, his only plan to get as far from the Morgawr as he could manage. He had no clear idea of where he was or where he should be trying to go. He knew he should be looking for a rain forest somewhere in the mountains, but there was no hope of doing that until it got light. He had the stars to guide him, although the stars were aligned differently in this part of the world and partially blocked by the spread of the single wing, so it was difficult to use his navigational knowledge.

Not that he was deterred by this. He was so grateful to be free that his euphoria made every potential problem save being captured again seem solvable. The single wing sped on without difficulty on the back of steady breezes off the Blue Divide. He had worried at first that he might have trouble keeping his carrier aloft, but it proved to be relatively easy to fly. The wing straps allowed him to bank to either side and change direction, and the bar that ran the length of the framework opened and closed vents in the canvas so that he could gain altitude or descend. So long as the winds blew and he stayed away from downdrafts and bad storms, he thought he would be all right.

He had time to think on his journey, and his thoughts were mostly of Ryer Ord Star. The more he mulled over her situation, the less happy he was. She was playing a dangerous game, and she had no way to protect herself if she was found out. Once the Mwellrets discovered he was missing, she would be the first person they would suspect. Nor was he convinced that she had a way to get off the ship if that happened. Was there a second single wing hidden somewhere aboard the airship? She had told him that she would follow later, but he wasn't sure it was the truth.

He wished now that he hadn't been so quick to accommodate her. He wished he had forced her to come with him, no matter what she thought Walker wanted from her. He had been so eager to get away that he hadn't pressed the matter. He didn't like what he remembered about the way she had looked at him at the end. It felt final—as if she already knew she wasn't going to see him again.

She was a seer, after all, and it was possible that in one of her visions she had seen her own fate. But if she knew what was going to happen, couldn't she act to prevent it? He didn't know, and after a while he quit thinking about it. It was impossible for him to do anything to help until he found the others, and then maybe they could go back for her.

But in his heart, where such truths have a way of surfacing, he knew it was already too late.

The sun rose, and he flew on. New light etched the details of the land below, and he began to look for something he recognized. It quickly became apparent to him that his task was impossible. Everything looked the same from up there, and he didn't remember enough about the geography from flying along the coast aboard the *Jerle Shannara* to know what to look for. He knew he should turn inland toward the mountains, but how far north should he fly before he did that? Ryer Ord Star had told him she was misdirecting the Morgawr at Walker's request, so the coast was the wrong place for him to be. He should be searching for a rain forest. But where? He could see neither the beginning nor the end of the mountains that ran down the spine of the peninsula. Clouds blanketed the peaks and screened away the horizon, giving the impression that the world dropped away five miles in. He couldn't tell how far anything went. He couldn't even be sure of his direction without a compass.

He could try using the Elfstones. They were seeking stones, and they could find anything that was hidden from the naked eye. But using them would alert the Morgawr, and he had seen enough of the warlock's abilities to know that he could follow magic as a hunter did tracks. Using the Elfstones might bring the warlock down on his friends, as well, should he manage to find them. He didn't think he wanted to bear the responsibility for that, no matter how desperate his own situation.

The sun brightened, and the last of night's shadows began to fade from the landscape. The air warmed, but was still cold enough that he wished he was wearing something warmer. He hunched his shoulders and turned the single wing farther inland, away from the chilly coastal breezes. Maybe he would spy the rain forest and his friends if he just gave himself a little more time.

He gave himself the entire day, spiraling inland in ever widening sweeps, searching the sky and ground until his head ached. He found nothing—no sign of the *Jerle Shannara* or his friends or a rain forest. He saw barely anything moving, and then only a few hawks and gulls, and once a herd of deer. As the day lengthened and the sun began to slip west, his confidence started to fail. He swept further into the mountains, but the deeper in he went the more confusing things became. He had been flying for eighteen hours with nothing to eat or drink, and he was beginning to feel light-headed. He couldn't remember the last time he had slept. If he didn't find something soon, he would have to land. Once he did that, he wasn't sure he could get airborne again.

He stayed in the air, flying into the approaching darkness, stubbornly refusing to give up. Soon, he wouldn't be able to see at all. If he didn't land, he would have to fly all night because it was too cloudy for the moon and stars to provide enough light for him to try to set down. Soon, he would have to use the Elfstones. He would have no choice.

He rolled his shoulders and arched his back to relieve the strain of holding the same position for so long. Dusk settled over the land in deepening layers, and still he flew on.

He had almost decided to give it up when the Shrikes found him. He was far enough inland that he wasn't expecting them, thinking himself safely away from the danger of coastal birds. But there was no mistaking what they were or that they were coming for him. Hunting him, he thought with a chill. Sent by the Morgawr to track him down and destroy him. He knew it instinctively. They sailed toward him in the silvery glow of the failing sunset, seven of them, long wings and necks extended, hooked beaks lifted like blades.

He swung away immediately and started downward in a slow glide, unable to make the single wing respond with any greater agility or speed. It was like canoeing in rapids; you had to ride the current. Opening the vents all the way would drop him from the skies like a stone. The single wing wasn't designed for quick maneuvers. It wasn't built to flee Shrikes.

He spiraled toward the land below, toward peaks and cliffs, defiles and ravines, already able to tell that there was nowhere safe to land. But there was no time to worry about it and nothing he could do to change things. The best he could hope for was to get down before the Shrikes reached him. His flight was over. All that remained to be seen was how it would end.

He was still almost a thousand feet up when the first Shrike swept past him, claws raking the canvas and wood frame, sending him skidding sideways with a sickening lurch. He straightened out and angled sharply away, casting about for the others. If he had been frightened before, he was terrified now. He was helpless up here, strapped into his flimsy flying device, suspended in midair, unable to outrun or hide from his pursuers.

A second Shrike attacked, slamming into the single wing with such force that it jarred Ahren to his bones. He dropped dozens of feet before leveling out, and when he did, the single wing's flight had turned shaky and uneven, and he could hear the flapping of torn canvas.

All about him, the Shrikes circled, beaks lifted, claws extended, eyes reflecting like pools of hard light in the darkness of their predatory faces.

Use the Elfstones!

But he couldn't reach them without releasing his grip on the control bar, and if he did that, he might go straight down. He also risked dropping the Stones, fumbling them away as he tried to bring them to bear. Nevertheless, he took the gamble, certain that he was doomed otherwise. He let go of the bar and plunged his right hand into his tunic, tearing open the drawstrings of the pouch to fish out the stones.

Instantly, the single wing went into a steep dive. The Shrikes attacked from everywhere, but the wing was skewing sideways so badly that they were unable to get a grip on it.

Shrieking, they dived past Ahren in a flurry of movement, wings whipping the air, talons extended, huge black shadows descending and then lifting away. He closed his eyes to sharpen his concentration, forcing his fingers to find and tighten about the Elfstones, drawing them clear.

He thrust his hand out in front of him, called up the power of the magic, and sent it sweeping out into the dark in a wall of blue fire.

The result was unexpected. The magic flooded the air with its sudden brightness, frightening the Shrikes but not harming them. Ahren, however, was sent spinning off into the void, the backlash from the magic nearly collapsing the single wing about his body. Belatedly, he remembered that the magic of the Elfstones was useless against creatures that did not rely on magic themselves. The Shrikes were immune to the power of the only weapon he possessed.

Still clutching the Elfstones, he tried to maneuver downward, diving between cliff faces so sheer that if he struck one, he would slide all the way to its base unimpeded. The Shrikes followed, screaming in frustration and rage, whipping past him in one series of near misses after another, the wake of their passing spinning him around until he could no longer determine where he was.

He was finished, he knew. He was a dead man. The whirl of land and sky formed a kaleidoscope of indigo and quicksilver, stars and darkness melding as he fought to slow his descent. A strut snapped with the sharpness of broken deadwood. His left wing shuddered and dipped.

Then something bigger than the Shrikes appeared at the corner of his eye, there for only a moment before the single wing spun him a different way. The Shrikes screamed anew, but the sound was different, and the Elven Prince detected fear in it. An instant later they were winging away, their dark shadows fading as quickly as their cries.

Something huge loomed over him, its shadow blacking out

the sky. He tried to look upward to see what it was, but it collided with his single wing, knocking it askew once more, then latched on to the frame. He fought wildly to free it, to regain some control, but the control straps refused to respond or the grapples release.

The Morgawr! he thought in terror. *The Morgawr has found me once more!*

Then a second shadow appeared, lifting out of the well of cliffs and valleys in a spread of massive wings and a shining of great, gimlet eyes.

"Let go, Elven Prince!" Hunter Predd called out through the haze of shadows, reaching up from Obsidian's back to catch hold of his dangling legs.

Ahren quit struggling and did as he was told, releasing first the control straps and then the buckles and ties that secured him to the harness. In a rush of wind and blackness, he slid down into the Wing Rider's arms, scarcely able to believe the other was really there. In a daze, he watched the single wing and its harness tumble away, a tangle of crumpled wreckage.

"Hold tight," Hunter Predd whispered in his ear, rough-bearded face pressing close to his own, strong arms fastening a safety line in place. "We have a ways to go, but you're safe now."

Safe, Ahren repeated silently, gratefully, and began to shake all over.

Hunter Predd's strong arms tightened about him reassuringly, and with Po Kelles and Niciannon leading the way, they flew into the night.

Miles away in the same darkness that cloaked the fleeing Wing Riders and the Elven Prince, Ryer Ord Star hung from the yardarm of *Black Moclips*, swaying gently at the ends of the ropes tied about her wrists. Blood coated her arms from the deep gouges the ropes had made in her flesh, and sweat ran down her face and body in spite of the cool night air. Her pain was all encompassing, racking her slender body from head to toe, rising and falling in steady waves as she waited to die.

"Walker," she begged softly, "please help me."

She had called to him all night, but this time he responded. He appeared out of nowhere, suspended in air before her, his dark countenance pale and haunted, but so comforting to her that she would have welcomed it even if it was nothing more than a mirage. Wrapped in his Druid robes, he was a shade come from death's gate, a presence less of this world than the one beyond, yet in his eyes she found what she was seeking.

"Let me go," she whispered, the words thick and clotted in her throat. "Set me free."

He reached for her with his one good arm, his strong hand brushing against her ravaged cheeks, and his voice was filled with healing.

—Come with me—

She shook her head helplessly. "I cannot. The ropes hold me."

—Only because you cling to them. Release your grip—

She did so, not knowing how exactly, only knowing that because he said so, she could. She slipped from her bonds as if they were loose cords and stepped out into the air as if she weighed nothing. Her pain and her fear fell away like old clothes she had tossed aside. Her heartache subsided. She stood next to him, and when he reached out a second time, she took his hand in her own.

He smiled then and drew her close.

—Come away—

She did so, at rest and at peace, redeemed and forgiven, made whole by her sacrifice, and she did not look back.

TWENTY-SIX

When he went to look for the Ahren Elessedil shortly after dawn, Bek Ohmsford found him sitting at the stern of the *Jerle Shannara*. They had been airborne for more than three hours by then, flying south through heavy clouds and gray skies, intent on reaching the coast before nightfall.

The Elven Prince glanced up at him with tired eyes. He had been asleep for almost twelve hours, but looked haggard even so. "Hello, Bek," he said.

"Hello, yourself." He plopped down next to Ahren, resting his back against the ship's railing. "It's good to have you back. I thought we might have lost you."

"I thought so, too. More than once."

"You were lucky Hunter Predd found you when he did. I heard the story. I don't know how you did it. I don't think I could have. Flying all that way without food or rest."

Ahren Elessedil's smile was faint and sad. "You can do anything if you're scared enough."

They were silent then, sitting shoulder to shoulder, staring down the length of the airship as she nosed ahead through ragged wisps of cloud and mist. The air had a damp feel to it and smelled of the sea. Redden Alt Mer and his Rovers had cut short the repairs to the *Jerle Shannara* last night, installed the recovered diapson crystals early this morning, and lifted off at first light. The Rover Captain knew that the Morgawr had some control over the Shrikes that inhabited the coastal regions of Parkasia, and he was afraid that the birds that had attacked Ahren would alert the warlock and lead him to them. He could have used another day of work on his vessel, but the risk of staying on the ground any longer was too great. No one was upset with his decision. Memories of the Crake Rain Forest were fresh in everyone's minds.

In the pilot box, Spanner Frew stood at the helm, his big frame blocking the movements of his hands as he worked the controls. Now and then he shouted orders to one of the Rovers walking the deck, his rough voice booming through the creaking of the rigging, his bearded face turning to reveal its fierce set. There weren't all that many of them left to shout at, Bek thought. He numbered them in his head. Ten, counting himself. Twelve, if you added in the Wing Riders. Out of more than thirty who had started out all those months ago, that was all. Just twelve.

Make that thirteen, he corrected himself, adding in Grianne. Lucky thirteen.

"How is your sister?" Ahren asked him, as if reading his mind.

"Still the same. Doesn't talk, doesn't see me, doesn't respond to anything, won't eat or drink. Just sits there and stares at nothing." He looked over at the Elf. "Except for two nights ago. The night you were rescued, she saved Quentin."

He told Ahren the details as he had done for everyone else, aware that by doing so he was giving hope to himself as much as to them that Grianne might recover, and that when she did, she might not be the Ilse Witch anymore. It remained a faint hope, but he needed to believe that the losses suffered and the pain endured might count for something in the end. Ahren listened attentively, his young face expressionless, but his eyes distant and reflective.

When Bek was finished, he said quietly, "At least you were able to save someone other than yourself. I couldn't even do that."

Bek had heard the story of his escape from *Black Moclips* from Hunter Predd. He knew what the Elf was talking about.

"I don't see what else you could have done," Bek said, seeking words that would ease the other's sense of guilt. "She didn't want to come with you. She had already made up her mind to stay. You couldn't have changed that."

"Maybe. I wish I were sure. I was so eager to get away, to get off that ship, I didn't even think to try. I just let her tell me what to do."

Bek scuffed his boot against the deck. "Well, you don't know. She might have gotten away. She might have done what she said she was going to do. The Wing Riders are out looking for her. Don't give up yet."

Ahren stared off into space, his eyes haunted. "They won't find her, Bek. She's dead. I knew it last night. I woke up for no reason, and I knew it. I think she realized what was going to happen when she sent me away, but she wouldn't tell me because she knew that if she did, I wouldn't go. She had promised Walker she would stay, and she refused to break her word, even at the cost of her life."

He sounded bitter and confused, as if his realization of that premonition defied logical explanation.

"I hope you're wrong," Bek told him, not knowing what else to say.

Ahren kept his gaze directed out toward the misty horizon, above the sweep of the airship's curved rams, and did not reply.

Redden Alt Mer walked down the main passageway below-decks to the Captain's quarters—his quarters, once upon a time—searching for his sister. He was pretty sure by now, having walked the upper decks without success, that she had retired once more to the temporary shelter assigned to the wounded Quentin Leah and the unresponsive Grianne Ohmsford. It was the witch Little Red would go to see, to look at and study, to contemplate in a way that bothered him more than he cared to admit. He was feeling better about himself since braving the horrors of the Crake to recover the lost diapson crystals, especially after hearing from Bek how the witch had wakened from her dead-eyed sleep long enough to do the unexpected and use her magic to help heal the Highlander. Big Red was feeling better, but not entirely well. His brush with death in the rain forest had left him hollowed out, and he wasn't sure yet what it would take to fill him up again. Recovering the crystals was a start, but he was still entirely too conscious of his own mortality, and given the nature of his life, that wasn't healthy.

But for the moment his concern was for his sister. Rue had always been more tightly wound than he was, the cautious one, the captain of her life, determined that she would decide what was best for those she felt responsible for, no matter the obstacles she faced. But, of late, she had begun to show signs of vacillation that had never been apparent before. It wasn't that she seemed any less determined, but that she seemed uncertain what it was she should be determined about.

Her attitude toward the Ilse Witch was such a case. In the beginning, there had been no question in his mind that as soon as she could find a way to do so, Rue would dispose of her. She would do so in a way that would remove all suspicion from herself, especially because of how she felt about Bek, but do it she would. Hawk's death demanded it. Yet something had happened to change her mind, something he had missed entirely, and it was impacting her in a way that suggested a major shift in her thinking.

He shook his head, wishing he understood what that something was. Since yesterday, when she had returned from the Crake with Bek after completing a mission he would have put a stop to in a minute had he known about it, she had come down here at every opportunity. She had taken up watch over the witch, as if to see what would happen when she woke, as if trying to ascertain what manner of creature she really was. At first, he had thought she was waiting for an opportunity to finish her off. But as time passed and opportunities came and went, he had begun to wonder. This wasn't about revenge for Hawk and the others; this was about something else. Whatever it was, he was baffled.

He pushed open the door to his cabin, and there she was, sitting next to Bek's sister, holding her hand and staring into her vacant eyes. It was such a strange scene that for a moment he simply stood there, speechless.

"Close the door," she said quietly, not bothering to look over.

He did so, then moved to where she could see him, and knelt at Quentin Leah's bedside for a moment, placing his fingers on the Highlander's wrist to read his pulse.

"Strong and steady," Little Red said. "Bek was right. She saved Quentin's life, whether she intended to or not."

"Is that what you're doing?" he asked, standing up again, giving the Highlander a final glance. "Trying to decide if it was an accident or not?"

"No," she said.

"What, then?"

"I'm trying to find out where she is. I'm trying to figure out how to reach her."

He stared at her, not quite believing what he was hearing. She was leaning forward as she sat in front of the witch, her face only inches away. There was no fear in her green eyes, no suggestion that she felt at risk. She held Grianne's hands loosely in her own, and she was moving her fingers over their smooth, pale backs in small circles.

"Bek said she was hiding from the truth about herself, that when the magic of the Sword of Shannara showed her that truth, it was too much for her, so she fled from it. Walker told him that she would come back when she found a way to forgive herself for the worst of her sins. A tall order, even to sort them all out, I'd think." She paused. "I'm trying to see if a woman can reach her when a man can't."

He nodded. "I guess it's possible it might happen that way."

"But you don't know why I have to be the one to find out."

"I guess I don't."

She didn't say anything for a long time, sitting silent and unmoving before Grianne Ohmsford, staring into her strange blue eyes. The Ilse Witch was little more than a child, Alt Mer realized. She was so young that any attempt to define her in terms of the acts she was said to have committed was impossible. In her comatose state, blank-faced and unseeing, she bore a look of complete innocence, as if incapable of evil or wrongdoing or any form of madness. Somehow, they had got it all wrong, and it needed only for her to come awake again to put it right.

It was a dangerous way to feel, he thought.

She looked over at him. "I'm doing it for Bek," she said, as if to explain, then quickly turned her attention back to Grianne. "Maybe because of Bek."

Alt Mer moved to where she could no longer see him, doubt clouding his sunburned features. "Bek doesn't expect this of you. His sister isn't your responsibility. Why are you making her so?"

"You don't understand," she said.

He waited for her to say something more, but she didn't. He cleared his throat. "What don't I understand, Rue?"

She let him wait a long time before she answered, and he realized afterwards that she was trying to decide whether to tell him the truth, that the choice was more difficult for her than she had anticipated. "I'm in love with him," she said finally.

He wasn't expecting that, hadn't considered the possibility for a moment, although on hearing it, it made perfect sense. He remembered her reaction to his decision to take Bek with him into the Crake while leaving her behind. He remembered how she had cared for the boy when Hunter Predd had flown him in from the mountain wilderness, as if she alone could make him well.

Except that Bek wasn't a boy, as he had already noted days earlier. He was a man, grown up on this journey, changed so completely that he might be someone else altogether.

Even so, he could not quite believe what he was hearing. "When did this happen?" he asked.

"I don't know."

"But you're sure?"

She didn't bother to answer, but he saw her shoulders lift slightly as if to shrug the question away.

"You don't seem suited to each other," he continued, and knew at once that he had made a mistake. Her gaze shifted instantly, her eyes boring into him with unmistakable antagonism. "Don't get mad at me," he said quickly. "I'm just telling you what I see."

"You don't know who's suited to me, big brother," she said quietly, her gaze shifting back to the witch. "You never have."

He nodded, accepting the rebuke. He sat down now, needing to talk about this, thinking it might take a while, and having no idea what he was going to say. Or should. "I thought what Hawk thought—that you were never going to settle on anyone, that you couldn't stand it."

"Well, you were wrong."

"It just seems that your lives are so different. If you hadn't been thrown together on this voyage, your paths would never have crossed. Have you thought about what's going to happen when you get home?"

"If I get home."

"You will. Then Bek will go back to the Highlands and you'll go back to being a Rover."

She exhaled sharply, let go of Grianne Ohmsford's hands, and turned to face him. "We'd better get past this right now. I told you how I feel about Bek. This is new to me, so I'm still finding out what it means. I'm trying not to think too far ahead. But here is what I do know. I'm sick of my life. I've been sick of it for a long time. I didn't like it on the Prekkendorran, and I haven't cared much for it since. I thought that coming on this voyage, getting far away from everything I knew, would change things. It hasn't. I feel like I've been wandering around all these years and not getting anywhere. I want something different. I'm willing to take a look at Bek to see if he can give it to me."

Redden Alt Mer held her gaze. "You're putting a lot on him, aren't you?"

"I'm not putting anything on him. I'm carrying this burden all by myself. He loves me, too, Redden. He loves me in a way no one ever has. Not for how I look or what I can do or what he imagines me to be. It goes deeper than that. It touches on connections that words can't express and don't have to. It makes a difference when someone loves you like that. I like it enough that I don't want to throw it away without taking time to see where it leads."

She eased herself into a different position, her physical discomfort apparent, still sore from her wounds, still nursing her injuries. "I wanted to kill the Ilse Witch," she said. "I had every intention of doing so the moment I got the chance. I thought I owed that much to Hawk. But I can't do it now. Not while Bek believes she might wake up and be his sister again. Not after all he has done to protect her and care for her and give her a chance at being well. I don't have that right, not even to make myself feel good again about losing Hawk.

"So I've decided to try to do what Bek can't. I've decided to try to reach her, to see where she is and what she hides from, to try to understand what she's feeling. I've decided to let her know someone else cares what happens to her. Maybe I can. But even if I can't, I have to try. Because that's what loving someone requires of you—giving yourself to something they believe in, even when you don't. That's what I want to do for Bek. That's how I feel about him."

She turned back to Grianne Ohmsford, lifted the girl's hands in her own, and held them anew. "I keep thinking that if I can help her, maybe I can help myself. I'm as lost as she is. If I can find her, maybe I can find myself. Through Bek. Through feeling something for him." She leaned forward again, her face so close to Grianne's that she might have been thinking of kissing her. "I keep thinking that it's possible."

He stared at her in silence, thinking that he wasn't all that secure himself, that he felt lost, too. All this wandering about the larger world had a way of making you feel disconnected from everything, as if your life was something so elusive that you spent all the time allotted to you chasing after it and never quite catching up.

"Go away and leave me alone," she said to him. "Fly this airship back to where we came from. Get us safely home. Then we can talk about this some more. Maybe by then we will understand each other better than we do now."

He climbed back to his feet and stood watching her for a moment longer, thinking he should say something. But nothing he could think of seemed right.

Resigned to leaving well enough alone, to letting her do what she felt she must, he walked out of the room without a word.

Still sitting with Ahren by the aft railing, Bek Ohmsford glanced over as Redden Alt Mer emerged from the main hatchway and turned to look at him. What he saw in the Rover Captain's face was a strange mix of frustration and wonderment, a reflection of thoughts that Bek could only begin to guess at. The look lasted only a second, and then Alt Mer had turned away, walking over to the pilot box and climbing up to stand beside Spanner Frew, his attention directed ahead into the shifting clouds.

"I heard that Panax stayed behind," Ahren said, interrupting his thoughts.

Bek nodded absently. "He said he was tired of this journey, that he liked where he was and wanted to stay. He said with Walker and Truls Rohk both gone, there was nothing left to go home to. I guess I don't blame him."

"I can't wait to get home. I don't ever want to go away again, once I do." The Elf's face twisted in a grimace. "I hate what's happened here, all of it."

"It doesn't seem to have counted for much, does it?"

"Walker said it did, but I don't think I believe him."

Bek let the matter slide, remembering that Walker had told him that his sister was the reason they had come to Parkasia and returning her safely home was the new purpose of their journey. He still didn't understand why that was so. Forget that he wasn't sure if they could do it or if she would ever come awake again if they did. The reality was that they had come here to retrieve the books of magic and failed to do so. They had destroyed Antrax, so there was some satisfaction in knowing that no one else would end up like Kael Elessedil, but it felt like a high price to pay for the losses they had suffered. Too high, given the broad scope of their expectations. Too high, for what they had been promised.

"Ryer said I was going to be King of the Elves," Ahren said softly. He gave Bek a wry look. "I can't imagine that happening. Even if I had the chance, I don't think I would take it. I don't want to be responsible for anyone else but me after what's happened here."

"What will you do when you get home?" Bek asked him.

His friend shrugged. "I haven't thought about it. Go away somewhere, I expect. Being home means being back in the Westland, nothing more. I don't want to live in Arborlon. Not while my brother is King. I liked being with Ard Patrinell when he was teaching me. I'll miss him more than anyone except Ryer. She was special."

His lips compressed as tears came to his eyes, and he looked away self-consciously. "Maybe I won't go home, after all."

Bek thought about the dead, about those men and women who had come on this voyage with such determination and sense of purpose. Who would he miss most? He had known none of them when he started out and had become close to all at the end. The absence of Walker and Truls Rohk, because they had been his mentors and protectors, left the biggest void. But the others had been his friends, more so than the Druid and the shape-shifter. He couldn't imagine what his life would be like without them or even what it would be like when he parted company with those who remained. Everything about his future seemed muddled and confused, and it felt to him as if nothing he did would be enough to clear away the debris of his past.

His gaze drifted along the length of the ship's deck, searching for Rue Meridian. She was the future, or at least as much of it as he could imagine. He hadn't seen much of her since their return from the Crake Rain Forest. There hadn't been time for visiting while they readied the *Jerle Shannara* for flight, their sense of urgency at the approach of the Morgawr consuming all of their time and energy. But even after setting out, she had kept to herself. He knew she spent much of her time looking in on his sister, and at first he had worried about her intentions. But it seemed wrong of him to mistrust her when she felt about him as she did. It felt small-minded and petty. He thought that she was reconciled to her anger and disappointment at Grianne's presence and no longer thought it necessary to act on them. He thought that because she loved him she would want to help his sister.

So he left her alone, thinking that when she was ready to come to him again, she would do so. He didn't feel any less close to her because she chose to be alone. He didn't think she cared any less for him for doing so. They had always shared a strong sense of each other's feelings, even in the days when they were first becoming friends on the voyage out. There had never been a need for reassurances. Nothing had changed. Friendship required space and tolerance. Love required no less.

Still, he missed being with her. He knew he could seek her out in Big Red's quarters and she would not be angry with him. But it might be better to let her find her own way with Grianne.

"Maybe I'll go home, too," he whispered to himself.

But he wasn't as sure about it anymore.

It was late afternoon when the Wing Riders reappeared, illumined by the red glare of the fading sun. The *Jerle Shannara* was less than an hour from the coast, and there had been no sign of the Morgawr's airships. With the return of the Wing Riders, Redden Alt Mer intended to turn his vessel south and begin working along the cliffs that warded the south end of the peninsula to where he could set out across the Blue Divide.

Hunter Predd brought Obsidian beneath the airship, released his safety harness, caught hold of the lowered rope ladder, and climbed to the aft railing. Alt Mer extended his hand, and the Wing Rider took hold of it and pulled himself aboard. His lean face was ridged with dirt and bathed in sweat. His eyes were hard, flat mirrors that reflected the sunset's bloodred light. He looked around the airship without saying anything, his callused hands flexing within their leather gloves, his arms stretching over his windswept head.

"We're maybe a day ahead of them," he said finally, keeping his voice low enough that no one else could hear. "They're north of us, strung out along the edge of the mountains and flying inland. They must think we're still there, from the look of things."

Alt Mer nodded. "Good news for us, I'd say."

He held out a water skin, which the Wing Rider accepted wordlessly and drank from until he had emptied it. "Ran out of water two hours ago." He handed it back.

"It will be dark in another hour. After that, we won't be so easy to track, especially once we get out over the water."

"Maybe. Maybe not. They tracked us easily enough from home and then inland here. The only time they had any real trouble was after you crashed. That doesn't sound like an evasion tactic you want to employ regularly."

Alt Mer grunted noncommittally as he looked out over the railing at the darkness behind them, finding phantoms in the movement of the clouds against the mountains. The Wing Rider was right. He had no reason to think they could evade the Morgawr forever. Their best chance lay in putting as much distance between themselves and their pursuers as they could manage. Speed would make the difference as to whether they would escape or be forced to turn and fight. Speed was what the *Jerle Shannara* offered in quantities that not even *Black Moclips* could match.

"One other thing," Hunter Predd said, taking his arm and leading him over to the far corner of the aft deck. There was no one else around now. Even Bek and the Elven Prince had gone below. "We found the seer's body."

Redden Alt Mer sighed. "Where?"

"Floating in the ocean some miles west of here. All broken up and cut to pieces. I wouldn't have known she was down there if not for Obsidian. Rocs can see things men can't."

He looked at Alt Mer with his hard, weathered eyes and shook his head. "You tell young Elessedil about her, if you can manage it. I can't. I've given out all the bad news I care to."

He squeezed Alt Mer's arm hard and walked away. Moments later, he was down the rope and back astride Obsidian, winging away into the darkness. Redden Alt Mer stood alone at the railing and wished he were going with him.

TWENTY-SEVEN

Flying through the night, the *Jerle Shannara* reached the tip of the peninsula at dawn. The Wing Riders had flown ahead to scout for resistance to her passage and had not encountered the Morgawr's airships. With no sign of their pursuers to discourage them, they set out across the Blue Divide for home.

From the first, they knew the return would be a journey of more than six months, and that was only if everything went well. Any disruption of their flying schedule, anything that forced them to land, would extend the time of their flight accordingly. So a certain pacing was necessary, and Redden Alt Mer wasted no time in advising those aboard of what that meant. They were down to thirteen in number, and of those, two were incapable of helping the others. Nor could Rue Meridian be expected to do much in the way of physical labor for at least several more weeks. Nor were the Wing Riders of much use in flying the airship, since they were needed aboard their Rocs to forage for food and water and to scout for pursuers.

That left eight able-bodied men—Spanner Frew; the Rover crew members Kelson Riat, Britt Rill, and Jethen Amenades; the Elves Ahren Elessedil and Kian; Bek Ohmsford; and himself. While Bek would be of great help to the five Rovers in flying the airship, the Elves lacked the necessary skills and experience and would have to be relegated to basic tasks.

It was a small group to man an airship twenty-four hours a day for six months. For them to manage, they were going to have to be well organized and extraordinarily lucky. Alt Mer could do nothing about the latter, so he turned his attention to the former.

He set about his task by drawing up a duty roster for the eight men he could rely upon, splitting time between the Elves so that there would never be more than one of them on watch at a time. At least three men were needed to sail the *Jerle Shannara* safely, so he drew up a rotating schedule of eight-hour shifts, putting two men on the midnight-to-dawn shift when the airship would be mostly at rest. It was not a perfect solution, but it was the best he could come up with. Rue was the only one who complained, but he deflected her anger by telling her that she could handle the navigation, which would keep her involved with sailing the vessel and not relegate her to tender of the wounded.

On the surface of things, they were in good condition. There was sufficient food aboard to keep them alive for several weeks, and they carried equipment for hunting and fishing to help resupply their depleted stock. Water was a bigger problem, but he thought the Wing Riders would be able to help with their foraging. Weapons were plentiful, should they be attacked. Now that they had replaced the damaged diapson crystals with the ones they had recovered from the Crake, they were able to fly the airship at full power. Since they were aboard the fastest airship in the Four Lands, no other airship, not even *Black Moclips*, should be able to catch them.

But things were not always as they seemed. The *Jerle Shannara* had endured enormous hardship since she had departed Arborlon. She had been damaged repeatedly, had crashed once, and was patched in more places than Alt Mer cared to count. Even a ship built by Spanner Frew could not stand up to a beating like that without giving up something. The *Jerle Shannara* was a good vessel, but she was not the vessel she had been. If she held together for even half the distance they had to cover, it would be a miracle. It was likely she would not, that somewhere along the way she would break down. The crucial question was how serious the breakdown would be. If it was too serious and took too long to correct, the Morgawr would catch up to them.

Redden Alt Mer was nothing if not realistic, and he was not about to pretend that the warlock would not be able to track them. As Hunter Predd had pointed out, he had managed to do so before, so they had to expect he would be able to do so again. It was a big ocean, and there were an infinite number of courses that they could set, but in the end they still had to fly home. If they failed to take a direct course, they were likely to find the Morgawr and his airships waiting for them when they got there. Getting back to the Four Lands before their enemies would give them a chance at finding shelter and allies. It was the better choice.

So he addressed the company as Captain and leader of the expedition and made his assignments accordingly, all the while knowing that at best he was staving off the inevitable. But a good airship Captain understood that flying was a mercurial experience, and that routine and order were the best tools to rely on in preparing for it. Bad luck was unavoidable, but it didn't have to find you right away. A little good luck could keep it at bay, and he had always had good luck. Given what the ship had come through to get to this point, he was inclined to think that his streak had not deserted him.

Nor did it do so in the weeks ahead. In the course of their travels, they encountered favorable weather with steady winds and clear skies, and they found regular opportunities to forage for food and water. They flew over the Blue Divide without need for slowing or setting down. Radian draws frayed, ambient-light sheaths tore loose, parse tubes required adjustments, and controls malfunctioned, all in accord with Alt Mer's expectations, but none of it was serious and all of it was quickly repaired.

More important, there was no sign of the Morgawr's airships and no indication that the warlock was tracking them.

Alt Mer kept his tiny crew working diligently at their assigned tasks, and if he felt they needed something more to occupy their time or take their minds off their problems, he found it for them. At first, their collective attitude was dour, a backlash from the hardships and losses suffered on Parkasia. But gradually time and distance began to heal and their spirits to lift. The passing of the days and the acceptance of a routine that was free of risk and uncertainty gave them both a renewed sense of confidence and hope. They began to believe in themselves again, in the possibility of a future safely back in the Four Lands and a life beyond the monstrous events of the past few weeks.

Ahren Elessedil emerged a little farther from his despondency each day. That he was damaged was unmistakable, but it seemed to Bek that the damage was repairable and that with time he would find a way to reconcile the loss of Ryer Ord Star. When Ahren learned of her death from Big Red, he seemed to lose heart entirely. He quit taking nourishment and refused to speak. He languished belowdecks and would not emerge. But Bek kept after him, staying close, talking to him even when he would not respond, and bringing him food and water until he started to eat and drink again.

Eventually, he began to recover. He no longer sought to blame himself for Ryer's death. He found it hard to speak of her, and Bek kept their conversations away from any mention of the seer. They spoke often of Grianne, who remained unchanged from when they had departed Parkasia, still a statue staring off into space, unresponsive and remote. They discussed what she had done for Quentin and what it meant to her chances for recovery. Ahren was more supportive of her than Bek would have expected, given the trouble she had visited on him, directly and indirectly. But Ahren seemed capable of unconditional forgiveness and infinite grace, and he displayed a maturity that had not been there when they had set out from Arborlon all those months ago. But then, Bek had been no more mature. Boys, both of them, but their boyhood was past.

Quentin continued to improve. He was awake much of the time, if only for short stretches, but he was still weak and unable to leave his bed. It would be weeks yet before he could stand, longer still before he could walk. He remembered almost nothing of what had happened in the Crake or anything of Grianne's healing use of the wishsong. But Bek was there to explain it to him, to sit with him each day, gradually catching small glimpses of the familiar smile and quick wit, finding new reasons with each visit to feel encouraged.

Bek spent time with Grianne as well, speaking and singing to her, trying to find a way to reach her, and failing. She had locked herself away again. Nothing he tried would persuade her to respond. That she had come out the first time was mystifying, but that she would not come a second time was maddening. He could think of no reason for it, and his inability to solve the riddle of her became increasingly frustrating.

Nevertheless, he kept at it, refusing to give up, certain that somehow he would find a way to break through, convinced that Walker had spoken the truth in prophesying that one day his sister would come back to him.

He spent stolen time with Rue Meridian, hidden away from the rest of the company, lost in words and touchings meant only for each other. She loved him so hard that he thought each time it ended and they separated that he could not survive letting her go. He thought he was blessed in a way that most men could only dream about, and in the silence of his mind he thanked her for it a hundred times a day. She told him that he was healing her, that he was giving her back her life in a way she had not thought possible. She had been adrift, she said, lost in her Rover wanderings, cast away from anything that mattered beyond the day and the task at hand. That she had found salvation in him was astonishing to her. She confessed she had thought nothing of him in the beginning, that she saw him as only a boy. She thought it important that he was her friend first, and that her deeper love for him was built on that.

She told him that he was her anchor in life. He told her that she was a miracle.

They spent their passion and their wonder when the night was dark and the company mostly asleep, and if anyone saw what they were doing, no one admitted to it. Perhaps for those who suspected what was happening, there was a measure of joy to be found in what Bek shared with Rue, an affirmation of life that transcended even the worst misfortunes. Perhaps in that small, but precious joining of two wounded souls, there was hope to be found that others might heal, as well.

So the days passed, and the *Jerle Shannara* sailed on, drawing further away from Parkasia and closer to home. Voracious sea birds circled the remains of meals consumed by sleek predators, and schools of krill swam from the wide-stretched jaws of leviathans. Far away on the Prekkendorran, the Races still warred across a plain five miles wide and twenty miles long. Farther away still, creatures of old magic slumbered, cradled in the webbing of their restless dreams and unbreakable prison walls.

But in the skies above the Blue Divide, the troubles of other creatures and places were as distant as yesterday, and the world below remained a world apart.

But even worlds apart have a way of colliding. Eight weeks into their journey, with the Four Lands still a long way off, Redden Alt Mer's fabled luck ran out. The sun was bright in the sky and the weather perfect. They were on course for Mephitic, where they hoped to use the Wing Riders to forage for fresh water and game while the airship stayed safely aloft. Alt Mer was at the helm, one of three on duty for the midday shift, with Britt Rill working the port draws and Jethen Amenades the starboard. The other members of the company were asleep below, save Rue Meridian, who was looking after Quentin and Grianne in the Captain's quarters, and Ahren Elessedil, who was weaving lanyards in one of the starboard pontoon fighting stations.

Alt Mer had just taken a compass reading when the port midships draw gave way with a sharp, vibrating crack that caused him to duck instinctively. It whipped past his head, wrapping about the port aft draw and snapping it loose, as well. Instantly, the masts sagged toward the starboard rail, the weight of their sails dragging them down, breaking off metal stays and pieces of crossbars and spars as they did so. Responding to the loss of balance in the sails and failure of power in the port tubes, the airship skewed sharply left. Alt Mer cried out a warning as both Rill and Amenades raced to secure the loose draws, but before he could right the listing vessel, it lurched sharply, twisting downward, sending Rill flying helplessly along the port rail and Amenades over the side.

They were a thousand feet in the air when it happened; Amenades was a dead man the minute he disappeared into the void. There was no time to dwell on it, so Alt Mer's hands were already flying over the controls as he shouted at Rill to grab something and hold fast. Without bothering to see if the other had done so, he cut power to all but the two forward parse tubes and put the ship into a steep downward glide. He heard the sound of heavy objects crashing into bulkheads and sliding along corridors, and a flurry of angry curses. As the airship finally righted itself, he opened the front end of the forward tubes, reversed power through the ports, and caught the backwash of the wind in the mainsail to bring up her nose.

Holding her steady against the tremors that rocked her, he eased her slowly into the ocean waters and shut her down.

Britt Rill staggered to his feet, Ahren Elessedil climbed from the fighting port, and all the rest poured out through the main hatchway and converged on Alt Mer. He shouted down their questions and exclamations and put them to work on the severed draws, broken stays and spars, and twisted masts. A quick survey under Spanner Frew's sharp-tongued direction revealed that the damage was more extensive than Alt Mer had thought. The problem this time did not lie with something as complicated as missing diapson crystals, but with something more mundane. The aft mast was splintered so badly it could not be repaired and would have to be replaced. To do that they would have to land, cut down a suitable tree, and shape a new mast from the trunk.

The only forested island in the area was Mephitic.

Alt Mer was as unhappy as he could be on realizing what this meant, but there was no help for it. He dispatched the Wing Riders to retrieve the body of Jethen Amenades, then called the others together to tell them what they were going to have to do. No one said much in response. There wasn't much of anything to say. Circumstances dictated a course of action they would all have preferred to avoid, but could do nothing about. The best they could do was to land far from the castle that housed the malignant spirit creature Bek and Truls Rohk had encountered and hope it could not reach beyond the walls of its keep.

They made what repairs they could, detaching the draws to the aft parse tubes and reducing their power by one-third. All of a sudden they were no longer the fastest airship in the skies, and if the Morgawr was tracking them, he would quickly catch up. The Wing Riders returned with Amenades, and they weighed him down and buried him at sea before setting out once more.

Setting a course for Mephitic, they limped along for all of that day and the two after, casting anxious glances over their shoulders at every opportunity. But the Morgawr did not appear, and their journey continued uninterrupted until at midday on the fourth day, land appeared on the horizon. It was the island they were seeking, its broad-backed shape instantly recognizable. Green with forests and grassy plains, it shimmered in a haze of damp heat like a jewel set in azure silk, deceptively tranquil and inviting.

From his position at the controls in the pilot box, Redden Alt Mer stared at it bleakly. "Let's make this quick," he muttered to himself, and pointed the horns of the *Jerle Shannara* landward.

They set down on the broad plain fronting the castle ruins, well back from the long shadow of its crumbling walls. Alt Mer had thought at first to land somewhere else on the island, but then decided that the western plain offered the best vantage point for establishing a perimeter watch against anything that approached or threatened. He assumed that the spirit that lived in the castle could sense their presence wherever they were, and the best they could hope for was that it either couldn't reach them or wouldn't bother trying if they left it alone. He dispatched the Wing Riders to search for food and water, then Spanner Frew, Britt Rill, and the Elven Hunter Kian to locate a tree from which to fashion a new mast. The others were put to work on sentry duty or cleaning up.

By sundown, everyone was back aboard. The Wing Riders had located a water source, Spanner Frew had found a suitable tree and cut it down, and the thing that lived in the ruins had not appeared. The members of the company, save Quentin and Grianne, sat together on the aft deck and ate their dinner, watching the sunset wash lavender and gold across the dark battlements and towers of the castle, as if making a vain attempt to paint them in a better light. As the sun disappeared below the horizon, the color faded from the stones and night's shadows closed about.

Alt Mer stood looking at the outline of the ruins after the others had dispersed. Kian was scheduled to stand guard, but he sent the Elven Hunter below, deciding to take his place, thinking that on this night he was unlikely to sleep anyway. Taking up a position at the *Jerle Shannara*'s stern, he left responsibility for keeping watch over the Blue Divide to Riat and gave his attention instead to the empty, featureless landscape of Mephitic.

His thoughts quickly drifted. He was troubled by what he perceived as his failure as Captain of his airship. Too many men and women had died while traveling with him, and their deaths did not rest easy with him. He might pretend that the responsibility lay elsewhere, but he was not the kind of man who looked for ways to shift blame to others. A Captain was responsible for his charges, no matter what the circumstances. There was nothing he could do for those who were dead, but he was afraid that perhaps there was nothing he could do for those who were still alive, either. His confidence had been eroding incrementally since the beginning of their time on Parkasia, a gradual wearing away of his certainty that nothing bad could happen to those who flew with him. His reputation had been built on that certainty. He had the luck, and luck was the most single important weapon of an airship Captain.

Luck, he whispered to himself. Ask Jahnon Pakabbon about his luck. Or Rucker Bont and Tian Cross. Or any of the Elves who had gone inland to the ruins of Castledown and never come back. Ask Jethen Amenades. What luck had Alt Mer given to them? It wasn't that he believed he had done anything to cause their deaths. It was that he hadn't found a way to prevent them. He hadn't kept his people safe, and he was afraid he had lost the means for doing so.

Sooner or later, luck always ran out. He knew that. His seemed to have begun draining away when he had agreed to undertake this voyage, so self-confident, so determined everything would work out just as he wanted it to. But nothing had gone right, and now Walker was dead and Alt Mer was in command. What good was that going to do any of those who depended on him if the armor of his fabled luck was cracked and rusted?

Staring at the dark bulk of the ruins across the way, he could not help thinking that what he saw, broken and crumbled and abandoned, was a reflection of himself.

But his pride would not let him accept that he was powerless to do anything. Even if his luck was gone, even if he himself was doomed because of it, he would find a way to help the others. It was the charge he must give himself, that so long as he breathed, he must get those he captained, those eleven men and women who were left, safely home again. Saving just those few would give him some measure of peace. That one of them was his sister and another the boy she loved made his commitment even more necessary. That all of them were his friends and shipmates made it imperative.

He was still thinking about this when he sensed a presence at his elbow and glanced over to find Bek Ohmsford standing next to him. He was so surprised to see Bek, perhaps because he had just been thinking of him, that for a moment he didn't speak.

"It won't come out of there," Bek said, nodding in the direction of the castle. His young face bore a serious cast, as if his thoughts were taking him to dark and complex places. "You don't have to worry."

Alt Mer followed his gaze to the ruins. "How do you know that?"

"Because it didn't come after me when I stole the key the last time we were here. Not past the castle walls, not outside the ruins." He paused. "I don't think it can go outside. It can chase you that far, but no farther. It can't reach beyond."

The Rover Captain thought about it for a moment. "It didn't bother us when we were searching the ruins, did it? It just used its magic to turn us down blind alleys and blank walls so that we couldn't find anything."

Bek nodded. "I don't think it will bother us if we stay out here. Even if we go in, it probably won't interfere if we don't try to take anything."

They stood shoulder to shoulder for a few moments, staring out into the darkness, listening to the silence. A dark, winged shape flew across the lighter indigo of the starlit sky, a hunting bird at work. They watched it bank left in a sweeping glide and disappear into the impenetrable black of the trees.

"What are you doing out here?" Alt Mer asked him. "Why aren't you asleep?"

He almost asked why he wasn't with Rue, but Bek hadn't chosen to talk about it, and Alt Mer didn't think it was up to him to broach the subject.

Bek shook his head, running his hand through his shaggy hair. "I couldn't sleep. I was dreaming about Grianne, and it woke me. I think the dream was telling me something important, but I can't remember what. It bothered me enough that I couldn't go back to sleep, so I came up here."

Alt Mer shifted his feet restlessly. "You still can't reach her, can you? Little Red can't either. Never thought she'd even try, but she goes down there every day and sits with her."

Bek didn't say anything, so Alt Mer let the matter drop. He was growing tired, wishing suddenly that he hadn't been so quick to send Kian off to sleep.

"Are you upset with me about Rue?" Bek asked suddenly.

Alt Mer stared at him in surprise. "Don't you think it's a little late to be asking me that?"

Bek nodded solemnly, not looking back. "I don't want you to be angry. It's important to both of us that you aren't."

"Little Red quit asking my permission to do anything a long time ago," Alt Mer said quietly. "It's her life, not mine. I don't tell her how to lead it."

"Does that mean it's all right?"

"It means . . ." He paused, confused. "I don't know what it means. It means I don't know. I guess I worry about what's going to happen when you get back home and have to make a choice about your lives. You're different people; you don't have the same background or life experience."

Bek thought about it. "Maybe we don't have to live our old lives. Maybe we can live new ones."

Alt Mer sighed. "You know something, Bek. You can do whatever you want, if you put your mind to it. I believe that. If you love her as much as I think you do—as much as I know she loves you—then you'll find your way. Don't ask me what I think or if I'm upset or what I might suggest or anything. Don't ask anyone. Just do what feels right."

He clapped Bek lightly on the shoulder. "Of course, I think you should become a Rover. You've got flying in your blood." He yawned. "Meanwhile, stand watch for me, since you're so wide awake. I think I need a little sleep after all."

Without waiting for an answer, he walked over to the main hatchway and started down. There was a hint of self-confidence in his step as he did so. One way or another, it would work out for all of them, he promised himself. He could feel it in his bones.

The company was awake and at work shortly after sunrise, continuing repair efforts on the damaged Jerle Shannara. Using axes and planes, Spanner Frew and the other two Rover crewmen took all morning to shape the mast from the felled tree trunk. It was afternoon before they had hauled it back to the ship to prepare it for the spars and rigging it would hold when it was set in place. The painstaking process required a careful removal of metal clasps and rings from the old mast so that they could be used again; the work would not be completed for at least another day. Those not involved were sent out to complete the foraging begun the other day by the Wing Riders, who had been dispatched to make certain the company was still safely ahead of the Morgawr.

They weren't. By late afternoon, the Wing Riders returned, landed their Rocs close by the airship, and delivered the bad news. The Morgawr's fleet was less than six hours out and coming directly toward them. In spite of everything, the warlock had managed to track them down once more. If the enemy airships continued to advance at their present pace, they would arrive on Mephitic shortly after nightfall.

Anxious eyes shifted from face to face. There was no way that the repairs to the *Jerle Shannara* could be finished by then. At best, if she tried to flee now, she would be flying at a speed that would allow even the slowest pursuer to catch her within days. The choices were obvious. The company could try to hide or they could stand and fight.

Redden Alt Mer already knew what they were going to do. He had been preparing since the night before, when he had decided that no one else was going to die under his command. Assuming the worst might happen, he had come up with a plan, suggested by something Bek had told him, to counteract it.

"Gather up everything," he ordered, striding through their midst as if already on his way to do so himself. "Don't leave even the smallest trace of anything that would suggest we were here. Put everything aboard so we can lift off. Hunter Predd, can you and Po Kelles find hiding places for yourselves and your Rocs offshore on one of the atolls? You'll need a couple of days."

The Wing Riders looked at each other doubtfully, then

looked at him. "Where will you be while we're safe and snug on the ground?" Hunter Predd asked bluntly. "Up in a cloud?"

Alt Mer smiled cheerfully. "Hiding in plain sight, Wing Rider. Hiding right under their noses."

TWENTY-EIGHT

By the time the Morgawr brought his fleet of airships to within view of Mephitic, darkness had eclipsed the light necessary for a search, so he had them anchor offshore until dawn. His Mwellrets supervised the walking dead who crewed the ships, giving them directions for what was needed before setting themselves at watch against a night attack. Such a thing was not out of the question. His quarry was close ahead, perhaps still on the island, her scent stronger than it had been in days, a dense perfume on the salt-laden air.

The following morning, when it grew light and he could see clearly, he set out to discover where she had gone. Leaving the remainder of his fleet at anchor, he flew *Black Moclips* in a slow, careful sweep over the island, searching for her hiding place.

His mood was no longer as dark and foul as it had been after the seer had died, when he had felt both betrayed and outwitted. The seer had tricked him into following blind leads and useless visions. The *Jerle Shannara* and her crew had escaped him completely, flying out of Parkasia through the mountains even as he was flying in. With the Ilse Witch safely aboard, they had gotten behind him and turned for home.

He had known what that meant. The Druid's vessel was the faster ship, much faster than anything the Morgawr commanded, including *Black Moclips*. He had lost the advantages of surprise and numbers both, and if he did not find a way to turn things around, he risked losing them completely.

But the Four Lands were a long way off, and fate had intervened on his behalf. Something had happened to slow the *Jerle Shannara*, allowing him to catch up. Even though she had gotten far ahead of him, he had still been able to track her. She had brought aboard her own doom in thc form of the Ilse Witch, and once that was done, her fate was sealed. Just as the little witch had tracked the Druid from the Four Lands through her use of the seer as her spy, so had he tracked her through her use of her magic. The scent of it, layered on the air, was pungent and clear, a trail he could not mistake. For a time, when the witch had escaped into the mountains with her brother, he had lost all track of her. He assumed she had simply ceased using the magic, though that was unlike her.

Then, only days before the Elven Prince had fled and he'd had the seer killed, there had been a resurgence of the use of magic deep in Parkasia's mountains. At the time, intent on following the seer's false visions, he had ignored it. But now he had the Ilse Witch's scent again, so strong there was no need for anything more. Small bursts of it permeated the air through which he flew, sudden fits and starts he could not explain, but could read well enough. Wherever she went, while she remained aboard the *Jerle Shannara*, he would be able to find her.

Her scent was present now, hanging in a cloud over the island, blown everywhere on the breeze. But did it lead away? Had they gotten off the island just ahead of him? That was what he must discover.

He cruised Mephitic from end to end, tracking the magic, following its trail. He determined quickly enough that it did not extend beyond the island's broad, low sweep. He felt a wildness building in him, an anticipation bordering on frenzy. They were here still; he had them trapped. He could already taste the witch's life bleeding out of her and into him. He could already imagine the sweetness of its taste.

So he swept the island carefully, flying low enough to read its details, seeking to uncover their hiding place, thinking that no matter how well they hid themselves, they could not hide the scent of his little witch's magic. They might even abandon their ship, though he could not believe they would be so foolish, but they were his for the taking so long as they kept the witch beside them. If the boy was her brother, as the Morgawr was now certain he must be, there was no question but that they would.

Even so, he could not find them. He searched from the air until his eyes ached and his temper frayed. He put Cree Bega and his Mwellrets at every railing and had them search, as well. They found nothing. They searched until midmorning, and then he brought the rest of the fleet inland and had them fan out and blanket the island from the air. When that failed, he had the Mwellrets disembark and under Cree Bega's command search on foot. He had them comb the forests and even the open grasslands, seeking anything that would indicate the presence of his quarry.

He had them search everywhere except the castle ruins.

The ruins presented a problem. Something was alive inside those walls, something birthed of old magic and not made of flesh and blood. In spirit form, it had lived for thousands of years, and it regarded those broken parapets and crumbling towers as its own. The Morgawr had sensed its presence right away and sensed, as well, that it might be as powerful as he was. He was not about to send the Mwellrets stumbling about in its domain unless there was good reason to do so. From the air, he had seen nothing to suggest that his quarry had gotten inside. That they could do so seemed doubtful, but if they had, there should be some sign of them.

The hunt continued through the remainder of the day without result. The Morgawr was furious. It was impossible that he had been mistaken about the scent of the magic, but even so he went back around in *Black Moclips*, well off the island, to see if he had misread it somehow. But the results were the same; there was no trail leading away. Unless they had found a way to disguise the Ilse Witch's scent—which they had no reason even to think of doing—they were still on the island.

By darkness, he was convinced of it. A tree had been cut down very recently, and shavings indicated that something had been shaped from it. A mast, the Morgawr guessed. A broken mast would explain why they had been forced to slow and why he had been able to catch up to them. The Mwellrets found tracks, as well, deeper into the trees where damp grasses and soft earth left imprints. There were fresh gouges on the plains across from the castle, as well, where an airship might have been moored.

Now there was no doubt in the Morgawr's mind that the *Jerle Shannara* and her company had been on Mephitic less than a day ago, and unless he was completely mistaken, they were still here.

But where were they hiding?

It took him only a moment to decide. They were inside the castle. There was nowhere else they could be.

He sent his searchers back aboard their ships and had them make a final pass over the dusk-shrouded island before moving back out to sea to drop anchor just offshore. There he set the watch, and while the Mwellrets went about the business of shutting down the airships and settling in for the night, he stood alone in the prow of *Black Moclips*, thinking.

He did not yet know what had happened to reunite the Ilse Witch with her brother. He did not know if she was now her brother's ally or simply his prisoner. He had to assume she was the former, although he had no idea how that could have happened. That meant she would have the support of not only her brother, but also the young Elessedil Prince and whoever else was still alive, as well. But she would not have the Druid to protect her, and the Druid was the only one who might have stood a chance against him. The others, even fighting together, were not strong enough. The Morgawr had been alive a long time, and he had fought hard to stay that way. The power of his magic was terrifying, and his skill at wielding it more than sufficient to overcome these children.

Still, he would be careful. They would know he was there by now, and they would be waiting for him. They would try to defend themselves, but that would be hopeless. Most of them would die quickly at the hands of his Mwellrets, leaving the few who possessed the use of magic for him to deal with. A few quick strikes, and it would be over.

Yet he wanted his little Ilse Witch alive, so that he could feed on her, so that he could feel her life drain away through his fingertips. He had trained her to be his successor, a mirror image of himself. She had become that, her magic fed by rage and despair. But her ambition and her willfulness had outstripped her caution, and so she was no longer reliable. Better to have done with her than to risk her treachery. Better to make an example of her, one that no one could possibly mistake. Cree Bega and his Mwellrets wanted her gone anyway. They had always hated her. Perhaps they had understood her better than he had.

His gaze lifted. Tomorrow, he would watch her die in the way of so many others. It would give him much satisfaction.

Radiating black venom and hunger, he stood motionless at the railing and imagined how it would be.

Crouched in the shadow of the crumbling castle walls, only a dozen yards from where the *Jerle Shannara* lay concealed, Bek Ohmsford watched the dark bulk of an airship pass directly overhead, then swing around and pass back again. It floated over the ruins like a storm cloud.

"That's *Black Moclips*," Rue whispered in his ear, pressing up against him, her words barely more than a breath of air in the silence.

He nodded without offering a reply, waiting until the vessel was far enough away that it felt safe to speak. "He knows we're here," he said.

"Maybe not."

"He knows. He would have moved on by now if he didn't. He searched the entire island and didn't find us, but he knows we're here. He senses it somehow. Tomorrow, he'll search these ruins."

They had been in hiding all day, ever since Redden Alt Mer had taken the *Jerle Shannara* inside the castle walls. It was a bold gamble, but one that the Rover Captain thought would work. If the creature that lived in the ruins had not bothered with them when they had searched for the key, it might not bother with them now, even if they set the *Jerle Shannara* down inside one of its numerous courtyards. So long as they did not try to take anything out, it might tolerate their presence long enough for them to deceive the Morgawr.

There was time to try his plan out before the warlock reached them, and so they did. They had been able to fly the *Jerle Shannara* into the ruins and set her down in a deeply shadowed cluster of walls and towers. Once anchored, they had stripped her of sails and masts and rigging, leaving her decks bare. When that was done, they had covered her over with rocks and dirt and grasses until from the air, astride a Roc, they could not see her at all and would not have known she was there.

Alt Mer knew they were taking a big chance. If they were discovered, they would have no chance of getting aloft with the masts and rigging and sails dismantled. They would be trapped and most probably killed or captured. But the Rover Captain was counting on something else, as well. When they had tried to penetrate the ruins on their way to Parkasia, the castle's spirit dweller had used its magic to turn them aside.

Each new foray took them down blind alleys and dead ends and eventually back outside. If that magic was still in place, it ought to work in the same way against the Morgawr and his rets. When they tried to come inside, they would be led astray and never get past the perimeter walls.

With luck, it should not come to that. With luck, the Morgawr should determine after a careful sweep of the island that his quarry had eluded him. There should be no reason to search the ruins from the ground if nothing was visible from the air.

But Bek knew it wasn't going to work out that way. Their concealment had been perfect, but the Morgawr's instincts were telling him that they were still on the island. They were whispering to him that he was missing something, and it wouldn't take him long to determine what it was. He would decide that they must be hiding in the ruins. Tomorrow, he would search them. It might not yield him anything, but if it did, the company of the *Jerle Shannara* was finished.

With Rue still pressing close, he leaned back against the cool stone of the old wall. *Black Moclips* had not returned, and the sky was left bright and open in its wake, a trail of glittering stars shining down through a wash of moonlight. The others of the company were inside the *Jerle Shannara*, kept there by Redden Alt Mer's strict order not to venture out for any reason. Bek was the sole exception, because an outside perspective was needed in case of an attempted ground approach and Bek was best able to conceal himself from the spirit dweller, should the need arise. Rue was with him because it was understood that wherever Bek went, she went, as well. They had been out there, hiding in the shadows, since early morning. It was time to go inside and get some sleep.

But Bek's mind was running too fast and too hard to permit him to sleep, his thoughts skipping from consideration of one obstacle to the next, from one concern to another, everything tied up with the dangerous situation facing them and what they might try to do to avoid it.

One concern, in particular, outstripped the rest.

He bent close to Rue. "I don't know what to do about Grianne." His lips pressed against her ear, his words a hushed whisper. Voices carried in the empty silence of ruins such as these, beyond even walls of mortar and stone. "If the Morgawr comes for her, she will have no way to protect herself. She will be helpless."

Rue leaned her head against him, her hair as soft as spider-webbing. "Do you want to try to hide her somewhere besides here?" she whispered back.

"No. He'll find her wherever we put her. I have to wake her up."

"You've been trying that for weeks, Bek, and it hasn't worked. What can you do that you haven't already done?"

He kissed her hair and put his arms around her. "Find out what it is that keeps her in hiding. Find out what it will take to bring her out."

He could sense her smile even in the darkness. "That isn't a new plan. That's an old one."

He nodded, touching her knee in soft reproach. "I know. But suppose we could figure out what it would take to wake her. We've tried everything we could think of, both of us. But we keep trying in a general way, a kind of blanket approach to bringing her out of her sleep. Walker said she wouldn't come back to us until she found a way to forgive herself for the worst of her wrongs. I think that's the key. We have to figure out what that wrong is."

She lifted her head, her red hair falling back from her face. "How can you possibly do that? She has hundreds of things to forgive herself for. How can you pick out one?"

"Walker said it was the one *she* believed to be the worst." He paused, thinking. "What would that be? What would she see as her worst wrong? Killing someone? She's killed lots of people. Which one would matter more than the others?"

Rue furrowed her smooth brow. "Maybe this was something she did when she first became the witch, when she was still young, something that goes to the heart of everything she's done since."

He stared at her for a long time, remembering his dream of the other night. It had been nagging at him ever since, reduced to a vague image, the details faded. It hovered now, just beyond his grasp. He could practically reach out and touch it.

"What is it?" she asked.

"I don't know. I think there's something in what you just said that might help, something about her childhood." He stared at her some more. "I have to go down and sit with her. Maybe looking at her, being in the same room for a while, will help."

"Do you want me to come with you?"

When he hesitated, she reached out and cupped his face in her hands. "Go by yourself, Bek. Maybe you need to be alone. I'll come later, if you need me to."

She kissed him hard, then slipped from his side and disappeared back into the bowels of the airship. He waited only a moment more, still wrestling with his confusion, then followed her inside.

There was no reason to think that this night would be different from any other, but Bek was convinced by feelings he could not explain that it might be. Nothing he had tried—and he had tried everything—had gotten so much as a blink out of Grianne from the moment he had found her kneeling with the bloodied Sword of Shannara grasped in her hands. Only when he broke down in frustration and cried that one time, when he wasn't even trying to make her respond, had she come out of her catatonia to speak with him. She had done so for reasons he had never been able to figure out, but tonight, he thought, he must. The secret to everything lay in connecting the reason for that singular awakening with the wrong she had committed somewhere in her past that she regarded as unforgivable.

He told Redden Alt Mer what he was going to do and suggested someone else might want to take up watch from one of the taller towers. Alt Mer said he would handle it himself, wished Bek good luck, and went over the side of the airship. Bek stood alone on the empty deck, thinking that perhaps he should ask Rue to help him after all. But he knew he would be doing so only as a way of gaining reassurance that he had done everything he could, should things not work out yet again. It was not right to use her that way, and he abandoned the idea at once. If he failed this night, he wanted it to be on his head alone.

He went down to the Captain's quarters and slipped through the doorway. Quentin Leah lay asleep in his bed, his breathing deep and even, his face turned away from the single candle that burned nearby. The windows were shuttered and curtained so that no light or sound could escape, and the air in the room was close and stale. Bek wanted to blow out the candle and open the shutters, but he knew that would be unwise.

Instead, he walked over to his sister. She was lying on her pallet with her knees drawn up and her eyes open and staring. She wore her dark robe, but a light blanket had been laid over her, as well. Rue had brushed her hair earlier that day, and the dark strands glimmered in the candlelight like threads of silk. Her fingers were knotted together, and her mouth was twisted with what might have been a response to a deep-seated regret or troublesome dream.

Bek raised her to a sitting position, placed her against the bulkhead, and seated himself across from her. He stared at her without doing anything more, trying to think through what he knew, trying to decide what to do next. He had to break down the protective shell in which she had sealed herself, but to do that he had to know what she was protecting herself from.

He tried to envision it and failed. On the surface, she looked to be barely more than a child, but beneath she was iron hard and remorseless. That didn't just disappear, even after a confrontation with the truth-inducing magic of the Sword of Shannara. Besides, what single act set itself apart from any other? What monstrous wrong could she not bring herself to face after perpetrating so many?

He sat staring at her much in the same way that she was staring at him, neither of them really seeing the other, both of them off in other places. Bek shifted his thinking to Grianne's early years, when she was first taken from her home and placed in the hands of the Morgawr. Could something have happened then, as Rue had suggested, something so awful she could not forgive herself for it? Was there something he didn't know about and would have to guess at?

Suddenly, it occurred to him that he might be thinking about this in the wrong way. Maybe it wasn't something she had done, but something she had failed to do. Maybe it wasn't an act, but an omission that haunted her. It was just as possible that what she couldn't forgive herself for was something she believed she should have done and hadn't.

He repeated to himself what she said when she woke on the night she had saved Quentin's life—about how Bek shouldn't cry, how she was there for him, how she would look after him again, his big sister.

But she had said something else, too. She had said she would never leave him again, that she was sorry for doing so. She had cried and repeated several times, "I'm so sorry, so sorry."

He thought he saw it then, the failure for which she had never been able to forgive herself. A child of only six, she had hidden him in the basement, choosing to try to save his life over those of her parents. She had concealed him in the cellar, listening to her parents die as she did so. She had left him there and set out to find help, but she had never gotten beyond her own yard. She had been kidnapped and whisked away, then deceived so that she would think he was dead, too.

She had never gone back for him, never returned to find out if what she had been told was the truth. At first, it hadn't mattered, because she was in the thrall of the Morgawr and certain of his explanation of her rescue. But over the years, her certainty had gradually eroded, until slowly she had begun to doubt. It was why she had been so intrigued by Bek's story about who he was when they had encountered each other for the first time in the forest that night after the attack in the ruins. It was why she hadn't killed him when she almost certainly would have otherwise. His words and his looks and his magic disturbed her. She was troubled by the possibility that he might be who he said he was and that everything she had believed about him was wrong.

Which would mean that she had left him to die when she should have gone back to save him.

It was a failure for which he would never blame her, but for which she might well blame herself. She had failed her parents and then failed him, as well. She had thrown away her life for a handful of lies and a misplaced need for vengeance.

He was so startled by the idea that it could be something as simple as this that for a moment he could not believe it was possible. Or that it could be something so impossibly wrongheaded. But she did not think as he did, or even as others did. She had come through the scouring magic of the Sword of Shannara to be reborn into the world, tempered by fire he could barely imagine, by truths so vast and inexorable that they would destroy a weaker person. She had survived because of who she was, but had become more damaged, too.

What should he do?

He was frightened that he might be wrong, and if he was, he had no idea of where else to look. But fear had no place in what was needed, and he had no patience with its weakness. He had to try using his new insight to break down her defenses. He had to find out if he was right.

His choices were simple. He could call on the magic of the wishsong or he could speak to her in his normal voice. He chose the latter. He moved closer to her, putting his face right in front of hers, his hands clasped loosely about her slender neck, tangling in her thick, dark hair.

"Listen to me," he whispered to her. "Grianne, listen to what I have to say to you. You can hear me. You can hear every word. I love you, Grianne. I never stopped loving you, not once, not even after I found out who you were. It isn't your fault, what was done to you. You can come home, now. You can come home to me. That's where your home is—with me. Your brother, Bek."

He waited a moment, searching her empty eyes. "You hid me from the Morgawr and his Mwellrets, Grianne, even without knowing who they were. You saved my life. I know you wanted to come back for me, that you wanted to bring help for me and for our parents. But you couldn't do that. There wasn't any way for you to return. There wasn't enough time, even if the Morgawr hadn't tricked you. But even though you couldn't come back, you saved me. Just by hiding me so that Truls Rohk could find me and take me to Walker, you saved me. I'm alive because of you."

He paused. Had he felt her shiver? "Grianne, I forgive you for leaving me, for not coming back, for not discovering that I was still alive. I forgive you for all of that, for everything you might have done and failed to do. You have to forgive yourself, as well. You have to stop hiding from what happened all those years ago. It isn't a truth that needs hiding from. It is a truth that needs facing up to. I need you back with me, not somewhere far away. By hiding from me, you are leaving me again. Don't do that, Grianne. Don't go away again. Come back to me as you promised you would."

She was trembling suddenly, but her gaze remained fixed and staring, her eyes as blank as forest lakes at night. He kept holding her, waiting for her to do something more. *Keep talking,* he told himself. *This is the way to reach her.*

Instead, he began to sing, calling up the magic of the wishsong almost without realizing he was doing so, singing now the words he had only spoken before. It was an impulsive act, an instinctive response to his need to connect with her. He was so close, right on the verge of breaking through. He could feel the shell in which she had encased herself beginning to crack. She was there, right inside, desperate to reach him.

So he turned to the language they both understood best, the language peculiar to them alone. The music flowed out of him, infused with his magic, sweet and soft and filled with yearning. He gave himself over to it in the way that music requires, lost in its rhythm, in its flow, in its transcendence of the here and now. He took himself away from where he was and took her with him, back in time to a life he had barely known and she had forgotten, back to a world they had both lost. He sang of it as he would have wanted it to be, all the while telling her he forgave her for leaving that world, for abandoning him, for losing herself in a labyrinth of treacheries and lies and hatred and monstrous acts from which it might seem there could be no redemption. He sang of it as a way of healing, so that she might find in the words and music the balm she required to accept the harshness of the truth about her life and know that as bad as it was, it was nevertheless all right, that forgiveness came to everyone.

He had no idea how long he sang, only that he did so without thinking of what he was attempting or even of what was needed. He sang because the music gave him a release for his own confused, tangled emotions. Yet the effect was the same. He was aware of her small shivers turning to trembles, of her head snapping up and her eyes beginning to focus, of a sound rising from her throat that approached a primal howl. He could sense the walls she had constructed crumble and feel her world shift.

Then she seized him in such a powerful embrace it did not seem possible that a girl so slender could manage it. She pressed him against her so hard that he could barely breathe, crying softly into his shoulder and saying, "It's all right, Bek, I'm here for you, I'm here."

He stopped singing then and hugged her back, and in the ensuing silence he closed his eyes and mouthed a single word.

Stay.

TWENTY-NINE

She had been hiding in the darkest place she could find, but in the blackness that surrounded her were the things that hunted her. She did not know what they were, but she knew she must not look at them too closely. They were dangerous, and if they caught even the smallest glimpse of her eyes, they would fall on her like wolves. So she stayed perfectly still and did not look at them, hoping they would go away.

But they refused to leave, and she found herself trapped with no chance to escape. She was six years old, and in her mind she saw the things in the darkness as black-cloaked monsters. They had pursued her for a long time, tracking her with such persistence that she knew they would never stop. She thought that if she could manage to get past them and find her way home to her parents and brother, she would be safe again. But they would not let her go.

She could remember her home clearly. She could see its rooms and halls in her mind. It hadn't been very large, but it had felt warm and safe. Her parents had loved and cared for her, and her little brother had depended on her to look after him. But she had failed them all. She had run away from them, fled her home because the black things were coming for her and she knew that if she stayed, she would die. Her flight was swift and mindless, and it took her away from everything she knew—here, to this place of empty blackness where she knew nothing.

Now and again, she would hear her brother calling to her from a long way off. She recognized Bek's voice, even though it was a grown-up's voice and she knew he was only two years old and should not be able to speak more than a few words. Sometimes, he sang to her, songs of childhood and home. She wanted to call out to him, to tell him where she was, but she was afraid. If she spoke even one word, made even a single sound, the things in the darkness would know where she was and come for her.

She had no sense of time or place. She had no sense of the world beyond where she hid. Everything real was gone, and only her memories remained. She clung to them like threads of gold, shining bright and precious in the dark.

Once, Bek managed to find her, breaking through the darkness with tears that washed away her hunters. A path opened for her, created out of his need, a need so strong that not even the black things could withstand it. She took the path out of her hiding place and found him again, his heart breaking as he watched his little dog lying injured beside him. She told him she was back, that she would not leave him again, and she used her magic to heal his puppy. But the black things were still waiting for her, and when she felt his need for her begin to wane and the path it had opened begin to close, she was forced to flee back into her hiding place. Without his need to sustain her with its healing power, she could not stay.

So she hid once more. The path she had taken to him was closed and gone, and she did not know what she could do to open it again. Bek must open it, she believed. He had done so once; he must do so again. But Bek was only a baby, and he didn't understand what had happened to her. He didn't realize why she was hiding and how dangerous the black things were. He didn't know that she was trapped and that he was the only one who could free her.

"But when you told me you forgave me for leaving you, I felt everything begin to change," she told him. "When you told me how much you needed me, how by not coming back to you I was leaving you again, I felt the darkness begin to recede and the black things—the truths I couldn't bear to face—begin to fade. I heard you singing, and I felt the magic break through and wrap me like a soft blanket. I thought that if you could forgive me, after how I had failed you, then I could face what I had done beyond that, all of it, every bad thing."

They were sitting in the darkness where this had all begun, tucked away in a corner of Redden Alt Mer's Captain's quarters, whispering so as not to wake the sleeping Quentin Leah. Shadows draped their faces and masked some of what their eyes would have otherwise revealed, but Bek knew what his sister was thinking. She was thinking he had known what he was doing when he found a way to reach her through the magic of the wishsong. Yet it was mostly chance that he had done so. Or perhaps perseverance, if he was to be charitable about it. He had thought it would take forgiveness to bring her awake. He had been wrong. It had taken her sensing the depth of his need.

"I just wanted to give you a chance to be yourself again," he said. "I didn't want you to stay locked away inside, whatever the consequences of coming out might be."

"They won't be good ones, Bek," she told him, reaching over to touch his cheek. "They might be very bad." She was quiet for a moment, staring at him. "I can't believe I've really found you again."

"I can't believe it either. But then I can't believe hardly anything of what's happened. Especially to me. I'm not so different from you. Everything I thought true about myself was a lie, too."

She smiled, but there was a hint of bitterness and reproach. "Don't say that. Don't ever say that. You're nothing like me, save that you didn't know you were an Ohmsford. You haven't done the things that I've done. You haven't lived my life. Be grateful for that. You can look back on your life and not regret it. I will never be able to do that. I'll regret my life for as long as I live. I'll want to change it every day, and I won't be able to do that. All of the things I've done as the Ilse Witch will be with me forever."

She gave him a long, hard look. "I love you, and I know you love me, too. That gives me hope, Bek. That gives me the strength I need to try to make something good come out of all the bad."

"Do you remember everything that happened now?" he asked her. "Everything you did while you were the Ilse Witch?"

She nodded. "Everything."

"The Sword of Shannara showed it to you?"

"Every last act. All of the things I did because I wanted revenge on Walker. All of the wrongs I committed because I thought I was entitled to do whatever was necessary to get what I sought."

"I'm sorry you had to go through that, but not sorry that I got you back."

She pushed her long dark hair out of her pale face, revealing the pain in her eyes. "There wasn't any hope for me unless I discovered the truth about myself. About you and our parents. About everything that happened to us all those years ago. About the Morgawr, especially. I couldn't be anyone other than who the Morgawr had made me to be—and who I had made myself to be—until that happened. I hate knowing it, but it's freeing, too. I don't have to hide anymore."

"There are some things you don't know yet," he said. He shifted uncomfortably, trying to decide where to start. "The people we're traveling with, the survivors of Walker's company, all have reason to hate you. They don't, not all of them anyway, but they have suffered losses because of you. I guess you need to know about those losses, about the harm you've caused. I don't think there's any way to avoid it."

She nodded, her expression one of regret mixed with determination. "Tell me then, Bek. Tell me all of it."

He did so, leaving nothing out. It took him some time to do so, and while he was speaking, he became aware of someone else entering the room, easing over next to him, and sitting close. He knew without looking who it was, and he watched Grianne's eyes shift to find those of the newcomer. He kept talking nevertheless, afraid that if he looked away, he would not be able to continue. He related his story of the journey to Parkasia, of finding the ruins and Antrax, confronting her, escaping into the mountains and being captured, breaking free of *Black Moclips* and the rets, coming down into the bowels of Castledown to find that Walker had already tricked her into invoking the cleansing magic of the Sword of Shannara, taking her back into the mountains, and finding their way at last to what remained of the company of the *Jerle Shannara*.

When he had finished, he looked over his shoulder to find Rue. She was staring at Grianne. The look on her face was indecipherable. But the tone of her voice when she spoke to his sister was unmistakable.

"The Morgawr has come searching for you," she said. "His ships are anchored offshore. In the morning, he will search these ruins. If he finds us, he will try to kill us. What are you going to do about it?"

"Rue Meridian." His sister spoke the other's name as if to make its owner real. "Are you one of those who have not forgiven me?"

Little Red's eyes were fierce as they held Grianne's. One hand came up to rest possessively on Bek's shoulder. "I have forgiven you."

But Bek did not miss the bitterness in her voice or the challenge that lay behind it. *Forgiveness is earned, not granted,* it said. *I forgive you, but what does it matter? You still must demonstrate that my forgiveness is warranted.*

He glanced at his sister and saw sadness and regret mirrored on her smooth, pale face. Her eyes shifted to where Rue's hand rested on his shoulder, and the last physical vestiges of the girl of six that she had been for all those days and nights of her catatonia vanished. Her face went hard and expressionless, the mask she had perfected to keep the demons of her life at bay when she was the Ilse Witch.

She looked back at her brother for just a moment. "I told you," she said to him, "that the consequences of my waking would not all be good ones." She smiled with cold certainty. "Some will be very bad."

There was a long pause as the two women attempted to stare each other down, each laying claim to something that the other wanted and could never have. A part of a past gone by. A part of a future yet to be. Time and events would determine how much of either they could share, but there was a need for compromise and neither had ever been very good at that.

"Maybe you should meet the others of the company, as well," Bek said quietly.

Beginnings in this situation, he thought, might prove tougher than endings.

At dawn, they stood together in the shelter of a tower's crumbling turret, Bek and Grianne and Rue, perched on its highest floor so that they could look out across the ruins to where the Morgawr's airships were beginning to stir. By now, Grianne had met all of the ship's company and been received with a degree of acceptance that Bek had not expected. If he was honest about it, Rue had proven to be the most hostile of the company. The two women were locked in some sort of contest that had something to do with him, but about which he understood little. Unable to deflect their mutual disdain, he had settled for keeping them civil.

Across the broad green sweep of the grasslands, the airships of the Morgawr were visible in the clear pale light of a sunrise that heralded an impossibly beautiful day. Bek saw the sticklike figures of the walking dead, standing at their stations, awaiting the commands that would set them in motion. He saw the first of the Mwellrets, cloaked and hooded against the light, emerging from belowdecks, climbing through the hatchways. Most important of all, he saw the Morgawr, standing at the forward railing of *Black Moclips*, his gaze, searching, directed toward the ruins where they hid.

"You were right," Grianne said softly, her slight body rigid within her robes. "He knows we're here."

The others of the company were settled in below, hiding within the hull and pontoons of the *Jerle Shannara*, waiting to see what would happen. Alt Mer knew of Bek's fears, but he could do nothing about them. The *Jerle Shannara* could not fly if they did not put up her masts and sails, and the noise alone of doing so would give them away. Even if the Morgawr tried to search the ruins, there was reason to think he would not find them, that the magic of the spirit dweller would refuse him entry and lead him back outside without his even realizing it, just as it had done to Walker. But that was a huge gamble; if it failed, they were trapped and outnumbered. Escape would be impossible unless they could overcome their enemies through means that at this point were a mystery.

Bek did not feel good about their chances. He did not believe that the Morgawr would be fooled by the magic of the spirit creature. Everything suggested otherwise. The warlock had tracked them this far without being able to see them and with no visible trail to follow. He seemed to know that they were hiding in the ruins. If he could determine all that, he would be quick enough to realize what the spirit dweller was doing to him when he tried to penetrate the ruins and would probably have a way to counteract it.

If that happened, they would have to face him.

He glanced at Grianne. She had never answered Rue's question about what she intended to do to stop the Morgawr.

In fact, his sister had said almost nothing past greeting those to whom she was introduced. She had not asked them if they had forgiven her, as she had asked Rue. She had not apologized for what she had done to them and to those they had lost. All of the softness and vulnerability that she had evidenced on waking from her sleep was gone. She had reverted to the personality of the Ilse Witch, cold and distant and devoid of emotion, keeping her thoughts to herself, the people she encountered at bay.

It worried Bek, but he understood it, too. She was protecting herself in the only way she could, by closing off the emotions that would otherwise destroy her. It wasn't that she didn't feel anything or that she no longer believed that she must account for the wrongs she had committed. But if she gave them too much consideration, if she gave her past too great a hold over her present, she would be unable to function. She had survived for many years through strength of will and rigid control. She had kept her emotions hidden. Last night, she had discovered that she could not let go of those defenses too quickly. She was still his sister, but she could not turn away from being the Ilse Witch either.

She was walking a fine line between sanity and madness, between staying out in the light of the real world and fleeing back into the hiding place she had only just managed to escape.

"We have to decide what we're going to do if he comes into the ruins and finds us," Bek said quietly.

"He is only one man," Rue said. "None of the others have his magic to protect them. The rets can be killed. I've killed them myself."

She sounded so fierce when she said it that Bek turned to look at her in spite of himself. But when he saw the look on her face he could not bring himself to say anything back.

Grianne had no such problem. "What you say is true, but the Morgawr is more powerful than any of you or even all of you put together. He is not a man; he is not even human. He is a creature who has kept himself alive a thousand years through use of dark magic. He knows a hundred ways to kill with barely a thought."

"He taught you all of them, I expect," Rue said without looking at her.

The words had no visible effect on Grianne, though Bek flinched. "What can we do to stop him?" he asked, looking to avoid the confrontation he could feel building.

"Nothing," his sister answered. She turned now to face them both. "This isn't your fight. It never was. Rue was right in asking me what I intended to do about the Morgawr. He is my responsibility. I am the one who must face him."

"You can't do that," Bek said at once. "Not alone."

"Alone is best. Distractions will only jeopardize my chances of defeating him. Anyone whom I care about is a distraction he will take advantage of. Alone, I can do what is necessary. The Morgawr is powerful, but I am his match. I always have been."

Bek shook his head angrily. "Once, maybe. But you were the Ilse Witch then."

"I am the Ilse Witch still, Bek." She gave him a quick, sad smile. "You just don't see me that way."

"She's right about this," Rue interrupted before he could offer further argument. "She has magic honed on the warlock's grinding stone. She knows how to use it against him."

"But I have the same magic!" Bek snapped, hissing in anger as he sought to keep his voice down. "What about Ahren Elessedil? He has the power of the Elfstones. Shouldn't we use our magics together? Wouldn't that be more effective than you facing the Morgawr alone? Why are you being so stubborn about this?"

"You are inexperienced at using the wishsong, Bek. Ahren is inexperienced at using the Elfstones. The Morgawr would kill you both before you could find a way to stop him."

She walked over to stand beside Rue Meridian, a deliberate act he could not mistake, and turned back to face him. "Everything that has happened to me is the Morgawr's doing. Everything I lost, I lost because of him. Everything I became, I became because of him. Everything I did, I did because of him. I made the choices, but he dictated the circumstances under which those choices were made. I make no excuses for myself, but I am owed something for what was done. No one can give that back to me. I have to take it back. I have to reclaim it. I can only do that by facing him."

Bek was incensed. "You don't have to prove anything!"

"Don't I, Bek?"

He was silent, aware of how untenable his argument was and how implacable his sister's thinking. She might not have anything to prove to him, but she did to a lot of others. Most important of all, she had something to prove to herself.

"I won't be whole again until I settle this," she said. "It won't stop if we escape. I know the Morgawr. He will keep coming until he finds a way to destroy me. If I want this matter ended, I have to end it here."

Bek shook his head in disgust. "What are we supposed to do while you go out there and sacrifice yourself? Hope for the best?"

"Take advantage of the confusion. Even if I am killed, the Morgawr will not emerge unscathed. He will be weakened and his followers will be in disarray. You can choose to face them or escape while they lick their wounds. Either is fine. Talk about it with the others and decide among you."

She leaned forward and kissed him on the cheek. "You have done everything you could for me, Bek. You have no reason to feel regret. I am doing this because I must."

She turned to Rue Meridian. "I like it that you are not afraid of anyone, even me. I like it that you love my brother so much."

"Don't do this," Bek pleaded.

"Take care of him," his sister said to Rue, and without an-other word or even a single glance back she walked away.

Ordering the rest of the fleet to remain anchored offshore, safely away from any attempts at sabotage, the Morgawr flew *Black Moclips* over the silver-tipped surface of the Blue Divide to the grassy flats of Mephitic. He landed his vessel and tied her off, leaving Aden Kett and his walking dead on board with a handful of guards to watch over them. Then, tossing a rope ladder over the railing of the starboard pontoon, he took Cree Bega and a dozen of his Mwellrets down off the ship and toward the castle.

They crossed the grasslands openly and deliberately, making no effort to hide their approach. If the survivors of the *Jerle Shannara* were hiding within the walls of the ruins, the Morgawr wanted them to see him coming. He wanted them to have time to think about it before he reached them, to let their anticipation build, and with it their fear. The Ilse Witch might not be frightened, but her companions would be. They would know by now how he feasted on the souls of the living. They would know how the Federation crew he had captured aboard *Black Moclips* had reacted while it was happening and what they looked like afterwards. At least one of them was likely to break down and reveal the presence of the others. That would save him time and effort. It would allow him to conserve his energy for dealing with the witch.

He told Cree Bega what he wanted. The Mwellrets were to follow his lead. They were not to talk. When they found their quarry, they were to leave the Ilse Witch to him. The others were theirs to do with as they wished. It would be best if they could kill them swiftly or render them unconscious so that they could be carried outside and disposed of.

Above all, they were to remember that there was something else living in the ruins, a spirit creature possessed of magic and capable of generating tremendous power. If it was aroused or attacked, it could prove extremely dangerous. Nothing was to be tampered with once they were inside, because the creature considered the castle its own and would fight to protect it. It cared nothing for the *Jerle Shannara* and her crew, however. They were not a part of its realm, and it would not protect them.

He said all this without being entirely sure it was true. It was possible that he was wrong and that the castle's inhabitant would attack for reasons the Morgawr could not even guess at. But no good purpose was served in telling that to the Mwellrets. All of them were expendable, even Cree Bega. What mattered was that he himself survive, and he had no reason to think that he wouldn't. His magic could protect him from anything. It always had.

His plan, then, was simple. He would find the witch and kill her, retrieve the books of magic from the airship, and escape. If he could achieve the former and not the latter, it would be enough. With the Druid dead, his little witch was the only one left who might cause him problems later. The books of magic were important, but he could give them up if he had to.

He began thinking about what it meant to have the last of the Druids gone. Paranor would lie uninhabited and vulnerable— protected by magic, yes, but accessible nevertheless to someone like himself who knew how to counteract that magic. It was Walker who had kept him at bay all these years. Now, perhaps, what had belonged to the Druids could be his.

The Morgawr permitted himself a smile. The wheel had come full circle on the Druids. Their time was over. His time was not. He need only dispose of one small girl. Ilse Witch or not, she was still only that.

Ahead, the broken-down walls and parapets of the ancient castle reared against the sunrise, stark and bare. His anticipation of what was waiting within compelled him to walk more swiftly to reach them.

THIRTY

Grianne Ohmsford walked through the empty corridors and courtyards of the old castle with slow, deliberate steps, giving herself a chance to gather her wits. In spite of what she had allowed Bek and Rue Meridian to believe, her decision to face the Morgawr alone was impulsive and not particularly well thought out. But it was necessary for all the reasons she had given them. She was the one he was looking for, and therefore the one who must confront him. She was the only one who stood a chance against his magic. She had done a lot of harm in her life as the Ilse Witch, and any redemption for her wrongs began with an accounting from the warlock.

She was still weak from her long sleep, but fueled by anger and determination. The truths about her life hovered right in front of her eyes, images made bright and clear by the magic of the Sword of Shannara, and she could not forget them. They defined her, and knowing what she had been was what made it possible for her to see what she must now become. To complete that journey, she must put an end to the Morgawr.

Silence cloaked her like a shroud, and the ruins bore the aura of a tomb. She smiled at the feeling, so familiar and still welcome, her world as she had known it for so many years. Shadows cast by walls and towers where sunlight could not penetrate spilled across the broken stone and cracked mortar like ink. She walked through those shadows in comfort, the darkness her friend, the legacy of her life. It would never change, she realized suddenly. She would always favor those things that had made her feel safe. She had found a home under conditions that would have destroyed others, had done so when everything she cared for had been taken away and all that was left was her rage, and she knew she would not be able to step away from that past easily.

That would not change, should she survive this day. Bek envisioned a returning home, a coming together of their new family, a settling into a quiet life. But his vision held no appeal for her and was rooted in dreams that belonged to someone else. Her life would take a different path from his; she knew that much already. Hers would never be what he hoped it might, because the reason for her recovery lay not so much with him—though he had brought her awake when no one else could—but with the Dark Uncle, the keeper of secrets and the bestower of trusts. With Walker Boh.

Dead now, but with her always.

She began to hum, wrapping herself in the feel of the ruins and the thing that lived within them. It was dormant at present, but as pervasive in its domain as Antrax had been in its. It was everywhere at once, its presence infused in the hard stone and the dead air. She knew from Bek that the way to deceive it was to make it feel as if you belonged. She would begin her efforts to achieve that now. Once she had thoroughly integrated herself, once she was accepted as just another piece of rubble, she would be ready to deal with her enemy.

It took only a little time and effort to create the skin she needed, the mask she required. She eased herself along the corridors, listening now for the sounds of the Morgawr and his rets. They would have reached the walls and begun looking for a way inside. Her plan for him was simple. She would try to separate him from his followers, to isolate him from their help. If she was to have a chance against him, she must get him alone and keep him that way. Cree Bega and his Mwellrets were no threat to her, but they could become the sort of distraction she had worried Bek and Rue Meridian might become. To win her struggle with the Morgawr, that must not be allowed to happen.

Already, she was beginning to feel a part of her surroundings, a thing of stone and mortar, of ancient time and dust.

She shed that part of her that was Grianne Ohmsford and reverted very deliberately to being the Ilse Witch. She became the creature she must to survive, armoring herself against what waited and concealing what was vulnerable. It demanded a shift in thinking, a closing off of feelings and a shutting away of doubt. It required a girding of self for battle. Such prosaic descriptions made her smile, for the truth was much darker and meaner. She was taking a different path from the one she had followed when her purpose in life was to see Walker destroyed, but this path was just as bleak. Killing the Morgawr was killing still. It would not enhance her self-respect. It would not change the past. At best, it would give a handful of those she had wronged a chance at life. That would have to be enough.

She was glad Bek was not here to see the change happen, for she believed it was reflected in her eyes and voice. It could be contained, but not hidden. Maybe this was how she must always be, split between two selves, required by events and circumstances to be duplicitous and cunning. She could see it happening that way, but there was nothing she could do about it.

There were sounds ahead now, the echoes of small scrapings and slidings, of heavy boots passing over stone and earth. They were still a long way off, but getting closer. The Morgawr was trying to penetrate the maze. As yet, he had not detected her presence, but it would not take him long. It would be best if she attacked him before he did, while he still thought himself safe. She could wait and see if the magic of the thing in the ruins might confuse the warlock, but it would probably be wasted effort. The Morgawr was too clever to be fooled for long and too persistent to be turned away for good. Redden Alt Mer's plan had been a reasonable one, but not for someone so dangerous.

She continued to hum softly, the magic concealing her not only from the dweller in the ruins but from those who hunted her, as well. She made her way toward them, sliding through the shadows, watching the open spaces ahead for signs of movement. It would not be long until she encountered them. She breathed slowly and deeply to steady herself. She must be cautious. She must be as silent as the air through which she passed. She must be no more in evidence than would a shade come from the dead.

Most of all, she must be swift.

Redden Alt Mer seemed almost resigned to the inevitability of it when he heard what Grianne Ohmsford had done. Standing on the aft deck of the *Jerle Shannara* with Bek and Rue, he made no response, but instead stared off into the distance, lost in thought. Finally, he told them to go back on watch and let him know if they saw anything. He did not look ready to summon any of the Rover crew to prepare for an escape should Grianne fail. He did not appear interested in doing anything. He heard them out and then walked away.

His sister exchanged a quick glance with Bek and shrugged. "Wait here," she said.

She disappeared below, leaving Bek to contemplate what lay ahead. He stood at the railing of the airship and looked up at the clear blue sky. Britt Rill and Kelson Riat stood together in the bow, talking in low voices. Spanner Frew was fussing with something in the pilot box, working through the heavy boughs they had laid down to hide it from the air. Alt Mer and the others were nowhere to be seen. Everything seemed strangely peaceful. For the moment, it was, Bek thought. No one would come for them right away. Not until the Morgawr had settled things with Grianne.

He thought about looking in on Quentin, but couldn't bring himself to do so. He didn't want to see his cousin while he was feeling like this. Quentin was smart enough to read his face, and he didn't think that would be such a good thing this morning. If Quentin knew what was happening, he would want to get out of bed and stand with them. He wasn't strong enough for that, and there would be time enough for the Highlander to engage in futile heroics if everything else failed. Best just to let him sleep for now.

Rue Meridian reappeared through the hatchway, buckling on her weapons belt with its brace of throwing knives, tucking a third into her boot as she came up to him. "Ready to go?" she asked.

He stared at her. "Ready to go where?"

"After your sister," she said. "You don't think we're going to stand around here doing nothing, do you?"

Not when she put it that way, he didn't. Without another word, they slipped over the side of the airship and disappeared into the ruins after Grianne.

Redden Alt Mer had been thinking about the company's situation all night. Unable to sleep, he had been reduced to pacing the decks to calm himself. He hated being grounded, all the more so for knowing that he couldn't get airborne again easily and was, essentially, trapped. He was infuriated by his sense of helplessness, a condition with which he was not familiar. Even though it had been his plan to hide in the ruins and hope the Morgawr didn't find them, he found it incomprehensible that he would actually sit there and do nothing while waiting to see if it worked.

When Bek's sister awoke, brought out of her catatonia after all these weeks, he knew at once that everything was about to change. It wasn't a change he could put a name to, but one he could definitely feel. The Ilse Witch awake, whether friend or enemy or something else altogether, was a presence that would shift the balance of things in some measurable way. To Alt Mer, that she had chosen to go after the Morgawr rather than to wait for the warlock to come to her seemed completely in character. It was what he would have done if he hadn't locked himself in the untenable position of hiding and waiting. The longer he stayed grounded, the more convinced he became that he was making a mistake. This wasn't the way to save either his airship or her passengers. It wasn't the way to stay alive. The Morgawr was too smart to be fooled. Alt Mer would have been better off staying aloft and fighting it out in the air.

Not that he would have stood a chance with that approach either, he conceded glumly. Best to keep things in perspective while castigating oneself for perceived failures.

He left the airship and climbed the tower into which he had sent Little Red and Bek to keep watch, but they weren't there. Confused by their absence, he looked down into the courtyard where the *Jerle Shannara* sat concealed, thinking he might spy them. Nothing. He looked off toward the surrounding courtyards and passageways, peering through breaks in the crumbling castle walls.

He found them then, several hundred yards away, sliding through the shadows, heading toward the front of the keep and the Morgawr.

For a second, he was stunned by what he was seeing, realizing that not only had his sister disobeyed him, but she was risking her life for the witch. Or for Bek, but it amounted to the same thing. He wanted to shout to them to get back to the ship, to do what they had been told, but he knew it was a waste of time. Rue had been doing as she pleased for as long as he could remember, and trying to make her do otherwise was a complete waste of time. Besides, she was only doing what he had been thinking he should do just moments earlier.

He walked to the outer wall of the tower and looked out across the grasslands. The Morgawr and his rets were already inside the castle, and the plains were empty save for *Black Moclips*, which sat anchored inland perhaps a quarter of a mile away. Beyond, clearly visible against the deep blue of the morning sky, the Morgawr's fleet hovered at anchor offshore.

He stared at the airships for a moment, at the way they were clustered to protect against a surprise attack, and an idea came to him. It was so wild, so implausible, that he almost dismissed it out of hand. But he couldn't quite let it go, and the longer he held on, the more attractive it seemed. Like a brightly colored snake that would turn on you once it had you hypnotized. Like fire, waiting to burn you to ash if you reached out to touch it.

Shades, he thought, he was going to do it.

He was aghast, but excited, as well, his blood pumping through him in a hot flush as he raced down the tower stairs for the airship. He would have to be quick to make a difference, and even that might not be enough. What he was thinking was insane. But there was all sorts of madness in the world, and at least this one involved something more than just standing around.

He burst out of the tower, leapt aboard the *Jerle Shannara*, and headed directly for Spanner Frew. The shipwright looked up from his work, doubt clouding his dark features as he saw the look on the other's face. "What is it?" he asked.

"You're not doing anything important, are you?" Alt Mer replied, reaching for his sword and buckling it on.

Spanner Frew stared at him. "Everything I do is important. What do you want?"

"I want you to go with me to steal back *Black Moclips*."

The shipwright grunted in disgust. "That didn't work so well for Little Red, as I recall."

"Little Red didn't have a good plan. I do. Come along and find out. We'll take Britt and Kelson for company. It should be fun, Black Beard."

Spanner Frew folded his burly arms across his chest. "It sounds dangerous to me."

Alt Mer grinned. "You didn't think you were going to live forever, did you?" he asked.

Then, seeing the other man's dark brow furrow in response, he laughed.

He left Ahren Elessedil and Kian to keep watch over the *Jerle Shannara* and set out with Spanner Frew, Kelson Riat, and Britt Rill for the outside wall of the castle. It didn't occur to him until he was well away from the airship that he might have trouble finding his way back. Not only were the ruins a confusing maze to begin with, but the spirit creature's magic was designed to keep intruders from penetrating beyond the perimeter. But there was no help for it now, and besides, he didn't think he would be coming back anyway.

He told his companions what he thought they needed to know and no more. He told them that they were going to skirt the ruins to their most inland point, well away from the view of those aboard *Black Moclips*, then sneak around to the far side of the airship, get aboard, and steal her away. If they could manage it, they would have a fully operational airship in which to make their escape. With luck, the Morgawr would not be able to give chase, and without him, the rest of the fleet would lack the necessary leadership to act.

It was all an incredible bunch of nonsense, if he thought it through, but since they were already moving to do what he had suggested, there wasn't enough time for much thought on the part of anyone.

He took them directly to the outer wall, then east and north along their perimeter to a gate that opened almost directly into a heavy stand of trees. He was moving quickly, aware of the fact that the Morgawr could encounter Grianne or Bek and Rue at any time, and once that happened, it might be too late for him to succeed in what he intended. Scooting out from the cover of the walls, the four Rovers gained the trees and worked their way through them until they were across the flats. From there, they followed a shallow ravine that allowed them to creep through the tall grasses until they were less than a hundred yards from their target.

Spanner Frew was huffing noticeably from the effort, but Kelson and Britt were barely winded. Alt Mer lifted his head for a quick look around. They were behind *Black Moclips*, and the Mwellrets he could see were all facing toward the ruins.

"Black Beard," he said to Spanner Frew, keeping his voice soft. "Wait here for us. If we don't make it, get back to the airship and warn the others. If we get aboard, come join us."

Without waiting for a response, he slithered out of the ravine into the cover of the grasses and began to crawl toward the airship. Kelson and Britt followed, all of them experienced at sneaking into places they weren't supposed to be. They crossed the open ground quickly, easing through gullies and shallow depressions, pressed close to the ground.

When Alt Mer could see the hull of the airship without lifting his head, he paused. The pontoon closest to him blocked their view of the rets on the main deck, but it blocked the rets' view of them, as well. Unless one of the rets came down into the fighting stations and peered over the side, the Rovers were safe. All they had to do now was to find a way to get aboard.

Alt Mer stood up carefully, signaled to the other two men to follow, and started toward the rope ladder. He passed under the hull of the airship, which, anchored by ropes tied fore and aft, floated perhaps two dozen feet off the ground. He paused to study the rope ladder, the easiest way onto the ship, but the one the rets would be quickest to defend. Beckoning Britt and Kelson to him, he whispered for them to move as close to the ladder as they could without being seen and to stand ready to board when he called for them.

Then moving to the bow of the airship, he took hold of the anchor rope and, hand over hand, began to haul himself up.

He reached the prow at the curve of the rams and peeked over the railing. There were four rets, two at the railing by the rope ladder, one in the pilot box and one aft. The hapless Federation crew stood around like sleepwalkers, staring at nothing, arms hanging limp at their sides. He felt a momentary pang of regret at what had to happen, but there was no way anyone could save them now.

He took a deep breath, heaved himself over the side, and charged across the deck toward the two closest Mwellrets. He killed the first with a single pass of his long knife, yelling for Britt and Kelson as he engaged the second. Both Rovers appeared up the ladder almost at once, grabbing his antagonist from behind and throwing him down. Alt Mer rushed the pilot box as the third ret snatched up a pike and launched it at him. The pike passed so close to his head that he heard the air vibrate, but he didn't slow. He went up the front of the box with a single bound, vaulted the shield, and was inside before the ret could escape. The ret swung at him with his broadsword in a desperate effort to stop him, but Alt Mer blocked the blow, slid inside the ret's guard, and buried the long knife in his chest.

The last ret tried to go over the side, but Kelson caught him halfway over the rail and finished him.

That wasn't so difficult after all, Alt Mer decided, aware that he had been injured in the struggle, both arms bleeding from slashes, his ribs bruised on his left side, and his head light with the blow it had taken from the first ret. He went back down to the deck, hiding the wounds as best he could. He ordered his men to throw the dead rets over the side, then go down the ladder and hide the bodies in the grass. It was a strange order, and they glanced at each other questioningly, but they didn't argue. They were used to doing what he told them to do, and they did so now.

As soon as they were safely over the side and on the

ground, he pulled up the ladder. Then he walked quickly to the anchor ropes, passing the dead-eyed Federation crew, who made no effort to stop him or even to look at him, and cut them both. As the ropes fell away, *Black Moclips* began to rise.

"Big Red!" he heard Spanner Frew call after him, lumbering across the grasslands in a futile effort to catch up. Below, Kelson Riat and Britt Rill were calling up to him, as well, shouting that the ropes were gone, that they couldn't reach him.

That was the general idea, of course. He didn't need any help with what he intended to do next. The sacrifice of his own life in furtherance of this wild scheme was more than enough.

Redden Alt Mer leaned over the side and waved good-bye.

THIRTY-ONE

She could hear them coming now, the scrape of their foot-falls, the hiss of their breathing, and the rustle of their heavy cloaks, the echoes reaching out to her through the silence. Grianne slowed to where her own sounds disappeared completely, lost in the concealment of her wishsong's magic. She disappeared into the stone walls and floors of the ruins, into its towers and parapets. She completed the transformation she had begun earlier, taking on the look and feel of the castle. She disappeared in plain sight.

The Morgawr had come to find her, but she had found him first.

She could feel the magic of the castle dweller working about her, changing the way the corridors opened and closed, shifting doorways and walls to confuse and mislead. It did so in arbitrary fashion, a function of its being that required no more thought than did her breathing. It was not yet aroused to do more, to lash out as it had at Bek and the shape-shifter when they had stolen the key from its hiding place. Thousands of years old, a thing out of the world of Faerie, it slumbered in its lair. If it sensed the presence of the Morgawr and his Mwellrets, or if it sensed her own for that matter, it did so in only the most subliminal way, and was not concerned by it.

That would change, she decided, when the time was right. In any arena in which she must do combat, weapons of all sorts were permitted.

She breathed slowly and evenly to quiet her pulse and her mind and to steady her nerves. She was at her best when she was in control, and if she was to overcome the Morgawr, she must take control quickly. Hesitation or delay would be fatal. Or any show of mercy. Whether or not to kill the Morgawr was not an issue she could afford to debate. Certainly he would be quick enough to kill her—unless he thought he could render her immobile and feed on her later.

She shuddered at the thought, never having gotten used to it or quite been able to put aside her fear and revulsion of what it would feel like. She had never thought she would be at risk and so never considered the possibility. It left her chilled and tight inside to do so now.

But she was still the Ilse Witch, cloaked in a mantle of steely confidence and hardened resolve, and so she choked off her revulsion and clamped down on her fear. The Morgawr had destroyed many creatures in his long lifetime and overcome much magic. But he had never had to face anyone like her.

She thought of the creatures she had destroyed in her turn and of the magics she had overcome. She did not like thinking of it, but could not help herself. The truths of her life were too recently revealed for her to close them away. One day, she might be able to do so with some of them, perhaps most. For now, she must embrace them and draw what strength she could from the anger they engendered. For now, she must acknowledge their monstrosity and remember that they were the consequence of the Morgawr's treachery. For a little while longer, she must be the creature he had helped create.

For a little while longer.

The words had a hollow feel to them, an ephemeral quality that suggested they could be blown away in a single breath.

But there was no more time for rumination. She spied movement through breaks in the stone walls, the bulky shapes of the Mwellrets sliding past the shadows of the sunless ruins.

She moved to intercept them, already laying the groundwork for separating them from the Morgawr, casting her magic in places that would draw his attention long enough for her to do what was needed.

Down through the corridors of broken rock they trudged, the Mwellrets and their dark leader. She could see him now, tall and massive and loathsomely familiar. He walked ahead, pointing the way for Cree Bega and his minions, testing the air for danger, for magic, for signs of her presence. He would already know about the spirit that warded the ruins, and he would be wary of it. His plan would be to find and engage her in single combat. He would expect her to be hiding with the company of the *Jerle Shannara*. He would not expect her to be hunting him as he was hunting her.

She used the magic of the wishsong to smooth the path he followed, to give him a sense of ease. It was a subtle effect, but one that, if he detected it, would not disturb him in a place where magic was rife. He knew he was being manipulated by the castle's dweller, and he would expect to be gently prodded in the direction the dweller wished him to go. In his arrogance, he would allow this, thinking he could compensate for it whenever he was ready. He would not suspect that she was there, acting as the dweller's surrogate, manipulating him for her own purposes. By the time he realized the truth, it would be too late.

When he neared, she found a place suitable to her intent and stepped back into the shadows to wait.

Seconds later, the Morgawr emerged from one of several corridors leading in, and she used the magic at once to suggest her presence in a chamber further on. He glanced up in response to the faint impression, leaning forward within the covering of his cowl as if to taste the air, sensing something he couldn't see, not quite sure what it was, only that it touched on her. He signaled for the Mwellrets, who were a dozen paces back, to hold up.

Come ahead, she urged him silently. *Don't be afraid.*

He slipped into the chamber on cat's paws, little more than a hint of dark movement in shadows that were darker still. He crossed the room in pursuit of her tease, cautious and deliberate, and disappeared down a corridor.

She left her hiding place and slid along the wall that followed the Morgawr's path, as deliberate and careful as he was, humming steadily, purposefully, keeping herself concealed. She could just hear the soft muttering of the rets behind her, but nothing of the warlock.

When she was all the way across the room and next to the corridor beyond, able to see the Morgawr's dark shape ahead, she turned back to the rets. Projecting the warlock's voice into their minds so that it seemed as if he were speaking, she summoned them ahead.

They came instantly, responding as she knew they would. But once they entered the room, she took them a different way. The ruins were a maze, and there were openings everywhere. She chose one that led away from the Morgawr, but gave the rets the impression they were still following him. Cree Bega's blunt, reptilian face lifted in doubt, gimlet eyes casting about for his leader. But, unable to find him, he continued on, following the thread she had laid out for him, moving steadily further away. Bunched together like cattle, they let themselves be herded into the chute she had chosen for them, and when they were all safely inside, she closed the gate. As quickly as that, the way back disappeared. She threw up a wall of magic that closed it off as surely as if it had never existed. The rets were in a corridor from which they could not escape without breaking through her magic or moving ahead down a series of twists and turns that would take them too long to navigate to be of any help to their leader.

Instantly, she turned into the passageway the Morgawr had taken, spied him turning toward her, and attacked, striking out with every last measure of power she could muster, hurtling it at him like a missile. The magic was a shriek in the silence, hammering into the Morgawr, throwing him back down the corridor and into a wall with such force that the ancient stones shattered from the impact. She went down the corridor in a rush, bursting into the room just in time to watch her handiwork disappear in a whiff of vapor.

It was only an illusion, she realized at once. It wasn't the Morgawr at all. She had been tricked.

She turned around to find him standing right behind her.

Bek and Rue Meridian heard the explosion from several chambers away while still winding through the maze in a futile effort to catch up with Grianne. The sound was like nothing either of them had ever heard, a sort of metallic scream that set their teeth on edge. But Bek recognized the source instantly; Grianne had invoked the magic of the wishsong. He screamed her name, then charged ahead heedlessly, abandoning any effort at a silent approach, anxious now just to get to where things were happening before it was too late.

"Bek, stop!" Rue called after him in dismay.

Too late. Rounding the corner of a twisting passageway hemmed in by walls so tall they left only a sliver of blue sky visible overhead, they ran right into Cree Bega and his Mwellrets. Rushing from opposite directions into a tiny courtyard littered with debris and streaked with shadows, they skidded to a stop. It happened so quickly that the image was still registering in Bek's mind as Rue whipped out both throwing knives and sent them whistling across the short space in a blur of bright metal. Two of the rets died on their feet as the rest charged.

They would have been finished then, if Bek, watching the massive bodies of the rets bear down on them, had not reacted instinctively to the threat. Calling up his own magic in a desperate response, he sent a wall of sound hurtling into his attackers. It caught up the rets as it had the creepers in the ruins of Castledown and sent them flying. Three got past, breaking in at the edges. Bek had only a moment to catch the glitter of their knife blades, and then they were on top of him.

Rue, swift, agile, and lethal, killed the first, ducking under his massive arms and burying her third throwing knife in his throat. She intercepted the second as well, but it bore her backwards, its momentum too great to slow. Bek saw her go down, then lost track as the final assailant crashed into him, knife slicing at his throat. He blocked the blow, screaming at the ret in defiance. His voice was threaded with the wish-song's magic; it exploded out of him in automatic response to his fear and anger and shredded the Mwellret's head like metal shards. The ret was dead before he knew what had happened, and Bek was scrambling back to his feet.

"Rue!" he called out frantically.

"Not so loud. I can hear you."

She hauled herself out from under the body of her as-sailant, but only with some difficulty. Blood covered her, a jagged tear down the front of her tunic and another down her left sleeve. Bek dropped to his knees next to her, shoving the dead Mwellret out of the way. He began searching through her clothing for the wounds, but she pushed him away.

"Leave me alone. I've broken my ribs again. It hurts just to breathe." She swallowed against her pain. "Bring me my knives. Watch yourself. Some of them might still be alive."

He pulled free the knife buried in the throat of the ret a few feet away, then crossed the courtyard to where the others lay in tangled heaps. The impact of striking the wall had smashed them so badly they were barely recognizable. He stared at them a moment, sickened by the fact that he was responsible for this, that he had killed them. He hadn't seen so many dead men since the attack on the company of the *Jerle Shannara* in the ruins weeks earlier. He hesitated a moment too long, thinking about the deaths here and there, and was suddenly sick to his stomach. He went down on his knees and retched helplessly.

"Hurry up!" Rue called impatiently.

He retrieved the other two throwing knives, carried them back and gave them to her, and again reached to bind her wounds. "Leave that to me," she said, holding him off.

"But you're bleeding!" he insisted.

"The blood isn't all mine. It's mostly the ret's." Her eyes were bright with tears, but her gaze steady. "I can't go any further hurting like this. You have to go on without me. Find your sister. She needs you more than I do."

He shook his head, suddenly concerned. "I won't leave you. How bad are you hurt, Rue? Show me."

She set her jaw and shoved at him again. "Not so bad that I can't get up and thrash you to within an inch of your life if you don't do what I tell you! Go after Grianne, Bek! Right now! Go on!"

Another explosion sounded, this one closer, the sound deeper and more ominous than before. Bek looked up in response, fear for his sister reflected in his eyes.

"Bek, she needs you!" Rue hissed at him angrily.

He gave her a final glance, then sprang to his feet and charged ahead into the gloom.

Redden Alt Mer swung the bow of *Black Moclips* toward the Blue Divide and the Morgawr's fleet, setting his course and locking down the wheel before leaving the pilot box. Down on the deck, he raised all the sails, tightened the radian draws, and checked the hooding shields on the parse tubes, making sure that everything was in good working order and could be controlled from the pilot box. A quick glance over the tips of the ramming horns revealed that nothing had changed ahead. The fleet still lay at anchor, and there was almost no movement on the decks. It was a lapse in judgment and discipline that he would make them pay dearly for.

He paused for a moment in front of Aden Kett and looked into the Federation Commander's dead, unseeing eyes. Like Rue, he had admired Kett, thought him a good soldier and a good airship Commander. To see him like this, to see all of them like this, was heartbreaking. Reducing men to puppets, to something less than the lowest animals that walked the earth, bereft of the ability to reason or act independently, was a monstrous evil. He thought he had seen more than enough kinds of evil in his life and wanted no more of this one. Perhaps he could put a stop to it here.

He went aft to the storage lockers and hauled out two heavy lines of rope and a pair of grappling hooks. Double-looping the lines through the eyes of the hooks, he carried one to each side of the rams and tied off the free ends to mooring cleats. Coiling the lines with the hooks resting on top so that they were ready for use, he went back up into the box.

He glanced back at the shoreline. Spanner Frew and the Rover crewmen stood at the edge of the bluff, staring after him in what he could only imagine was disbelief. At least they weren't shouting at him to come back, calling unwanted attention to themselves and to him. Maybe they had figured out his plan and were just watching to see what would happen.

For a moment, he found himself thinking of the Prekkendorran and all the airship raids he had survived under much worse conditions. It heartened him to imagine that he might survive this one, too, even though he couldn't see how that was possible. He looked up at the brilliant morning sky, a depthless blue expanse that seemed to open away forever, and he wished he had more time to enjoy this life that had been so good to him. But that was the nature of things. You got so much time and you made the best of it. In the end, you needed to feel that the choices you had made were mostly the right ones.

He adjusted his approach to the anchored fleet so that it

would appear he intended to pass by them on their port side. The first faint stirrings of life were visible now, a few of the rets moving to the railings to look out at him. They recognized *Black Moclips* and were wondering why they didn't see any of the Mwellrets or the Morgawr. It helped that Kett's Federation crew was visible, the men who had taken her ashore, but it would keep them from acting for only a few moments more.

Redden Alt Mer pulled back on the levers to the thrusters. Drawing down power from the light sheaths through all twelve of the radian draws, *Black Moclips* began to pick up speed.

Ahren Elessedil heard the explosion, as well, standing on the deck of the dismantled *Jerle Shannara* with the Elven Hunter Kian. Save for Quentin Leah, who'd been sedated by Rue Meridian to make certain he stayed quiet, they were alone now on the airship. Quentin had suffered a setback in recent days, his injuries worsening once more after seeming to heal. He did not appear to be in any serious danger, but he was running a fever and had developed a tendency to hallucinate that often provoked loud outcries. So Rue had given him the sleeping potion to help him rest.

But the explosion might have brought him awake, so Ahren left Kian topside and went belowdecks to see after the Highlander. He wished he didn't have to stay aboard the airship, that he could go out with the others and see what was happening. It was bad enough when Bek and Rue left, but now the Rovers had all disappeared, as well, and with only the taciturn Kian and the sleeping Quentin Leah for company, he felt like he had been deserted.

He ducked his head into the Captain's quarters long enough to reassure himself that Quentin was all right, then went back down the passageway and upstairs again. Kian was standing at the port railing, looking off into the ruins.

"See anything?" Ahren asked him, coming alongside.

Kian shook his head. They stood together listening, then heard a second explosion, this one of a deeper sort. There were sounds of fighting, as well, distant but clear, the bright, sharp clang of blades and sudden cries of injured or dying men. More explosions followed, and then silence.

They waited a long time for something more, but the silence only deepened. The minutes ticked away, sluggish footfalls leading nowhere. Ahren grew steadily more impatient. He had the Elfstones tucked in his tunic and his broadsword belted at his waist. If he had to fight, he was ready. But there would be no fighting so long as he stayed here.

"I think we should go look for them," he said finally.

Kian shook his head, his dark face expressionless. "Someone has to stay with the airship, Elven Prince. We can't leave her unguarded."

Ahren knew Kian was right, but it didn't make him feel any better. If anything, it made him feel worse. His obligation to the company required him to stay aboard the *Jerle Shannara* even when it made him feel entirely useless. It wasn't so much that he was anxious to fight, but more that he didn't want to feel as if he wasn't doing his part. It seemed to him that he had failed as a member of this company in every conceivable way. He had failed his friends in the ruins of Castledown when he had run away. He had failed Walker by not being able to recover the Elfstones in time to help him in his battle with Antrax. He had failed Ryer Ord Star by leaving her behind when he escaped *Black Moclips* and the Morgawr.

He was particularly bothered by the death of the seer. Big Red had smoothed out the rough parts, but there was no way to soften the impact. Ahren's sense of guilt went unrelieved. He had been in such a rush to escape that he had let himself believe the lie she told him without questioning it. She had sacrificed herself for him, and to his way of thinking it should have been the other way around.

He sighed with sad resolution. It was too late to change what had happened to her, but not too late to make certain that it didn't happen to someone else. Yet what chance did he have to affect anything stuck back here on the *Jerle Shannara* while everyone else went off to fight his battles for him?

There were more explosions, and then a huge grinding sound that rolled through the ruins like an avalanche. The ground shook so heavily that it rocked the airship and sent both Elves careening into the ship's railing, which they quickly grabbed for support. Blocks of stone tumbled from the battlements and towers of the old castle, and new cracks appeared in the walls and flooring, opening like hungry mouths.

When the grinding ended, it was silent again. Ahren stared into the ruins, trying to make sense of things, but there was no way to do that from here.

He turned to Kian in exasperation. "I'm going to have a look. Something's happened."

Kian blocked his way, facing him. "No, Elven Prince. It isn't safe for you—"

He gave a sharp grunt, and his eyes went wide in shock. As Ahren watched in confusion, Kian took two quick steps toward him and toppled over, eyes fixed and staring. Ahren caught him as he fell, lowering him to the ship's decking. The haft of a throwing knife protruded from his back, the blade buried to the hilt.

Ahren released him, rushed to the railing and peered over. A Mwellret had hold of the rope ladder and was climbing its rungs. The dark, blunt face lifted into the light, the yellow eyes fixing on Ahren. It was Cree Bega.

"Little Elvess," he purred. "Ssuch foolss."

Unable to believe what was happening, Ahren backed away in horror. He glanced down quickly at Kian, but the Elven Hunter was dead. There was no one else aboard, save Quentin, and the Highlander was too sick to help.

Too late, he thought to cut the ladder away. By then, Cree Bega was climbing onto the deck across from him.

"Musstn't be frightened of me, little Elvess," he hissed. "Doess little Elvess thinkss I mean them harm?"

He stepped over to Kian and pulled out his knife. He held it up as if to examine it, letting the blood run down the smooth, bright blade onto his fingers. His dark tongue slipped out, licking the blood away.

Ahren was frantic. He backed all the way to the pilot box before he stopped, fighting to control his terror. He couldn't use the Elfstones, his most powerful weapon, because they only worked to defend against creatures of magic. Nor could he run, because if he ran, Quentin was a dead man. He swallowed hard. He couldn't run anyway, not if he wanted to retain even a shred of self-respect. It was better that he died here and now than flee again, than fail still another time to do what was needed.

"Givess me what I wantss, little Elvess, and perhapss I will let you live," Cree Bega said softly. "The bookss of magic. Hidess them where, Elven Prince?"

Ahren drew his broadsword. He was shaking so badly he almost dropped it, but he breathed in deeply to steady himself. "Get off the ship," he said. "The others will be back in minutes."

"Otherss are too far away, foolissh little Elvess. They won't come thiss way in time to ssave you."

"I don't need them to save me." He made himself take a step toward the other, away from the pilot box, away from the almost overpowering temptation to run. "You're the one who's alone."

The Mwellret started toward him, coming slowly, dark face expressionless, movements almost languid. *Don't look into his eyes,* Ahren reminded himself quickly. *If you look into a Mwellret's eyes, he will freeze you in place and cut your throat before you know what is happening.*

"Doess ssomething sseem wrong, little Elvess?" Cree Bega whispered. "Afraid to look at me?"

Ahren glanced at the ret in spite of himself, looking into his eyes, almost as if the question required it of him, and in an instant Cree Bega sprang. Ahren slashed at the other in desperation to ward him off, but the Mwellret blocked the blow. The throwing knife sliced across Ahren's chest, cutting through skin and muscle as if they were made of paper. Burning pain flooded through the Elven Prince as he pushed the other away, dropping into a crouch and whipping the sword back and forth to clear a space between them.

Cree Bega slid clear, watching him. "Esscapess uss once perhapss, little Elvess, but not twice. Little sseer made that misstake. Sshall I tell you what we did to her? After the Morgawr gave her to uss? How sshe sscreamed and begged for uss to kill her? Doess that make you ssad?"

Ahren felt a roaring in his ears, a tremendous pressure from the rage he felt building inside, but he would not give way to it because he knew that if he did, he was a dead man. He hated Cree Bega. He hated all the rets, but their leader in particular. Cree Bega was a weight around his neck that would drag him to his death if he didn't cut it loose. The Elven Prince was not the boy he had been even a few weeks ago, and he was not going to let the Mwellret win this contest of wills. He was not going to panic. He was not going to be baited into foolish acts. He was not going to run. If he died, he would do so fighting to defend himself in the way that Ard Patrinell had taught him.

He went into a defensive stance, calling on his training skills, his concentration steady and absolute. He kept his eyes averted from the ret's, kept himself fluid and relaxed, knowing that Cree Bega would want to make this next pass his last, that the ret would try to kill him quickly and move on. Ahren wondered suddenly why the ret was alone. Others had come into the ruins. Where were they? Where was the Morgawr?

He edged to his left, trying to put the Mwellret in a position that hemmed him between the railing and the mainmast. Blood ran down Ahren's chest and stomach in a thin sheet and his body burned from the wound he had received, but he forced himself to ignore both. He dropped his blade slightly, suggesting he might not quite know what to do with it, inviting the other to find out. But Cree Bega stayed where he was, turning to follow Ahren's movements without moving away.

"Sshe died sslowly, little Elvess," he hissed at Ahren. "Sso sslowly, it sseemed sshe would take forever. Doess it bother you that you weren't there to ssave her?"

Ahren went deep inside himself, back in time, back to where he practiced his defensive skills with Patrinell on this very deck, all those long, hot days in the boiling sun. Ahren could see his friend and teacher still, big and rawboned and hard as iron, making the boy repeat over and over the lessons of survival he would one day need to call upon.

That day had arrived, just as Patrinell had forecast. Fate had chosen this time and place.

Cree Bega lunged for him, a smooth, effortless attack that took him to Ahren's left, away from his sword arm and toward his vulnerable side. But Ahren had anticipated that this was how the ret would come at him. Guided by the voice of his mentor whispering in his mind, buttressed by the hours of practice he had endured, and sustained by his determination to acquit himself well, he was ready. He kept his eyes on Cree Bega's knife, squared his body away, angled his sword further down, as if to drop his guard completely, then brought it up again when the other was too far committed to pull back, his blade slipping under Cree Bega's extended arm, cutting through to the bone, and continuing to slide up across his chest and into his neck.

The Mwellret staggered back, the knife dropping away from his nerveless fingers, clattering uselessly on the wooden deck. A gasp escaped his open mouth, and his blank features tightened in surprise. Ahren followed up instantly, thrusting with his sword, catching Cree Bega in the chest and running him through.

He yanked his weapon free and stepped away as the other staggered backwards to the railing and hung there. No words came out of his open mouth, but there was such hatred in his eyes that Ahren shrank from them in spite of himself.

He was still struggling to look away when the other sagged into a sitting position and quit breathing.

THIRTY-TWO

If she hadn't already been using the magic of the wishsong to conceal her presence, Grianne Ohmsford would not have survived. The Morgawr was right on top of her when she turned, and his hand shot out to grip and hold her fast. But her defenses were already up, and her magic deflected his effort just enough that it was turned aside. As she jerked away, his blunt nails scraped across her neck, tearing open her skin. She threw up a wall of sound between them, shrieking at him in anger and shock, but his own magic was in place, as well, his black-cloaked form shielded by it, just as it must have been shielded all along. She had thought to catch him off guard when she separated him from the Mwellrets, but he was too experienced. He had created an illusion of himself for her to attack, and she had almost paid the price for her carelessness.

Spinning away from him in a haze of sound and movement, she dropped into a crouch by the far wall, breathing hard. He made no effort to come after her, remaining in place by the chamber entry, watching her, measuring the effect of his appearance.

"Did you think I wouldn't be expecting you, my little Ilse Witch?" he asked softly, the words smooth and almost gentle. "I know you too well for that. I trained you too well to think that you wouldn't come looking for me."

"You lied to me," she replied, barely able to contain her

rage. "About the Druid, about my parents and Bek, about my whole life."

"Lies are sometimes necessary to achieve our purposes. Lies make possible what we would otherwise be denied. Do you feel yourself ill-used?"

"I feel myself made into something loathsome." She took a tentative step left, looking to find an opening in his defenses. She could feel his power building, swirling all around him like heat off a fire. He would come at her shortly. She had been too slow, too confident, and she had lost the advantage of surprise.

"You made yourself what you are," he told her. "I merely gave you the opportunity to do so. You were wasting your life anyway. Your father chose to keep you from the Druid, and for that I was grateful. Trying to keep you from me, as well, was a mistake."

"He knew nothing of you! You killed him and my mother for no reason! You stole me away to make me your tool! You used me for your own purposes, and you would have done so forever if I had not discovered the truth!"

He gave a small lift of his shoulders as if to disclaim his guilt for anything of which she had accused him. His tall frame bent toward her as if to throw its shadow across her like a net. "How did the Druid persuade you of the truth, little witch? You never would have believed him before. Or was it your brother who told you?"

She did not care to explain anything to him, did not want even to speak with him. She wanted him gone from her life, from the earth she walked, and from her memory as well, were it possible. She hated him with such passion that it seemed to her that in the closeness of their shared space she could smell the stench of him—not the rankness of body odor, but the putrefaction of evil. Everything about him was so revolting to her that it was impossible to think of doing anything other than distancing herself in any way she could.

"You shouldn't have come after me," she told him, taking another sideways step, building her own magic in response to his.

"You shouldn't have betrayed me," he replied.

The power of her wishsong was born of earth magic, absorbed from the Elfstones by her ancestor, Wil Ohmsford, and passed on to his descendants. It could do almost anything once mastered by its wielder, from taking life to restoring it. But the Morgawr possessed magic very like it and every bit as powerful. His was rooted in the essence of his being, rather than extracted from the earth. Conceived at his birth in the dark reaches of the Wilderun, he the warlock brother of the witch sisters, Mallenroh and Morag, it had been fueled by his hunger for power and honed by his experiments with living creatures. Twisted by a special form of madness, he had sought for a way to increase the power of his birthright, and by so doing, the years of his life.

He found that way early on, when he was still quite young, discovering that feeding on the lives of others invested him with their life force. Stealing away their souls increased his vitality and strength; it fed his hunger in a way that nothing else could. It was easy enough, he had told the Ilse Witch long ago, once you got over your revulsion for what it required.

All those years she had tolerated this madness because she thought him her ally in achieving her greatest goal—the destruction of the Druid Walker. She had known what he was, and still she had allowed herself to be his creature. She had subverted herself for him when reason told her she should not. She had done so in the beginning because it seemed her only choice; she was homeless and still a child. But she had matured quickly, and that excuse had long since ceased to be a reasonable one for why she had stayed so long with him, or would be with him still if not for Bek. Nor could she claim that because she was a child, she'd had no other choice but to be what he made her. In truth, she had embraced his efforts freely, adopted his thinking and his ways, and hungered to be a part of his madness, his coveted power. That made her as guilty as he was.

"I am taking back my life." The tension she felt caused her to shiver. "I am taking back what you stole."

"I let no one take anything from me," he replied. "Your life is mine, and I will give it up when I choose to do so and not before."

"This time the choice is not yours to make."

He laughed softly, a swirl of dark cloth as he gestured disdainfully at her. "The choice is always mine. Laying claim to your life was good for you, little witch, until you sought power that wasn't yours. You would pretend that you are better than I am, but you are not. You are no freer of guilt, no nobler of purpose, no higher of mind. You are a monster. You are as cold and dark as I. If you think otherwise, you are a fool."

"The difference between us, Morgawr, is not that I think I am better than you. The difference is that I recognize what I am, and I understand how terrible that is. You would go on as you are and not regret it. Even if I am able to change myself, I will look back at what I was and regret it always."

"Your time for regret will be short, then. Your life is almost over."

There was a fresh edge to his voice, one infused with anticipation. He was getting ready to attack. She could feel it in the movement of the air, in its crackle and hiss as the magic he summoned began to break free of its restraints.

As a result, she wasn't where he expected her to be when he lashed out. She had eased to the side, leaving just a shadow of herself behind to draw him out. Feeling the backwash of the magic's power, watching the whipsaw effect of his fury cause the wall behind her to rupture, she struck back at him with shards that would have ripped him apart had he not already made his own warding motion in response.

Trading ferocious assaults, they quickly turned the chamber into a smoking, debris-clogged furnace, the heat and sound intense and suffocating. But they were more evenly matched than either had expected, and neither could gain the upper hand.

Then the Morgawr simply disappeared. One moment he was there, his great form shadowy and fluid behind a screen of smoke and heat, and the next he was gone. Grianne slid back to her right, not wanting to give him a chance to come at her from another direction. She tested the air, searching for him, but the trail of his body heat told her he had fled from the room.

She went after him at once. If he was running, his confidence was breaking down. She did not want to give him a chance to recover. A fierce anticipation flooded through her. Maybe now she could put an end to him.

Black Moclips was closing on the Morgawr's fleet when Redden Alt Mer decided to take a look for something he was already pretty certain wasn't still aboard. He did it on a whim, having not even thought of it until now, remembering it because of something Ahren Elessedil had told him when they had talked about Ryer Ord Star, wanting suddenly to discover if it was true.

So he climbed down out of the pilot box, the controls locked, the airship on course, and walked past the living dead of the Federation and climbed down into the aft fighting station in the port-side pontoon. He walked back to where the ram began its upward curve, removed a panel on the side of the hull, and peered inside.

There it was, against all odds, in spite of his certainty it wouldn't be, still in the same condition in which it had been installed, neatly wrapped and ready for use. *You never know,* he mused.

He carried it out and laid it on the deck, piecing it together in moments, wondering why he bothered. Because it was there, he supposed. Because he lived in a world where a man's fate was often determined by chance, and he had believed in the importance of chance all his life.

Back in the pilot box, he saw the sail-stripped masts of the Morgawr's fleet begin to loom ahead of him like trees in a winter forest. A few sails were still unfurled to permit the airships to hover, but most were rolled and cinched. Mwellrets clustered against the railings, peering intently at him as he neared, trying to figure out why *Black Moclips* was coming back and why they couldn't see the Morgawr or their fellow rets. They were not yet concerned, however. He didn't seem to pose a threat. He wasn't flying directly at them, instead pointing off to their port side and slightly away, as if intending to fly out to sea.

Black Moclips was traveling very fast now and still picking up speed. She was doing better than thirty knots, flying through the clear morning sky like a missile launched from a catapult, skimming the back of a gentle southerly wind, the ride smooth and easy. Sea birds flew at him and banked away, as if sensing that trouble rode his shoulder, but he only smiled at the thought.

When his speed reached forty knots and he was less than a quarter of a mile off the fleet's port side, he went back down to the main deck and threw the heavy ropes and grappling hooks over the side. They swung out and away, trailing the vessel like monstrous fishing hooks. *An apt analogy,* he thought wryly. He sprinted to the pilot box, seized the controls, opened the starboard tubes, and raked the sails hard to port. *Black Moclips* swung sharply left, the sudden movement throwing most of the crew sprawling across the deck, where they remained, staring at nothing. Alt Mer ignored them, straightening out the airship and picking up new speed, heading directly for the Morgawr's fleet, the barbed ends of the grappling hooks glinting in the sunlight as they swung back and forth like lures. Aware that they were being attacked, the Mwellrets were racing about like frightened ants now. Sails were being run up, lines fastened in place, and anchors weighed. The Mwellret guards were trying frantically to get their dead-eyed crews to their stations. But in stealing their lives, the Morgawr had also stolen their ability to respond quickly. They weren't going to get under way in time.

Black Moclips was a brute among Federation warships, not particularly large, but blocky and powerful. She went through the Morgawr's fleet as if it were a stack of kindling, her battering rams and hull snapping off masts like pieces of kindling, the grappling hooks tearing apart sails and shredding lines. Half of the airships lost power immediately and plummeted into the ocean. The rest spun away, damaged and fighting to stay aloft. If they hadn't been so stupid about it, the rets would have put their ships down in the water right away, but they lacked the experience that would have taught them to do so.

The shock of multiple collisions rattled *Black Moclips* to her mastheads, tearing huge holes in her hull and collapsing her forward rams. Both grappling hooks had torn free somewhere along the way, leaving entire sections of decking and railing in splinters. Alt Mer was thrown to the back of the pilot box and lost control of the craft completely. He struck his head on the retaining wall, bright splashes of color clouding his vision. But he scrambled up again anyway, hands groping for the steering levers.

In seconds, he had *Black Moclips* swinging back around for a second pass. He could see clearly now the damage he had inflicted on the Morgawr's fleet. Airships lay in pieces in the water, some of them burning. Debris and bodies were scattered everywhere. A few survivors clung to the wreckage, but not many. Most were gone. He tried not to think of it. He tried to think instead of the lives he was saving, concentrating on his friends and shipmates and his promise to protect them.

Back toward the remainder of the fleet he sailed, picking up speed as he approached. One or two airships were under way now, and he made for them. His purpose was clear. By the time he was finished, not one of them would be left. He intended to sink them all and leave the Morgawr and whoever was with him stranded on Mephitic.

He couldn't do this, of course, if there was any chance at all that the ships he was attacking might be repaired. He had to destroy them utterly. He had to decimate them.

There was only one way to do that.

He wished Little Red could be here to see this. She would appreciate the simplicity of it. He glanced over his shoulder at the island, but he was too far away now to make out anything clearly. Smoke and ash rose off the damaged fleet in waves, obscuring his view. A dingy gray haze masked the clear blue of the morning sky, and the fresh salt air smelled of burning wood and metal.

His speed was back up to better than thirty knots as he bore down on the ships still flying. He corrected his course to allow for what he intended, a pass that would take him directly into their midst, but lower down this time. Only one of those remaining had managed to get all her sails up and her anchor weighed, but she was floundering in dead air and smoke. Smoke roiled off the decks of three others.

Alt Mer threw off his cloak and unsnapped his safety line. Mobility was his best ally at this point. He closed down the parse tube exhausts, but locked the thrusters all the way forward to keep drawing down power from the light sheaths. No airship Captain would do this unless he wanted to blow his vessel to pieces. The power generated by the radian draws had to be expelled from the tube exhausts or they would explode and take the airship with them.

Not to mention everything within shouting distance.

He held *Black Moclips* on course, letting the power build inside the parse tubes until he could see smoke and fire breaking through the seams. *They just need to hold together a little longer,* he thought. He took a deep breath to steady himself. The Morgawr's airships loomed right ahead.

"Time to move on," he whispered.

Moments later, *Black Moclips* tore through the hulls of the remaining airships like an enraged bull through stalks of corn in an autumn field, and exploded in a ball of fire.

Bek Ohmsford raced through the ruins after his sister, heedless of the noise he was making because no one could hear him anyway over the sounds of the battle being fought somewhere just ahead. Sharp cracklings and deep booms echoed through the stone corridors of the ancient castle, breaking down centuries-old silence and walls alike, the exchanges of magic powerful enough to cause the earth itself to vibrate beneath his feet. Grianne had found the Morgawr, or it might be the other way around, but the battle between them had begun in either case, and he needed to be a part of it.

Except that he had no idea what to do once he was, and it was a problem he couldn't afford to delay solving for long. After he found his sister, he was going to have to do something to help her. But what sort of help could he offer? His mastery of the wishsong's power was a poor second to her own. She had already warned him that he stood no chance against the Morgawr, that the warlock's experience and skill were so vast that Bek would be swiftly overwhelmed.

So what was he going to do that would make a difference? How was he going to avoid being the distraction she had told him she could not afford to have him be?

He didn't know. He knew only that he couldn't stay behind and let her face the Morgawr alone. He had gone through too much to find and heal her to let something bad happen to her now.

The sounds ahead quieted, and he slowed in response, listening carefully. He was in a gloom-shrouded part of the castle, its walls towering over him, corridors narrow and high and rooms cavernous. The ceilings were vaulted and multitiered, and the dark shadows they cast were alive with unexplained movement. He eased along one wall, walking softly, once again trying to hide his approach. Smoke rolled through the chambers, and the air had a burnt smell to it.

He quieted his breathing. Everything was still. What if it was over? What if the Morgawr had won and Grianne was dead? He went cold at the prospect, casting it away from him as he would a poisonous snake, not wanting to touch it. That was not what had happened, he told himself firmly. Grianne was all right.

Nevertheless, he moved ahead more quickly, anxious to make certain. He was surprised that the enormity of the struggle hadn't roused the castle's dweller. With so much sound and fury invading its privacy and so much damage inflicted upon its keep, Bek would have thought the spirit furious enough to retaliate. But there was no indication of that happening, nothing in the air to trigger a warning, nothing in the feel of the stone to suggest danger. For whatever reason, the spirit was not responding. Bek found it puzzling. Maybe it was because the spirit reacted only to attempts to take things away, as it had with Bek and Truls. Maybe that was all it cared about—keeping possession of its treasures. Maybe the fact that the walls and towers that made up its domain were collapsing didn't mean anything to it, no more so than when they crumbled as a result of time's passage.

He had an idea then, sudden and unexpected, of how he might use his magic against the Morgawr. But he had to find him first, and he sensed that time was running out.

But finding the warlock did not take him as long as he had expected. The silence was shattered moments later by a rough-edged sound that reverberated through the stone walls, a quick and sudden rending. He went toward it at once, following its echoes as they died away, hearing voices. He reached a break in the walls, and through it saw his sister and the Morgawr locked in combat. The warlock had trapped her and was holding her fast by the sheer force of his magic. She was fighting to break free—Bek could see the strain on her smooth face—but she could not seem to bring her magic to bear in a way that would allow her to do so. The Morgawr was squeezing her, crushing her, closing off air and space and light, the darkness he wielded a visible presence as it closed.

Bek saw the Morgawr's hand reach for Grianne, stretching the fabric of her protective magic to touch her face. Grianne's head snapped away, and she wrenched at the shackles that had trapped her. The Morgawr was too strong, Bek saw. Even for her, for the Ilse Witch, he was too powerful. His fingers extended, and Bek could see the sudden hunching of his shoulders as he forced his way closer. His intent was unmistakable. He meant to feed on her.

Grianne!

There was no time left for Bek to think about what he wanted to do, no time for anything but doing it. He threw out the magic of his wishsong in an enveloping cloak that settled over the Morgawr like spiderwebbing, a faint tickling that the warlock barely noticed. But deep within the heart of the ruins, where even the Morgawr could not penetrate, the castle's dweller stirred in recognition. Up from its slumber it surged, fully awake in seconds, sensing all at once that something it had thought lost for good was again within reach. It roared through its crumbling walls, down its debris-strewn corridors, and across its empty courtyards. It paid no heed to the *Jerle Shannara* or to the living or the dead men who surrounded her or to what was taking place just offshore over the Blue Divide. It paid no heed to anything but the creature that had roused it.

The Morgawr.

Except that it didn't see the warlock for what he was. It saw him for what Bek had used the magic of the wishsong to make him appear. It saw him as the boy who had stolen its key weeks earlier, who had teased it with boldness and tricked it with magic.

Mostly, it saw him as a thief who still had that key.

The Morgawr had only a moment to look up from Grianne, to realize that something was terribly wrong, and then the spirit was upon him. It swept into the Morgawr like a whirlwind, ripping him away from his victim, bearing him backwards into the closest wall and pinning him there. The Morgawr shrieked in fury and fought back with his own magic, tearing at the wind, at the air, at the magic of the dweller, mad with rage. Bek screamed through the thunderous roar for Grianne to run, and she gathered herself and started toward him.

Then, almost inexplicably, she turned back.

Bracing herself, she threw her own magic at the Morgawr, lending strength to the castle dweller's efforts to crush him. The sound was so terrifying, so wrenchingly invasive, that Bek put his hands over his ears and scrunched up his face in pain. Reptilian face twisting with shock and fury, arms windmilling to gain purchase where there was none to be had, the Morgawr jerked upright as the combined magics ripped through him. For a moment, he held them at bay, girl and spirit both, his dark heart long since turned to stone, his mind to iron. He would not be beaten by such as these, the bright glare of his green eyes seemed to say. Not on this day.

Then the stone behind him cracked wide, and he was thrust inside the fissure. The opening ran deep and long, through multiple tiers of blocks set by its builders centuries ago to form a support wall for towers and ramparts now mostly gone. Thrashing against his imprisonment, the Morgawr fought to escape, but the pressure of the magics that held him fast was enormous.

He could not break free. Bek could see it on his face and in his eyes. He was trapped.

Slowly, the stone began to seal again. The Morgawr

shrieked, striking at it with his magic, chunks of it falling away beneath the sharp edges of his power. But not enough stone could be shredded or slowed, and the gap narrowed. Bit by bit, he was squeezed as he had sought to squeeze Grianne. Little by little, he was crushed more tightly by the dwindling space. Now he could no longer move his arms to gesture, to invoke his spells, to trigger his magic's release. His body twisted frantically, and his shrieking rose to inhuman levels.

When the walls closed all the way, the fingers of one hand were still protruding from a tiny crack. They twitched momentarily in the fresh silence that settled over the ruins. When they finally went still, the crack had disappeared and the wall was leaking blood.

The explosions from land and sea had brought the Wing Riders out of hiding on the distant atoll. They flew their Rocs into the clear morning air and banked toward the dark smudges of smoke rising off the ruins of the ancient castle, then turned again at the sight of more smoke rolling over the waters of the Blue Divide. They caught a glimpse of the Morgawr's freshly smoldering airships and watched in shock as *Black Moclips* flew into them. Then everything disappeared in a massive explosion that filled the air with fire and smoke and created a shock wave so strong it could be felt miles away.

Hunter Predd could not tell what had transpired beyond the obvious. Hiding from the Morgawr had clearly not worked, but the nature of the battle being fought now was hard to judge. Catching sight of Spanner Frew and two of the Rover crew standing at the shore's edge, he banked Obsidian toward them, with Po Kelles and Niciannon following right behind. More explosions sounded, parse tubes giving way to the pressure of overheated diapson crystals as the destruction of the Morgawr's fleet continued. The Wing Riders swept downward to the island, landed close to the Rovers, jumped from their birds, and rushed over.

"What's happened?" Hunter Predd asked the shipwright. Seeing the other's dazed look, he took hold of his arm and turned him about forcibly. "Talk to me!"

Spanner Frew shook his head in disbelief. "He flew right into them, Wing Rider. He hooded the crystals, drew down enough power to destroy a dozen airships, and he flew right into them. All by himself, he destroyed them. I can't believe it!"

Hunter Predd knew without having to ask that the shipwright was talking about Redden Alt Mer. He looked out over the Blue Divide into the billowing clouds of smoke. Pieces of airships floated on the water, twisted and blackened. The water itself was on fire. There was no sign of an airship aloft and no sign of life in the water.

He stood with Po Kelles and the Rovers and stared in silence at the carnage. Big Red had found a way to stop them after all, he thought with a mix of admiration and sadness.

"Maybe he got out in time," he said quietly.

None of the others replied or even looked at him. They knew the truth of it. No one could survive an explosion like that. Even if you somehow managed to jump clear, the fall would kill you; the fire and the debris would finish you if it didn't.

They stared out into the heavy clouds of smoke, transfixed. None of them wanted to believe that Redden Alt Mer was really gone. None of them wanted to believe it could end like this.

It was quiet now, the morning gone still and peaceful. The explosions had stopped, even from the castle behind them. Whatever battles had been fought, they were over. Hunter Predd found himself wondering who had won. Or maybe if anyone had.

"We'd better see what's happened to the others," he said.

They were just turning away, when something appeared out of the roiling clouds of black smoke. At first, the Wing Rider thought it was a Roc or a War Shrike and wondered where it had come from. But it wasn't the right size and it wasn't flying in the right way. It was something else altogether.

"Black Beard," he whispered softly.

The flying object began to take shape as it emerged from the haze, slowly becoming recognizable for what it was, floundering badly, but staying aloft.

It was a single wing.

"Shades!" Spanner Frew hissed.

The man who flew it still had the luck.

THIRTY-THREE

A little more than five months later, the man with the luck and those he had sworn to protect were safely home again. Redden Alt Mer stood at the rail of the *Jerle Shannara* and stared out into the misty twilight of the Dragon's Teeth, thinking for the first time in weeks of his harrowing escape from the destruction of the Morgawr's fleet, reminded of it suddenly by a hunting bird winging its way in slow spirals through the mist that drifted down out of the mountains. His thinking lasted only a moment. That he had found a way through the fire and smoke and explosive debris still amazed him and didn't bear looking at too closely. Life was a gift you accepted without questioning its generosity or reason.

Still, he would not want to risk his luck like that again. When he returned to the coast and March Brume, he would still fly airships, but he would fly them in safer places.

"What do you suppose they are talking about?" Rue asked, leaning close so that her words would not carry.

Some distance off in the gloom, Bek Ohmsford stood with his sister, two solitary figures engaged in a taut, intense discussion. Their argument, pure and simple, transcended the parting that was taking place. Those who watched from the airship, those few who still remained—Ahren Elessedil, Quentin Leah, Spanner Frew, Kelson Riat, and Britt Rill—waited patiently to see how it would end.

401

"They're talking about the choice she has made," he answered quietly. "The choice Bek can't accept."

They had flown in from the coast yesterday, the Wing Riders Hunter Predd and Po Kelles leaving them there to return home to the Wing Hove, their mission complete, their pledge to provide scouting and foraging for the expedition fulfilled. How invaluable their help had been. It was hard to watch them make that final departure, hard to know they wouldn't still be warding the ship. Some things he got so used to he couldn't imagine life without them. It was like that for Alt Mer with the Wing Riders.

Still, he would see them again. Out along the coast, over the Blue Divide, on calmer days and under better circumstances.

They would have returned Ahren Elessedil and the Blue Elfstones to Arborlon and the Elves, then flown the Elven Prince home to face his brother, but for the insistence of Grianne Ohmsford that they come first to the Dragon's Teeth, to the Valley of Shale and the Hadeshorn. She would hear no arguments against it. She owed something to Walker, she told them. She must come to where the dead could be summoned and spoken with, to where the shade of the Druid could tell her the rest of what she must know.

When she had told them why, they were stunned into silence. Not even Bek could believe it. Not then and clearly not now.

"She might be mistaken about this," Rue continued obstinately. "She might be taking on more than was ever intended of her."

Alt Mer nodded. "She might. But none of us thinks so, not even Bek. She was saved for this, made whole by the Sword of Shannara and her brother's love." He grimaced. "I sound almost poetic."

She smiled. "Almost."

They watched in silence again. Bek was gesturing furiously, but Grianne was only standing there, weathering the storm of his anger, calm resolution reflected in her stance and lack of movement. She had made up her mind, Alt Mer knew, and she was not someone who could be persuaded to change it easily. It was more than stubbornness, of course. It was her certainty of her destiny, of what was needed of her, of what was expected. It was her understanding of what it would take for her to gain redemption for the damage she had done to so many lives in so many places for all those years that she had been the Ilse Witch.

When this is done, he thought, *nothing will be the same again for any of us; our lives will be changed forever. Perhaps the lives of everyone in the Four Lands will be changed, as well.* What waited in the days ahead was that compelling—a new order, a fresh beginning, a reaching into the past to find hope for the future. All these would come about because of what happened here, on this night, in the mountains of the Dragon's Teeth, in the Valley of Shale, at the edge of the Hadeshorn, when Grianne Ohmsford summoned the shade of Walker.

So she had promised them.

He found it hard to argue with someone who believed she was meant to be Walker Boh's successor and the next Druid to serve the Four Lands.

Bek was having none of it. He had gone through too much in bringing his sister safely home again to let her wander off now, to place herself at risk once more—at greater risk perhaps than ever.

"You assume that you are meant to achieve something that even Walker could not!" he snapped, willing her to flinch in the face of his wrath. "He could not return for this, could not save himself to make the Druid order come alive. Why do you think it will be any different for you? At least he was not universally despised!"

He threw out the last few words in desperation and regretted them as soon as they were spoken. But Grianne did not seem bothered, and she reached out to touch his face gently.

"Don't be so angry, Bek. Your life does not lie with me in any case. It lies with her."

She glanced toward the *Jerle Shannara* and Rue Meridian. Stubbornly denying what he knew was true, Bek refused to look. "My life is not the subject of this discussion," he insisted. "Yours is the one that's likely to be thrown away if you go through with this. Why can't you just come home with me, find a little peace and comfort for a change, not go out and try to do something impossible!"

"I don't know yet exactly what it is I am expected to do," she answered calmly. "I only know what was revealed to me through the magic of the Sword of Shannara—that I am to become the next Druid and will atone for my wrongs by accepting that trust. If through my efforts a Druid Council is formed, as Walker intended that it should be, then the Druids will have a strong presence again in the Four Lands. That was why I was saved, Bek. That was what Walker gave his life for, so that I could make possible the goals he had set for himself but knew he would not live to see fulfilled."

She stepped close to him and placed her slender hands on his shoulders. "I don't do this out of foolish expectation or selfish need. I do this out of an obligation to make something worthwhile of a wasted life. Look at me, Bek. Look at what I have done. I can't ignore who I am. I can't walk away from a chance to redeem myself. Walker was counting on that. He knew me well enough to understand how I would feel, once the truth was revealed to me. He trusted that I would do what was needed to atone for the harm I have visited on others. How wrong it would be for me to betray him now."

"You wouldn't betray him by becoming who you should have been in the first place if none of this had happened!"

She smiled sadly. "But it did happen. It did, and we can't change that. We have to live with it. I have to live with it."

She put her arms around him and hugged him. He stood rigid in her embrace for a few moments, then little by little, the tension and the anger drained away until at last he hugged her back.

"I love you, Bek," she said. "My little brother. I love you for what you did for me, for believing in me when no one else would, for seeing who I could be if I was free of the Morgawr and his lies. That won't change, even if everything else in the world does."

"I don't want you to go." His words were bitter with disappointment. "It isn't fair."

She sighed softly, her breath a whisper in his ear. "I was never meant to come home with you, Bek. That isn't my life; it isn't the life I was meant to live. I wouldn't be happy, not after what I have been through. Coran and Liria are your parents, not mine. Their home is yours. Mine lies elsewhere. You have to accept this. If I am to find peace, I have to make amends for the damage I have done and the hurt I have caused. I can do this by following the destiny Walker has set for me. A Druid can make a difference in the lives of so many. Perhaps becoming one will make a difference in mine, as well."

He hugged her tighter to him. He sensed the inevitability of what she was saying, the certainty that no matter how hard he argued against it, no matter what obstacles he presented, she was not going to change her mind. He hated what that meant, the loss of any real chance at a life as brother and sister, as family. But he understood that he had lost most of that years ago, and he couldn't have it back the way it was or even the way it would have been. Life didn't allow for that.

"I just don't want to lose you again," he said.

She released him and stepped away, her strange blue eyes almost merry. "You couldn't do that, little brother. I wouldn't allow it. Whatever I do, however this business tonight turns out, I won't ever be far away from you."

He nodded, feeling suddenly as if he were just a boy again, still small and in his sister's care. "Go on, then. Do what you need to do." He gave her a quick smile. "I'm all argued out. All worn out." He looked off into the sunset, which had become a faint silver glow in the gathering dark, and fought back his tears. "I'm going home, now. I need to go home. I need for this to be over."

She came close once more, so small and frail it seemed impossible that she could possess the kind of strength a Druid would need. "Then go, Bek. But know that a part of me goes with you. I will not forget you, nor my promise not ever to be too far away."

She kissed him. "Will you wish me luck?"

"Good luck," he muttered.

She smiled. "Don't be sad, Bek. Be happy for me. This is what I want."

She tightened her dark robes about her and turned away. "Wait!" he said impulsively. He unstrapped the Sword of Shannara from where he wore it across his back and handed it to her. "You'll know what to do with this better than I will."

She looked uncertain. "It was given to you. It belongs to you."

He shook his head. "It belongs to the Druids. Take it back to them."

She accepted the talisman, cradling it in her arms like a baby at rest. "Good-bye, Bek."

In moments, she had started her climb into the mountains. He stood watching until he could no longer see her, all the while unable to overcome the feeling that he was losing her again.

Rue Meridian watched him return to the airship across the broken rock of the barren flats on which they had landed, his head lowered into shadow, fists clenched. Clearly, he was not happy about how things had turned out with his sister. Anger and disappointment radiated from him. Rue knew what he had asked of Grianne and knew, as well, that he had been refused. She could have saved him the trouble, but she supposed he had to find it out for himself. Bek was nothing if not a believer in impossibilities.

"He looks like a whipped puppy," Big Red mused.

She nodded.

"At least we can go home now," he continued. "We're finished here."

She watched Bek approach for a moment longer, then left her brother's side, climbed down the rope ladder, and walked out onto the flats. She didn't think Bek even saw her until she moved to block his way and he looked up to find her standing right in his path.

"I've been thinking," she said. "About your home, the one you were born in. It wasn't too far from here, was it?"

He stared at her.

"Do you think we could find where it was, if we went looking?"

His puzzlement was clear. "I don't know."

"Want to try?"

"It's only ruins."

"It's your past. You need to see it."

He glanced toward the airship doubtfully.

"No," she said. "Not them. They don't have time for such things. It would be just you and me. On foot." She let him consider for a moment. "Think of it as an adventure, a small one, but one for just the two of us. After we find it, we can keep going, walk south through the Borderlands along the Rainbow Lake down to the Silver River, then home to the Highlands. Big Red can fly Quentin to Leah on the *Jerle Shannara*, then take Ahren on to Arborlon."

She stepped closer, put her arms around him and her face next to his. "I don't know about you, but I've had enough of airships for a while. I want to walk."

He looked stunned, as if he had been handed a gift he hadn't expected and didn't deserve. "You're coming with me? To the Highlands?"

She smiled and kissed him softly on the mouth. "Bek," she whispered, "I was never going anywhere else."

Grianne Ohmsford spent the larger part of the night climbing into the foothills below the Dragon's Teeth, seeking to reach the Valley of Shale before dawn. She might have had Alt Mer fly her in on the airship, but she wanted time alone before summoning the shade of Walker. Besides, it was easier to say her good-byes now rather than later, particularly to Bek. She knew it would be hard to tell him she wasn't going with him, and it had been. His expectations for her had always been his own and never hers, and it was difficult for him to give them up. He would come to understand, but only in time.

She found the darkness familiar and comforting, still an old friend after all these years. Wrapped in its protective concealment, given peace by its unbroken solitude, she could think about what she was doing and where she was going; she could reflect on the events that had led her to this place and time. The destruction of the Morgawr had not given her the satisfaction she had hoped for. She would need more than revenge to heal. Her Druid life might provide her with that healing, though she knew it would not do so in the traditional way. It would not soothe and comfort her. It would not erase the past or allow her to forget she had been the Ilse Witch. She was not even assured of the nurturing rest of a good night's sleep. Instead, she would be given an opportunity to balance the scales. She would be given a chance at redemption for an otherwise unbearable past. She would be given a reason for living out the rest of her life.

She did not know if that would be enough to salvage her damaged psyche, her wounded soul, but it was worth a try.

By midnight, she was approaching her destination. She had never been here before and did not know the way, but her instincts told her where she needed to go. Or perhaps it was Walker who guided her, reaching out from the dead. Either way, she proceeded without slowing, and found in the simple act of moving forward a kind of peace. She should have been frightened of what waited; she knew one day the fear she could not seem to put a name to would catch up to her, would make itself known. But her feelings now were all of resolution and commitment, of finding a new place in the world and making a new beginning.

When she reached the rim of the Valley of Shale, coming upon it quite suddenly through a cluster of massive boulders, she stopped and gazed down into its bowl. The valley was littered with chips of glistening black rock, their shiny surfaces reflecting the moonlight like animal eyes. At the valley's center, the Hadeshorn was a smooth, flat mirror, its waters undisturbed. It was an unsettling place, all silence and empty space, nothing living, nothing but herself. She thought it a perfect place for a meeting with a shade.

She sat down to wait.

Everyone despises you, Bek had told her. The words had been spoken with the intent of changing her mind, but also to hurt her. They had not succeeded in the former, but had in the latter. Did still.

With dawn an hour away, she went down into the valley and stood at the edge of the lake. From what she had been shown by the magic of the Sword of Shannara, she understood what had happened to Walker in this place and would happen now to her. There was a power in the presence of the dead that was disconcerting even to her. Shades were beyond the living and yet still held sway over them because of what they knew.

The future. Its possibilities. Her fate, with all of its complex permutations.

Walker would see what she could not. He would know the choices that awaited her, but would not be able to tell her of their meaning. Knowledge of the future was forbidden to the living because the living must always determine what that future would be. The best the dead could do was to share glimpses of its possibilities and let the living make of them what they would.

She stared off into the distance, thinking that she didn't care to know the future in any case. She was here to discover if what the magic had shown her was real—if she was meant to be a Druid, to be Walker's successor, to carry on his work. She had told Bek and the others that she was, but she could not be sure until she heard it from the Druid's shade. She wanted it to be so; she wanted to be given a chance at doing something that would matter in a good way, that would help secure the work Walker had begun. She wanted to give him back something for the pain she had caused him. Mostly, she wanted to think that she was useful again, that she could find purpose in life, that things did not begin and end with her time as the Ilse Witch.

She glanced down at the waters of the Hadeshorn. *Poison,* the magic of the Sword of Shannara had whispered. But she was poison, too. She bent impulsively to dip her hand into the dark mirror of moonlight and stars but snatched it back as the waters began to stir. At the center of the lake, steam hissed like dragon's breath. It was time. Walker was coming.

She straightened within the dark folds of her cloak and waited for him.

"I did not think to see you again, little brother," Kylen Elessedil declared, sweeping into the room with his customary brusqueness, not bothering with formalities or greetings, not wasting unnecessary time.

"Your surprise is no greater than my own," Ahren allowed. "But here I am anyway."

It had been two days since he had said good-bye to Quentin Leah in the Highlands and three since Grianne Ohmsford had walked into the Dragon's Teeth. Afterwards, Ahren had flown west with the Rovers aboard the *Jerle Shannara* to Arborlon, thinking the whole time of what he would say when this moment came. He knew what was expected of him—not only by those with whom he had traveled, but also by himself. His was arguably the most important task of all, certainly the most tricky, given the way his brother felt about him. The boy he had been when he had left to follow the tracings of Kael Elessedil's map would not have been able to handle it. It remained to be seen if the man he had become could.

That he had been met by Elven Home Guard and brought to this small room at the back of the palace, quietly and without fanfare, testified to the fact that his brother still regarded him mostly as a nuisance. Kylen would tolerate his return just long enough to determine if anything more was necessary. The reappearance of Ahren was no cause for celebration absent a recovery of the Elfstones.

"Where is the Druid?" his brother asked, getting right to the point. He walked to the curtained windows at the back of the room and looked out through the folds. "Still aboard ship?"

"Gone back into the Dragon's Teeth," Ahren answered. It was not a lie exactly, just a shading of the truth. Kylen didn't need to know everything just yet. In particular, he didn't need to know how things stood with the Druids.

"Were you successful in your efforts on this expedition, brother?"

"Mostly, yes."

Kylen arched an eyebrow. "I am told you return with less than a quarter of those who went."

"More than that. Some have gone on to their homes. There was no need for them to come here. But, yes, many were lost, Ard Patrinell and his Elven Hunters among them."

"So that of all the Elves who went, you alone survived?"

Ahren nodded. He could hear the accusation in the other's words, but he refused to dignify it with a response. He did not need to justify himself to anyone now, least of all to his brother, whose only disappointment was that even a single Elf had survived.

Kylen Elessedil moved away from the window and came over to stand in front of him. "Tell me, then. Did you find the Elfstones? Do you have them with you?"

He could not quite hide the eagerness in his voice or the flush that colored his fair skin. Kylen saw himself empowered by the Elfstones. He did not understand their demands. He might not even realize that they were useless in most of the situations in which he would think to use them. It was the lure of their power that drew him, and the thought of it obscured his thinking.

Still, it was not Ahren's problem. "I have them. I will give them to you as soon as I am certain we are clear on the terms of the agreement Father and Walker reached."

Anger flooded his brother's face. "It is not your place to remind me of my obligations! I know what my father promised! If the Druid has fulfilled his part of the bargain—if you have the Elfstones and a share of the Elven magic to give to me—then it shall be done as Father wished!"

His brother made no attempt to hide the fact that he thought everything was intended just for him rather than for the Elven people. Kylen was a brave man and a strong fighter, but too ambitious for his own good and not much of a politician. He would be causing problems with the Elven High Council by now. He would have already angered certain segments of his people.

"The Elfstones will be yours by the time I leave," Ahren said. "The magic Walker sought to find requires translation and interpretation in order to comprehend its origins and worth. Those Elves who go to become Druids in the forming of the new council can help with that work. Two dozen would be an adequate number to start."

"A dozen will do," his brother said. "You may choose them yourself."

Ahren shook his head. "Two dozen are necessary."

"You test my patience, Ahren." Kylen glared at him, then nodded. "Very well, they are yours."

"A full share of the money promised to each of the men and women who went on this expedition must be paid out to the survivors or to the families of the dead."

His brother nodded grudgingly. He was looking at Ahren with something that approached respect, clearly impressed, if not pleased, by his younger brother's poise and determination. "Anything else? You'll want to keep the airship, I expect."

Ahren didn't bother answering. Instead, he reached into his pocket, withdrew the pouch containing the Elfstones, and handed it to his brother. Kylen took only a moment to release the drawstrings and dump the Stones into his hand. He stared down wordlessly into their depthless blue facets, an unmistakable hunger in his eyes.

"Do you need me to tell you how to make the magic work?" Ahren asked cautiously.

His brother looked over at him. "I know more about them than you think, little brother. I made a point of finding out."

Ahren nodded, not quite understanding, not sure if he wanted to. "I'll be going, then," he said. "After I gather supplies and talk with those I think might come to Paranor." He waited for Kylen to respond, and when he didn't, said, "Goodbye, Kylen."

Kylen was already moving toward the door, the Elfstones clutched in his hand. He stopped as he opened it, and looked back. "Take whatever you need, little brother. Go wherever

you want. But, Ahren?" A broad smile wreathed his hand-
some face. "Don't ever come back."

He went out through the door and closed it softly behind him.

It was dawn off the coast of the Blue Divide, and Hunter
Predd was flying on patrol aboard Obsidian. He had slept almost continuously for several days after his return, but because he was restless by nature, he required no more time
than that to recover from the hardships of his journey and so
was back in the air. He never felt at home anywhere else, even
in the Wing Hove; he was always anxious to be airborne, always impatient to be flying.

The day was bright and clear, and he breathed deeply of the
sea air, the taste and smell familiar and welcome. The voyage
of the *Jerle Shannara* seemed a long time ago, and his memories of its places and people were beginning to fade. Hunter
Predd did not like living in the past, and thus discarded it
pretty much out of hand. It was the present that mattered, the
here and now of his life as a Wing Rider, of his time in the air.
He supposed that was in the nature of his occupation. If you
let your mind wander, you couldn't do what was needed.

He searched the skyline briefly for airships, thinking to
spot one somewhere in the distance along the coast, perhaps
even one captained by Redden Alt Mer. He thought that of all
those he had sailed with, the Rover was the most remarkable.
Lacking magic or knowledge or even special skills, he was
the most resilient, the one nothing seemed to touch. The man
with the luck. Hunter Predd could still see him flying, miraculously unscathed, out of the smoky wreckage of the Morgawr's fleet aboard his single wing. He thought that when
nothing else could save you in this world, luck would always do.

Seagulls flew across his path, white-winged darts against
the blue of the water. Obsidian gave a warning cry, then
wheeled left. He had seen something floating in the water,

something his rider had missed. Hunter Predd's attention snapped back to the job at hand. He saw it now, bobbing in the surf, a splash of bright color.

Perhaps it was a piece of clothing.

Perhaps it was a body.

He felt a catch in his throat, remembering a time that suddenly did not seem so long ago after all.

Using his hands and knees to guide the Roc, he flew down for a closer look.

Please read on for a taste of
HIGH DRUID OF SHANNARA: JARKA RUUS
by Terry Brooks

She sat alone in her chambers, draped in twilight's shadows and evening's solitude, her thoughts darker than the night descending and heavier than the weight of all Paranor. She retired early these days, ostensibly to work but mostly to think, to ponder on the disappointment of today's failures and the bleakness of tomorrow's prospects. It was silent in the high tower, and the silence gave her a momentary respite from the struggle between herself and those she would lead. It lasted briefly, only so long as she remained secluded, but without its small daily comfort she sometimes thought she would have gone mad with despair.

She was no longer a girl, no longer even young, though she retained her youthful looks, her pale translucent skin still unblemished and unlined, her startling blue eyes clear, and her movements steady and certain. When she looked in the mirror, which she did infrequently now as then, she saw the girl she had been twenty years earlier, as if aging had been miraculously stayed. But while her body stayed young, her spirit grew old. Responsibility aged her more quickly than time. Only the Druid Sleep, should she avail herself of it, would stay the wearing of her heart, and she would not choose that remedy anytime soon. She could not. She was the Ard Rhys of the Third Druid Council, the High Druid of Paranor, and while she remained in that office, sleep of any kind was in short supply.

Her gaze drifted to the windows of her chamber, looking west to where the sun was already gone behind the horizon, and the light it cast skyward in the wake of its descent a dim glow beginning to fail. She thought her own star was setting, as well, its light fading, its time passing, its chances slipping away. She would change that if she could, but she no longer believed she knew the way.

She heard Tagwen before she saw him, his footfalls light and cautious in the hallway beyond her open door, his concern for her evident in the softness of his approach.

"Come, Tagwen," she called as he neared.

He came through the door and stopped just inside, not presuming to venture farther, respecting this place that was hers and hers alone. He was growing old, as well, nearly twenty years of service behind him, the only assistant she had ever had, his time at Paranor a mirror of her own. His stocky, gnarled body was still strong, but his movements were slowing and she could see the way he winced when his joints tightened and cramped after too much use. There was kindness in his eyes, and it had drawn her to him from the first, an indication of the nature of the man inside. Tagwen served because he respected what she was doing, what she meant to the Four Lands, and he never judged her by her successes or failures, even when there were so many more of the latter than the former.

"Mistress," he said in his rough, gravel-laced voice, his seamed, bearded face dipping momentarily into shadow as he bowed. It was an odd, still gesture he had affected from the beginning.

He leaned forward as if to share a confidence that others might try to overhear. "Kermadec is here."

She rose at once. "He will not come inside," she said, making it a statement of fact.

Tagwen shook his head. "He waits at the north gate and asks if you will speak with him." The Dwarf's lips tightened in somber reflection. "He says it is urgent."

She reached for her cloak and threw it about her shoulders. She went by him, touching his shoulder reassuringly as she passed. Within the stairwell, beyond the sound of her own soft footfalls, she heard voices rise up from below, the sounds of conversations adrift on the air. She tried to make out what they said, but could not. They would be speaking of her; they did so almost incessantly. They would be asking why she continued as their leader, why she presumed that she could achieve anything after so many failures, why she could not recognize that her time was past and another should take her place. Some would be whispering that she ought to be forced out, one way or another. Some would be advocating stronger action.

Druid intrigues. The halls of Paranor were rife with them, and she could not put a stop to it. At Walker's command, she had formed this Third Council on her return to the Four Lands from Parkasia. She had accepted her role as leader, her destiny as guide to those she had recruited, her responsibility for rebuilding the legacy of the Druids as knowledge givers to the races. She had formed the heart of this new order with those few sent under duress by the Elven King Kylen Elessedil at his brother Ahren's insistence. Others had come from other lands and other Races, drawn by the prospect of exploring magic's uses. That had been twenty years ago, when there was fresh hope and everything seemed possible. Time and an inability to effect any measurable change in the thinking and attitudes of the governing bodies of those lands and Races had leeched most of that away. What remained was a desperate insistence on clinging to her belief that she was not meant to give up.

But that alone was not enough. It would never be enough. Not for someone who had come out of darkness so complete that any chance at redemption had seemed hopeless. Not for Grianne Ohmsford, who had once been the Ilse Witch and had made herself Ard Rhys to atone for it.

She reached the lower levels of the Keep, the great halls that connected the meeting rooms with the living quarters of those she had brought to Paranor. A handful of these Druids came into view, shadows sliding along the walls like spilled oil in the light of the flameless lamps that lit the corridors. Some nodded to her; one or two spoke. Most simply cast hurried glances and passed on. They feared and mistrusted her, these Druids she had accepted into her order. They could not seem to help themselves, and she could not find the heart to blame them.

Terek Molt walked out of a room and grunted his unfriendly greeting, outwardly bold and challenging. But she could sense his real feelings, and she knew he feared her. Hated her more than feared her, though. It was the same with Traunt Rowan and Iridia Eleri and one or two more. Shadea a'Ru was beyond even that, her venomous glances so openly hostile that there was no longer any communication between them, a situation that it seemed nothing could help.

Grianne closed her eyes against what she was feeling and wondered what she was going to do about these vipers—what she could do that would not have repercussions beyond anything she was prepared to accept.

Young Ceryson Scyre passed her with a wave and a smile, his face guileless and welcoming, his enthusiasm evident. He was a bright light in an otherwise darkened firmament, and she was grateful for his presence. Some within the order still believed in her. She had never expected friendship or even compassion from those who came to her, but she had hoped for loyalty and a sense of responsibility toward the office she held. She had been foolish to think that way, and she no longer did so. Perhaps it was not inaccurate to say that now she merely hoped that reason might prevail.

"Mistress," Gerand Cera greeted in his soft voice as he bowed her past him, his tall form lean and sinuous, his angular features sleepy and dangerous.

There were too many of them. She could not watch out for all of them adequately. She put herself at risk every time she walked these halls—here in the one place she should be safe, in the order she had founded. It was insane.

She cleared the front hall and went out into the night, passed through a series of interconnected courtyards to the north gates, and ordered the guard to let her through. The Trolls on watch, impassive and silent, did as they were told. She did not know their names, only that they were there at Kermadec's behest, which was enough to keep her reassured of their loyalty. Whatever else happened in this steadily eroding company of the once faithful, the Trolls would stand with her.

Would that prove necessary? She would not have thought so a month ago. That she asked the question now demonstrated how uncertain matters had become.

She walked to the edge of the bluff, to the wall of tress that marked the beginning of the forest beyond, and stopped. An owl glided through the darkness, a silent hunter. She, too, hunted. She felt a sudden connection with him so strong that she could almost envision flying away as he did, leaving everything behind, returning to the darkness and its solitude.

She brushed the thought aside, an indulgence she could not afford, and whistled softly. Moments later, a figure detached itself from the darkness almost in front of her and came forward.

"Mistress," the Maturen greeted, dropping to one knee and bowing deeply.

"Kermadec, you great bear," she replied, stepping forward to put her arms around him. "How good it is to see you."

Of the few friends she possessed, Kermadec was perhaps the best. She had known him since the founding of the order, when she had gone into the Northland to ask for the support of the Troll tribes. No one had ever thought to do that, and her request was cause enough for a convening of the council of the nations. She did not waste the opportunity she had been given. She told them of her mission, of her role as Ard Rhys of a new Druid Council, the third since Galaphile's time. She declared that this new order would accept members from all nations, the Trolls included. No prejudices would be allowed; the past would play no part in the present. The Druids were beginning anew, and for the order to succeed, all the Races must participate.

Kermadec had stepped forward almost at once, offering the support of his sizeable nation, of its people and resources. Prompted by her gesture and his understanding of its importance to the Races, his decision was made even before the council of nations had met. His Rock Trolls were not imbued with a strong belief in magic, but it would be their honor to serve as her personal guard. Give them an opportunity to demonstrate their reliability and skill, and she would not regret it.

Nor had she ever done so. Kermadec had stayed five years, and in that time became her close friend. More than once, he had solved a problem that might otherwise have troubled her. Even after he had left for home again, his service complete, he had remained in charge of choosing the Trolls that followed in his footsteps. Some had doubted the wisdom of allowing Trolls inside the walls at all, let alone as personal guards to the Ard Rhys. But she had walked in darker places than these and had allied herself with creatures far more dangerous. She did not think of any Race as predisposed toward either good or evil; she saw them all only as being composed of creatures that might be persuaded to choose one over the other.

Just as she saw the members of her Druid order, she thought, though she might wish it otherwise.

"Kermadec," she said again, the relief in her voice clearly evident.

"You should let me rid you of them all," he said softly, one great hand coming to rest on her slim shoulder. "You should wash them away like yesterday's sweat and start anew."

She nodded. "If it were that easy, I should call on you to help me. But I can't start over. It would be perceived as weakness by the governments of the nations I court. There can be no weakness in an Ard Rhys in these times." She patted his hand. "Rise and walk with me."

They left the bluff and moved back into the trees, perfectly comfortable with each other and the night. The sights and sounds of Paranor disappeared, and the silence of the forest wrapped them close. The air was cool and gentle this night, the wind a soft whisper in the new spring leaves, bearing the scent of woods and water. It would be summer before long, and the smells would change again.

"What brings you here?" she asked him finally, knowing he would wait for her to ask before speaking of it.

He shook his head. "Something troubling. Something you may understand better than I do."

Even for a Rock Troll, Kermadec was huge, towering over her at close to seven feet, his powerful body sheathed in a barklike skin. He was all muscle and bone, strong enough to rip small trees out at the roots. She had never known a Troll to possess the strength and quickness of Kermadec. But there was much more to him. A Maturen of thirty years, he was the sort of man others turned to instinctively in times of trouble. Solid and capable, he had served his nation with a distinction and compassion that belied the ferocious history of his Race. In the not so distant past, the Trolls had marched against Men and Elves and Dwarves with the single-minded intent of smashing them back into the earth. During the Wars of the Races, ruled by their feral and warlike nature, they had allied themselves with the darker forces in the world. But that was the past, and in the present, where it mattered most, they were no longer so easily bent to service in a cause that reason would never embrace.

"You have come a long way to see me, Kermadec," she said. "It must be something important."

"That remains for you to decide," he said softly. "I myself haven't seen what I am about to reveal, so it is hard for me to judge. I think it will be equally hard for you."

"Tell me."

He slowed to a stop in the darkness and turned to face her. "There is strange activity in the ruins of the Skull Kingdom, mistress. The reports come not from Rock Trolls, who will not go into that forbidden place, but from other creatures, ones who will, ones who make a living in part by telling of what they see. What they see now is reminiscent of other, darker times."

"The Warlock Lord's domain, once," she observed. "A bad place still, all broken walls and scattered bones. Traces of evil linger in the smells and taste of the land. What do these creatures tell you they see?"

"Smoke and mirrors, of a sort. Fires lit in darkness and turned cold by daylight's arrival. Small explosions of light that suggest something besides wood might be burning. Acrid smells that have no other source than the fires. Black smudges on flat stones that have the look of altars. Markings on those stones that might be symbols. Such events were sporadic at first, but now occur almost nightly. Strange things that of themselves alone do not trouble me, but taken all together do."

He breathed in and exhaled. "One thing more. Some among those who come to us say there are wraiths visible at the edges of the mist and smoke, things not of substance and not yet entirely formed, but recognizable as something more than the imagination. They flutter like caged birds seeking to be free."

Grianne went cold, aware of the possibilities that the sightings suggested. Something was being conjured up by use of magic, something that wasn't natural to this world and that was being summoned to serve an unknown purpose.

"How reliable are these stories?"

He shrugged. "They come from Gnomes for the most part, the only ones who go into that part of the world. They do so because they are drawn to what they perceive in their superstitions as sacred. They perform their rituals in those places because they feel it will lend them power. How reliable are they?" He paused. "I think there is weight to what they say they see."

She thought a moment. Another strangeness to add to an already overcrowded agenda of strangeness. She did not like the sound of this one, because if magic was at work, whatever its reason, its source might lie uncomfortably close to home. Druids had the use of magic and were the most likely suspects, but their use of it in places beyond Paranor was forbidden. There were other possibilities, but this was the one she could not afford to ignore.

"Is there a pattern to these happenings?" she asked. "A timing to the fires and their leavings?"

He shook his head. "None that anyone has discerned. We could ask the Gnomes to watch for it, to mark the intervals."

"Which will take time," she pointed out. "Time best spent

looking into it myself." She pursed her lips. "That is what you came to ask me to do, isn't it? Take a look for myself?"

He nodded. "Yes, mistress. But I will go with you. Not alone into that country—ever—would I go. But with you beside me, I would brave the netherworld and its shades."

Be careful of what you boast of doing, Kermadec, she thought. *Boasts have a way of coming back to haunt you.*

She thought of what she had committed herself to do in the days ahead. Meetings with various Druids to rework studies that members of the order would undertake. Those could wait. Overseeing the repairs to the library that concealed the Druid Histories—that one could not happen without her presence, but could wait, as well. A delegation from the Federation was due to arrive in three days; the Prime Minister of the Coalition was reputed to lead it. But she could be back in time for that if she left at once.

She must go, she knew. She could not afford to leave the matter unattended to. It was the sort of thing that could mushroom into trouble on a much larger scale. Even by her appearance, she might dissuade those involved from pursuing their conjuring. Once they knew that she was aware of them, they might go to ground again.

It was the best she could hope for. Besides, it gave her an opportunity to escape Paranor and its madness for a few days. In the interval, perhaps a way to contend with the intrigues might occur to her. Time and distance often triggered fresh insights; perhaps that would happen here.

"Let me tell Tagwen," she said to Kermadec, "and we'll be off."